SIZE

by

A. W. Gray

AN ONYX BOOK

ONYX
Published by the Penguin Group
Penguin Books USA Inc., 375 Hudson Street
New York, New York 10014, U.S.A.
Penguin Vooks Ltd. 27 Wrights Lane,
London W8 5TZ, England
Penguin Books Australia Ltd. Ringwood,
Victoria, Australia
Penguin Books Canada Ltd, 2801 John Street,
Markham, Ontario, Canada L3R 1B4
Penguin Books (N.Z.) Ltd, 182–190 Wairau Road,
Auckland 10, New Zealand

Penguin Books Ltd. Registered Offices:
Harmondsworth, Middlesex, England

Size was previously published in a Dutton edition, and simultaneously in Canada by Fitzhenry and Whiteside, Limited, Toronto
First Onyx Printing, July, 1990
10 9 8 7 6 5 4 3 2 1

The excerpt from *In Defense of Judges* by A. W. Gray appeared previously in the Dutton hardcover edition of this novel.

REGISTERED TRADEMARK—MARCA REGISTRADA

Printed in the United States of America

PUBLISHER'S NOTE
This is a work of fiction. Names, characters, places, and incidents either are the product of the author's imagination or are used fictitiously, and any resemblance to actual persons, living or dead, events, or locales is entirely coincidental.

PRAISE FOR A. W. GRAY AND HIS NOVELS

"ONE OF THE BEST CRIME NOVELISTS PRODUCING TODAY!"

—*San Antonio Express News*

"THAT TRUE-BLUE TEXAS COMBINATION OF GOOD-OL' BOY COUNTRY CHARM AND BULL."

—*Dallas Morning News*

"GRAY WRITES WITH A PEN DIPPED IN HEMLOCK. REPULSIVE FAT CATS, UNSCRUPULOUS POLITICIANS AND SHAMELESS HYPOCRITES ARE TAKEN FOR A LOVELY RIDE."

—*The New York Times Book Review*

"COLORFUL CHARACTERS, SHARP DIALOGUE . . . GRAY WRITES WITH SAVVY ABOUT THE CRIMINAL WORLD."

—*United Press International*

"RAW, FUNNY, AND ADDICTIVE."

—*Detroit Free Press*

"LIGHTNING QUICK . . . LITERATE AND TOUGH IN THE ELMORE LEONARD MODE!"

—*Publishers Weekly*

For Chuck McGuire
and Ole Dick Martin
Guys I owe

1

Sizemore Brandon's conclusion re the federal prosecutor after studied observation of the clean-shaven face, the slightly jutted jaw, and the pink, fresh-scrubbed skin: a Class-A Prick.

"Please state your full name for the record," the prosecutor said, one elbow leaning on the railing that surrounded the witness box. His black suitcoat was unbuttoned, his waist narrow, his starched shirt the color of high-grade cocaine. The court reporter's machine, operated by a skinny guy in horn-rimmed glasses, stopped its muted clatter.

Size gave his name, including the middle one, Fred. A chubby, bald man in the top row of the amphitheatre, the A in the gilt lettering that spelled out GRAND JURY ROOM directly above his smooth scalp, sat forward and regarded Size like, Boy, have we ever got us one here.

"And," said the prosecutor in a strong New York accent, "do you currently reside at three-two-four-eight Shady Brook Lane, here in Dallas? In apartment"—he glanced at the three-by-five index card he held between his thumb and forefinger—"number three-two-four?"

Size said that he did.

The prosecutor strolled to a polished dark wood table which was big enough to sort mail but now held only a single legal-size sheet of paper. The paper rattled slightly as he held it out so that Size could read it. It was a form: "Wherefore" and "Know all men by these presents," with some blanks filled in.

"And are you the same person who is named in this subpoena?"

Size ran his thick freckled fingers through his hair as he leaned forward and read the form carefully. You never knew. Finally he said, "Yes, sir, that's me."

"And have you previously served two separate sentences in the Texas Department of Corrections, in Huntsville?" The prosecutor was moving faster now, up-tempo.

Size thought that one over. Hell, it was a public record. "Well, the last one was on Ramsey II, two years."

"For the record and for the information of the grand jurors," said the prosecutor with a tight smile, "Ramsey II is a *maximum security* farm unit within the Texas penal system. Now, Mr. Brandon, so you'll know and to save time, a grand jury proceeding is a little different from regular courtroom procedure. That is, I can ask you questions and from time to time the members of the panel may have questions of their own. Is that clear?"

"Yes." Size knew that, and Gurney had told him a lot more a few minutes ago out in the corridor. Like that he couldn't have his attorney present, and that the grand jury could consider hearsay evidence and other good stuff. Real necktie party.

"That's good, Mr. Brandon." The prosecutor swept the grand jurors with his gaze, an expression on his face that said he was about to tell them one strictly between him and them. He said to Size, "Now I'll begin by asking you, are you acquainted with Mr. James Patrick Fontenot?"

Size thought, Who, me? Know Pecos Jimmy? He knitted his bushy red brows in concentration and took a sheet of paper from the side pocket of his tan Ultrasuede sports coat. He unfolded the yellow ruled slip, adjusted the microphone that sat before him on the rail, and read, "I claim my right under the Fifth Amendment of the U.S. Constitution and Article One of the Constitution of the State of Texas and respectfully refuse to answer on the ground that any answer I might give could implicate me in an ongoing criminal investigation.''

''Oh, come *on.''* This from a blonde grand juror in her forties. She was sitting in the front row dressed in flamingo red, neck to knee, with heavy gold bracelets on both wrists and large gold rings on her fingers. Her lipstick and nails were matching shades of scarlet, and she had thick calves and heavy thighs. ''Aren't you his driver or bodyguard, whatever?'' Her bleached hair touched her shoulders. She beamed at the prosecutor as if she expected him to pat her on the head.

Size thought, she wants him to fuck her. He read them the page again.

The prosecutor scratched his chin, feeling a slight stubble and wondering if he should start shaving twice a day, as he listened to the witness claim his Fifth Amendment rights in a deep East Texas twang. Sizemore Brandon, his massive arms and tree-trunk legs tight against his sports coat and navy knit slacks, had a red sideburn-to-sideburn Abe Lincoln beard. Good old country boy, the kind they told the prosecutor to watch out for when he transferred down from the Southern District of New York. Size held the page in both hands, as if he were singing in a choir.

As Size finished reading the prosecutor poured himself a goblet of ice water from a chrome pitcher. He sipped, then smacked his lips thoughtfully. ''Mr. Brandon,'' he said when Size had finished, ''is it your intention to take the Fifth Amendment to any questions whatsoever regarding your relationship with Mr. James Patrick Fontenot?''

The two locked stony gazes for an instant. Then Size broke out in a toothy smile. He read the page a third time.

An irritated snap in his walk, the prosecutor strode to the table and pulled a dark leather attaché case from underneath. He opened it with a bang. Then he dug inside, coming up with a sheaf of papers which were stapled together and thumbing through them. For the third or fourth time today they told him: Sizemore Fred Brandon, b. Commerce, Texas, 7/14/49. Red hair, blue eyes, pale complexion. 6′4″ 260 lbs. ID mark, tattoo on upper left arm, bust of caricature bulldog, letters USMC. Served in United States Marine Corps, 1969–1972, honorably discharged, attained rank of corporal. 1974, Forney, Texas, convicted Auto Theft, served eight months eleven days Texas Department of Corrections. 1978, Dallas, Texas, Assault on a Police Officer, served two years three months TDC, paroled August 1980. Lists current occupation as professional poker player, holds IRS Gambling Tax Stamp. Education one year, Kilgore Junior College. No dummy.

The prosecutor murmured, "Time out." Then in his loud Yankee courtroom voice, "Ladies and gentlemen, we are taking a brief recess. Please bear with us. Mr. Brandon, I'll remind you that you're under subpoena. Don't leave the building, sir." With that he marched out of the room, heels clicking. His black shoes were polished like mirrors.

The blonde grand juror watched Size climb down from the witness box and exit after the prosecutor. Size took his time about it, moving with a bearlike grace, his arms slightly akimbo, and his palms to the rear like muscled hams. The woman thought, God, what a beast. Wonder how many people he's killed? And what his favorite method is. A gun? An ice pick? Sweet Jesus, with that build he looks like a neck-breaker. Her breath caught slightly and she felt a tingling sensation on the insides of her thighs.

Outside in the green-carpeted hallway Size almost collided with a couple of people—a young female clerk in a short skirt who was hustling along with a stack of file folders; a harried-looking gray-haired man who gave him a quick annoyed glance, started to say something, then after giving Size the once-over thought better of it—on the way to one of the long wooden pews that lined both sides of the corridor. He sat down, rested an arm on the seat back and crossed his legs. Seated directly across from him was a young pregnant girl with water-swollen knees and a splotchy complexion. She was chewing gum slowly. There was a white porcelain drinking fountain on the wall close to her and Size directed his gaze at it.

A man in a charcoal Armani suit sat next to Size on the bench. He was half bald, and what hair he did have was neatly and closely barbered. He looked in good shape, like a jogger. He wore a slim gold Piaget watch, and a full-karat diamond sparkled on his right ring finger. He leaned forward, rested his forearms on his thighs, clasped his manicured hands together, and turned to Size. "How's it going?"

Size's broad upper lip was shaved. He said, "Not for shit, Beaumont. You shoulda seen it. Four times last night I turn trips in pots you can't jump over. Got every one of 'em beat. Stool beat me twice in a row on hands he should have thrown in, never played the fuckers. Son of a—"

"Not the poker game, Size." Beaumont blinked his watery eyes. He looked as if he had a touch of hay fever. "I mean in there, in the grand jury room. What's happening, what do they want with you?"

"I ain't sure. Tell you one thing, though, they're wanting a piece of Pecos Jimmy. Wanting it bad."

"It figures. Well, it's in our best interest for you to—" Beaumont stopped in mid-sentence as the federal prosecutor approached, walking in a near goose step, like a palace guard. He pointedly ignored Size and stuck out a hand in Beaumont's direction. Beaumont stood and gripped it.

The prosecutor smiled warmly. "Henry Mitchell, Mr. Gurney. Your reputation precedes you, sir. I'm so pleased."

"Likewise, Mr. Mitchell," said Beaumont Gurney. "My, I guess this is quite a change for you after all those years in New York."

Size watched the chubby knees of the pregnant girl and thought, These two rigging up a fucking *golf game* or something? The Fed ought to—bad as Gurney plays.

Mitchell was saying, "And we seem to have a twofold problem here, Mr. Gurney. Number one, of course, is your client. He isn't cooperating. The other problem, and I hate to bring this up, frankly, but we need to know what your function is. Are you Mr. Brandon's lawyer for the duration, or will you be switching to Pecos Jim—to Mr. Fontenot? Should we proceed against him, of course.''

Gurney folded his arms, deadpanning it. ''Oh? Does this investigation involve Jim Fontenot, Mr. Mitchell?''

Mitchell didn't speak for a moment. Then he said, ''A few minutes, Mr. Gurney. I'll get back to you.'' He turned on his heel and marched away, raising a hand and snapping his fingers as he did. A slim guy with short brown hair, who was wearing a dark J. C. Penney suit, got up from another bench and fell into step behind the prosecutor. The two men did a snappy column-left into an anteroom off the corridor.

The anteroom held a scarred bookcase that contained red-bound volumes of the United States Code, West's *Federal Practice Digest*, and the *Federal Reporter, Second Series*. Dead center between the four walls was a round conference table surrounded by six straight-backed chairs. There was a Mr. Coffee on the table, black dregs in the bottom of the clear glass pot. The two men sat down.

The prosecutor leaned forward. ''The FBI isn't going to like this, Sam. But I'm going to give him the letter.''

Sam rolled his eyes and licked his thin lips. He nervously unbuttoned his coat as he said, ''I knew it. I said to the Agent-in-Charge this morning, 'Bet Mitchell gives him the letter.' Six weeks, Henry. Six fucking weeks, the last two, eight hours a day, just to get the subpoena served on this creep you're wanting to give immunity.''

''You don't have to tell me, Sam. It's tough on me to do it, too, but—''

''Tough? I'll give you tough, Henry.'' Sam leaned back, lifting the front legs of his chair from the carpet and hooking his thumbs through two of his front belt loops. ''A week I hang outside his apartment and he doesn't show, right in the middle of July with this suit on and sweating my ass off. I hung around there so much that the bikini-bunnies around the pool started to figure me for some kind of flasher. So you play golf, Henry? Like at Great Southwest, out in Grand Prairie by Six Flags?''

"Lord, yes. It's a toughie. Got a par-five finisher that—''

"I don't play no golf, Henry. But I get word that sooner or later this Brandon's going to show up at Great Southwest Golf Club, so I pull a few strings and get a guest card. Five days in a row I play that fucking golf course. Don't nobody want to play with me on account of I pull my clubs around on a handcart and wear Hush Puppies golf shoes and won't bet nothing. Also I lose a lot of balls, you know what I mean?''

"Goodness yes, Sam. You know you really should take a few lessons before you—''

"That ain't the point, Henry. Finally on the fifth day this big-ass Brandon shows. Him and his buddies drive up in these Eldos and Mercedes and pile into these nifty electric carts. They got Mexican forecaddies, no less, to find their balls in the rough, a broad with an ass that won't quit—she's wearing shorty-shorts and driving this monster cooler of iced-down beer and shit around with them—and there I stand in these Hush Puppies golf shoes with a bunch of cut-up golf balls. But it's *him,* Henry. I've finally spotted the dirtbag. So you know what I do?''

"I hope you called the U. S. Marshall, Sam. Jesus Christ.''

"Bingo. Nice and legal, ain't no way this creep's gonna duck the subpoena. Yeah, I call the marshal and then hide out in the trees like some kind of fucking Natty Bumpo and tail these thugs around the golf course until the marshal shows. Which is about two hours, time this marshal gets through with his coffee break and shit. The marshal gets there, they're playing number seven, the tight hole alongside the condos. I give the marshal the papers—he's a young, gung-ho sprout decked out in boots and Stetson and crap—describe Brandon to him and point him in the right direction. A few minutes later the marshal comes back grinning like a possum saying, I got him. So—''

''*Perfectamente,* Sam.'' The prosecutor made a circle with his thumb and forefinger. ''We've had a lot of trouble with improper service of subpoenas lately and—''

The agent cocked his head. He was poker-faced with slate-gray eyes. ''You think it's *'perfectamente,'* Henry? I ain't through. So anyway, this marshal comes back grinning and I take a peek over his shoulder at the thugs playing golf. And you know what? He's served the papers on the fucking *Mexican,* Henry—the caddy. I look and this Mexican in overalls is standing in the fairway with a nine-iron in one hand and the subpoena in the other like, *que* the fuck *paso?* And this Brandon creep is bent over close to the green raking a sand trap like he's the groundskeeper or something. Best I can figure, these thugs see the marshal coming in his Roy Rogers getup, figure out he's the law, and finger the Mex as Brandon. So I say, 'You dumb shit, that ain't the guy,' and we have to do it all over. But we got it done, Henry. And now after all that you're telling me you're going to give him immunity? Bull*shit,* Henry, is all I can say.''

Mitchell took the pot from the Mr. Coffee, swishing it around by the handle and studying the thick black dregs as they swirled in the bottom. ''Sam, I know this is irritating to you. But I've got the ultimate responsibility in this case and it's my ass, not yours, if something goes wrong. It's sad, but sometimes you have to let a few little fish out of the net in order to land the big ones. You may have read about a case I handled in the Southern District of New York. The Carmino Family. We let a few guys off, sure, but the dons went down in that one.'' He set the pot back in its niche and grinned. ''Did they ever.''

''You—'' Sam hesitated, his jaw slack, then plunged on. ''Henry, I've been working with you on this case what—six months? Ever since you came to Texas. And you want to know how many times I've heard about the Carmino Family? Once a week, minimum. Look,

Henry, this ain't no fucking New York. This is Texas. There ain't no family here, no outfit guys. This is a *gang* is all, just Pecos Jimmy Fontenot and these other creeps. And—well shit, Henry, you're wanting to give immunity to a guy we figure for two hits—three, if he did the jukebox man got stuffed in the Wurlitzer last year. It doesn't wash, Henry, and I'm asking you please, don't let this scumbag walk."

The prosecutor shook his head. "Sorry, Sam, but no soap. Look, what have we got on this Brandon we can make stick? Income tax evasion, maybe a mail fraud count or two if he mailed in his returns? Hell, Sam, the murders you're talking aren't even *federal* crimes. We didn't do all of this work so that some State of Texas prosecutor can step in and get all of the gravy. Look, with Pecos Jimmy Fontenot you're talking RICO and continuing criminal enterprise, a lot of good stuff. But to get it we need testimony, Sam. You know that. Which brings us to Sizemore Brandon. I'm sorry, Sam, but that's the way it is. I'm giving him the letter." He folded his arms with finality.

The FBI agent looked the prosecutor over for a moment, wanting to say, Yeah, and a RICO prosecution is going to get your name in the paper, isn't it, asshole? But he didn't. Instead he let his breath out slowly. What the hell, it was only a job. "Whatever you say, Henry. Whaddya say we get some fresh java in here?"

Size could figure a few things out for himself. Like that the advice Beaumont Gurney was giving him might not be the best thing for Sizemore Brandon. Gurney was Pecos Jimmy's lawyer, so listening to him was a lot like getting a tip from a bookmaker on which team to bet on. You're betting against the fucker, he's going to give you a winner?

Size zeroed in on the pregnant girl's jaw moving up and down in rhythm as he said, "Okay, Beaumont, so they give me this immunity, say anything I tell them in there"—he jerked his big head in the direction of the floor-to-ceiling grand jury room entrance—"can't be used against me, and I tell 'em, fuck off, I ain't talking. And then what happens?"

Gurney smiled a soft, it-won't-be-so-bad smile. "Oh, they'll take you in front of the judge—Judge Barefoot Sanders is ramrodding the grand jury this session, I think—and he'll order you to talk. Then if you refuse to say anything he'll jail you for contempt. Four months, five tops. No time, really."

"It ain't no time to you, Beaumont, 'cause you ain't the guy what's going to be doing it." Size shifted on the bench so that he was half-facing Gurney. Gurney reminded Size of the dentist at Ramsey II, the one who told him it wasn't going to hurt a bit then yanked so hard on a tooth that Size barreled out of the chair and broke the dentist's nose. Size said, "What about Pecos Jimmy? What's he say?"

"Well you know, Size, I'm not supposed to converse with Jimmy, not while I'm representing you on this matter. It would mean a breach of legal ethics. But knowing Jimmy as we both do, I'm sure you'd win his appreciation if you don't say anything. He'd take care of you, I'm sure of that."

Size gave a snort. "You're not supposed to—The fuck you mean, Beaumont? Pecos Jimmy's paying you. I ain't."

Gurney looked up and down the corridor as though he was about to break into a liquor store. "That's on the q.t., Size. Officially you're paying me and Jimmy's just loaning you the money. I wouldn't—"

"You wouldn't shit, Beaumont. Look, any way you want to slice it up it comes out the same way. I'm betting that Jimmy ain't giving you any cash, either. What do you get, Beaumont, a week's free play against the baseball line? Fuck it, I'm going to talk to Jimmy myself before I decide what to do."

Gurney's eyes narrowed. He played with the big diamond on his finger as he said, "I wouldn't advise that, Size, especially not now. If the FBI sees you talking to Jimmy they're going to claim a conspiracy to obstruct justice. Trust me, I've seen it before."

Size started to say, "The fuck, trust you—" But

before he could, Henry Mitchell goose-stepped toward them from the direction of the anteroom, the FBI agent Size had seen at the golf course ambling along behind him. The prosecutor snapped to a halt in front of Gurney. "Good news for your client, Mr. Gurney. We're giving him immunity to testify. I've just dictated the letter over the phone. One of the girls in the office is typing it up right now and it'll be here shortly."

Size looked at the prosecutor and rolled his eyes. Visible over Mitchell's shoulder, the FBI agent raised a hand and waggled his fingers, a shit-eating grin on his face. Size looked away. Jesus Christ.

Gurney said, "Well, of course, counselor, I haven't had time to confer with my client on that possibility. I'll need some time to do so."

"Of course." The prosecutor checked his watch. "There are some special clauses in the letter I've dictated and I expect it will take fifteen or twenty—Mr. Brandon? Mr. Brandon, sir, where are you going? I'll remind you that you've been instructed not to leave the building."

Several paces down the hall, Size turned. "Well, ain't nothing in your subpoena says I can't take a piss, is there, Mr. Fed?"

"No. Sam, accompany Mr. Brandon. We wouldn't want him to get lost now, would we?"

The FBI agent moved alongside Size, dwarfed by his bulk. "After you, Mr. Brandon," he said.

Size rubbed the back of his thick neck. "Yeah? Well okay, so long as you don't try to grab my peter or nothing." The two strolled off like buddies forever.

Across the hall the pregnant girl stopped chewing gum. She had stringy brown hair. "Ssst! Ssst! Hey, mister."

Gurney quizzically raised his eyebrows. "Are you talking to me, Miss?"

"Yeah," the girl said. "That big red-headed guy? He one of the Dallas Cowboys?"

Henry Mitchell was glad he didn't have to spend a lot of time trying to get one-up on Beaumont Gurney. It was a tough go. Henry had gone through P. S. 239 in the Bronx and struggled through N.Y.U. Gurney had gone to the University of Texas on a baseball scholarship (pitching a three-hitter in the third game of the '62 College World Series against Arizona State), had turned down a Red Sox farm club offer because he didn't need the money, and breezed through law school at Harvard. Henry Mitchell had tried thirteen cases in his career (he was bullshitting Sam somewhat; he'd worked on the Carmino Family trial all right, but only doing book research for the guys who really tried the case). Beaumont Gurney, thirty-eight, had beaten the Feds eight times. Unheard of, a strong enough record for the boys in the U. S. attorney's office to start looking around for something to indict Gurney on.

Mitchell was sizing up Gurney, envying the forty-dollar razored hairstyle, the Armani suit that cost five hundred bucks off the rack (Henry knew—he'd looked one over, tried it on, then forgotten about it when he figured out what a point-and-a-half on the unpaid balance of five hundred dollars would come to every month). He was wondering what the Piaget had cost Gurney when the girl came down the hallway carrying the immunity letter for Sizemore Brandon.

Actually she pranced. She was the new girl the Civil Service Commission had sent over. About twenty-five, with soft brown curls and a wiggle in her high-heeled, tight-skirted walk as she came down the corridor from the elevators. Mitchell made a mental note to find out more about her as he took the letter and pretended to read it over, watching the movement of her backside as she walked away.

"I think you'll find this in order, Beaumont," Mitchell said, handing the letter to Gurney. As Gurney read it over, Mitchell thought, Well, that's some progress—calling him Beaumont, already on a first-name basis with a bigshot Texas lawyer. Wonder what kind of fees a high-dollar hood like Pecos Jimmy Fontenot pays?

Gurney rolled his wrist and held the letter facedown as he checked the Piaget, holding it between a thumb and forefinger to steady it on his wrist. "Time's marching on, Henry. You don't suppose they've gotten lost, do you?" He righted the letter and went on reading.

Mitchell felt a slight twinge of panic, picturing the look on the chief prosecutor's face if Mitchell had to explain why his star witness had disappeared, then relaxed as he realized he could point the finger at the FBI. Although—

"I'd better check on them. Back in a minute, Beaumont."

As the federal prosecutor marched away, Beaumont Gurney shifted the letter from one hand to the other, murmuring, "Hope there're plenty of stalls in there. Jesus Christ—"

The men's room door creaked slightly as Henry Mitchell opened it and looked along the row of gleaming white urinals, the mirror that ran the length of the wall over the five sinks. A young guy was cocking his head at different angles as he combed his hair in the mirror. Mitchell went to the rear and peered out the window, looking through the thick wire screen at the gray stone structure of One Main Place, at the traffic going one way east on Commerce Street, like a row of Tonka toys.

He said to the young guy at the mirror, "Excuse me. You seen a couple of guys, one a monster with a red beard, the other a slim, short-haired guy around forty?" He leaned on the windowsill and crossed his feet at the ankles.

The water was running, the air full of the odor of disinfectant tablets in the urinals. The guy gave his long brown hair a final swish with the comb, turned the water off, and started to say something. Before he could speak, Sam's tenor voice called out, "Over here, Henry. The one in the center."

The prosecutor went to the door of the stall and jiggled it. It was locked. Sam said, "You'll have to go under or over, Henry. It's latched from inside. Come on, I ain't taking a shit in here."

Mitchell looked around. The young guy was watching with his jaw slack, the black comb poised in midair. Mitchell grinned sheepishly, feeling foolish, shrugged, then got down on all fours and peered underneath the door.

Sam was on his knees by the commode. He was hugging its base with his arms. His wrists were handcuffed together and the toilet bowl was too big around for him to lift his arms over it. His pants were down around his ankles, and he was wearing knee-length black socks and white boxer shorts. The area around his right eye was puffy-red, swelling. The eye was beginning to close.

"Tell you what, Henry," Sam said. "You give this creep immunity you get yourself a bodyguard. A big one, to keep me from whipping your ass when I get out of here."

2

The pretty blonde had a sweeping Veronica Lake wave in the front of her hair. Its softness covered approximately one third of her right eye. The eye was crystal blue. It peeped seductively from beneath the overhanging locks as she thoughtfully drew out the crusty center membrane of a crab claw from between lightly clenched, even white teeth. She chewed slowly, savoring the just-right garlic butter sauce that no place could make like the Egyptian—the odd name for the best Italian restaurant west of New York and south of Chicago. She sipped some red Chianti. Then she watched the candle flicker inside the clear glass lamp on the center of the tablecloth as she said vacantly, "Wow, Harold. You've *got* to be kidding."

The man across from her was wearing a pale blue suit with matching tie and a navy silk breast pocket handkerchief. His nails were perfectly manicured and his silver-gray sideburns clipped as if they had been measured with rulers. His expression indicated that he wasn't kidding at all. "Far from it, Suzy. I'm sick to death of the secrecy. I want to show you off to the world, not just the private dining room in the Egyptian. I took the bull by the horns. Diane knows everything now, and what a relief it was to get everything off my chest. Let her have it all. You'll see, Suzy, it'll work out." He reached across the table and patted her hand gently.

Suzy thought fleetingly about the six hundred dollar rent on her apartment. It had just been paid; she had a month. Or a little more counting the ten-day grace period. The title to the Vega was in her name, free and clear. She pictured Harold's frantic thrusts, his high, catlike *yeowwwl!* as he neared climax. Rolling her eyes she said, "You *told* her? Jesus Christ—"

"I know what you're thinking, Suzy." He lit a Marlboro. The soft shadows thrown by the candles flickered on the dark red velvet wallcovering. Visible through the doorway that led to the main dining room, a red-jacketed bartender was briskly shaking locked mixing cups. The taped music was an orchestrated version of "Arrividerci Roma." The dripping crab claws were in a foot-high pile in a gleaming metal serving platter on the table between them. Suzy reached almost timidly for another one as Harold went on. "Yes, I've become so much a part of you that I can feel what you're thinking. And you're right, it isn't easy for me. Tadder's just started Harvard and I think Norma wants to go to school back east. Randolph-Macon, perhaps. There's a lot of equity in the house, Diane will get that. And the lake house *and* the stocks. But my company's doing well, Suzy, we can make it. We don't even have to keep living in Dallas if you don't want to. I want the world to be yours. And I know there's a lot of difference in our ages, darling, but love can bridge the gap. This has been coming on in my heart for a long time. It isn't a sudden decision on my part, Suzy. I've thought it out, believe me I have."

She brushed the blonde lock away from her eye. It softly fell back into place. Suzy looked like a girl watching a scene from *Halloween—The Night He Came Home* as she said, "Sudden? *Sudden!* It's a pile of shit, Harold."

He raised an eyebrow. His lips parted in surprise. "Huh?"

"Well yes, it's—" Suzy took another bite of crabmeat, wanting to give herself time to think. God. From the highest-kicking Tyler J.C. Apache Bell—long flowing strides, white boots marching one in front of the other, flashing legs, pleated skirt six inches below the pantyline, short hem popping from side to side with the movement of her hips—to this. Mistress (God, couldn't there be another word for it?) to Harold. Harold with his damned insurance office, his overstuffed wife. Harold, just enough guts to slip by for a quick—*quick?* God, world-record—bang a couple of times a week; never, thank the Lord, enough gumption to make a night or a weekend of it. Harold on a *full-time* basis? God.

She swallowed. "It's just sex between us, Harold. You've said so yourself a thousand times. No hangups, tie-ups. Wow, you're the guy who'd never give up his wife and family. How can you—"

"We all say things, Suzy. Things we don't mean. I was trying to hide my feelings, it's true. But being devil-may-care just isn't me. I know that now. I've taken the plunge. I'm all yours, darling."

Three men came in from the dining room. One had shoulder-length hair, wore a sleeveless black T-shirt, jeans, and high black boots. There were tattoos on his beefy arms: one a script HARLEY-DAVIDSON, the other a skull and crossbones with ROAD WARRIOR written underneath. The other two men were in western shirts, hats and boots. All three looked around, staring a moment at Suzy and Harold. Then they went back into the bar. Suzy saw the motorcycle guy saying something to the bartender, who looked in her direction.

"Devil-may—" Suzy crossed her legs and brushed crumbs from the slacks of her pale yellow pants suit. She was wearing a red flouncy bandanna around her neck. "Oh, hell, Harold. How can you be mine? I don't want you. Jesus Christ, you're screwing everything up."

The three men came back into the private dining room, this time joined by two more guys and two women. One girl had waist-length black hair combed straight, wore tight jeans molded around her strong legs and buttocks and a sleeveless black T-shirt, like the guy's shirt, only hers had a big silver eagle painted on its front. The eagle's wings were taut against big round breasts. She wore high black leather boots with silver buckles at the ankles. She carried a blue plastic crash helmet under her arm. She had one tattoo, the same HARLEY-DAVIDSON as the motorcycle guy. Her mouth was a wide, cruel, bright-red slash.

One of the two new guys walked with a half-strut. He wore a soft gray Stetson tilted at a cocky angle, a Levi's western-cut navy suit, gray lizard cowboy boots, a gray shirt, and black string tie. He was slim and square-shouldered, around forty. There was a big Rolex watch on his wrist, and Suzy caught the glint of diamonds as he moved his arm. She cocked her head and arched an eyebrow. *What's this?* The motorcycle guy and the motorcycle girl pushed two tables together. The group sat down around them. The guy with the Rolex propped a knee against the edge of the table and snapped his fingers. A waiter appeared as if by magic. The guy stroked the brim of his gray Stetson as he gestured toward Suzy and said something.

"—and you're really cutting me, Suzy," Harold was saying. His voice was cracking. Suzy thought, Jesus, Harold is looking older and older. "Deep, clear to the quick. My heart is aching for you, and you just. . . ." He covered his eyes with a hand, his shoulders heaving.

Suzy leaned sideways and peered around Harold at the group at the two tables. "Could you move over a little, Harold? I'm trying to see."

The waiter approached and stood by the table. A linen napkin was draped over his forearm. He was thin and had a pencil moustache. "Sorry, folks. We'll have to ask you to move into the main dining room."

Harold lifted his head. His eyes were wet. "Move? I don't understand."

"It's Tuesday, sir. The private dining room is reserved every Tuesday for Fontenot Motors. Sales meeting. That's Mr. Fontenot over there." He indicated Gray Hat with the Rolex, who winked at Suzy. Fontenot had a handlebar moustache and white teeth, like the villain who tied Little Nell to the railroad track. But he was cute. Suzy thought about the diamonds on the Rolex and blushed slightly.

"Well, I don't care what day it is," said Harold. "We're not moving. Not for the Hell's Angels, or whoever they are.'' The motorcycle girl heard. She sneered at Harold's back.

The waiter said, ''I'd advise you to go on, bud. Mr. Fontenot don't like nobody horning in.''

Harold stood and squared his shoulders. Suzy thought, God. Harold said, ''Mr. Fontenot? Well, just who the hell is Mr. Fontenot?''

The waiter's glance darted to the other table and back at Harold, like the shifty look of a nervous rat. ''Who's—''

''King's 'X', Mickey,'' Fontenot said loudly from across the room. ''C'mere.''

The waiter went over and bent his skinny head next to Fontenot, who whispered something to him. Fontenot glanced at Suzy as he talked to the waiter. The waiter came back.

To Harold, the waiter said, ''Mr. Fontenot changed his mind. He says since you don't want to give up your table you don't have to. You just have to leave. The lady can stay at the table.'' He glanced at Suzy.

''Well, I—'' sputtered Harold. ''Okay. To save any trouble we'll go. Those types of people aren't worth getting upset over. Come on, darling. We'll finish our conversation outside.''

Suzy wasn't looking at him. Her elbows were on the table, her chin resting lightly on her intertwined fingers. Her crystal-blue gaze was on Gray Hat with the Rolex. Fontenot was returning the look. Suzy stuck out her full lower lip and blew a puff of air upward. The soft Veronica Lake wave rose in the quick gust, then settled back down over her eye.

Without looking at Harold, Suzy said, ''Bye, Harold. It's been swell.''

Suzy settled back in the padded leather chair next to Pecos Jimmy Fontenot and tried to figure out what was going on. This certainly wasn't like any sales meeting that she had ever seen. Which wasn't too many. But she'd shorthanded the minutes on a couple of sales meetings down at Harold's office before Harold saw that he couldn't make heads or tails of her transcriptions and decided to start paying her rent instead. But at Fontenot Motors' sales meetings nobody seemed to want to talk about selling anything.

First there was the motorcycle girl, Yucca-baby. Suzy wondered if Yucca was her first name or her last name. The girl that strutted in front of Suzy in the Apache Belles' lineup was called Tara-baby, but Tara wasn't her name at all. What was Yucca-baby doing? She sat at the table with her silver-buckled ankle resting on her knee and her shin parallel to the floor. The motorcycle guy sat on Yucca-baby's right. His name was Tommy and he said everything from the side of his mouth. On Yucca-baby's left was a tiny red-headed girl with big, scared-doe eyes. Sometimes Yucca-baby would whisper to Tommy, scratching her tattoo as she did. Then the two of them would snicker and Yucca-baby would poke Tommy in the ribs or pinch his thigh. Then sometimes Yucca-baby would bend to her left and whisper something in the redhead's ear. The redhead's eyes would widen and she'd give a smile that Suzy couldn't figure out. Was it a happy smile or a scared smile? Then Yucca-baby would pinch the redhead's thigh. Pretty freaking hard. Strange.

The three guys in western hats and shirts and jeans were named Chester, Winslow, and Slim. Slim was a colored guy with salt-and-pepper kinky hair, a wide gray moustache and big white teeth. His western shirt was red with pink flowered quilting at the shoulders. He was pretty skinny, and Suzy thought that was probably why they called him Slim. How odd—a nigger cowboy. Slim drank Orange Tommy, a mixture of wine and orange juice that came in a squat brown bottle. He never said a word, just sat and sipped. Maybe just polite or timid, being the only colored person at the table.

Chester and Winslow were like two peas in a pod. Even dressed alike—blue denim shirts and straw cowboy hats with upturned brims and creases down the center. They both had big guts and drank Coors. Once Chester tried to start the nearest thing to a business conversation that Suzy heard all afternoon. He told

Pecos Jimmy that Slats over at the Red Devil was knocking down on the jukebox take, whatever that meant. Pecos Jimmy told Chester to shut up. This was supposed to be a business meeting, wasn't it? Suzy thought that was a pretty strange way for Pecos Jimmy to act. But since Pecos Jimmy was having the skinny waiter set a fresh Jack Daniels and water in front of her every five minutes, Suzy didn't have much time to think about anything. She was getting drunk. God.

And this guy Jimmy Fontenot. Pecos Jimmy, cute name. And a pretty cute guy, but boy was he different. He kept smoothing his handlebar moustache with a forefinger. When he'd lean close to Suzy she could smell his lime aftershave. Once he put his hand on her leg and squeezed. He murmured softly, "Firm. Nice, baby, I like that." She giggled and said, "Sure it's firm. You should have seen me high-kicking with the Apache Belles." He asked her what club that act was in. Suzy couldn't believe that anybody didn't know what the Apache Belles were. Not anybody who'd ever heard of the Cotton Bowl.

As the afternoon wore on Suzy decided that weird as he might seem, Pecos Jimmy was pretty generous. A wild and crazy guy. All of these people kept coming into the Egyptian to see him—men in business suits, a couple of young girls in jeans, one deeply tanned sandy-haired guy in yellow golf slacks and a blue knit Izod shirt, a suntan line on his left wrist and below that a pale white hand. People stopped by to see Pecos Jimmy one by one. Pecos Jimmy greeted each and all alike, getting to his feet, shaking hands. "Hiya, Doris—Sally—Hey, Bo! Howsa putter workin', buddy? Naw, business ain't been too good—Size? You talkin' about Size Brandon? Shit, you kiddin'? Size, he's my boy. I ain't worried—"

Then, while whoever-it-was was standing there, Jimmy would say to Yucca-baby, "Tally up, Yucca."

Yucca-baby would half-smile, fish a small spiral pad from her snug jean pocket, glance at whomever was standing there (sneering at the men, leering at the women), and read off a figure. Like, "Twenty-five hundred your way, Jimmy,'' or ''Pay the man a dime, Jimmy.'' And whatever Yucca-baby read off, Jimmy did it. Collect or pay, fishing a wad of bills out of his pocket that made Suzy bug-eyed. Collecting from the people, adding money to his roll. Or paying out, grinning while he did it, all the while joking, kidding around. Suzy sipped cool Jack Daniels, crunching ice between her teeth, and thought, Wow, what a way to run a car business, huh?

And after he paid out or collected, whichever, Jimmy would wave a hand expansively toward the other tables in the room and say, ''What's your pleasure? On Pecos Jimmy's tab, huh?'' Partyingest man that Suzy had ever run across.

In about an hour and a half the private dining room was full of chattering, laughing, good-time people. Mickey, the skinny waiter, was running back and forth with drinks, ice tinkling in them, and trays of crab claws, lasagna, and spaghetti carbonara with a creamy white bacon sauce. And Jimmy was squeezing Suzy's hand, rubbing her leg, as he said to Mickey, ''Whatever they want, huh, Mickey? Anything. Nothin' too good for a friend of Pecos Jimmy.''

One man came by who Pecos Jimmy got into a little argument with. By then Suzy had quite a buzz on. Things were foggy. Maybe the guy didn't like the car that he'd bought. Who knows? The guy was short, fat, and red-faced.

Breathing in quick gasps like he was out of breath, the guy said, ''No way, Jimmy. It wasn't on the square, I ain't payin'. Fuck you and your fifteen-cent line.''

Fifteen-cent line? Suzy guessed that the guy meant Pecos Jimmy's cars were pretty cheap. Why would a man like Pecos Jimmy sell cheap cars?

Pecos Jimmy didn't say anything, just folded his hands on the table and looked at the man. Suzy wondered if Pecos Jimmy's feelings were hurt.

Then the guy said, ''So don't bug me about it, see? You'll be wastin' your time.'' Then he turned around and stalked out through the bar.

Pecos Jimmy shrugged, chuckled, and stroked his moustache. "Jesus Christ," he said. "Slim."

Slim wiped the back of his hand across his shiny ebony forehead. Then he said, "Sho', boss." He set his Orange Tommy on the table and ambled off in the same direction the fat man had gone.

Pecos Jimmy said loudly, "Nothin' to it, folks. Just a little misunderstandin' is all. Absolutely nothin' to worry about."

Everybody went on eating and drinking.

Slim came back in a few minutes. He tipped his western hat and sat back down, handing Pecos Jimmy a wad of money across the table. Slim said, "Half, boss. Rest next Tuesday. He'll be here." He swigged more Orange Tommy.

Suzy thought that Slim was pretty diplomatic for a colored man. Solving problems like that, she thought sleepily as her eyes half-closed and she rested her head on Pecos Jimmy's shoulder. Wow. Slim must be the Customer Service Department—

It was getting dark when Beaumont Gurney nosed his midnight-blue Lincoln Town Car into a head-in parking place in front of the Egyptian. Coming within a gnat's whisker of hitting the rear bumper of Pecos Jimmy Fontenot's snow-white Biarritz, then wincing and bracing himself, he let out a sigh as he eased on into the parking space without nicking the Caddy. Pecos Jimmy was never satisfied with one space, the prick; the Biarritz's rear wheel was a good foot over the painted line.

Gurney reached inside the left breast of his charcoal suit, took the Beretta out, and locked it up in the glove compartment. Gurney had taken to carrying the piece a couple of years ago. It was shortly after Jubie Cardenas's sentencing hearing, the one where Cardenas had said to Gurney, "Man, one-ah these days you going to wake up with a second asshole over the one you was born with." There wasn't much chance of Cardenas giving Gurney a second asshole anytime soon, not with Cardenas sneering and spitting as he went off cuffed and chained between two marshals to do thirty years of federal time, but the remark set Beaumont Gurney to thinking about it, and that's when Gurney started carrying the Beretta. Let some Mexican dope dealer try and give Beaumont Gurney a second asshole after Gurney had put a couple of slugs into the fucker, huh?

Gurney eased the Lincoln's door open, being careful not to bang the side of Pecos Jimmy's Cad, and squeezed out to stand in between the cars. Sun going down, but the heavy air was still hot as a pizza oven. Looking across the street and to the west Gurney could see the grass-covered grounds around the Dr. Pepper plant, beyond that the white building front at Bekins' Van and Storage, and farther on down the way, the Mockingbird Lane bridge over North Central Expressway. Freeway lights glowed in the dusk.

On the adjacent corner to the east, across Greenville Avenue, the Kip's Restaurant parking lot was full. Visible through Kip's glassed-in entryway people sat on couches and waited in line for tables. The Big Boy stood grinning on the corner in front of Kip's thrusting a juicy burger on a sesame seed bun over his head with a chubby hand, his happy cartoon face telling the world there wasn't any better. Gurney threw a broad wink in the direction of the Big Boy and went into the Egyptian.

There were four occupied tables in the front dining room, three by couples and one by two women in their forties in pants suits and with brightly painted nails. The women gave Gurney the once-over as he went by.

Behind the bar was a long row of bottles, their reflections in the long polished mirror like double vision, silver pouring spouts corked into their necks. On a stool with an elbow propped against the bar's foam padding sat Joe Campisi. Campisi was the Egyptian's owner, a short, grinning Italian guy. Right now he was shooting the shit with a pudgy brunette waitress in a black dress and white apron. Gurney raised a hand—Hiya, Joe—then lifted his eyebrows in a silent question. Campisi nodded and jerked his head in the direction of the private dining room entrance in the rear. Gurney went on past the bar and through the door.

Back here there was a crowd. Gurney recognized Bo Petrie at one of the linen-covered tables. Not many years back Petrie was a comer on the pro tour with a million-dollar swing and a putting stroke smooth as buttermilk; now he hustled two-bit muny course games and fought a long-lost battle with a sports-betting habit. Petrie gave Beaumont Gurney a tanned, crooked, happy-drunk grin and waved. The half-full and empty glasses on the table, plus the long-haired, leggy girls on either side of him, said that Petrie'd booked a winner this week. Next week he'd be nursing draft beer and sitting alone at the bar.

Yucca-baby was there, too. She had her beefy, almost manlike arms folded on a table in front of her. She was drinking Coors from a can and pitching woo at a tiny red-headed broad. Gurney grinned at her. Yucca-baby acknowledged him with eyes like lumps of dull coal.

Gurney scanned the rest of the room, nodding and smiling at the faces he recognized; most of them he couldn't put together with a name. Just seen them around. Noticing a few hard-line bettors reminded Gurney that it was Tuesday. Settle-up day. A little twinge of panic chilled through him as he tried to remember whether he owed Jimmy or if he had money coming. Then he relaxed. Okay, yeah, Sunday night it was, Nolan Ryan dragging the hummer up from yesteryear and blowing it by the Padres. Big winner, made Gurney a little ahead this week. He squinted and looked around some more.

There was a hard pull on Gurney's sleeve. Close on his right a deep voice said, "Hey, Bo. Bo Gurney, drag yo' Perry Mason ass over here an' have a beer wif us po' folk."

It was Slim Burdine, sitting just feet away at a table, a Stetson tilted back off his glistening black forehead. Slim showed Gurney a gold tooth in a wide grin. There was a white woman, black hair, not bad looking, sitting by Slim with her arm looped through his. Gurney remembered that he hadn't seen Slim since he'd beaten the extortion beef. Seems the state witness in the case forgot to show.

Gurney stepped closer and patted Slim on the shoulder. "You know me," Gurney said. "Never pass up a free one. But I can't. Business calling. Where's Jimmy, Slim? I need to jaw with him."

The woman giggled and scooted closer as Slim put a hand on her thigh. "Shee-it, Bo, Jimmy's entertainin'. Behind the curtain in the *private* room. Yonder way." He indicated a corner of the room that was cordoned off by thick blue drapes. "Where my Sizemo', Beaumont? We figgered Size to show up same time as you."

"Yeah, well that's what I need to see Jimmy about. Size. Jimmy's not tied up to where he can't talk, is he?"

Slim's pink gums showed as he cackled, "Mist' Pecos Jimmy'd *like* to get tied up by what's back there with him. But naw. Go on back. Say Bo, Size—he ain't got no shit storm? Hey, Bo, say he don't."

"Not now," said Gurney over his shoulder, starting to walk away, weaving through the crowded tables, headed for the closed curtains. "Won't, either, unless the Feds run across him. Stay cool, Slim."

Gurney hesitated for just an instant before pulling a drape aside and entering the curtained-off area. He hoped that Jimmy was in a good mood. Gurney had to make a quick decision. Was what he had to say important enough to butt in on whatever Pecos Jimmy was doing? Pecos had a nasty temper at times. Yeah, this was important. The curtains parted and fell instantly back into place as Gurney entered.

Pecos Jimmy had the kind of look about him that Gurney had never seen before, not in the whole—what, fifteen years? As if Pecos was spaced out on something. His gray Stetson was on his head at a strange angle, the narrow front of the brim sort of cockeyed and above his left cheek instead of his nose. His black string tie was undone and hanging loose, his collar unbuttoned, big Adam's apple sticking out. He was sitting on one side of a linen-covered table, a small round one. An uncapped Pearl longneck was sitting in front of him, next to it a half-full glass of tea-colored beer. The beer had been sitting there a long time. It was flat, all the bubbles gone. There was a lit Pall Mall cigarette in Jimmy's hand, smoke drifting up and vanishing in the air, but he didn't seem to be smoking it. Just sort of staring at the lengthening gray ash.

The blonde across the table from Jimmy was probably a knockout. At least she had a knockout body, good legs in a snug yellow pants suit and a filmy red scarf tied loosely around a slim model's neck. But Gurney couldn't see her face. Her arms were crossed on the white tablecloth and she'd buried her face in them. Long straight honey blonde hair hung in cascades, touching the tablecloth and billowing around her arms. Her fine breasts moved gently in unison with slow, even sleep-breaths.

Gurney pulled up a soft-bottomed leather chair and sat down. "Damn, Jimmy. You look like you lost your best friend."

Without looking at Gurney, Jimmy Fontenot said, "Well, maybe I did. You're gonna give me some bad news, Beaumont." The ash fell from the cigarette and broke up on the table. Absently, Pecos Jimmy brushed the ashes away and stubbed the butt in a glass tray. "You've got to. Nothing good's happened all day. The bettors beat me like a tom-tom this week. I've picked up this girl here looks like Jayne Mansfield, gotten her all to myself, and look at her. Broad's too drunk to do so much as a hand job. So what's the bad news?"

The blonde moved slightly and murmured something as Gurney said, "Well, it could be bad news somewhere down the line. But not yet. Size Brandon did a disappearing act right in the middle of the grand jury hearing. Son of a bitch couldn't just run, he had to beat the shit out of an FBI agent on the way out. Jesus Christ, Jimmy, five hours I've spent with the most boring damn Yankee assistant U.S. attorney you ever saw. I'm trying to smooth things over, but I don't think I'm doing any good."

Pecos Jimmy didn't seem to have heard. His gaze was dully directed across the table at the long blonde hair as he said, "What's an Apache Belle, Beaumont?"

"It's a drill team. You know, a bunch of girls in short western outfits that do routines and stuff. They're from Tyler Junior College, do a halftime performance every year at the Cotton Bowl."

Pecos Jimmy stroked his moustache. "Jesus Christ. Five million broads, I gotta pick a pep squad cutie. Where'd Size go to? Number one. And number two, what are those Feds trying to do to me?" He looked away from the girl and, for the first time, at Gurney. He looked a little scared. Gurney had never seen Jimmy when he looked frightened.

"Hey, Jimmy, it isn't that bad. I know what they're trying to do. The prosecutor, Mitchell, was about to pee in his pants to tell me about this great case he's got on you. RICO. Continuing criminal enterprise. What they've got to do to convict you is prove two overt acts on your part—you know, stuff you did in conspiracy with others, things like that. But I don't think they can dig up a case unless Size testifies for them. And Size takes a powder on them, standup guy. So here we are. Not so bad."

"Not so bad, huh?" said Pecos Jimmy, turning once again to stare ahead of him at nothing. "It's not so bad that my buddy, a guy I've known since both of us were no bigger than a minnow, that he's maybe going to jail to keep from talking about Pecos Jimmy? You don't think that's bad, Beaumont? Well, I do. It gets me right here." He put a clenched fist to his breastbone.

The blonde raised her head, showing a pretty porcelain face with a soft wave of hair down over one eye. She smiled lazily at Gurney, yawned, and went back to sleep.

"You've got to be realistic, Jimmy," Gurney said. "Size is well paid for what he does. And you've picked a good man for the job. To get a RICO conviction they've somehow got to tie you into certain things—

laundering illegal money, putting it into legitimate businesses, things like that. As far as most folks know, Size has been doing all of the deals on his own. There's nobody to tie Jimmy Fontenot into any of it *but* Size. Without testimony from him the Feds don't have a leg to stand on. Besides, I'm not even sure they can find him again, not if he doesn't want them to."

Pecos Jimmy's eyes were actually brimming with tears. Gurney couldn't believe it. Pecos Jimmy said, his voice breaking slightly, "God, I don't know if I can take it if Size has to go to jail again because of me. It'll be what, the *third* time? Look, Beaumont, I don't care what anybody says. I'm no heartless bastard. I got feelings. You know what we're talking about here, what Size Brandon means to me? Jesus, if it wasn't for him I'd have never made it past the sixth grade in one piece. I'd have gotten killed. Shit, I'm through being a heel where Size is concerned. I've got to get him off the hook. That's what I'll do. Let the Feds take me—I can cop a plea, do maybe two or three years. God knows old Size has done enough time on account of me."

Gurney played with the sparkling diamond on his finger. "Now I wouldn't advise you to jump into anything, Jimmy. Two or three years? I don't think you understand. The Feds aren't after you for the fun of it. They start grand jury investigations and all that, they're after you bigtime. Jesus, Jimmy. If they could get Size to open up I think you'd be looking at thirty years. Minimum."

It took just an instant for it to sink in. Pecos Jimmy's jaw dropped. He snapped his head around to look at Gurney. "Thirty—? Goddam, Beaumont, thirty fucking years? For no more'n I've done? You're shitting me."

"I'm afraid not," Gurney said. "The Feds go after a guy, they do it for keeps."

"And you're telling me Size Brandon, he's the only one can make a case against me?"

"Absolutely, Jimmy. The way I understand your organization, there's no doubt about it."

Pecos Jimmy's eyes narrowed. He reached up and straightened the gray Stetson on his head, brim point now directly over his slim nose. "Well, where's the dirty sonofabitch hiding? Size Brandon, Beaumont, where's he at?"

3

Size strolled out of the Federal Building acting as if he had all the time in the world to get where he was going and he didn't really care whether he made it or not. It was the only way to go. He was fucked anyway if they spotted the FBI in the john before Size got outside, so what the hell. Take it easy. Acting as though he was running from something would be his second mistake today. The first mistake was listening to Beaumont Gurney and coming here in the first place. He should have taken a powder the second they laid the subpoena on him.

So Size rode the elevator to the lobby with some hatless and coatless civil servants in short-sleeve white shirts and dark ties and played one of the boys. When one guy wondered if the new pay raise was going to be effective retroactively to the beginning of the pay period, Size said that he hoped to hell it was. The guy said, "Well, seeing as how the president didn't sign the raise until last Friday they probably can't get it into the computer on time." Size said, "You think so? Hell, that'll be tough." Then the guy said, laughing, "Guess Reagan's too busy trying to remember what he knows about giving guns to the contras to sign the raise, ha, ha." Size said, "Yeah, what's a contra going to do with a gun anyway? He don't know how to shoot the fucker. Give him a blowgun or a spear to chuck." The guy gave Size a funny look as the elevator doors opened into the building lobby.

A. U.S. marshal was checking people through a metal detector as they came in through the revolving doors from Commerce Street. He was fifty or so, wearing gray slacks, a blue blazer, and a Fifties-style white-sidewall haircut. As he moved back and forth in front of the rectangular wooden pass-through, he limped slightly. Size walked up just as the guy was going through a woman's purse, dumping keys, compact, and Kleenex out on a small table.

The woman was saying, "I'm just for God's sake trying to pick up a few forms from the IRS. I'm sure not a spy. Do I look like a spy?" She had frosted hair, was short and chubby and wore round-framed glasses. Her arms were folded and one of her feet was doing a toe-tap.

"I know, lady," the marshal said, "believe me. Nobody's a spy. Five hundred, maybe a thousand folks a day say the same thing. We're not looking for spies. We're looking for kooks, guys that—"

"Excuse me," said Size, trying to sound dumb.

"Just a minute, buddy . . . Like I say, kooks. Three or four times a day somebody calls up and makes a threat. Against judges mostly. This judge or that judge. Hey, you know up north they're trying out a system where the judge sits in court inside a bulletproof bubble? We need twice the marshals we got. We can't serve civil papers or warrants or even hunt guys what have walked off from prison camps. All we got time to do anymore is guard the judge. Here, lady." He gave the woman her purse. She rolled her eyes and headed for the bank of elevators, heels clicking. To Size the marshal said, "Yeah, what's up? Don't tell me—you're not a spy. That's a joke, son."

Size thought, Jesus Christ, this yo-yo's guarding the judge? Who's guarding the guy? Anybody wants a judge knocked off, it'd be like falling off a log. He said, "Listen, can you tell me how to get to Reunion Arena?" He stood as close as he dared, the guy might be nearsighted. Make sure this marshal gets a good look.

"Yeah. Say, you must be new in town, not knowing where the arena is. Just go west, to your left. Six or seven blocks, through the underpass."

Size said thanks, went out into the street and headed

east, picturing the old marshal telling them, "He went thataway. Yeah, I *thought* there was something funny about the big red-headed guy. What is he, a spy?"

Size hadn't gone a full block before his collar was damp and sticking to his neck. The sun was getting just close enough to the horizon to cover the sidewalks along the western curb of the street in shade. As Size made a right on Akard Street and entered the shadows he stripped off his Ultrasuede coat and loosened his collar. He folded his yellow tie and stuck it in the breast pocket of the coat, folding the coat over his forearm. A man without legs, bearded and wearing a blue Texas Rangers baseball cap, was on a wooden platform with metal wheels, the wheels scraping as he propelled himself along using his hands and arms like oars. Size did a little hop-step as he quickened his pace and passed the legless guy.

Size was thinking, Helluva predicament. Feds going to lock me up if I don't stick around and talk. 'Course I ain't going to, me and Pecos go way back, but Jesus Christ. First the car, Pecos steals it and I get busted driving the damn thing out to dinner. Eight months lockup, and by the time I hit the street Jimmy's gone and organized things, I'm working for *him* instead of the other way around. Then the poker game thing. What a deal, huh? Jimmy's in the back running the game, snatching the take out of the pot, me watching the door like I'm supposed to. Plainclothes cop—Jesus Christ, little fat guy looks like he couldn't hit himself in the ass with a paddle, no wonder we don't spot him as the law the couple of times he played in the game—this plainclothes cop walks up and flashes a warrant on me. What the fuck can I do? It's let him in, bust up the game for good, or figure out a way to stop him. So I deck the fucking guy, only way I can see. Just a little tap, didn't break nothing. Two-and-a-half—count 'em, two-and-a-half fucking years—that one costs me. Pecos Jimmy—shit, the cop forgets about him and his poker game the second I let him have it. The whole deuce-and-a-half Jimmy keeps running the game. So when I get out this time, what does Jimmy do? Gives me another fucking job is all. We're buddies, Jimmy, sure. But Jesus Christ, there's got to be a limit.

The sidewalk wasn't crowded, just a few women in pairs and three window-shopping and some men in business suits hustling along swinging briefcases. Size checked his watch. It wasn't three yet. Another hour before the rush. Sweat was beginning to run down his forehead in rivulets as he crossed with the light at Akard and Jackson, walked a block and a half to his right and entered a glass-fronted office in an old red brick building, five stories high with dirty windows. There was a huge sign over the door, eight-foot-high letters that said: LEON HUNDLEY BAIL BONDS—NEED A FRIEND? The sign was iridescent yellow with black letters. It was visible from the old county jail windows a block away atop the courthouse.

Inside, the sun slanted through the windows and made parallelogram-shaped outlines on the dusty tile floor. The windows had dirty streaks that made little shadows in the bright outlines. A waist-high wood counter ran the length of the room and separated the reception-waiting area from the office proper. Size was conscious of the chugging of the air conditioner; the suddenly cool air made goose bumps on his arms. A stack of slick-paper brochures was on the counter. Size picked one up and looked at it. A skinny guy, jug-handle ears, clean-shaven, Jewish features, was pictured grinning over a caption that said, "Leon Hundley—The Working Man's Candidate. City Council, Precinct 4." Size snorted to himself and put the brochure back on the counter.

In back of the counter, Jez Radley was sitting in a swivel chair behind a scarred brown desk. She was on the phone, fiddling with the harlequin-framed glasses that hung on a silver chain around her neck. "I know, sweetie. Jail's no fun, that's what we're here for. But I've got to have money, honey. Pays the rent. Tell you what—you have your cousin come down here with half the money, I'll trust you for the rest. Deal?" She was wearing a navy sleeveless sweater that outlined little rolls of fat poking out around her bra straps.

Size went through the creaky swinging counter gate and sat down across from her. The chair groaned under his weight. Jez was listening to whoever was on the phone. Size pictured a desperate-looking guy in the phone booth at the jail with other guys in line behind him saying, "Hurry it up, Buddy." Jez Radley winked at Size. She had stubby brown lashes and didn't wear eye makeup. Finally she said, "Sorry, sweetie. It's the best I can do. Let me hear from you, okay?" She hung up, saying to Size, "It's only Tuesday. You're early."

"I ain't collecting. Where's Leon?"

There was a calendar on the wall behind her that advertised an insurance company—INTERNATIONAL FIDELITY. She hadn't torn the last month off as yet; the calendar was still showing May. She said, lisping slightly, "Leon?" She put on her glasses and blinked. "Last time I looked he was in his office. He's thinking about slashing his wrists." She had a pleasant round face that always looked to Size as if she was about to bust out laughing. "Oh, and even if you're not here to collect, I've got something for you . . . you big pansy."

"The paper this morning said I'm an alleged enforcement man. Don'tcha read, Jez? What you calling me a pansy for?"

She gave a twinkly half-grin. Jez was a broad without much looks and had a weight problem—not really a bad one. But she grew on you, with the way she smiled and got under your skin. She didn't look too bad when she dressed up, either—Jez wore clothes pretty good. Size figured Leon to be head over heels for Jez and didn't blame him. She said, "The guy at the paper doesn't know you, sweetie. I do. And you're a pansy. A marshmallow. Here." She took a brown letter-size envelope out of her desk and tossed it to him.

Size caught the envelope, feeling its cushiony softness, tore it open, and looked inside. There was a small stack of bills, mostly twenties. "Huh? I didn't win no bets this week."

"Size. Jesus Christ. It's from Benny, honey, Benny Sands. He thought you'd drop by here and left it for you."

"Aw. Benny. Sure." Size took the money and stuffed it in his pocket without counting it. "He owes me from pool."

Jez's moon-face softened. She shook her head. "Pool? Benny already told me, you big galoot. I *thought* Benny came up with his kid's bond money awfully fast. What's the deal, Size? Leon and I wanted to give Benny credit to begin with. So he's down and out, we all know Benny for a lot of years. He's good for it. But no, you won't give the okay. You got real hardass about it, like this"—she tucked her chin and deepened her voice, mimicking—"what the fuck does Benny think this is, his birthday? Broke my heart to turn poor old Benny down, it really did. So today Benny comes in to drop off the envelope and it turns out he borrowed the bond money from you. You big pansy."

Size waved a huge paw in the air as though he was batting away a mosquito. "Aw, Jez, you know it ain't good business to be giving credit on bond money to a bunch of brokes. Jimmy don't like it. But what I want to loan Benny out of my own pocket, that's between Benny and me." He looked serious. "Look, Jez, don't say nothing about this to anybody. I wouldn't want it to get around, okay?"

"Size, you dumbo, when are you going to wake up? Always Jimmy this and Jimmy that. Jesus Christ, can't you see Pecos Jimmy's just using you? Wise up. Let *him* take a little risk—he's making all the money. It's none of my business, honey, I know. But Jimmy's way in the back holding the purse strings and it's your big dumb butt up front on the line. And if you think Jimmy Fontenot gives a flip what happens to you, you're crazy."

He felt his neck flushing. Jesus, she was right. Quickly, he said, "I've been thinking about it, Jez. Hey, look, I gotta see Leon, okay?" Brushing her off, he got up, lumbering across the room to the frosted glass-paned door at the rear, feeling her stare and not looking at her. He knocked once on Leon's door and went in.

Leon Hundley looked as though Yom Kippur had been canceled. His dark eyes had the sad soft look that comes with worry and with pity. And Leon hadn't ever pitied anybody in his life. His long, slightly crooked nose was pointed down at a form on his desk. There was a logo on the form that began with a big, three-dimensional block E.

As Size sat down, Leon said, "I thought you were over at the federal grand jury today. I'm not expecting to see you for a while."

"Yeah, well, I went, Leon, but I cut it short. I need a lift. And the piece I left here—the Luger. You know Daisy Mae's, out on Harry Hines Boulevard? Sure you do, Benny Sands works there. That's where my car is. I hooked a ride downtown with Beaumont Gurney."

Leon looked up from the form he'd been going over. His hair was jet black, cut short and parted on his left. The politician look. Size liked Leon better the other way, with the long hair and the full beard, the open-necked shirts and medallions. Today Leon had on a blue suit and red tie. He said, "Well, at least *somebody's* through with the federal grand jury. It's trouble I'm afraid I got, Size—that special grand jury that's been investigating the condos along I-30? Jesus Christ, the word is my number's about to come up."

"Yeah? You ain't kidding? That's tough, Leon. I-30 condos, I seen that in the paper. You in on that scam?"

Leon's eyes softened and saddened even more. "It was an *investment* is all. One of my campaign contributors brought it to me. Joint venture, forty acres. Jesus Christ, we buy the land on Monday, sell it on Thursday. Turned a profit of two hundred grand—two jumbos."

"What's wrong with that?"

"Nothing. It's the *goy* Savings and Loan, the schmucks." Leon turned the form around so that Size could read it. Underneath the block "Empire Savings" was printed Mortgage Loan Application." It was a Xerox of the original, with Leon's signature on the bottom of the page. "Empire Savings, the schlock outfit in Mesquite, they financed the whole shmear. They got to wheeling and dealing so fast that the FSLIC shut them down and took them over, then started going over their loan files with a fine-tooth comb. Jesus Christ, it's everybody ever bought a lot on I-30 they're getting. Just last week a doctor in town got *five years,* can you believe it? You know Phil Burleson. He's my lawyer. Phil says they can prosecute anybody who ever filled out a loan application. I knew it. It was too good to be true."

"Look, Leon," Size said, "I'm in kind of a hurry. The piece, huh? Say, what kind of a beef is that, selling forty acres? Don't sound like much to me."

Leon reached into the bottom drawer of his desk. It was old and scarred, same as Jez's. The Luger was in a white nylon shoulder rig that fit like parachute straps. The Luger's weight made a soft thump, muffled by the cushioned nylon. Size stood and struggled into the holster, one arm at a time, as Leon said, "I wouldn't have believed it myself. It's a charge called 'False Statement to Get a Loan.' Sounds like horseshit, but *five years?* Jesus Christ, I'd be better off doing the kind of things you and Pecos Jimmy are into. At least then they'd have to prove I did something, not just filled out a loan application." His thin jaw worked nervously.

"Say, Leon, get my coat for me. It's by Jez's desk out front, I don't want to go walking around wearing this piece where anybody can see me." Size slapped the Luger, now snug and heavy under his left armpit. His palm stung. He cocked his head. "And whaddya mean, 'the kind of things' me and Jimmy are into? Shit, Leon, I never made no false statement to get a loan. The fuck kind of a guy you think I am, anyway?"

"Watch out, Leon!" Size jammed his feet against the passenger-side floorboard, bracing himself and hitting an imaginary brake pedal. He shut his eyes. The brakes squealed. The car came to a jolting halt, Size feeling his weight thrust hard forward, then abruptly backward against the cushioned seat. He opened his eyes and looked. The rear bumper of the Ford pickup in front of them was maybe six inches from the red Caddy's nose. "Jesus, you want me to drive?" Visible beyond the pickup was the overpass and cloverleaf ramp leading from westbound Elm Street onto Stemmons Freeway going north. The red brick Texas School Book Depository was on the right, the grassy green knoll around the Kennedy Memorial on the left. People walked in groups on the lawns, gawking and taking pictures of the stone memorial and the depository across the street. Up on Stemmons, cars, trucks, and buses were moving at a good clip.

Leon was clutching the wheel with both hands in a death grip. The Seville's A/C was blowing cool wind, and he had an old Dionne Warwick tape playing on the wraparound stereo. Bert Bacharach tunes—"Do You Know the Way to San Jose?" Leon kept his foot on the brake and turned to look at Size. "Do I want you to drive? It might be better that way. Then when we get arrested I can claim you're holding me hostage. You walked out on the grand jury? I haven't got enough trouble with I-30 condos, now I'm aiding an escape? How come you don't tell me these things?"

"I didn't want you to worry about me. Stay to the right, Leon. Jesus, that was close."

The supercab jerked and moved on. The Seville smoothly climbed the long curve upward and around to the right, rolling into a northbound freeway lane. A bearded guy in overalls, thumb cocked, was standing at the freeway entrance. He sneered at the Caddy as it went by.

"Look, Size, you mean a lot to me. If it wasn't for you I'd never have the bail bond business. But what do you think the voters would say about Leon Hundley driving a man who just escaped from a federal grand jury out to a strip joint? It's an image I'm keeping."

"It's an image you're keeping, Leon. It's an image Pecos Jimmy's keeping. So how come I ain't keeping a fucking image? How come I'm running around doing dirty work and going to jail all the time and everybody else is keeping up an image? Go to the right again up here, Leon. Take the tollway ramp over to Harry Hines Boulevard. It's faster that way.'' He scratched his red beard, figuring it probably had to go. Maybe a dye-job on the hair.

''I don't know how come, Size. Man does what he wants. He grows up, gets older, learns things. You don't seem to. You're still with the poker games, the night life. So settle down.''

Size blinked as the afternoon sun glinted sharply from the Seville's hood. As they wound to the left, Lemmon Avenue with its shade trees on both sides overhead, he said, ''So maybe someday I'm gonna, Leon. Find a good broad, get married. For now I can't think about that. For now I've got to get ahold of Pecos Jimmy, find out what I'm gonna do about this grand jury shit.''

Harry Hines Boulevard changed in a hurry. One minute they were rolling along between manicured grassy slopes with glass-walled office buildings on both sides. Scant blocks farther on were warehouses, factories with smokestacks, the Seville's front suspension jiggling over tar-filled cracks in the pavement.

''I can be straight with you, can't I?'' Leon said. ''I mean, we're close enough friends I can tell you what's what. You got a chance, I think you should help the Feds. Tell them what they want to know.''

Size's jaw slackened. He turned in the seat, facing Leon's profile and resting a beefy forearm on the seat-back. The Luger pressed against his ribcage as he said, ''Jesus Christ, Leon. I can't believe that's coming from you. Be a stool pigeon? I'd never—Jesus Christ, you're getting soft in the head.''

''Soft I might be in the head. But I think it's the only chance you've got. The shmucks—the Feds—they're never going to let up. You think Pecos Jimmy Fontenot would take the heat for you if it were the other way around? Get serious.''

''I'm getting serious, Leon. And being a snitch ain't the answer. Never has been and never will be. Jez been talking to you?'' Size didn't really have to ask. He already knew.

Leon looked straight ahead, veering the Seville's nose slightly to go around a gray-haired man in a blue jumpsuit who was crossing the street. The first in a long row of topless bars was coming into view on the right—Texas Darlin', a white-fronted, tiltwall stucco building with a sign in front of it on a tall pole. The sign pictured a tall gal in a bikini who was wearing a huge ten-gallon hat and twin holstered pistols at her waist. She was outlined in red neon.

Leon said, ''If I'm talking to Jez about it, it's for your own good. She's a good woman, Size. She's got compassion. And she worries about you. Thank God she doesn't know the whole story, about the guys getting killed. Jesus Christ, I guess your head is hard enough that you'd take the rap for Pecos Jimmy on that, too.''

Size's chin lifted. ''Now let's don't be talking about nobody getting knocked off, Leon. You don't know nothing about that. I ain't told you nothing about that. If anybody's dead it's 'cause of something they did and . . . shit, Leon, just don't talk about nobody dying, okay?''

''So all right, already. Daisy Mae's, you said? That's about the fourth joint down the line. There's no point in talking to you about anything. You're not going to change—it's what I told Jez. Here we are, Daisy Mae's.''

The Seville crunched gravel as it came to a halt in front of another white tiltwall stucco. It's sign showed a Dogpatch scene: Daisy Mae with her arms around Li'l Abner's neck, her shapely leg lifted in the air and Li'l Abner showing a silly grin. Size's tan Riviera was parked close to the street; about thirty cars and pickups were in the dusty parking lot between the Riviera and the front entrance.

Leon was sad-eyed once again as he said, ''No, you're not going to do anything based on advice from anybody. You're Size Brandon, that's all I can say about it. You going to leave town, or what?''

Size opened the Seville's door and turned to Leon. Sudden heat blasted into the Seville's interior and mixed with the frosted cool of the A/C. The Dionne Warwick tape played on. "I ain't sure, Leon. I got to talk to Jimmy before I do anything, maybe get a little money together. Right now I'm thinking I probably will go somewhere. I'll keep in touch. And Leon"—he reached over and gave Leon's shoulder a playful shove—"don't worry. I'll be okay. You got any sense, you'll take that Jez and marry her. Man can do a lot worse." He stood up on the gravel, started to close the door, then stuck his big head back inside the car and gave Leon a toothy grin. "And whatever you do, don't make no more false statements to get loans. Let's watch that shit, huh?"

The song was "Seduce Me Tonight" from *Flashdance,* blaring from wide-open speakers in all corners of the club and behind the shimmering gold curtain at the rear of the stage. A leggy, small-breasted brunette was doing a loose-jointed disco shuffle in spike heels and a gold lamé G-string, a smile on her face as she gave an extra-hard bump in the direction of a chubby man in a blue suit. He wore thick rimless glasses and had thin brown hair. He was sitting in a chair near the stage, and dollar bills were folded over the temples of his glasses. The stripper did a slow, rhythmic dip before him, squatting and bouncing on her haunches to the music. She snatched his glasses off. After she'd tucked the money carefully inside the waistband of the G-string, she rubbed the glasses on her inner thighs and, smirking, over her crotch. She laughed and replaced the glasses on his nose. The fat guy covered his ears with his hands and stuck out his tongue. He threw back his round head and howled. The stripper giggled, stood, and went on with her bumps and grinds.

In the club's entryway, Benny Sands said to Size, "*Cover charge?* For you? I'm not charging you any, come on in." He held out the ten-dollar bill that Size had just given him. Benny was sitting hunched over on a stool behind a black-painted wood counter. A small lamp sat on a flexible metal neck at his side, the shaded bulb about a foot over the countertop. The prominent red veins in Benny's huge nose stood out in the artificial light. "You coulda saved me a trip, though. If I'd known you were coming by I'd've never gone downtown and dropped the money off with Jez. Jesus Christ, two-and-a-half to ride a city bus downtown and back, can you believe it? C'mon, Size. Take it. Here." He kept his skinny hand extended, offering the money.

Size was leaning his elbow on the counter, being careful not to let the lapel of the Ultrasuede fall away from his chest to expose the Luger. A small white sign on the wall said that the carrying of firearms where alcoholic beverages were sold was a felony. His huge hand engulfing Benny's, squeezing it into a fist around the ten-spot, Size said, "How many times I gotta tell you, Benny? Everybody pays. Even Pecos Jimmy, if he comes in. That way you don't have to worry about, hey, do I charge this guy, let that guy skate, or what? Gimme my change." There was a half-full glass on the counter, clear liquid with bubbles rising. As Benny opened a drawer to fish out bills and jingled change, Size scowled, picked up the glass, and sniffed. Seven-up.

Benny said grinning, "Thirty-seven days. Every time I walk into the meeting, Doc Beeler—you know Doc, plays poker?—Doc looks like he's gonna faint. But I'm making it, I got to."

Which was the same thing that Size was thinking, that Benny had to quit for good this time if he was going to have any chance at all. The last time that Size had taken Benny Sands to the hospital to dry out the doctor had said that Benny's liver was getting bigger. Size said, "How 'bout this job, Benny? It making things tough, sitting here looking at the booze flowing around?"

"I was afraid that it might. But I ain't letting you down, Size, not after all you done. It ain't easy for a man my age to get honest work doing anything, and I ain't stealing no more. And you know what? I'm damned if I don't think maybe this job makes it easier. Hell, walking down the street I see booze everywhere anyhow. Either a bottle or a sign advertising it. But in here I see the bad end of drinking, ain't a day goes by we don't bum's-rush a drunk or two. Keeps me thinking about it, what's gonna happen to me if I take a drink."

Size thought about it, too, looking around as his eyes got used to the dark and the shapes at the tables began to take form. At the bright points of red glow on cigarettes, at the waitresses jiggling back and forth toting trays of fresh drinks and carrying the empties away. The leggy brunette finished her act and was now hustling through the club toward the dressing room behind the bar, hugging her clothes in a bundle to her bare chest. "Splish Splash," the old Bobby Darin rock 'n' roll tune that came out before "Mack the Knife," was pouring from the speakers. A short, tanned peppy blonde in tight cut-off jeans and a pink T-shirt was bebopping on stage. The fat guy was still sitting stageside. He was clapping and whistling.

"How's your boy?" Size said.

Benny bent over to close the cash drawer. The lamp made his scalp glisten through the thin layer of gray hair combed straight back from his forehead. "Kenny? Oh, great. And the burglary, hell, it was all a mistake. Kid didn't do it, Size, the law's just hassling him. Wasn't for you he'd still be in jail."

Size knew that was horseshit, about it being a mistake, but said, "Glad to hear it, Benny. Listen, I got to go in the office and make a call. See you in a minute, huh?"

"Yeah, sure. You got a key?"

Size extracted a big ring from his pocket, twenty or thirty keys of all shapes and sizes jingled. He nodded. Then Benny said, chuckling, "I guess my memory don't work so good. One more time, how you pronounce the name on the license?"

"It's *Boo-dro,* Benny. And don't forget it, Jesus Christ. Anybody from the Alcoholic Beverage Commission comes in you're Moey Boudreaux, and don't fuck up trying to pronounce the 'ro'—it's a dead give-away. The last four guys running this joint was all named Moey Boudreaux. If the state boys find out there ain't no Moey Boudreaux it's gonna cost ten grand for another license, the time we pay the lawyer and shit."

"I'll remember, Size. If they come in and ask, I'll remember good, just like you say." Benny's eyes were shiny.

Size winked. "I ain't worried, Benny. If I was, you wouldn't be sitting here. I gotta make that call now." He turned and strolled through the darkened club, side-stepping tables, feeling the carpet give as he walked on it, nodding to a thin guy in a denim shirt who was tending bar, and going around the bar and through the swinging door at the rear.

There was a ten-foot corridor that led to the office, wooden walls and ceiling painted black. A single seventy-five-watt bulb glowed overhead. The music filtered in from the club, now slowing to "I Just Called to Say I Love You." Out of habit Size bent over to check the crack under the office door. The light inside was off.

There was a single door in the corridor besides the one to the office, about halfway between the office and the slatted, swinging door exit. It opened. The leggy brunette stripper, now wearing a tight silver cocktail dress, stuck her head around the frame and said, "I need to talk atcha, big man."

Size turned the key in the lock, feeling the click as the button on the other side of the knob popped out. Without looking at the stripper, Size said, "Hiya, Gloria. Say, can't it wait? I'm kind of busy."

"Won't take long. It's Tina, my girlfriend. She got busted last night, wants to know if you can make bail."

"You know the answer to that. She don't work here, we can't help her." He swiveled his massive head toward her. She was out in the hallway now. The dress was really short, at mid-thigh, and Gloria's legs were too skinny for the outfit. "By the way," he said, "I was watching that fat guy and the act with the glasses. You ain't selling a little pussy outta here, are you?"

Gloria struck a one-foot-in-front-of-the-other, hip-swinging pose. "What if I was? Don't it look like it's worth something?"

"Look, Gloria, I ain't got time for games. Either you are or you ain't. You bring any heat down on this club you're gonna be sorry. No drugs and no hooking, that's the rules. What you do on your own time is your business. You keep it in mind, huh? You fuck up our license and your friend in jail's gonna be the lucky one." He opened the office and went in. Gloria stuck her tongue out at the closed door.

The office was a tiny eight-by-ten. It held a rolltop desk with deep scars in the wood, as if somebody had been whittling on it. The brown paint was flaking on the wall behind a lumpy couch. The desk's top was open, revealing a dog-eared checkbook, some yellow copies of bills impaled on an upright metal spike, and a plain black phone.

Size sat down, the desk chair groaning and squeaking under him. He reached out and rested his big freckled hand on the phone, then took it away. He stared at the receiver, thinking, Here I am. Now what the fuck do I do? Call Jimmy at—yeah, today's Tuesday, call him at the Egyptian. And tell him what? Talk stupid, like Brando in—whatsit, *On the Waterfront?* Jimmy, I coulda been a contender, only gotta say it, "con-ten-dah," just the way Brando said it. Otherwise it might not sound stupid enough. Keep right on playing Pecos Jimmy's rummy, a big dumb shit like Lenny in *Of Mice and Men*? That seemed to be the picture everybody had, and Size was tired of it. Tired of fronting and covering for Jimmy as he had ever since the fourth fucking grade in Commerce, Texas—Jimmy, a skinny little kid sniveling and hiding behind Size while Size bluffed out a gang of kids who wanted to whip Jimmy's ass for him. Wanted to whip him because Jimmy's mouth was a lot bigger than he was.

Tired of playing the dumbass as he was, Size sure

wasn't going to testify for any stuffed-shirt federal prosecutor. Split, that was the answer—get up a little bankroll and disappear into the sunset. For good this time, go somewhere and do something that didn't involve fronting for Pecos Jimmy Fontenot. Do anything.

Size shook his head. Right now wasn't the time to talk to Pecos Jimmy about money. Trying to talk to Jimmy while he was paying off this guy, collecting from that guy—hell, it was a waste of time. Yeah, wait a while. And don't talk to Jimmy over the phone, you never know who's listening in on what anymore. Wait till after dark, after Jimmy's through with settle-up day, and meet him face to face somewhere.

Size poked around inside the desk, found a pen and pad and wrote a note. Tell Jimmy to meet him at . . . yeah, Reverchon Park, under the big oak trees behind the backstop on the softball field. Jimmy'd know the spot, same place where they met the slick little dark guy from Bogotá that time. Midnight sharp, wasn't no way anybody'd be hanging around Reverchon Park that time of night. 'Cept a few queers maybe, and Size had a little medicine for them if they tried to fuck around any. Yeah, meet Pecos Jimmy there and talk things over, make Jimmy see how it was best for Size to just disappear for good. He read the note over. It was okay, got the point across. Size folded it up and put it in his pocket.

A portable TV, a little color Zenith, was on a rolling stand next to the couch. Size turned it on and fiddled with the tuner. Silly, zany music played. A cartoon. Yogi Bear—shit, another big dumb bastard. Size changed the channel, *click, click.* A black-and-white scene from an old movie appeared. Glenn Ford and Sidney Poitier, staring at each other across a high school classroom, Poitier saying, "Mr. Dadier, huh? Sounds like 'Daddy-o' to me, Teach." Size remembered the flick—*Blackboard Jungle,* and it wasn't bad. He folded his hands behind his head and leaned back in the swivel chair to watch.

* * *

Around nine-thirty Size went up front and said to Benny Sands, "Look, I need you to make a little run for me. You can drive my car."

Benny was still sitting on the stool by the front door. The crowd had thinned, only about ten guys in the place now, most of the guys buying drinks for strippers and waitresses who sat at the tables with them. The fat guy in glasses by the stage was gone. So was the leggy brunette, Gloria. A big-boned redhead was on the stage, completely nude, doing a dance to "Love Potion Number 9." She was slowly peeling a banana.

Benny said, "Sure, Size, anything for you. But who's gonna watch the door while I'm gone?"

"I'll do it." Size reached in his pocket and handed Benny the folded note. "Now here's what you do. Go over to the Egyptian and find Pecos Jimmy. He'll be in back, in the private dining room. Just give him the note and leave. Don't tell him nothing about where you got the note or where I am."

Benny licked his thin lips, tiny sprouting whiskers around his mouth standing out in the beam from the shaded lamp. He shook the near-empty glass in his hand and watched melted ice cubes shift in the bottom as he said, "Shit, Size, you know Jimmy better than I do. You think he's gonna let me walk up, hand him a note, and leave? Naw, he'll have questions."

Benny was stalling. A little thing like delivering a note to a guy shouldn't bother him. Raising his voice slightly to be heard over the music, Size said, "Well, yeah, he might, Benny. But that ain't no problem. Just tell him if has any questions to ask me when he sees me." Benny was still watching the glass, as if he couldn't take his eyes away from it. Size cocked his head to one side. "It ain't going over to see Pecos Jimmy that's bothering you. What is it, Benny?"

With a shrug of his narrow stooped shoulders, Benny said, "I hate to ask for favors."

"Try me. I might say yes and I might say no, but asking don't cost nothing."

"It's Kenny. I been working every night and ain't gotten to see my boy any. If I'm going to be out running you an errand, I was wondering if you'd mind if I stopped by Kenny's place and saw him. You know, check on the boy."

The kid, huh? Poor old Benny'd wasted a lot of his life chasing around after a bottle, now he was going to waste a lot more of it fretting over a punk who wasn't worth shooting. But what could you say, it was his boy. Size grinned, finally saying, "Sure, Benny. No sweat. Look, you got a little time off coming anyway. Stop off on your way back from taking the note. I got until midnight or so, how's that?"

Benny brightened visibly and stood up. Might be Size's imagination, but it looked as though the old man was standing a little straighter. Maybe the sorry, no-good kid needed somebody to lean on. Everybody should have that feeling at some time or other.

Benny said, "Man, you don't know how much I appreciate it. And don't worry none, I won't take long. Just enough time to see how the boy's doing, okay?"

Size fooled with his key ring, finding the ignition and trunk keys to the Riviera and twisting them off the ring. "No problem, Benny. Always glad to help, huh?" Then he handed the two keys over, getting a kick out of the little-kid look on Benny's wrinkled old face. He followed the old man outside and stood on the curb, his hands in his pockets, to watch Benny go.

Watching the shuffle-gaited walk in the faded khaki pants that were a size too big, the wrinkled elbows below short sleeves that Benny rolled up one turn as if he was still living back in the Fifties, Size thought that if he had problems he just had to look at guys like Benny Sands to see what real troubles were. Size watched Benny pause under the lighted sign, the sky a dull black overhead as Li'l Abner hugged Daisy Mae, grinning like a fool. He watched Benny fumble around as he got the key into the Riviera's lock, opened the door, and climbed awkwardly behind the wheel. Size found himself wondering if Benny Sands was going to make it this time, or if another dumb stunt by the kid was going to set Benny to drinking again. Found himself wondering about Benny, right up to the instant the Riviera exploded.

The starter chugged twice. The Riviera's nose bucked up and down, hard. The sound of the bomb going off reached Size's ears like a thunderclap as the Riviera's hood flew up and banged into the windshield. Glass splintered and flew. Size could see Benny's head recoil, silhouetted in light from cars passing on Harry Hines Boulevard. Then a red and orange ball of flame rose instantaneously skyward and the Riviera vanished behind a wall of raging fire and billowing black smoke.

Size was running. He didn't have any memory of starting to run, just knew that his feet were thudding and crunching in dusty gravel and his breath was whistling between his teeth in quick bursts. Halfway to where the Riviera burned and smoked he was clawing inside the front of his jacket, feeling the cold butt of the Luger as he brought it out: a reflex, there wasn't any apparent reason for drawing the gun. It was just that something bad was happening, Size had a gun, and he was ready to use it without really thinking about it. As he neared the flaming Riviera a blue Dodge van parked next to it caught fire also. Flame spurted from underneath then wrapped the van's length and width in a seething blanket of flickering orange. Heat singed his face. His eyes watered and his nostrils burned.

He stood before the burning Riviera, squinting and peering through the black smoke. He couldn't see Benny Sands, just stood helpless and watched the car's hood twist and melt. Size felt an odd kind of relief for Benny, that Benny wouldn't have to worry anymore about his worthless kid, or taking a drink, or anything else. Cars all along Harry Hines Boulevard were stopping, drivers rubbernecking and gawking. To Size's rear a couple of guys—one short and chubby in western clothes, the other a stringbean in a navy blue suit—came out of Daisy Mae's, stopped in their tracks, and stared in disbelief. Two or three faraway voices shouted things that Size didn't understand.

Sudden images came to Size. Grand juries, the Feds.

The FBI agent, the asshole sneer on his face as Size handcuffed him to the toilet. It occurred to Size that he'd better get the fuck out of there. His eyes shifted back and forth as he tried to make up his mind which way he should go. Sudden white light flashed in the corner of his eye and something zinged and kicked gravel at his feet. There was a second flash and something sizzled past his ear, inches away.

Size looked toward the flashes. A black four-door Continental was across the street, parked parallel, windows down. Another flash came from the Continental's rear window. Size crouched down as the bullet whined overhead. Behind him the short fat man who had just come out of Daisy Mae's went down, clutching his throat, blood spurting from between his fingers. The other guy, the blue-suited beanpole, yelled, "He's hit! The sonofabitch shot him!" and charged back inside Daisy Mae's.

Suddenly Size was dead calm, his gaze steady on the Continental. A bare beefy female arm was visible on the driver's side, sticking out the open window. Size could make out the shape of a tattoo on the arm; inside the car the arm's owner had long, straight black hair. Size aimed and pulled the Luger's trigger, feeling his arm jerk as he snapped a shot off in the Continental's direction.

Size hoarsely screamed, "Goddam you, Yucca. You bitch! It was just Benny, he wasn't hurting nobody."

The Continental burned rubber and careened onto southbound Harry Hines, narrowly missing a halted pickup whose driver was staring at the burning Riviera across the street. Two more flashes came from the Continental's rear window. One of the bullets kicked a small piece of rock against Size's cheek. A siren began to wail from far away, drawing closer.

The sound of the siren startled Size into action, sent him running back toward Daisy Mae's, running past the throat-shot man and hearing his gurgling death rattle, feet digging hard as he ran around the corner of the white stucco building headed for the open spaces to the rear. Size was moving too fast and breathing too hard to have the slightest idea where he was going, just heard the siren howling louder and knew he had to get away. As he ducked around the corner of the building a third car, an Olds, burst into flame and dark smoke billowed skyward.

Behind Daisy Mae's was a weed-infested hill, railroad tracks running north and south at its crest. Size charged up the slope and across the tracks, stumbling slightly on a cross-tie and angling down the embankment on the other side among scrubby trees. He looked back, breathing hard, with his heart pounding as if it were coming through his breastbone. Over the railroad tracks the dark horizon glowed red. Size moved deeper in among the trees.

Fifteen minutes later Sizemore Brandon sat down on a wooden bench on Lemmon Avenue and waited for a bus. The Luger was holstered. There were a few grass stains on his tan ultrasuede coat and some stickers on his pants leg. He reached down and picked off the stickers, the ones he could feel.

He'd had time to think about it. Only three guys knew where Size's Riviera had been parked. Benny Sands had been one. Leon was another, the last guy in the world who would want anything to happen to Sizemore Brandon. The third guy was Beaumont Gurney.

Air brakes hissed as the bus pulled to a stop. There was a lone passenger, a black woman in a floppy hat who was sitting to the rear. A sign on the bus's side advertised HERTZ RENT-A-CAR. Size got on and dropped money in the slot. He felt the driver's slitted gaze on him from under the plastic-billed cap, could practically hear the guy thinking, Big dumb-looking sonofabitch, wonder if this is a stick-up?

Size nodded to the driver and grinned. "Nice evening."

The driver returned the greeting, pulled the lever, and the doors hissed closed. The bus chugged slowly away from the curb and into sparse traffic.

4

Jessica Rogers used her fork, carefully nudging the turnip greens aside and scooping up a glob of stuck-together macaroni and cheese. She stuffed it into her mouth to go along with the roast beef she was chewing, then added a swallow of milk to give some moisture to the concoction. Her right braid of brown hair came dangerously close to dipping into the milk as she squirmed around to look at the clock on the wall. "It's five till, Mom. Can we watch Fonzie?"

Merrillee Rogers sawed grimly at her roast beef with the E-Z-Carve knife that Oscar had bought from a TV ad by calling an 800 number. In the ad the thing had cut through a tin can as if it were hot butter. As Merrillee used extra muscle to separate a bite-sized piece of meat she wondered dully why Oscar hadn't packed the frigging knives off to stay with Miss Lay-Your-Husband. She lifted her hazel-eyed gaze across the table to Jessica, then quickly averted her glance from the sickening mess in her daughter's mouth. Merrillee said evenly, "You know the rules, Jessie. No TV until after dinner. And don't talk with your mouth full—it's disgusting." Merrillee's cloth napkin fluttered off her lap to the red-and-white-patterned linoleum tile. She bent to pick it up and replaced it over her bare tanned thighs.

Jessie screwed up her face. "Daddy lets me."

Merrillee put down her knife and fork, keeping her tone on an even keel. "Your father lets you do a lot of things, Jessie. Including combing his girlfriend's hair. Not when you're at home. Now eat your dinner. Your turnip greens, too, young lady."

Jessie swallowed, giggled, and rolled her eyes, saying, "I forgot you don't like me to talk about what Daddy does. Will I have time to watch Fonzie before nursery school?"

"Probably. We'll need to leave home by seven. And it isn't a nursery school, Jessie. It's a nighttime babysitter. Nursery school is where you learn something."

Something, Merrillee thought, besides how to strew toys from one end of the house to the other. She briefly pictured Fonzie, *"Hey, hey, hey,"* with his stupid thumbs in the air, curse of her own generation and now reincarnated on afternoon reruns to haunt her own five-year-old as well. Her face softened. "Are you liking Mrs. Tallon's, honey?" Picturing a squealing, giggling bunch from five-year-olds down to toddlers, shitty diapers and all, she wondered how Mrs. Tallon kept from being fitted for a straightjacket.

Jessie wrinkled her just-like-Oscar's freckled nose. "It's *fu*-un, Mom. I play with Freddie. Freddie's got an eye in his stomach."

"A what?"

"An eye, Mom. It's right here"—she raised her pink T-shirt, the one that said GRANDMA'S GENIUS in white letters across the front, and pointed at her navel—"right where Daddy says the Indian shot me."

Merrillee struggled to remember the family psychologist's instructions. Stay calm. Above all, stay calm. She wondered how the family psychologist would fare with Jessie as she said, still evenly, "It isn't where the Indian shot you, Jessie. It's your navel. And nobody's got an eye there. Everybody's got a navel there. Eat your dinner." A thought came to her and she suddenly arched an eyebrow, raising her voice an octave as she said, "What *else* did Freddie show you? Besides his navel?"

"He does, *too*, have an eye in his stomach." Jessie raised a small cupped hand over her head. "And he can raise it way up here to make it look at you, too. It's on a fucking stalk."

"Jessie! Don't use that word. Did Freddie teach you that, too?" Merrillee pictured a kid with an eye in his

stomach and a vocabulary from a smut movie. Ridiculous.

Jessie's eyes opened wide, innocent. Hazel, like Merrillee's. "What word, Mom?"

"You know very well what word, Jessie. Who taught it to you?"

Jessie smiled a sly, little-girl smile and pushed her plate away. "I'm finished," she said softly. "Can I watch TV now?"

Merrillee glanced at the half-eaten plate of food, the good-for-you turnip greens untouched. Bribery's a no-no. Something you never do with a child. Never, never, never. To hell with it, she had to know. "First tell me, Jessie. Then you can watch Fonzie."

Jessie looked deep in thought. Beyond her Merrillee saw two days' worth of plates, cups and saucers, and dirty iron skillets showing above tepid soapy water in the sink. Beyond the sink was the kitchen window through which she used to watch Oscar mow the back yard. Oscar with his shirt off, smooth brown shoulders square, hands on the handle bouncing up and down behind the chugging Briggs and Stratton rotary.

Merrillee said, "I'm waiting, Jessie."

"*Weh*-ell. I guess I heard it over at Daddy's." Then, quickly, "But Daddy told me not to say the word, either, Mom. I forgot. Sort of."

Merrillee felt a surge of—satisfaction? She couldn't help it, that's what it was. Folding her arms and tapping one small foot, Merrillee said, "All right, Jessie. You may go."

Merrillee stepped into the black bikini briefs, pulled them up, and snapped the elastic band at her waist. She turned sideways to the full-length mirror and struck a one-knee-bent pose. The steamy frost from the shower was still clinging lightly to the glass and she thought about wiping it off, then changed her mind. The frost gave the pose a filmy effect, like a *Playboy* layout she'd seen of Joan Collins. She threw back her shoulders, faintly hearing the "Happy Days" theme that meant Fonzie was about to ride off into the sunset until tomorrow. The music filtered into the bathroom dressing area through the closed master bedroom door. Merrillee arched her back and inhaled, tilting her chin at a saucy angle. Not bad at thirty-two. Not quite "Charlie's Angels" material, a little too prominent with the cheekbones, a little too muscled in the thighs. But pretty damned good. She winked at herself and put on her costume, the mesh hose, cutesy thigh-length skirt pleated in alternating black and gold, gold blouse with a western-style black string tie at the throat. And the logo on the pocket over the breast. She went into the bedroom and plopped her bottom on the king-size, picking up the white Princess phone and punch-dialing. She lit a filtered Virginia Slim, put her gold lighter on the nightstand, blew a plume of smoke in the air and held her breath while the other line rang.

Oscar answered in person. Merrillee relaxed, the dread of having to go through Miss Lay-Your-Husband leaving her.

Merrillee said, "Your daughter said, 'fucking stalk.' "

Twanging guitars in the background, Waylon For-Christ's-Sake Jennings. Oscar said, "Hold on." Then, "Turn down the stereo, hon." A pang of jealousy, dammit, shot through Merrillee. Then he said, "Fucking what?"

The sun's dying rays slanted through the bedroom window, dust particles swirling in the beam. Outside the window the square-patterned sprinkler threw clear droplets on emerald green Bermuda grass that needed mowing. Merrillee thought fleetingly about the water bill. "Stalk. With an eye on it."

"Merrillee? Are you drunk?"

"Being drunk isn't *my* bag, Oscar. Anyway, 'stalk' isn't the problem. It's 'fucking.' She says she heard it from you."

Silence. Merrillee set the cigarette in a glass ashtray and watched smoke drift up from its end. Finally Oscar said, "She didn't hear it from me. She heard it from Barney. She sneaked up on us."

"Barney? Barney who?"

"Barney Prather. He's with the Gaming Commission. We were playing poker. And he said, 'fucking queen,' not 'fucking stalk.' Jessie was supposed to be asleep. I look up and there she stands with her teddy bear. What do you do?"

"It's a Care Bear," Merrillee said, "Bedtime Bear. And that's nice, Oscar. Four months behind in child support you're playing poker. Big-time Charlie."

Oscar coughed, muffled, Merrillee picturing him with his hand cupped over his mouth, away from the phone. Then he said, "You've got the wrong idea, Merrillee. I'm about to make a deal, a sale maybe, on the Slipper Casino. If I can put the deal together, my commish is enough to catch up on my payments to you. There's a little snag in getting the buyers approved by the Gaming Commission. To smooth things over you have to do a little entertaining—you know that."

Merrillee thought, I'll bet. Entertainment including Miss Lay-Your-Husband and a couple of chickies from the "Hallelujah Hollywood" chorus line, Oscar big-timing it, getting drunk and losing his money to a just-as-drunk official from the State of Nevada. "What's the 'snag,' Oscar? As if I didn't know."

"The usual stuff. They think that the buyers have mob connections."

"Jesus Christ, Oscar. It's always mob connections. Why don't you sell a casino to Pat Boone, somebody like that?"

"Pat Boone doesn't buy casinos. Pat Boone starts boys' clubs. As long as you're in a getting-on-my-case mood, I may as well get on yours. Charlie Dorsett was by the office. He said he went to the Golden Nugget to see Steve-O the other day, and who does he see but you? My ex-wife. Serving *cocktails*, no less. Don't you know what that does to my image around town?"

Merrillee stretched out, lying on her back and looking at the ceiling. The quilted bedspread was cool on her neck. It seemed to her that the side of the bed she slept on had sunk lower than the other side. "Steve-O who?"

"Steve-O. Steve-O Winn. The guy who owns the hotel where you work. Serving cocktails."

She sighed. "I *know* who you mean, Oscar. His name is Steve. Only if you ever got an appointment with him you'd have to call him Mr. Winn. Jesus Christ, who do you think you're trying to impress?"

Sure it was a put-down, and Merrillee felt a twinge of conscience. But not much of one. Probably about the same amount of guilt that Oscar'd felt when he'd blown what little reserve they had left financing Miss Lay-Your-Husband's blackjack habit. Merrillee thought: Now Oscar's going to get indignant.

Indignantly, Oscar said, "Me? *Impress?* I don't have to try to impress anyone. I know some big names in this town, Merrillee. Some *big names.* I've got connections. And I've got to hear about you from an asshole like Charlie Dorsett? Right in my own office, *two clients* sitting there. Charlie gets this smirky look on his face and says"—switching to a high falsetto— " 'Boy, things must be tough on Merrillee, Oscar. She served me a drink at the crap table at the Nugget. I gave her a ten-dollar tip, I sure do hope it helps out.' Five'll get you ten the lard-ass was on the phone to both clients before the day was out. Jesus Christ, Merrillee, you've got a degree from UCLA. Use it."

She briefly remembered the touch of Charlie Dorsett's fat clammy hand as he did his damnedest to put two five-dollar chips down the front of her uniform. It gave her goose bumps. She started to tell Oscar about it, then changed her mind. This conversation wasn't getting anywhere. "Happy Days" would be over by now and Jessie would be in here any minute jumping up and down on the bed. Softly, Merrillee said, "Look, Oscar, I'm really not trying to do anything to damage your business. But facts are facts. A major in English lit in Vegas will buy you a cup of coffee if you have fifty cents to do it with. I can't *afford* to teach. I need a lot of income just to keep this house up, and working at the Nugget is the only thing I've found that'll make ends meet. But I didn't call to talk to you about that. It's Jessie. Poor little thing, she's not reacting well to this broken home bit, Oscar. She's—she's making up the most godawful stories you ever heard. She's getting to be a holy terror. I know I'm being lax, working at night. But I don't know what else to do. It's breaking my heart, Oscar. All I'm asking is that you hold your lifestyle down to a dull roar when your little girl is visiting you. Is that too much to ask?''

''Of course it isn't. But I don't need instructions on how to handle my own daughter, Merrillee. She's just fine when she's with me.''

Merrillee thought, What's the frigging use? Oscar'd never been able to see past the end of his nose when we were married, why should I expect anything different now? Oscar was—Oscar. Maybe Miss Lay-Your-Husband did me a favor. Nobody was ever going to love Oscar as much as *Oscar* loved Oscar. She said, ''Well, I'm glad she's fine. Look, thanks for visiting with me about it. I've got to sign off and go to work now, so I'll have to say goodbye.'' She hesitated, then as an afterthought added, ''Oh, and Oscar? Good luck with the Slipper Casino. Go get 'em, huh?''

Merrillee kept her eyes downcast as she said softly to Mrs. Tallon, ''I'm not making excuses. Really. And I'm not trying to give you a sob story. I'll have your money for you when I pick Jessie up in the morning.'' Adding to herself, If it's a good night—otherwise at least half, for sure.

Mrs. Tallon had white hair that was tinted beauty-shop blue. She was pleasant enough as she said, ''I have to set deadlines, Mrs. Rogers. I'm sure you understand. The arrangement you're making will be satisfactory so long as we understand that tonight is the limit. Tomorrow I'll have to say no.'' A very businesslike sixtyish woman in a long black dress with a white flower print, holding her plastic-framed eyeglasses in one hand and tapping the tip of one temple gently against her front teeth. And darting a fleeting, disapproving glance at Merrillee's mesh hose.

A young black girl was standing nearby holding her

pigtailed daughter's hand, not seeming to pay any attention to Merrillee. Merrillee wondered if it was an act, wondered if the black girl had heard. She thought her name was Cicely, and thought she was the prettiest black girl she'd ever seen—long false eyelashes and a tiny waist highlighting a figure that would stop traffic. Cicely's daughter had frizzy hair and was around Jessie's age. Cicely worked Keno at Caesar's and didn't seem to have any trouble paying Mrs. Tallon. Probably doing some hooking, a lot of the Keno girls on the Strip did. Right now Merrillee didn't think it was such a bad idea.

Merrillee said, "I won't let you down, Mrs. Tallon. You're being wonderful, waiting as long as you have."

Mrs. Tallon nodded and went over to talk to the black girl.

The room was wall-to-wall kids, around thirty in all, a few babies with chubby legs sticking out below rubber pants that puffed out around diapers, other toddlers in Pampers with little bands of tape holding them together at the tummy. Jessie was the center of attention to one little boy and two little curly-haired girls. She was hugging Astro Barbie to her chest, the slender doll in a silver space outfit.

Jessie indicated the boy. "He's my friend Freddie, Mom."

The kid was a towhead, his wide grin showing one front tooth missing. He was wearing jean shorts and a yellow He-Man T-shirt. Merrillee felt her gaze wandering in the vicinity of Freddie's navel. She thought, Jesus Christ, I'm losing my mind.

Merrillee nodded. "Hi, Freddie, glad to know you. I've got to go to work now, Jessie. Give Mommy kisses."

She bent down as Jessie came to her and threw warm little arms around her neck. Jessie gave her mom a wet smacky kiss on the cheek. "I love you, Mommy. Bunches and bunches."

Merrillee's cheeks were suddenly damp with tears. "Me, too, precious. God, do I ever."

5

The well-stacked, in-super-shape-for-forty woman from Sioux Falls, South Dakota, who'd never seen anything like it in her life, took two red five-dollar chips from her stack of six and dropped them confidently on the Come line. "The man from south of the border knows something. Let it all ride."

The logger from Coos Bay, Oregon, his thick neck red over a checked open-neck shirt, chewed lightly on a Hava-Tampa and considered what the woman from South Dakota had said. He had all the numbers covered, taking odds, and was showing a two hundred dollar profit. He finally said, from between teeth that were clenched around the butt of the cigar, "Jesus Christ, lady, I think you're right. Let 'em go, let 'em go. Roll them bones, Mr. Chili-choker."

The four-deep crowd around the green felt table edged closer, men in suits and men in jeans, women in jewels and furs and girls in midriff-baring halters, even one tanned brunette in a blue bikini and a T-shirt over it that came to just above her navel, yelling, squealing, getting their bets down. A young guy with brown hair to his shoulders, wearing a brown cloth sports coat with patches on the elbows, watched through mirrored sunglasses as he said, "Eighteen in a row, no seven. God almighty. I heard about a run at Caesar's went thirty-three rolls. But I haven't *seen* one this long, not that I can remember." He marked something down on a tiny spiral pad.

The pit boss, a skinny black-haired guy with a monstrous Adam's apple, wearing a gold blazer with the Golden Nugget logo on the breast pocket, sat on his stool and watched with folded arms through sleepy lidded eyes. He glanced at the stickman, the dealers shuffling stacks of chips one-handed, *click-click-click,* watched the bets on the line and in the Come rectangle as he droned, "Eee-o-leven, good for the Field and last Come. The gentleman from Colombia has it going, folks. Dice still his, place your bets. Still your roll, Senor."

Senor Emilio Garza Burista, long clipped sideburns graying, salt-and-pepper moustache perfectly trimmed, selected two clear red dice from the six cubes offered by the curved stick. He glanced at the long double rows of black chips in the trays in front of him, at his six-inch stack of blacks on the Pass line, and quickly checked the smaller piles of hundred-dollar chips behind the 4, 5, 6, 8, 9, and 10 across the top of the board. He shook the dice between chubby olive hands and held them out to the woman from Sioux Falls, South Dakota. She flashed even white teeth in a hesitant smile, then blew lightly on them. Senor Burista gave her his most winning Julio Iglesias grin. Bending to his left he said to Junior Gomez, in Spanish, "Tell the woman I pay two hundred dollars American for a good blowjob."

Junior Gomez winced, thinking, This was El Paso I'd know just where to take him. To the lady he said, "He says, thank you. He thinks you'll bring him luck."

She nodded and smiled.

Senor Emilio Garza Burista said, still in Spanish, "You see. Money buys all women. It is the same here as in Bogotá."

Junior played with the heavy gold chain around his throat. The chain supported a big round medallion that dangled over his nearly hairless breastbone. The medallion was engraved with a helmeted image of Cabeza de Vaca. "You are very wise in the ways of women, Senor," Junior said, not wanting to lay it on too thick, but after four days still not sure how to take the Colombian. Was the guy kidding or not? The ticket, that's what Junior called Senor Emilio Garza Burista. Called him that to Manny Cervantes back in El Paso, called him that to Dolores, too. The ticket to living off the fat, to never having to do any more stickups or anything else that would put Junior Gomez back on the Texas Penitentiary work farm. Junior'd had plenty of that shit. Didn't matter how dumb it sounded, what the Colombian had to say, Junior was staying on Burista's good side. If Burista wanted to stand up in the middle of the crap table and take a piss, man, Junior was going to act as if it were the very thing to do.

Burista was wearing a lightweight navy sports coat, a Hart-Shaffner, which had a red satin lining, and a red and yellow and green flowered Hawaiian shirt with the neck open and the pointed collar outside the collar of the sports coat. He wore a beveled gold, diamond pinky ring. "People of the United States should come to Colombia and learn to handle women. Here I see the woman telling the man what to do. The men are like burros. We have young strong women on the plantation. They work. During the day they mash the leaves together with kerosene, take the powder to the lab for the ether treatment. Work hard. Nights we can go to the cabins and fuck them if we want. It is better that way." His hairline receded to the top of his head, his forehead was dark and shiny. He was a good six inches shorter than Junior's six feet. Burista was round, like a short dark penguin. He rubbed the dice between his palms, still looking back and forth from Junior Gomez to the woman from South Dakota, who now looked uncertain. Like she was trying to figure out what the guy was saying in Spanish.

Junior said to the woman in English, "He thinks you're a living doll, lady."

Junior pictured Dolores back in El Paso, dark flashing eyes, thrusting high boobs, open-toed spike pumps and designer jeans, talking hip, Texas-style. Tried to picture Dolores stomping in coca leaves and kerosene, and going to a dirt-floored cabin at night to wait for a guy who looked like Burista to come along and lay the old pork to her. It was a tough thing to picture. He agreed with Burista in Spanish. "Yes, it is much better in your country." He wondered briefly what a field-hand broad smelled like.

The Coos Bay logger yelled, "Hey! You rubbing the spots off of 'em. Throw the fuckers," drawing a few sharp looks from the girls.

Burista glanced at the logger, then back to Junior. *"Que dice el?"* said Burista.

Junior said to the logger, loudly, "Hey, man. He's gonna. Keep your shirt on." Then, to Burista in Spanish, "He feels you are a very good shooter of the dice." Junior wore a black silk shirt, open to the fourth button and tapered to fit snug over his bulging pectorals and narrow waist. Two hundred push-ups a day, five hundred situps and crunches in his cell for the whole last year in T.D.C. Dolores stroking his back the other night in El Paso, saying, "God, sugar, they really manned you up in there."

"I always do well with the dice," said Burista to Junior. Then Burista smiled at the logger, said, "Thank you" in English (Junior had heard the Colombian say "eggs," "iced tea," and "young pussy" in English and wondered what else Burista knew), and tossed the dice. They ricocheted off the studded rubber at the other end of the table, bounced and danced on the green felt, and came up six-five. The crowd hooted, whistled, clapped, and cheered. Dealers paid off Come bets, stacking chips next to chips, and Burista grinned and shrugged as if there was nothing to it. Junior glanced past the opposite end of the table, past the rows of slot machines, people madly pumping handles, past twenty or thirty blackjack tables—about half in action and the other half with dealers waiting with folded arms—to the poker room. The entrance to the poker room was an arc, a row of lights overhead like the gate to the state fair midway. There were six or seven poker games in progress, players hunched over guarding their hands. Junior's attention returned to the crap game, where the starch-shirted, black-tied dealer was setting a pile of blacks in front of Burista, Junior thinking, Luckiest fucker since Nick the Greek.

* * *

Denver Phil Madison thought, Sucker on a roll, and turned his birdlike head around, darting a glance in the direction of the whoops and hollers. He'd seen a million of 'em, a million scenes like that one on the other side of the casino from the poker room, crowd pumped up high as a kite while one man plays King for a Day. Or King for a Minute, depending on how long the dice stay hot. The current hero was a greaser, a short pudgy olive-complexioned guy with a high-domed forehead; next to the crapshooter another chili pepper, an Erik Estrada type with the open-chested black tight shirt and pants that looked like they'd split if he ever sat down. Denver Phil hoped the dice cooled off pretty quick, so the yelling would die down and this pigeon across from him would get his head back in the poker game.

Feeling a slight pop in the base of his neck, Denver Phil Madison said, "It's eighty to you, pal. Come on, I raised. What you going to do?"

What Denver Phil Madison saw: In the center of the oblong, brown canvas-covered table, a good-size pile of red Golden Nugget five-dollar chips, quite a few twenty-five dollar greens mixed in, all in a pot that Denver Phil would make to be seven, eight hundred dollars. On his immediate right the house dealer, a skinny blond kid named Sandy, still with pimples on his face, bridge-size plastic deck face down in front of him. In front of the deck the straight-in-a-row, face-up Texas Hold-Em spread, nine-ten of clubs, deuce of diamonds, five of hearts, king of spades.

On the other side of Sandy, Stevie Wonder's slim hands, pasty white gambler's hands. Couldn't see all of Stevie Wonder, him leaning back in his chair and hidden from view behind Sandy the dealer; could just see Stevie Wonder's hands and Stevie Wonder's forty-dollar bet, a neat stack of chips right in front of his hands. Stevie'd been on a roll of late, had been able to quit his job dealing at the Stardust and had gone to playing Hold-Em poker on a full-time basis. Stevie was the kind of guy who could be holding anything from nothing to the nuts. Right now Denver Phil was figuring Stevie for nothing.

What Denver Phil Madison saw when he turned up the corners of his two-card hand and peeked at them: the king-ten of hearts. To go with the king and ten on the board, the top two pair. Beyond Denver Phil's cupped hands his neat stack of Golden Nugget chips that totaled eighty dollars, his raise over Stevie Wonder's lead bet. Beyond that the pile of discarded hands; around the table most of the other players looking off, not paying any attention, their hands folded, cards thrown in. A couple of them shooting the shit about a hand that was played last week.

Directly across the table from Denver Phil: The A-1, first-class, sucker-pigeon. Big bull-necked sonofabitch, black wild hair that came down over his forehead as if Ringo Starr'd been pumping iron for twenty years or so. Thick black eyebrows, a clean-shaven, wide-eyed face. The poker hustler's dream. But this pigeon was being a pain in the ass, kept staring over at the tamale-cooker at the crap table, rubbernecking, not watching what the fuck was going on in the poker game he was playing in. Had been that way all afternoon, big gorilla paying more attention to the two greasers over at the crap table than to his own business. And winning, the dumb-luck sonofabitch, sometimes not even looking at his hand before the cards were all out, turning up his cards and dragging the pots as if he knew what he was doing. At first Denver Phil had thought the big sucker was watching what's her name—Merrillee—the leggy, auburn-haired cocktail girl who was over there waiting on the crap table. And Denver Phil couldn't have blamed the pigeon for that, she was some stuff to look at. But no, it was the two greasers he was watching.

This hand though, Denver Phil had the sucker right where he wanted him.

A little louder, Denver Phil Madison said, "Come *on,* man. Get in the game."

Sandy, the dealer, added, "Eighty dollars to you, sir. Call, raise, or fold."

The big bastard looked familiar. Denver Phil had seen him somewhere. Could be anywhere, sucker like that, with as much Hold-Em poker as Denver Phil had played around the country. In a deep-voiced Texas drawl, the pigeon said, "Huh? To me?" Then peeped at his hand, Denver Phil thinking, Jesus Christ. Sucker doesn't even know what the fuck he's holding. Then the pigeon slid his cards facedown under a single chip and said, "I think I'll raise. Yeah. I'm raising." And stacked a hundred and twenty dollars in chips out front, the forty-dollar limit raise.

On Denver Phil's right, Stevie Wonder muttered, "What the hell?"

The big sucker started watching the crap game and the greasers again. As if Sandy and Denver Phil and Stevie Wonder and this twenty-and-forty-limit Texas Hold-Em poker game weren't even here.

Stevie Wonder folded, just what Denver Phil expected. Stevie snatched his two-card hand up, held the cards between his first and middle fingers and twirled them to the center of the table with the rest of the discards. Stevie said, "I guess you've got king-ten beat. I had the top two pair, Jesus Christ—" He sounded really pissed off.

Which was exactly what Denver Phil Madison was holding, the top two pair. Denver Phil snorted, not being able to resist saying, "Shee-it, Stevie. You'd have had the top two pair, wild horses couldn't have drug you out of this pot. Nothing's what you had. A stone fucking cold-ass bluff. You think we just got off the boat from the old country, or what?"

Stevie Wonder leaning forward. Now Denver Phil could see Stevie's square handsome Polack face, Stevie peering at him around Sandy. Stevie jerked his head in the direction of the big muscled-up sucker across the table, saying, "Yeah, well, since you got it all figured out, you call the fucker. All afternoon he's beat you, now in the middle of the night he's still knocking your brains out. Go on, Denver, shovel some more chips over to the man. He looks like he could use them.'' This is Stevie's Southern California, Gardena lo-ball way of speaking.

Which was just about the situation, the big Beatle-haired sucker from somewhere down in Texas sitting behind foot-high stacks of red and green chips. Sitting there stupid-looking, wearing a pale-blue golf shirt with—can you believe it?—Mickey Mouse on the pocket, straight from Disney World, his oversized arms and shoulders stretching the shirt out of shape. Sitting there as if he was in a trance, watching the two greasers over at the crap table, not even taking his eyes off them when Merrillee's long tanned legs came into his line of vision. Pigeon of the week, this big galoot, and if he sat here at this poker table long enough Denver Phil was going to have all those stacks or reds and greens in front of him. Send the big galoot home C.O.D.

Denver Phil looked the pigeon over, trying to get a tell—a face twitch or movement—some kind of sign to what the sucker might be holding. He couldn't. How the fuck can you read a man who don't even know the poker game is going on? Seen over the sucker's head, at the back of the cardroom, the electronic Keno board was flashing numbers. To the right of that, the scoreboard said the Dodgers had scored in the seventh, led the Mets 3–2.

Finally Denver Phil said, ''Yeah? Well, I'm calling you. What you got?'' And added another forty dollars in chips to the stack in front of him, setting them down nice and easy, pro-poker style.

The big sucker acted as if he didn't hear, kept gazing toward the crap table.

''Hey!'' Denver Phil yelled. ''I called you, man. Showtime.''

The pigeon started, his big head moving slightly as he said, ''Huh? Oh, me? Well I got''—he looked at his hand—''two deuces. And there's a deuce out there in the middle. That's three deuces, ain't it?'' He flipped them face-up and there they were. Deuce-deuce, a heart and a diamond.

The sucker wins again.

Sandy gave Denver Phil Madison an apologetic smile as he shoved the pot to the musclehead. Denver Phil started doing a burn, then closed his eyes tight and shook the anger off, quickly. Playing pissed-off poker's a sure way to get broke.

Narrowing his eyes, Denver Phil said, "Say. Ain't I seen you? In Dallas, maybe. Playing down on Greenville Avenue? With Bob Hooks? Charlie Harrelson, Cowboy Wolford. Gilbert Hess, Junior, guys like that?"

The big sucker looked thoughtful. "Gilbert who?" Then he grinned, stacking his chips even higher. "Yeah, well. I might know one or two of them guys."

Junior Gomez had this picture. It was nestled somewhere in a bureau drawer back in El Paso, underneath a pile of torn losing Juarez dog track tickets and some nude black-and-whites of Dolores that *Playboy* had sent back with a rejection slip. The *Playboy* turndown had made Dolores pouty for a while until Junior convinced her that the only difference between Dolores on a double bed with cotton stuffing poking out of the mattress and Barbi Benton on a postered king-size among satin pillows was in the background and the airbrush job. This had brightened Dolores up. "Hey, man! Maybe *Playboy* like one of me doing it with a donkey, huh?"

Anyway, this picture was one that Junior was really careful with, only bringing it out at parties early-on, before everybody got so drunk or coked-up that the photo got in danger of somebody using it to scrape up a line, or of somebody shooting a hole in it. The picture was seventeen years old. It was of four guys, in color, the emerald-green fairways of Horizon Hills C. C. in the background. The two guys in the center were leaning on drivers, both wrists crossed on top of the shaft. The one on the right was short, bald, and fat, Mr. Executive-on-the-Links, gut so big he couldn't get around on the ball; had this terrible slice, you could tell. But the center guy on the left—here the looker would get closer, squinting—naw, can it be? It *is*! Jesus Christ, Lee Trevino. Ole Super Mex himself, can ya believe it? The same familiar tire-ad grin, thick dark hair protruding from underneath a yellow-billed golf cap.

That's where Junior Gomez would say, "And who's *this?*" pointing to the happy, proud-as-tequila gangly kid next to Trevino, the kid leaning on Trevino's big green sharkskin bag. The looker would say, really excited, "Man, you're shitting me. You caddied for *Super Mex?* Wow, what a *trip!* Here, hero, how 'bout a toke?"

The part of the story that Junior Gomez always left out was what happened on Number Twelve, about the fourth or fifth time Trevino had to carry the bag himself while Junior Gomez dragged along behind, panting. Trevino had said, "Son, I'm gonna have to do this, you're gonna have to learn to hit a nine-iron," making the knot of twenty or thirty spectators bust out laughing and making Junior Gomez see red. Man, that big green fucking bag with its four wedges and three putters was heav-*eee*. Junior had stopped dead in his tracks, hands on fifteen-year-old skinny hips, and said real loud, "*Chingarro*, from now on you can do both, carry the bag and hit them nine-irons, too." He then stalked off the course, after first shooting the finger to Trevino's back, forgetting all about the two dozen brand-new Faultless 100s he'd pocketed when ole Super Mex wasn't looking. The next day he sold the balls in downtown El Paso for more than he was going to get for lugging that heavy-ass bag for four hours in the boiling sun. Which pretty well established Junior's philosophy. If you can't eat it or screw it and it doesn't run too fast, then *steal it*, man. It's bound to be worth *something*.

The problem was, Junior had been pedaling backwards. Every time he made a few good scores in a row, something would happen. Like somebody'd finger him, or somebody'd write his license number down, something like that. Then the lawyer would get all the money while Junior packed off to Ysleta County Jail or Texas Department of Corrections, depending on whether the current beef was a misdemeanor or a felony.

This last little stretch, a two-to-ten liquor store burglary that the Ysleta County prosecutor had tried to enhance into a twenty-five year habitual number, Junior had gotten pretty lucky on. Two times, double lucky. The first time had to do with observation. The second lucky break had to do with David Ruiz, whom Junior had never met in his life.

When the first break came he was sweating it out down at the county, awaiting trial. Really sweating, a hundred and ten and no A/C. He'd had a visit from Dolores that morning and was feeling pretty low, Dolores tilting her saucy olive-complexioned chin, narrowing her long-lashed black eyes as she said into the phone, "Man, you kidding? You get twenty-five years, you seen the last of this little twat." Then she slammed the receiver down and sashayed out with her solid rump twitching while Junior watched helpless through inch-thick bullet-proof plastic with chicken wire embedded in it.

In the afternoon Junior's lawyer had come by—Horace Ortiz was his name, pretty smooth little ex-assistant D.A. who'd quit the county and gone on his own about the same time all the Chagra brothers had gotten killed or gone to the federal pen. The burly deputy sheriff escorted Junior into the attorney visiting booth—rows of barred openings with little tables on either side where the lawyer could hand the prisoner papers to sign and maybe slip him a joint or two—at two P.M. Horace was wearing a light tan sports coat over a navy Izod knit shirt. He tapped a gold mechanical pencil against the edge of a legal pad. Junior's bare feet shuffled in plastic jail sandals as he sat down. There were lawyers meeting with clients on both sides of them.

"Junior. How you doing, man?"

"*Que tu piensas, hombre?* Not worth shit, Horace. Dolores says she's taking a powder."

"Yeah, well, maybe I talk to her, huh?"

Junior scratched his neck, reaching under the collar

of his tan jumpsuit. There was a frayed hole in the collar. A glob of sweat rolled down his cheek, from his hairline. "I know how you'd talk to her, Horace. Like, move a little closer, little jalapeño, we talk about ole Junior's fee, huh? I not feeling so good. So what you want?"

Horace Ortiz fingered his thick brushy moustache. "You're cutting me to the quick, Junior. Would I do that?"

"In a minute from New York, Horace. Like I say, what you want? We in the middle of a fly-swatting contest back in the cell."

"Well . . ." Horace unwrapped a stick of Doublemint and popped it in his mouth. As he chewed he said, "Four fucking months, I'm still dying for a smoke. Look, Junior, we got to face facts. They're not good facts. They got fingerprints, three half-gallons of Chivas at your pad, still with the store sticker on them. We're fucked for high and can't go low. Best I can do is make a deal, maybe get the habitual charge dropped. They've filed the bitch, it's twenty-five minimum. Maybe I can do something about that."

"So talk a fucking deal. I cop to a trey, maybe a nickel even. I ain't proud."

Horace put his chubby fingertips together. "Junior. You been down the line before. They *pendejos*, sorry bastards. They're not going to talk any two, three, even five-year deal. Twenty maybe, fifteen minimum, just so there won't have to be a trial and the judge won't have to get pissed off. If you want to talk short-time, you're going to have to give them something."

"Like what? Another burglary, stickup?"

"Junior. They're not going to make a deal, one burglar for another burglar. Look, you know any dope dealers?" Horace looked expectant.

"This is El Paso, Horace. I'm a Mexican, just like you. Sure, yeah, I know dope dealers. Dope dealers kill guys."

Junior knew that Horace understood, the part about dope dealers killing guys. Lee Chagra, a big El Paso lawyer, was killed in his office by a heroin man. Ever since that had happened most El Paso criminal lawyers kept a pistol in the drawer right by the receipt book. Horace had a Llama .380.

Horace said, "Now, Junior, here's my thinking. You come up with a good dope case I'll take it to the Feds. If the Feds need you they'll put the pressure on the county for us. And you won't have to worry too much, the Feds will put the dope dealer away until he's too old to give you much shit when he gets out. But it's got to be a big case, Junior. A really *big case.*"

Junior pictured himself gasping for air under deep Rio Grande currents, his feet planted in concrete. Then he pictured Dolores, her twitching butt as she left the visiting room. "Let me sleep on it, Horace," Junior said.

Horace Ortiz put the ruled yellow pad, still blank, in his leather attaché case and snapped it closed. He stood. "You think. I'll be back in a couple of days." He started to leave, then turned, looking thoughtful, his big sad eyes gazing at the floor. "Junior. You finger one of my clients, I'll have to represent him. I can't be your lawyer, too. It would be a breach of ethics. So tell you what. You give up a client of mine I'll get Manny Nunez, from up the street, to represent you. You won't have to worry about paying Manny, I'll take care of him. Know what I mean?" He left.

And that was the time that observation helped Junior Gomez. What he'd observed: Roberto Torres, guy he'd known since grammar school, renting some mini-warehouse space on the West Side, out near the interstate that went to La Tuna. Since a friend of Dolores, Rosie Valenzuela, did some hustling over in Juarez for Roberto Torres, Junior knew that Roberto was in the cocaine business. So Junior put two and two together. Sure, it was a guess, but right on the money. The real bonus for Junior came when Roberto Torres didn't take to his cache being surrounded by DEAs, FBIs, and whatnot, and decided to open up on the Feds with an Uzi. Real bloodbath. It bought Roberto Torres and two federal agents some cemetery space, not to mention Junior some peace of mind about Roberto Torres looking him up. Junior copped a plea to the state, really disgusted about having to do a nickel but in no position to hold out for a trey.

Junior made his third trip through T.D.C. in-processing—a two-week stay at Huntsville Diagnostic Unit, solid lockdown except for testing (Junior knew the ropes—he flunked one of the tests on purpose so he could get his third G.E.D. and collect twenty-five dollars from the state), showers, and meals eaten with his nose in the corner while guards yelled bloody murder in his ear; and another week up the street at Goree Unit for mustering out to a prison farm, keeping his eyes and ears open. If there was any word out about his giving Roberto Torres up to the Feds, he'd have to be careful. Being careful really didn't amount to much at T.D.C., just trading bags of commissary coffee for two more than the standard number of three homemade shanks, keeping two of the knives in bed with him and rigging a makeshift cowbell over his cell door at night that would clang if anybody tried to slip up on him. There wasn't any word out on Junior. Relieved, he took his assignment to Wynne Unit Farm without really caring one way or the other where he did his time.

On Wynne Farm, his first parole hearing was a turndown, not too surprising for a three-time con, but his second hearing two months later had given him a July release date. It was sixty days away when Junior, shirtless and in white boxer undershorts, was resting in between sixty-push-up sets, sitting on the hard bottom bunk in the five-by-nine, third-tier cell. His cellie, a Dallas stickup man named Lupe, was down in the day room watching TV. Junior's flat, muscled belly was rising and falling slowly. Night was coming fast, the cell-block darkening, the automatic ceiling lights glowing dim. Up and down the tiers countless ghetto-blasters were tuned to countless different stations, creating a loud jumble of sound. Suddenly a big shadowy form filled the open cell doorway. No warning, just a huge body standing there.

Junior's heartbeat quickened. His three shanks were

under the upper-bunk mattress, just out of reach. Junior said, gasping slightly, "I got steel in my hand, man, you want to fuck around any."

A high-pitched feminine chuckle. "Hey, Junior Gomez. You ain't got no steel, *chingarro.* You got something plenty good, though, I been watching. Hey, you don't need no steel wid me, Junior."

Junior squinted. "Hippo?"

"Yeah, it Hippo, man. Your homeboy, El Paso-grown Hippo Mendez. Hometown girl."

"I don't fool wid no stick-pussy, Hippo," Junior said.

A high-pitched giggle. Hippo looked down. "Ain't it a shame, ain't it a shame. Naw, big Junior, I got all I can handle right now. I need to talk, man."

"So talk, brudda. You smoke?" Junior stood, got two rolled menthol Kite cigarettes from his bunk. Hippo lit one, his fat cheeks making shadows in the flare of Junior's match. He was wearing rouge.

Hippo Mendez inhaled, blew it out. His huge belly quivered under a white cloth shirt. "I got a heavy number, Junior. Big-time dude, South American dude, *quiere hablar* with a connect in El Paso. Pretty quick. When you make parole?"

"July."

Hippo grimaced, shaking his head. *"Chinga tu madre!* I not think that soon enough. Listen, Junior. You know Roberto Torres?"

Junior said, too quickly, "Yeah, I know Roberto since grammar school, man." He started to add that Roberto was dead, then decided he'd better not.

"Roberto's gone home, man. Took two fucking feds with him, but he's gone."

Junior was glad he hadn't mentioned it. "No shit. Fucking Roberto, huh?"

"Yeah. Roberto, he was doing business with this man. Man's big-time. The real thing. He's moving three, four kilos a month through Roberto Torres, just as much through a guy in Brownsville, another one in Miami. There's this stash, somewhere in El Paso. I don't know where. Man says it's a hundred kilos. What he's looking for is somebody can move the powder now that Roberto's gone. But it's gotta be soon. Real soon. I can't do a thing, honey, I don't hit the street for another two years. But if I set the man up with somebody I want some bread laid on me. Put in my prison account, you know. Hey, Junior man, I can buy some real pretty young things in here if I got plenty of commissary to spread around."

Hippo was talking in low, soft tones, barely audible over the jumbled loud music from the radios. If Junior were to close his eyes he'd think he was listening to a woman, the way Hippo said things. Briefly, Junior tried to remember whether Hippo was a fag on the street, before he went to prison. Junior didn't think so. He said, "Where this man at, Hippo?"

Hippo took a drag from his cigarette, the end glowing hot. Visible over his round shoulders the automatic lights were slowly brightening, casting reflections on the steel railing on the catwalk outside Junior's cell. "Man's right here on Wynne," Hippo said. "Antonio Garza, only that not his real name. Look, a lot of these guys get busted at the border, nobody knows who's who. The real Antonio Garza, he's doing a long federal beef up at La Tuna, only up at La Tuna they think Antonio Garza's this man. It's a switch. You know—man's paying Antonio to go do his federal time while the man comes here, says he's Antonio, does four months. The man's getting out next week. But that hundred kilos in El Paso, it's *hot*, man. Man needs to move it quick. If you're going to be here until July, that's too late."

Junior was figuring. Most jail talk was bullshit, but even if what Hippo was saying were only half-true—shit, a hundred kilos, that's—

Junior said, "Tomorrow I talk to this man, Hippo."

Hippo shrugged. "It's okay, but I know what the man's going to tell you." He licked his lips. "Junior, honey. You sure you don't want to? Hippo make you feel real good, man."

Junior felt quick revulsion, then it subsided. He

said, "Tell you what, Hippo. You get me the deal with this man. Then we might talk."

At first Junior Gomez thought that Hippo Mendez had been putting him on. This guy? Little short round dude, olive skin puffy, the guy sort of hanging around the edge of the yard as if he was hoping nobody was going to beat the shit out of him. Looking around sort of scared—at the black guys playing basketball, hot-dogging it, doing leaping two-handed stuffs; at the guys lifting weights, grunting, their veined muscles standing out.

Junior said, "Hippo Mendez told me you looking for somebody out of El Paso."

At first the little guy didn't realize Junior was talking to him. So Junior repeated himself, a little louder, and the guy said, "Hippo? *Con permiso, no hablo ingles.*" White jail pants too long, rolled up at the cuffs, potbelly.

Junior wondered about the guy, wondered if he really couldn't speak English or if he was just saying he couldn't. The guy's Spanish sounded educated, not Tex-Mex. No border greaser, this guy.

Junior said in Spanish, "Yes, sir, Hippo Mendez. He says that you may need a friend in El Paso. Roberto Torres was my friend. He is missed."

A gray-uniformed guard, eyes hidden behind mirrored sunglasses, sat in a gun tower overlooking one end of the yard, a brick lighthouse affair. The short guy darted a glance at the tower, then said to Junior, "Do not look at me as we talk." The two cons turned back-to-back, Junior watching the basketball while the little man kept his gaze on the grunting, straining weightlifters.

Barely moving his lips, the guy who was posing as Antonio Garza said in Spanish, "Someone told the police about Roberto Torres. They shot him down in the streets like a filthy dog. I will find this person who talks to policemen, and he will die. Slowly, ever so slowly. I have given my word."

This wasn't a timid guy, not at all the way he looked.

This was a guy who was used to giving orders and who was used to having them carried out. Still looking at the basketball game, Junior Gomez said, "I, too, have an interest in this person. Is it for this reason that you need *un amigo* in El Paso?"

It was a few seconds before the guy answered. "Hippo Mendez has already told you why I need an *hombre* who is familiar with El Paso. Do not play games with me. I cannot use you, not if I must wait until July. I depart this prison on Thursday next. The man I use must be ready by that time."

Junior decided to change the subject, get away from talking about when he was hitting the street. Maybe he could stall the guy a couple of months. He said, "How does one know about you, sir? That you are really a man to be trusted?" hoping the guy wouldn't say anything else about when Junior was going to be ready.

Junior watched the little round man out of the corner of his eye, saw the guy stiffen, stand up straighter, heard him murmur, "If you like, you may inquire about Emilio Garza Burista of Colombia. Now you know, you and two other men in this prison. The other men I know will not give me away. Think about that. If the *policia* here discover my identity, then you will die also, my friend. I give my word on that as well."

Junior didn't need to check the guy out, not if he was who he said he was. Burista. He knew the name. Hell, who that had been around any didn't? Junior thought, Can't let a guy like this buffalo me, back me down. He said, "I don't talk to the police, old man. Do not think or say that I do. If I do business with you it will not be through fear. Let us have that understood between us."

Seconds passed. Burista didn't answer. Junior turned to face him, briefly conscious of the guard in the tower. Junior said, "Let's have it understood that—"

Burista wasn't there. He was nowhere in the yard, either. Junior looked around carefully. A couple of cons, a fat white guy and a skinny black with rotten teeth, gave Junior sideways glances. As if they thought he was some kind of lunatic, standing there talking to thin air.

Emilio Garza Burista. Big—no, man, the *biggest*—supplier. Owned plantations at just the right altitude, seven thousand feet, and with just the perfect amount of annual rainfall to make the coca plant thrive. Jesus Christ. Burista, right here on Wynne Farm? What a knockout. Junior knew a pilot, Red Weston, who'd done a little business in Colombia, who'd described Burista's coca fields that stretched into the distance so far you couldn't see from one end to the other. Had his own army, guys with Uzis and sawed-off Ithaca 12-gauges, Double-O buck-loaded, patrolling around the clock. Even the Bolivian government was scared shitless to go out there. Jesus, Emilio Garza Burista doing business with *Roberto Torres?* How can you figure?

Junior hustled back to his cell—down the long corridor past the chow hall where something was cooking that smelled like boiled jockstraps, knocking on the bulletproof window to wake up the guard long enough for him to throw the lever that clanged the steel cell-block doors open, then hop-stepping up the two steel flights of stairs to the third-tier catwalk—his mind going a mile-a-minute. Goddam, there had to be a way. Hundred kilos. Maybe Dolores . . . Naw, that Junior wasn't *that* dumb—let a broad like Dolores get her hands on that kind of money and it's bye-bye, see you later. Hey, what about—? Junior made a sharp column-left and entered the tiny cell, a glimmer of a plan starting to form.

He had company.

"Junior-boy." Donkey Rivers looked up from Junior's open foot-locker, lightly tossing a can of Star-Kist tuna from hand to hand. Donkey's coal-black face didn't look friendly.

Junior sensed movement beside him. He turned as a giant black guy, features like stone and eyes like slits, edged his way around to block the open doorway. Fear knotted in Junior's belly as he looked back at Donkey Rivers. His voice quavering slightly, Junior said, "What the fuck you doing in my locker, Donk?"

Donkey rose from his haunches to stand, still holding the tuna. His nickname came from his ears, like ebony jug handles. He said, "You don't see me payday, Junior-boy, so I come to see you. All's I find is this one stinking can of fish. So what happened to my smokes you owe me—the ten decks? You ain't been around to see Donkey. That ain't real smart, Junior-boy."

Junior tried to think of something—anything—to say. "My girl, Donk. Dolores, she late sending money to me. It be here tomorrow, hey?"

The guy behind Junior gave a low, guttural chuckle as he pricked Junior with cold, welded steel, made in the prison shop and sharp enough to shave hairs. Junior felt the point, right next to his spinal cord. His breath sucked in.

Donkey Rivers said, "Your whore not paying, that not Donkey's problem. You fucking with Donkey, Junior-boy. Hey, I don't make these deals. You do. I give you five decks you give me ten. You don't pay, you pay with your blood, that the deal." He had one gold tooth. Junior's wide-eyed gaze shifted to the corner of the upper bunk, where his own steel lay hidden under the mattress.

From outside and far below a deep male voice, amplified over a loudspeaker, said, "Gomez, Albert. Inmate one-one-seven-three-six-eight-four. Answer up, Gomez."

Donkey Rivers glanced at the guy behind Junior. Suddenly a strong, beefy arm encircled Junior's throat, the knife now digging into his ribs.

"You answer up careful, Junior-boy. You give us away you dead, you hear?" Donkey Rivers said.

The monster-man let go, the foul odor of sweat filling Junior's nostrils. Rubbing his windpipe, Junior yelled, "Yeah, boss?"

"Come on down, Gomez," the voice droned. "Your release is here. You're moving out today. Another of you fucking punks on the loose thanks to David Ruiz and that brainless federal judge up in Tyler. Come on, Gomez. You not down here in one minute I'm forgetting I ever heard of you."

It took an instant for it to sink in. Then, elation spreading through him, Junior Gomez walked out of the cell and down the catwalk. After four or five steps he turned and looked back. Donkey Rivers was peering around the corner, a grimace on his black face and hate in his eyes.

"You be good now, Donk," Junior said. "And be careful who you loan shit to, huh?"

Junior Gomez sat in the cushioned front seat and blessed David Ruiz. Only con he ever heard of who won a suit against a prison system, but what a suit it was. Federal judge turning them out in droves. Long live Dave Ruiz, wherever the fuck he was now.

Dolores was really wiggling around a lot today, constantly running a red-nailed hand underneath the hem of her short, tight jean cut-offs to adjust her panties, propping tiny bare feet on the Buick Park Avenue's dashboard, crossing her bare legs, then uncrossing and recrossing them. "This is getting *old*, Junior. Why we have to be here? How come you didn't just leave your phone number with the dude?" Then she put the back of her hand against the passenger-side window, middle finger extended, as she said, "Up yours, asshole!"

The recipient of the finger, a balding guy with a front tooth missing who had just come down the exit stairs leading from Huntsville's Walls Unit with his release papers in his hand, kept leering at Dolores's legs as he went by. There were three guys following him, all in prison hand-me-down release outfits, and two more guys coming out the exit door at the top of the steps.

Junior kept his hand over the car's steering-column ignition switch—or at least over the hole in the column where the switch had been before Junior had popped it out as a preliminary to hot-wiring the car in downtown Houston on the night of his release. All the way out to El Paso to pick up Dolores, and then back to

Huntsville, a fifteen-hundred-mile round trip in three days. Jesus, he was tired. He said, "How many times I got to tell you, babe? This deal is too big to wait on a phone call. It's for all the marbles, so I won't have to go to jail no more and so you and me can live off the fat. And so you won't be fucking any more lawyers. Like Horace Ortiz."

She scratched a firm brown thigh. "I *told* you, sugar, I was thinking about you. I was just lonely is all. Besides, you should call a girl up, let her know when you're coming." Across the street was a huge used clothing store, a big sign in the front window that said, T. D. C. RELEASE CHECKS CASHED HERE. Guys in old clothes were coming down the ramp and crossing the street in an ever-increasing stream.

"You know I ain't pissed off at you, babe," Junior said. Then he laughed. "Besides, it's almost worth it, the look on Horace when he saw me. Shit, he was looking out over the top of that fucking sheet like Kilroy was there."

That broke Dolores up. She doubled over, holding her sides. Between giggles she said, "Yeah, and what you said to him. Old Horace lying there naked, scared to death, and you say"—more titters—" 'Horace, how you doing, man?' God, sugar, you ought to be on television. I thought I'd just—"

She stopped in mid-sentence as Junior suddenly held up a hand. He opened the Buick's door. The A/C was blowing softly and Willie was low-volume on the radio. "Blue Eyes Cryin' in the Rain." Junior stood up outside and shouted over the top of the car, *"Senor! Padron! Aqui. Aqui en el carro!"*

Senor Emilio Garza Burista came down the steps in a faded blue sports coat that was too big in the shoulders and hung nearly to his knees. He was carrying a battered pasteboard suitcase. He stopped and regarded Junior over the Buick's roof with big, sad eyes. Burista looked as if he was deep in thought. He glanced into the car at Dolores, at her feet on the dash, her muscled thighs.

Finally Burista said, *"El hombre de El Paso. Tu sabes donde esta un poco* young pussy?"

Under thick curly hair, Junior's handsome face broke out in a grin. He made a little gesture with his head in Dolores's direction. *"Que tu piensas de ella?"* Junior said. *"Esta bien?"*

Dolores showed Junior a quizzical arched eyebrow. He nodded to her. She looked to Burista, brushing her fingers through jet-black waves that cascaded to her waist as she half-smiled and shrugged her slim shoulders.

6

Merrillee came to a halt that made her leather soles squeal like tires. A glass on the round plastic tray that she was carrying turned over, ice spilling and tinkling. She blinked. Hard.

It was him all right. Oscar, sitting right at the end of the horseshoe-shaped bar sipping a cool one, a tall gin and tonic. Oscar with his long graying sideburns and clipped moustache, rugged (dammit!) handsome features and sporting a movie-star tan over a rich-colored blue sports coat and white silk shirt.

Next to Oscar, of course—ta-*ta!*—Miss Lay-Your-Husband in the flesh (God, there were times when Merrillee couldn't even remember the little tramp's name). Miss Lay-Your-Husband, dress cut low, breasts snuggled in a push-up bra as if she was churning milk on a government contract. A blush makeup on her vacant pixie face, lips in a bow, lips made for saying, "Jeepers," and, "I like mink," and, "Wow, your jism sure does taste *different*, man."

Oscar lifted his glass and gave a little toast in Merrillee's direction. She nodded curtly, blinked again, and continued on to the waitresses' station with her shapely butt twitching. Why, hello, Oscar. You sorry bastard.

She set her tray down and said to Freddy, the bartender, "Cutty neat, water back, two whiskey sours, a Michelob with, one Tom Collins. Jesus Christ—"

Freddy went into action, grabbing bottles with chrome pouring-spouts corked into their necks, scooping ice, free-pouring one drink, using the liquor-gun on another. Freddy was black-haired, big-shouldered, and narrow-waisted. Merrillee had first thought he was coming on to her until she realized that Freddy was a pimp. He said, "Guy down there"—jerking his head in the direction of Oscar and Miss Lay-Your-Husband—"has been asking about you, toots. Says he wants to see you. Hell, he's got one girl. You're not into double-headers are you, Merrillee?"

"Not yet," she said. "He's my ex, and the girl is why he *is* my ex. Fill the orders, will you, Freddy?" Visible through the open entry-way to the left, the crowds were streaming back and forth down Fremont Street. Merrillee could see the million dollars in cash that sat in a glass case at the entrance to Binnion's Horseshoe, to the right of that the glittering neon of the Fremont Hotel across the way.

While Freddy made the drinks, Merrillee bounced along the bar to where Oscar was sitting. "My, Oscar," she said, "fancy meeting you. You still entertaining, trying to make a sale? This your buyer?" She glanced at Miss Lay-Your-Husband, who smiled, too dumb to know when she was being put down.

Oscar swiveled to face Merrillee, one elbow on the padded bar rim. He chewed lightly on a swizzle stick as he said, "All low blows accepted, Merrillee. Nothing—and I mean nothing—is going to upset me tonight. We're celebrating. I've made a deal. Charlotte. Tell the lady."

Charlotte Lay-Your-Husband, the tops of her boobs quivering, breathed, "It's true. Oscar has sold the Slipper Casino. Closed another big deal. We're having din-din here in the Golden Nugget. At Lily Langtry's. You know, sweet and sour goodies and all that? And then—well, Oscar's going to make an honest woman out of me. Can you be-*lieve?*" Charlotte batted long false lashes as Merrillee felt a wave of nausea.

Merrillee thought, Honest? Oscar's going to *marry* this airhead? Not even Oscar. Surely not. But the look on Oscar's face told her different. God, he was going through with it.

Merrillee said, more subdued, "Well. Congratulations." Then, suddenly thinking of Jessie, "And congratulations on the deal, Oscar. This probably isn't the time to bring this up, but when do you get your money? We're really hurting, Jessie and I."

Oscar averted his gaze just a hair, just enough so that he wasn't looking directly at Merrillee. Miss Charlotte L.Y.H. turned her back, spinning the stool around and putting her elbows on the bar. Down the way, Freddy raised his head from filling Merrillee's order to watch Charlotte's boobs. A couple of guys seated at the bar were doing the same.

Oscar cleared his throat. "Well, Merrillee, that's one reason why I wanted to see you. It's about the payments. Now that I'm going to be a married man, I simply can't afford them. I want to see if we can't work something out. Without going back to court, I mean."

Quick anger boiled in Merrillee. So that was it. Jesus, the food at Lily Langtry's wasn't *that* good, not for them to come all the way downtown to the Golden Nugget. She should have known something like this was coming. The sorry bastard.

Tapping the toe of one spike-heeled foot and folding her arms, Merrillee said, "Oh? And just what did you have in mind? A reduction in the payments that you haven't been making anyway? Really, Oscar?"

A chime in back of the bar dinged. Freddy nodded and winked. Merrillee's order was ready. Quickly, she said, "I've got to serve drinks now, Oscar. I'm really sorry if it embarrasses you for me to be working here, but I do need to make some money. *Really* need to now, it would appear. Excuse me for a moment, will you? But don't go away. Believe me, I'm just *dying* to hear this." With that she spun on her heels to march over and pick up the tray. As she headed for the gaming tables she was conscious of Miss Lay-Your-Husband leaning close to Oscar to kiss his ear.

The Spanish guy was still winning, an evil-but-interesting-looking little round man in a navy sports coat with a red satin lining, rubbing the dice as though he loved them, tossing them out on the green felt, and every time they came up natural getting a wide-eyed look like, "What'd you expect?" Carrying on a running pow-wow with his Latin-lover buddy, this one a mite *too* pretty, an oily-handsome guy with one eye on the shooter and the other on the rows of hundred-dollar chips in the racks. Merrillee thought, Keep your hand on your wallet, Mr. General Santa Ana. Senor Tight Pants there will pick your pocket for you if you aren't careful.

God, the crowd around the table was even bigger than before, five-deep now, some betting with the shooter, a few tourist types just gaping at the action. Look, Matilda. See the funny little spic? Watch, he's about to break the fucking bank.

Merrillee circled the outskirts of the mob, holding her loaded-down tray off to one side, looking for an opening. Drawing some hungry looks from some guys, some of them leering at her over their women's shoulders, one guy yelling, "Hey, mama, where'd you get them *laigs?*" She didn't mind it. What the hell, it was *recognition,* dammit. Beat sitting around picturing Oscar rooting and sweating on top of Miss Charlotte L.Y.H. The sorry bastard. She nodded here and there and painted on a smile, remembering one veteran waitress—Dolly was her name—telling her, "Act *interested,* darlin'. Don't make any difference if he's ninety, toothless, and got the syph. It's where the tips come from, giving them a little hip and showing them a little leg."

She finally gave up looking for an alleyway, took a deep breath, and elbowed her way in amongst them. Nodding and grinning all the while. "Pardon me, miss." "Excuse me, sir." "Oh? You think it's cute now, you should see it when I've got room to wiggle it a little more." *That* leering guy she gave a little bump with her hip, thinking, Take that, Oscar. You sorry bastard.

She delivered the whiskey sours to two women, a tall redhead and a hotsy, deeply tanned brunette who was wearing a navel-length yellow T-shirt over a red bikini. The shirt had SPRINGSTEEN—STILL THE BOSS written in white script across the front. Merrillee noticed some age wrinkles around the brunette's eyes. Merrillee thought, This honey's got a few too many miles on her to be groovin' with Bruce. The brunette ignored Merrillee. The redhead hesitated, then dropped a dollar chip on the tray. Merrillee waded on into the crowd, thinking, Oh, boy, the Trump sisters.

The Michelob beer went to a beefy man in an open-necked checked shirt. His thick neck was red, big freckles showing, and he had a cigar in his mouth that was smoked down to a half-inch of charred stump. He was standing at the crap table next to a light-haired woman with a forty-year-old face and a body that would be the envy of a lot of twenty year olds. The man was playing green twenty-five-dollar chips, the woman five-dollar reds. As the man took the beer, barely glancing at Merrillee as he tossed her a five-dollar tip, the woman yelled, "Goddam, twenty-four in a row. Go, Batista, go," sounding a little bit drunk. Merrillee thanked the guy for the tip, then elbowed her way around them through the crowd to where the short round shooter was raking in the chips and the would-be Valentino in the tight pants was keeping a close eye on the winnings.

The hot shooter—Merrillee had no idea what the guy might be winning, but each rack on the rail held a hundred black, and there were six of them—got the Tom Collins. He took it and sipped, ignoring cries of "Shoot 'em" and "Don't let 'em cool off" as he eyed Merrillee. He leaned over and said something to Tight Pants in Spanish, Tight Pants looking her over as well, as if she were some kind of cheesecake, prancing in place as he did, one hip cocked higher than the other. Tight Pants reached for the Cutty neat with one hand, the water back with the other.

Merrillee fleetingly pictured freshman Spanish class at U.C.L.A., the prof—Senorita Poles, a short chubby woman who'd never been to Mexico or Spain—standing in front of the window, Pauley Pavilion and the stately trees of Westwood in the background. Seemed a hundred years ago. To the short chubby dice-shooter Merrillee said, smiling, *"Usted gustas su tiempo en Vegas?"* Pretty sure that her accent stunk and not certain if *gustas* went with *usted* or *tu.* Feeling sort of silly.

At her side, Tight Pants set the glass of water on the rail, put his hand on her elbow and whispered in her ear. His cologne smelled like sticky maple syrup and his touch made her skin crawl. "I speaka de English, baby. And the man wants to lay you, not hear a bunch of broken gringo Spanish."

Merrillee's gaze met Tight Pants's, his eyes black and soulless. Who did this greaser think he was talking to? She opened her mouth to tell him to fuck off, but before she could the pudgy shooter reached into a rack and plunked five black chips onto her tray, giving her a broad wink as he did.

Now Tight Pants whispered, "That's just a down payment, angel. It's room fourteen seventy-nine. You get off your shift, you come up there. Knock once, count to four, knock again. There's plenty more C-notes in it, more where those come from than you'd ever believe. Oh, and sugar—I'd be sure to show up if I was you." He gave her elbow a pretty hard squeeze, then let go.

Merrillee stood there not knowing what to say or even what to think. Tamale-cooker son of a bitch! Oily, too-pretty Mexican guy turning his back and watching the action at the crap table, the dealers stacking chips next to chips and the stickman rolling dice around in the curve of his flexible wooden pole; the Mexican guy watching the action as if he'd forgotten that Merrillee was even standing there. Sounds came to her that she didn't really hear: the jumbled crowd noises, the drone from the pit boss as he called off the numbers on the galloping dominos, the *ching-ching!* and *rinnnggg!* of the slots.

Merrillee felt just about as repulsed as she felt mad. If somebody like, say, Robert Redford or Paul Newman, somebody like that, walked up and offered five hundred bucks for a lay, that's one thing. But these two guys? For a fleeting instant she pictured the dumpy round Spanish guy standing there with his olive-complexioned belly hanging out over size forty-four boxer shorts (God, she was sure that's what he'd wear—boxer shorts, and black socks held up by garters) while he pawed and yanked at her clothes and mouthed dirty Spanish words in her ear. While the other guy, Tight Pants, stood by and watched and waited his turn in the saddle—or worse yet, stood there and played with himself while he snapped a picture or two. *GOD!*

But still, there were these five black chips on her tray. Five hundred dollars, enough to pay Mrs. Tallon (God, it was embarrassing, having to face that woman and be in her debt day after day), maybe enough left over to hire a private sitter for Jessie for a week or two, to relieve some of the pressure that empty-pockets Oscar was putting on her by not paying her. God, she needed money. *Had* to have money. Couldn't live without it.

At Merrillee's elbow a harsh, gravelly female voice said, "Listen, dearie, are you fucking deaf?"

Merrillee turned. A tall, bony woman with graying hair was standing there in a pink pants suit, peering fiercely through a silver-rimmed pince-nez like the reincarnation of Auntie Mame. Merrillee said timidly, "Oh. I beg your pardon?"

"Sweetie, I'm not giving out any five-hundred-dollar tips," the woman said, "but I would like a *drink*, miss. Is that too much to ask? A dry sherry?" She glanced haughtily at the chips piled on Merrillee's tray.

Merrillee felt a hot flush spreading over her neck as she gulped, tucked the black chips in her tip box, and quick-stepped on her way to fill the woman's order.

"And really, Merrillee," said Oscar, "I think that my offer of half the former payments is more than fair. Especially considering"—he patted Miss Lay-Your-Husband's knee and gave her a sideways puppy-dog look that made Merrillee want to gag—"that Charlotte is willing to do her part in taking some of the responsibility for Jessie off your hands."

Merrillee practically had to bite her tongue to keep

from saying, "No thanks, I'd just as soon not have my five year old coming home in her very own G-string with pasties on her little nipples." Instead she glanced fleetingly at Charlotte, Charlotte with the wide-eyed, hello-world expression, then said to Oscar, "I'm sure that *you* think it's fair, Oscar. But I wouldn't dream of saddling your new wife with Jessie, not when she's going to have her hands full with getting used to you. And as for the fifty percent payments—well, Oscar, fifty percent of zero is still zero. I'd just as soon have a hundred percent of zero."

They were at a corner table in Yosemite Sam's, the Golden Nugget's casino-side coffee shop, Oscar and Charlotte side by side and Merrillee alone across from them. She'd gotten Patti, a dumpy, thick-thighed pep-perpot of a redhead whose eyes had gotten round as saucers when she'd seen the black chips in Merrillee's tip box, to deliver the dry sherry to the woman. Merrillee was taking a break to listen with half an ear to Oscar's half-baked reasons for not paying her and wondering what Tight Pants was going to say when she gave the five hundred dollars back. She must have lost her mind to begin with for taking it. God, if she was going to have a career as a hooker it wasn't going to start with a Latin version of Laurel and Hardy.

Oscar said, getting really testy, "Now that's only temporary, Merrillee. Jesus, you know that. The very idea. That you'd insinuate I might not pay you. A man with my reputation." The interior of the restaurant was dimly lit, more like a bar than a coffee shop. Western paintings hung on the walls: rustlers rustling cattle, firing blazing sixshooters in the air; Indians on the warpath, shooting flaming arrows from the backs of painted horses.

"Well, as a good-faith measure, Mr. Name Around Town," Merrillee said, "how about playing a little catch-up right now? Maybe a hundred dollars or so? Lord, Oscar, you're going to spend that much on dinner tonight."

Charlotte looked suddenly alarmed. "Wow, that's not all, is it?" She slid her arm around Oscar's shoulders.

"A *hundred dollars?* What about the show afterward?"

At first Merrillee thought it was some sort of imbecile humor, then her jaw dropped as she realized that the little dip was serious. She smiled at Charlotte, then said in the tone she usually reserved for Jessie, "Well really, it's only temporary, Charlotte. Like Oscar says, just until the big 'commish' comes rolling in."

Charlotte, relieved, said to Oscar, "Oh. That's nice, poopsie."

Poopsie? God, even Oscar looks embarrassed.

Oscar said, "Okay, Merrillee. Okay, I'll give you a check." He reached inside his coat, pulled out his checkbook, and started to write one out with his gold bigshot pen.

Merrillee's hear sank. The last two checks she'd gotten from Oscar had bounced like Super Balls. She said, "Oh, don't bother, Oscar, I can wait until you have the cash." She saw his shoulders sag in relief. "Look, I've got to get back to work. You two have fun."

She stood, picking up her round plastic serving tray and snapping a mental picture for posterity, burning it into her brain. A picture of Oscar, an image of how pitiful, how utterly low-down *silly* Oscar looked right now, fawning and bowing to an overstuffed pair of boobs and nothing more. A brainless child maybe half his age. In the future, this picture was all that Merrillee was going to need. So long, Oscar. Hello, world.

Merrillee turned to go and spotted Patti through the open restaurant entryway coming through the casino toward the restaurant. Patti's red curls were lengthening and springing as she hurried along between the rows of jingling, clanging slot machines, flesh quivering on mesh-stockinged thighs beneath her short pleated skirt, her uniform identical to the one Merrillee was wearing. Patti had all the moves, the cocktail waitress's wiggle-walk, the expert dodging of men and women as they pulled on silver handles on both sides of her. She carried her tray balanced on one arm. She hustled into the dimness of the restaurant, stood a moment while her eyes got accustomed to the darkness. Her expression brightened as she spotted Merrillee. Patti came over.

Her lipstick was the same shade of flaming red as her hair. "Any time, hon. Hey, Merrillee, where do you get these dudes? I carry the drink over to the woman—Jesus, what a hatchet-face—and this Mexican guy goes, 'Hey, where's the other chick?' I go, 'Won't I do?' Kind of flirting, you know. He acts real pissed off. Good-looking guy, but nas-*tee*, I'll say. Anyway, this little fat dude that can't speak English? I don't think he's a Mexican, he looks a little different. Anyway, the guys says something—I don't speak any Spanish, Merrillee, but it's obvious the guy's got the hots for somebody, and I don't think it's me, dammit. The short of it is that the guy gets the Mexican guy to write a note and gives me *fifty dollars* to bring it to you." She handed Merrillee a folded slip of paper from inside her tip box. "God, Merrillee. I never saw so many black chips. What is he, a king?"

There were only a few feet of carpet separating them from where Oscar sat with his bride-to-be. Merrillee tried not to, but darted a glance in their direction anyway. They'd heard, all right, and it was a toss-up as to which one looked the most interested. Merrillee felt an involuntary grin tugging at the corners of her mouth as she took Patti by the arm and guided her away from Oscar's table to near the restaurant entrance.

"Patti, I don't know the guy, either. He just—Look, Patti, you want to make another tip? Take these to the guy, the short one. I don't want to have to see him."

She stacked the five black chips on Patti's tray, then laid the note on her own tray and opened it clumsily, one-handed. The mirth over Oscar's look left her and a silent chill made her quiver as she read silently, "Don't forget, girlie. It's 1479. One knock, count four, knock again. You want to learn some Spanish?" She looked up. Patti was gazing longingly at the black chips, like she'd fallen in love.

Without raising her head, her eyes still on the chips, Patti said, "Wow, Merrillee, I can't. The guys are gone already. They got one of the security guards to escort them over to the cashier's cage. God, all these black chips."

Denver Phil Madison finally got just the one he'd been looking for: the eight of spades. Out it fell on Fifth Street, the final card in the Texas Hold-Em spread. It lay there, pretty as a *Penthouse* centerfold, next to the queen, jack, three, and four. Two hearts, one spade, a club, and a diamond. Denver Phil was holding a nine and ten in his palm, a queen-high straight that couldn't be beat no matter what anybody else happened to have. Awright, you all-muscle, no-brain, Beatle-haired motherfucker from Texas. You want to play Denver Phil?

Keeping a poker face, acting as though he didn't even notice the eight of spades, Denver Phil kept up the patter. "Yeah, and Jimmy Chagra sat next to me one time. Over across the street at the Horseshoe, playing no-limit. His bodyguard was carrying a million in cash, right there in a blue zip-up tote bag. Lessee, I believe that was the same year they say Jimmy paid Charlie Harrelson to ice the federal judge down in San Antone. You say you know those guys, huh?" Goddam, the big man was still staring off into space, over to where the two greasers were still winning at the crap table. Denver Phil turned his head, a quick jerky move, like a roadrunner. Jesus, they were finally going to quit, the Erik Estrada type motioning for a security guard, the soft round guy picking up trays in both hands that were loaded with black chips. Denver Phil looked back across the poker table to the big man, zeroing in on the tiny image of Mickey Mouse above the guy's breast pocket, thinking about the nine-ten in his palm and trying not to sound anxious as he said, "It's your bet, big fella. Come on, let's play poker." Drumming his fingers, acting cool about it.

"Me?" said the guy. "Oh. Oh, I fold." He tossed his cards into the discard pile.

Denver Phil couldn't believe the guy. Denver's jaw nearly hit the table. "You *what*? Man, ain't nobody bet nothing. How can you fucking get out?'' Glancing at the nine-ten once more, he began to realize he wasn't going to get any play. Jesus Christ.

''They ain't? Nobody bet nothing, huh? Well, it's too late, I already thrown my hand in. It's your pot, I guess.'' The muscle man lumbered to his feet, stacking huge piles into chip trays as he said, ''Look, I got to run. I'm cashing in. Enjoyed playing with you guys.''

As the big man carried his winnings away, Denver Phil took one last, longing glance at the nine-ten. Then he threw in the hand in disgust as Sandy, the dealer, shoved a tiny pot to him: Denver's winnings, a fraction of what he'd lost to the musclehead.

Sandy said, ''Well, it's about time you won one.''

Stevie Wonder leaned forward, peering around Sandy. Stevie said, ''What'd you have, Denver?''

Denver Phil Madison played with the tiny pile of red and green chips. He gazed helplessly at the ceiling. ''I didn't have nothing, Stevie,'' he said. ''Not one fucking thing.''

7

First Merrillee thought about giving the five black chips to Patti, having Patti take the money up to room 1479 and giving it back to the guy. But that wouldn't work. What if the guys raped her? Worse yet, what if Patti didn't go up there at all, just pocketed the money and kept going? The look that Tight Pants had given Merrillee—the smiling face over soulless eyes, like the grin of the dead—was stuck in her mind. No, whatever else she did, Merrillee wasn't about to let those guys think she'd taken their money and they'd been had. Not *those* two.

She stood in line at the cashier's window and watched a girl—a hip-looking college type in a tailored gold pants suit, complete with the Nugget's emblem over the breast—count out bills and change to a short pudgy woman with gray hair. The woman's yellow slacks were too tight. "Second machine down the line on the left, hon," the woman was saying to the cashier. "The Bally Double-Jack. Two small jackpots it paid, and the three cherries must've come up a hundred times."

The cashier smiled impersonally at the woman, then gave the woman's flabby back a bored, sleepy look as she left, fat thighs moving in a near-waddle. Merrillee was next in line.

The cashier pursed her lips in a silent whistle when she saw the blacks, then gave Merrillee a knowing wink through the bars of the cage. "Good night on the floor, huh?" The fine ends of her sandy-colored hair waved like tendrils.

Merrillee half-smiled, not saying anything, suddenly feeling like everyone in the place was looking at her. The girl inside the cage dropped the chips in a drawer, then popped five new hundreds on the counter, crisply peeling them out one at a time. She counted them twice, then handed them through the bars as she said, "Here's hoping there's more where these came from. Jeez, I've got the wrong job."

Merrillee was carrying a small zippered handbag. She opened it and stuffed the money in as she turned away from the window, then gasped in shock.

There was a black guy standing behind her. Close, so close that her elbow brushed against him. He was wearing faded jeans, tight around his narrow waist, and a pullover blue sweatshirt with the sleeves cut off about two inches below his shoulders. His arms were black, sinewy thick ropes, veins standing out like roads on a map. His kinky hair was salt-and-pepper gray, receding over a high glistening forehead. Merrillee was conscious of the sick-sweet odor of hair-gel as she looked at the guy's eyes, nearly dropping her purse and breaking into a terrified run.

One eye was glass. It stared unseeing straight ahead. Its gray pupil was hazy, like a color on a marble. The other eye was dark, almost black, bloodshot and red-rimmed. As the glass eye remained stationary in his head, the seeing eye alternated its gaze between stares at the edges of the hundred-dollar bills that poked out of her purse and hungry glances at her legs. With the urge to run gone, she now felt as if she was standing in cement. She felt an eerie fascination, the same crawling sensation she'd felt the first time she'd seen a live Gila monster.

Hoarsely, the black guy said, "Move please, lady. I've got to get by." Then he shouldered his way leisurely around her and to the cashier's window. He was holding a single red five-dollar chip, clutched in a deathgrip.

Merrillee exhaled slowly, feeling almost faint, then got a hold of herself and took off at a quick pace through the hubbub of the casino. She turned to her left and started up the long, slot-machine-lined corridor for the elevators, moving amid the click of the handles and the whirring spin of the wheels as she thought, God, what's *wrong* with me? The poor guy was just trying to cash his last five bucks in, and there I'm staring goggle-eyed like he was a circus freak. She pictured the dull glass eye and shuddered again.

Leaving the Golden Nugget's loud casino for the stillness of the hotel proper was a pretty spooky sensation in itself, and Merrillee changed her mind three or four times on the way. She passed by the rows of slot machines and came abreast of the first-floor lounge on her left. It was quiet inside the half-full bar, with serious drinking going on, expectant-looking guys leaning on their elbows and saucy-butted hookers giving lazy come-ons. Merrillee couldn't understand why the two Hispanic guys hadn't just come down here to the lounge. Flashing their five hundred dollars around the bar would have bought them all the action they could handle. She watched a bartender, a potbellied guy with curly gray hair, shake mixing cups as she thought, Why me? God, every girl in that bar has probably got a dildo in her purse along with who-knows-what-else, primed and ready for action.

She walked by the gift shop, hurrying now, feet flashing along in white spike-heeled sandals. The casino sounds had faded completely and the half-inch padding underneath the carpet muffled even her light footsteps. Eerie. Not half a minute ago she was in noisy bedlam. There weren't any customers in the gift shop. The salesclerk, a young, chubby, gum-chewing girl, was on the stool behind the counter reading a paperback of *Salem's Lot*, by Stephen King. Goody, thought Merrillee, just what I needed. Vampires yet. The gift shop held racks of red and blue and yellow T-shirts that had the Golden Nugget logo emblazoned on the chest, a loaded paperback book rack, and counters laden with shiny souvenirs—toy dice and roulette wheels.

Merrillee didn't have the slightest idea what she was going to do. Slide the money under the door and run? It was the best idea she could think of, but what if the guys didn't find the money? What if the maid picked it up? No, she had to have proof—*Proof?* God, Merrillee, what are you going to do, ask the guy for a receipt?

Maybe she could go up there and act so stupid that the guys would get turned off and demand their money back. Like maybe point at their dongs when they were hanging them out and say, "God, they're so *tiny.* Cutest little things I *evah saw.*" Giggle at them. God, what if it made them so mad that they broke her arms or something? Every idea that she had seemed a little dumber than the last one. She touched the elevator button. The doors slid noiselessly open. She walked inside and pressed the button for the fourteenth floor. The doors closed and she felt the pull of gravity as the car rose.

The elevator walls were mirrored glass; she checked the front, back, and side views of herself. Back straight, muscular thighs side-by-side. Marvelous Merrillee, hooker of the month. God. The elevator stopped, the doors opened, and a lump rose in her throat as she started down the hall. It was silent as a tomb.

The lush carpet was red with a gold flower pattern. There were paintings of Wild West scenes along the walls. An old man who was wearing a hearing aid passed her going in the opposite direction, giving her the once-over as he went by. She decided wearily that she'd had plenty of once-overs for one night.

She came to room 1479, stopping and just standing there, reading the number over and over to herself, stalling for time. Maybe it wasn't the right room, maybe the guy had written down the wrong number. Maybe the guys were too busy for her, tired out from their all-day stand at the crap table, relaxing and having a few drinks while they kicked around the current tamale prices. Maybe they'd rather not be bothered. Maybe she ought to quit making excuses to herself and get it over with. She took a deep breath and bent to put her ear to the crack between the door and the frame. Dead silence, with a little rushing sound in the background, like listening to a seashell.

She dug the hundred-dollar bills out of her purse and held them ready. Here, Senor Tight Pants, here's your money back. Some kidder you are. That's what she'd do, hand him the money the moment he came to the door and zippo, walk away fast before he could stop her. Her knees were wobbly-weak as she put out a tentative fist and knocked softly.

As she listened to the *snap-snap* of the locks and watched the doorknob turn, Merrillee wet her lips. She was about to say, I'm sorry, there's been a mistake, as she handed the money over. She was drawing in her breath to say just that when the door opened wide, a strong brown hand clamped her wrist then literally yanked her into the room as the door closed behind her.

Just like that, and just that quickly. One second she was standing there in the stony silence of the Golden Nugget hallway, the next second she was inside the room. The hand grabbed her too fast and jerked her too suddenly for her to put up any resistance; she had to follow her own stiffly extended arm into the room, moving her feet quickly to keep from stumbling and falling on her face.

Tight Pants let go of Merrillee's wrist, giving her his mirthless grin as he said, "Well, here we are. Good girl." Then said something over his shoulder in Spanish, out of the side of his mouth. Merrillee caught "*mamon.*" God, the Spanish word for blowjob. Her roommate in college had been from a well-to-do L. A. Mexican family and had used the word a lot of times, usually when she came in after a date. Like, I gave Johnny a little *mamon.* God.

Merrillee's mind raced, desperately looking for some way, *any* way, to get out of this as she took in the thick red drapes and listened dully to the faint whisper of the air conditioning. She was in a two-room suite. Through the connecting open doorway she could see the corner of a monster king-size covered in quilted red and two posh stuffed velvet chairs. Just like the room she was in. The light was on in the john, the bulb reflecting on the glassed-in shower.

These two were sure as hell ready for some kind of party. A rolling room-service tray on one wall was laden with two full-to-the-brim ice buckets, a quart of Cutty, the seal broken and a couple of brown-liquid inches gone, and an unopened fifth of Jack Daniels Black. The painting in the room was of a couple of moustachioed cowpokes unbuckling their gunbelts as a half-dressed Indian maid with waist-length black hair cowered terrified against one wall of an adobe hut. God, like they'd had it painted just for them.

Tight Pants had changed into something more comfortable. He wore navy shorts with the Izod 'gator grinning evilly on one leg and a pink, skintight tank top. His legs were smooth and brown, almost hairless. There was a faded purple tattoo on his upper right arm, two fanged snakes writhing and hissing. He was drinking Scotch from a clear plastic cup, with ice. He raised the cup to his lips and leered at her over the rim.

And on the edge of the king-size, grinning crookedly at her, sat—*him.* God, he was actually wearing them! Thin, calf-length, black stretch-sox, held up by elastic garters below the knee, and blue cloth boxer shorts. Size forty-four, at *least,* olive-skinned gut hanging out over the waistband. There was a long surgical scar running from a point just below his breastbone to below his puffy navel, where the scar disappeared underneath his shorts. He stroked his moustache, sipped his Scotch, then said something in Spanish to her. There were a lot of hundred-dollar bills piled on the bedspread next to his fat hip, and he gestured toward them with his head as he spoke. Lot more where these came from, sugar.

Merrillee's hand trembled as she held out the money she'd brought, held it out in the general direction of Tight Pants. She said, "Look—" Her voice caught and she had to clear her throat before saying, "Look. This has all been a big mistake. I'm not a call girl, or whatever you think I am. So I'm returning your money. Here—the money. See?"

Tight Pants scratched his hard belly, not saying anything, making no move to take the bills from her.

Finally Merrillee's hand dropped weakly to her side.

On the bed, El Black Sox said, *"Que dice ella?"* With his round head cocked slightly to his left.

To the guy on the bed, Tight Pants muttered, *"Momentito."* Then, to Merrillee, "You got any idea who you're trying to fuck around, little lady? Not just me. Me, Junior Gomez, I ain't nothing. But *him?* You want to go home with your ass still behind your twat, I think you better change your tune. But fast."

Merrillee thought, *Junior*? Last name in the world she would have picked for this guy. She began to get scared. Really scared. All through the walk down the silent hallways and the elevator ride she'd been . . . apprehensive? Nervous? Both of those. But what she was feeling now was pure, choking terror. She shot a wide-eyed glance at the closed hallway door. She'd never be able to move fast enough to get around Junior Gomez and out of this room. Never in a million years. God, why hadn't she brought a hotel security guard up here with her? Even a hooker has sense enough to have her pimp nearby in case any trouble starts. Merrillee thought, How can I be so everloving *dumb*?

The guy named Junior stepped in close to her now and slid his arm, almost lovingly, around her shoulders. He put a thumb and forefinger on opposite sides of the nape of her neck and squeezed, sudden, hard pressure. Tears of pain leaped into her eyes.

His cold stare never wavered as he said to her, "Come on, sister. We going to walk over and see the man." Then broke into a stream of rapid Spanish that Merrillee was too terrified even to try to understand. He kept the squeeze hold on the back of her neck as he directed her halting, staggering footsteps toward the bed. The soft round guy, his gut hanging out, leaned back and rested on his elbows. His lip curled in a sneer as he waited.

Now anger, a pure downright *mad,* began to crowd

its way through Merrillee's fear and despair. Two real brave cats here, about to gang up on a poor defenseless woman and terrorize her into doing God knows what to them, just for the pure hell of it. The sorry bastards. She didn't know exactly what, but she was going to do *something*, something so that these two Latin perverts weren't going to have near the fun doing this to her that they thought they were going to have. She was—she was—

She was going to kick this Mexican asshole who was hurting her right square in the balls, that's what she was going to do.

She planted her feet firmly in the carpet and raised her elbow, jamming it as hard as she could into the flesh of Junior's upper arm. He grunted in pain and shock and let go of her. The drink that he'd been carrying in his free hand slopped and sloshed onto the rug. Merrillee was conscious of a glazed, curious look on the round Latin on the bed as she spun in Junior's direction.

The Mexican guy, Junior, looked more puzzled than hurt. His dark brows knitted as he rubbed his bicep where she'd elbowed him. He half-smiled and started to say something. As he opened his mouth, Merrillee took a hopping stride with her left foot and swung her strong right leg, her white spike-heeled sandal flashing in the air as she buried her right toe in Junior's crotch like a ballerina trying a soccer-style placekick.

She did it without thinking. Merrillee had thought several times about taking some self-defense classes—woman alone, all that—but she'd never gone through with it. Nothing like that could ever happen to *her*. Now that it had, she was acting strictly out of frenzied instinct. Feeling pain and kicking hell out of whoever was inflicting it on her. Her foot thudded into Junior's crotch with a satisfying crunch.

Junior howled like a car-struck dog and doubled over. He fell to his knees, his eyes shut tight and tears streaming down his cheeks. Then he flopped to the floor and rolled over to one side. He began to moan.

Merrillee blinked in surprise. Surely it couldn't be

this easy. A few nights ago she'd watched a late-night softcore on the cable, "Angel of H. E. A. T." (or was it angel *in* heat?), starring Marilyn Chambers. Marilyn had disposed of half the spies in Europe, stopping for four or five good bangs in between, and it all had seemed pretty silly. Now by God, it was all coming to pass. Make way for Mad Merrillee, Angel of Ball-kicking. Where's the other tamale-cooker son of a bitch? Lemme at him.

Her muscles tensed as she whirled to face the guy on the bed. He was sitting there with his mouth wide open like a flytrap with a moustache. As Merrillee took a determined step in his direction he held out both trembling hands. The Scotch was in one, liquid sloshing and dribbling, and the other was palm-outward in a pleading attitude. He began to beg in Spanish. She couldn't understand the words, just the high, whiny tone.

God, she couldn't attack a little fat man who couldn't even speak English. She was aware that she still held the five one-hundred-dollar bills, now crumpled and wadded in her clenched fist. She tossed them at the guy as she said, "Here. Your money. Like I was trying to say, I just wanted to bring it back to you." Not even slowing down the guy's string of gibberish. One of the bills hit his nose and danced down onto his lap.

On the floor, Junior Gomez's groans were subsiding into whimpers. Merrillee decided that she'd better get moving, suddenly feeling a little sorry for Junior. She said, "Don't worry. You'll be okay." Then added, "I think," as she unbolted the door and left. The round man was staring vacantly after her from the bed. He hadn't moved; one of the crumpled hundreds was still balanced precariously on top of his quivering right thigh.

She felt drained once she was in the hallway. She felt as if she wanted to lie down. She took a deep breath as she gathered her strength and took a couple of steps in the direction of the elevator. Then she froze as a deep voice behind her said, "Hey, where you going?" in a Texas-sounding drawl.

She turned like a granite statue. Jesus H. Christ, where did *this* guy come from? The hallway had been empty. She was sure of it. Then, *poof,* here's this guy. There was a small alcove a few feet down the hall. Merrillee decided that that's where he'd been hiding as she looked the guy over and began to get scared again.

Holy manoley, this guy was a monster. Like a pro wrestler or something. Big, square-jawed, clean-shaven face under a Beatle haircut. Not an ugly face, she couldn't help noticing, just sort of unreal, like a handsome cartoon character. And a shirt with—God, Mickey Mouse, on the pocket. The guy was too much. And wow, was he big.

The guy said, "I need to talk to you."

She stood and stared, afraid after all she'd been through she might faint. Normally she probably would have at least asked the guy what he wanted. But not now. Not after the crap with the two Latins. What was this guy, one of their buddies?

She screamed, "You bastard! You lay one hand on me and I'll kick your nuts off." Then she ran off in the direction of the elevator, praying that he wouldn't follow.

Running at full stride in high heels was impossible; all she could manage was a rapid, jarring half-step. Her heels were absorbing the impact and were throbbing by the time she made the right-angle turn that led to the elevators. She wanted to look back to see if the monster-man was following but didn't dare. As she approached the three side-by-side elevator doors she was praying. Please, God. Just once let one of these frigging doors be open.

One was. It was the center door and Merrillee hopped into the car with a thud and pressed her thumb against the first-floor button. The doors began to slide closed as the big man huffed and puffed around the corner and started for her.

She watched in a helpless trance. The opening between the sliding doors grew narrower and narrower and the guy loomed bigger and bigger. His craggy features were set in concentration. He reached out to try to stop the closing doors, saw he wasn't going to make it. He tried pumping the DOWN button in the hallway between the doors, huge bicep rippling as he did. The guy disappeared from view as the doors thudded softly together. The car started down.

Merrillee sank back against a mirrored wall and listened to the blood pounding in her ears. She closed her eyes, conscious that she'd somehow hung onto her purse through the ruckus, feeling it against her hip. She thought of Jessie. God, sweetheart, Mommy nearly bought the farm. Thinking of Jessie made her picture Mrs. Tallon as well. Could she pay the woman? Yes, she'd made just enough in tips, without El Black Sox's five hundred bucks. She was only going to have about ten dollars left over, but at least after everything else that had happened tonight she wasn't going to have to be embarrassed again. Thank God for small favors.

By the time she exited from the elevator she'd calmed down some. Still pretty jittery and still plenty scared, but at least in control of herself.

Everything looked normal, the check-in desk on her left, the lounge in the other direction, the gift shop in between. The shop's lights were turned off. She looked at a digital wall clock, its outline in the shape of a covered wagon, and realized with a jolt that it had only been fifteen minutes since she'd gone up. God, it seemed like ten years. When she got home—if she ever did—she might sleep for a week.

She left the Golden Nugget by the double glass doors in front of the check-in desk and walked along Fremont Street away from the action, away from the glittering intersection that held the Nugget, Horseshoe, Fremont Hotel, and Four Queens on its corners. The crowd thinned as she click-clicked her way down the sidewalk: even downtown Vegas mellows some at four in the morning. There was a sportsbook across the street and Merrillee could see through its front glass windows, could see behind the counter where the odds showed on boards, the baseball lines, the racetrack numbers across the country. A sleepy-looking guy in a soiled white shirt was taking money from a bent old Chinese woman, selling her a betting slip. Baseball bet, Merrillee thought, the Orientals are crazy about the sport. On the other side of the sportsbook, on the opposite sidewalk from Merrillee, two hookers—a chatty black girl and a doe-eyed, dark-haired white—were making their proposition to a fat man in a blue suit. The guy was staggering drunk, Merrillee noticed as she hustled across an intersection. The lot where she parked her Mustang was just a half-block farther on.

Merrillee felt better. The desert night air was cool and crisp, and it was bringing her around. She was feeling nearly normal now, even returning a smile from a woman in designer jeans who went by in the opposite direction. She pictured Junior groaning and clutching at his crotch; she even giggled slightly at the thought, putting the back of a hand over her mouth as she did.

Her parking was paid in advance. She fast-stepped onto the gravel lot, feet crunching, and passed the unpainted attendant's booth with its single light bulb glowing inside. The green Mustang sat at the end of a long vacant row of parking places. It was an old one, a '76, the low-slung sports model with bucket seats and the shift on the floor. Merrillee kept it in pretty good shape; the streetlights reflected its polished hood and fenders. She took the keys from her purse and bent to unlock the door, thinking fleetingly of Oscar and Miss Lay-Your-Husband and wondering when she was going to get some money from the sorry bastard. Be a while, with the blissful wedding and all.

The black man with the glass eye, the one she'd seen at the casino pay window, walked up behind her. He put one hand on her shoulder and held the point of a stiletto against her ribs with the other.

He said, "You scream, you fucking dead, you heah? Where you got all that money, honkie bitch? You turn around slow now."

God, it was the voice. Panic was in her mouth like

bitter bile as she turned slowly, trying not to wince visibly at the sight of the dead, sightless eye, not able to help averting her gaze from his face. She smelled the sick-sweet scent of hair gel again.

He said, " 'S'matter, lady, you don't like my eye or something? Maybe you like it on top of you, watch it while I fuck you, huh?"

She gasped.

Where had he come from? She was pretty sure that nobody had followed her when she left the Nugget. She'd have sensed it, surely she would have. Cruel rotten luck, it just had to be. That this wretch—down, probably, to his last five dollars in the form of the single red chip that Merrillee'd seen clutched in his hand—had happened to see her. Had stayed hidden in the shadows and watched her come down that long dark street as if she didn't have a care in the world, and remembered her—remembered the wad of money that she'd stuffed in her purse as she left the cashier's window. Whatever little demon it was who lived within Merrillee gave a sardonic chuckle that echoed throughout her system.

The dead glass eye was in the periphery of her vision as she said, "Here. Here's all I have. Please leave me alone." Then moved only her arm, holding the rest of her body rigid with fear as she offered him her small zippered purse.

Beyond him she couldn't see anyone on Fremont Street, only darkened building fronts. The light still shone from the parking lot attendant's tiny booth, but there didn't seem to be anybody there, either.

He yanked the purse out of her hand and jammed it into his pants pocket, still holding the stiletto's point against her. "How come you not watching me, bitch? I said I want you look at me, white bitch." He put more pressure on the knife point, so much that Merrillee wondered in terror if he'd punctured her skin. He reeked of cheap street wine. Harsh, distance-runner breathing was interspersed with his guttural snarls.

Merrillee forced herself to turn her head and look

directly at him, flinching at the sight of his face, his breath now in her nostrils like sewer air. "Why—why, see, I'm looking at you." Tearfully begging now, her voice hoarse. "You have my money. Please. Please leave me alone."

Like most women—and like most, not talking about them much—Merrillee had had nightmares of scenes just like this one. Spine-crawling, horrible dreams that made her wake up shrieking in the middle of the night. None of the dreams could match this; no words could tell the pure horror of the moment; and she wasn't going to be able to wake up and make this nightmare disappear.

Merrillee's keys were stuck in the Mustang's lock. He reached around her and creaked the door open. The car's interior light suddenly illuminated his face, his nose casting a shadow over his bloodshot seeing eye. He said, "You get in that fucking back seat. You move now." He prodded her with the knife. She now felt a drop of wetness where the point touched her.

Slowly, inch by inch, her knees wobbling with fright, Merrillee backed into the Mustang. As she put her foot in the car, never taking her gaze away from his face, he folded the front seatback forward. She began to edge her way into the cramped backseat. "God in heaven, please don't do this," she said. He didn't answer, just pressed harder against her with the knife point.

She tried to make herself relax, tried to think of something far away—her job, Oscar, anything. If it's going to happen, keep your mind off it. Above all, don't anger him into really hurting you. Maybe he's really not going to do it. Maybe once you're inside the car, sitting in the backseat, he'll just slam the door and run away. Maybe—

He started to climb in after her.

Merrillee sat dumb as a stone, her back rigid, and watched him struggle his way in. The muscles under the popping veins on his forearms writhed like boas. There were damp spots at the underarms of his sweat-shirt, threads dangling from the cut-off sleeves like light blue moss. His big lips were pulled back from piano-key teeth in an insane grin. His bloodshot seeing eye showed a wild gleam.

Merrillee started to close her eyes, thinking, Dear God, at least I won't have to watch it happen to me. Just as her lids started to shut the light out, the black man gave a strange strangled squawk like a chicken. Merrillee couldn't help herself, she had to see; she opened her eyes wide as something behind him pulled the collar of his sweatshirt tight around his neck and yanked him backward, out the door of the Mustang, like a limp rag doll.

His arms flailed as he grabbed for purchase on the seatback. His thick tongue lolled, the sweatshirt collar digging in around his windpipe. Then he went out, falling in a tangle of arms and legs, grunting in pain as he slammed down on the gravel.

For seconds Merrillee was too stunned to move. She'd shrunk back as far as she could in the backseat, the window handle digging into the muscles of her back. It was the pressure from the handle that finally made her snap to. Then she struggled in the narrow backseat to get to where she could see what was going on outside the car. As she did, the black man's wide back blocked her view as he slammed against the side window with so much force that the Mustang rocked hard on its springs.

A deep but mellow voice said in a heavy Texas drawl, "Man, are you fucking *crazy*? You wave that two-bit pigsticker at me one more time and I'll jam it so far up your ass you'll have a built-in toothpick. Say, don't nobody want you around here. You drag your—"

God, it was the monster from the hallway at the Golden Nugget. There he stood like Conan, giant shoulders and arms silhouetted in the faint streetlights and brighter glow from the attendant's shack. Standing there in a fighter's attitude, hamlike fists upraised in the classic boxer's pose, biceps the size of thighs. And Jesus God—Merrillee blinked twice to make sure her eyes weren't fooling her—his hair was falling off! The dark wave of Beatle locks had slid down over one of his ears, short crew cut hair sticking out of his exposed scalp like tiny quills. So the guy was wearing a wig. God, with that body he might be a refugee from a circus. In spite of herself, Merrillee giggled.

The black man had had plenty. His seeing eye now round and wide, he charged around the back of the Mustang, feet thudding, and disappeared down the block.

The giant watched him go. Then a sudden, cartoon-like embarrassment spread over his face as he reached up and righted his wig. His dignity restored, he lumbered over to the Mustang, bent over, and peered inside. He was grinning a toothy grin. "Hey. You all right? Don't worry about that guy none, I think he's got someplace to go."

It all came down on her at once and she began to sob. She couldn't help it. Salty tears filled her eyes and cascaded down her cheeks as she covered her face with her hands, her shoulders heaving.

A giant freckled hand nudged her shoulder. She looked up, sniffling. A spotless white hanky—God, with embroidering around the edges—was in the hand.

"Here," he said, "this'll help you turn off the faucet, huh?"

She took it. As she daintily blew her nose, the giant took the keys out of the door and got in behind the wheel. The Mustang lurched under his weight.

"We got business to talk over, sister," he said. "Whaddya say we grab a bite?"

He gunned the engine and careened out of the parking lot, Merrillee bouncing around in the backseat, her jaw slack in astonishment.

This broad sure didn't act like any hooker that Size had ever run across. Must be Vegas. Must be like they said, the prime stuff hanging around where the action is, following the big bucks.

And here she was, sitting across the booth from him at Denny's on the Strip with the rippling up-and-down gaudy neon spire in front of the Dunes Hotel over her shoulder in the background. Sitting prim and proper with her knees side-by-side under the table, linen napkin draped over her lap like in the English movies, lifting her coffee cup to her lips and sipping without even blowing to cool the hot stuff off. Finishing-school moves. Like—what's her name?—yeah, Penelope Turner. Old man owned the furniture store back in Commerce, Texas, had more bread than anybody in the county. Always Penelope, never Penny, 'cause Penny would sound too much like she was from Commerce. Penelope Turner, packed off to Hockaday School for Girls over in Dallas, then on to S.M.U. and married off to some bigshot lawyer and living in a big house out in Highland Park. Yeah, this broad here, she carried herself a whole lot like old Penelope Turner.

She sure didn't talk like no hooker, either. No gum chewing, no dumb-sounding "*Wouldya* be-*lieve,*" or corny half-baked dirty jokes that weren't even funny. Just straight-on, no-nonsense talk with a saucy—yeah, even sexy—little tilt to her chin; perfect diction, just the way an English teacher'd talk. If Size didn't know better he'd swear this broad had a little class.

And some kind of looks. Soft auburn hair in waves that framed her face, legs in mesh stockings like a plum show horse. She'd have 'em hanging from the rafters back at Daisy Mae's. Yep, thought Size, bet this hooker is cleaning up around here.

And ballsy. Playing the act to the hilt, not giving away nothing.

She replaced her cup in the saucer with a soft glassy clink. "I'm sorry, but you're wrong. And I'd really like to help you, believe me. God knows you probably saved my life. But it was all a mistake, me being up there. I'm telling the truth. I've never laid eyes on the two before, Mr.—What did you say your name was?"

"Size. Uh, Fred Size, only nobody uses my first name." Jesus, what was the wop name on the driver's license in his pocket? He couldn't even remember. Good thing he'd never tried being an FBI. "Look," he went on, "how about if I give you a day or two to check me out? See that I'm not a vice cop or nothing. I can understand that the wig might make you jumpy, like I ain't on the square."

"That you're not a—?" Her sudden laughter tinkled like a dinner bell. "Well, the only picture I've got in my mind of a vice cop is what I've seen on TV. Which certainly isn't you. You've shaved. You don't look as though you need a bath, and you aren't wearing a Woodstock or Willie Nelson T-shirt. And you're the one who's out in left field as far as someone's identity goes, not me. I'm just not a hooker. Sorry to disappoint you." She looked a little more irritated, rolling her eyes slightly as she took another sip of coffee.

She'd said it straight-out, no twitch in her hazel eyes. Broad was *good.* Size pushed his plate of scrambled eggs and sausage links aside, nearly untouched, as he said, "Aw, I don't mean that you're a *full-time* hooker or nothing. Don't get me wrong. I'm sure you do okay hustling drinks, too. But look, sister, you don't have to put on no act with me. I know plenty of hookers, and ain't nothing wrong with it. I'm trying to make you a deal that'll let you make more money than you can make turning a trick. Ain't nothing to it, easy as pie." Size grinned as if he was offering the keys to the city.

The waitress, a sweet-faced pudgy girl with stringy brown hair, stopped at the booth. She was carrying a round glass coffeepot. Merrillee offered her cup. The girl poured fresh, then moved on to another table. Denny's was half-full, most of the customers sleepy-drunk, trying to get sober. The sky was lightening from black to gray over the roof of the Hilton Hotel as the blue-white stars winked off, one by one. It was five A.M. In anther hour the desert summer heat would take over.

Merrillee was saying, "I don't know anything about turning tricks. I don't even really know anything about being a cocktail waitress—it's only my second month. And what if I was what you seem to think I am? Why would I open up to you? All I really know about you is that you hide out in hallways, chase women onto elevators, and beat up muggers. And you wear a Beatle wig. What is it that I can find out about these two guys that you can't find out for yourself, snooping around?" She folded her arms in front of her. She wore one simple, gold-beveled ring on her right hand. No nail color, a clear lacquer polish.

Cagey as hell, this broad. Playing the old "What if I was?" game, trying to get Size to open up to her without really committing herself. Girl was okay. Size said, "Well, if you did just happen to be interested"—he threw her a big, we-both-know-you-are wink—"then I'd just want a little info. Look, sweetie, the Colombian guy has a lotta dough. You'd want to be balling him all you could anyway, right?"

She arched an eyebrow.

He went on, "But you ain't going to fall in love with the guy, so what's it to you if you double your money giving me what I want to know? Look, somewhere down the line those two guys are gonna have some company. From outta town. I just want to know when it's coming is all. No big deal." He grinned and waved a big paw like a friendly honey bear.

Her lip twitched slightly just before she sat up a little straighter in the booth and said, "It probably isn't any big deal to you. But it sure would be one to me. Look, Mr. Size, I'm trying very hard not to get mad at you because you came along and saved me from God knows what. And it's getting very difficult. So for the last time, I'm not a hooker. I know a whole lot less about those men than you do, that's obvious. And this conversation isn't getting us anywhere. It's really, really late and I've got to pick my daughter up from the—''

She broke off in mid-sentence and her expression changed from forced calm to sudden real distress. As if a mask had fallen away.

''What is it?'' Size said.

She was trying hard to put the mask back on, but it wasn't working. ''Oh, it's—'' she started to say, then, ''Oh hell, it *is* something, too. My purse. The guy ran away with my purse, every last cent I've got. I can't even pay my little girl's baby-sitter.'' A tear ran down her smooth cheek.

Size brightened. Cool one, this broad. ''Yeah? Well okay, if that's the way you want to do it. How 'bout if I pay the bill for you? Sure, I seen hookers that work it like that. Like they really ain't taking money for— Aw, you know what I mean. Don'tcha?''

Merrillee gently shook Jessie awake. It was quite a job. Jessie slept heavily; she would squirm and wiggle down in the bed and hug the grinning blue Care Bear tighter to her chest. Sometimes after a long night on her feet Merrillee would feel a tug of irritation when she tried to wake Jessie up. But not tonight. Spending plenty of time getting her daughter ready to go would let Merrillee avoid the knowing haughty glances from Mrs. Tallon while the big man, Size, paid Merrillee's bill.

Jessie finally sat up, yawned, and stretched her tiny arms, her hands balled into little fists. She smiled a sleepy child-smile, ''I dreamed about Fonzie, Mom. Is it time to go?'' She was in pink nylon jammies that said BE NICE—I'VE HAD A HARD DAY in script across the front.

Gently, Merrillee said, ''Yes, it's time, punkin. Do

you have to go to the bathroom before we leave?'' She felt a little testy with herself for asking the age-old Mommy-question. God, her own mother *still* asked it sometimes, when Merrillee was visiting in L.A. But she was worried some; Jessie had been into bedwetting of late. Nerves, the doctor said. Jessie giggled and said no, she didn't need to, her voice hushed by the throb of the window-unit air conditioner.

There was only one other child still in the nursery, a frizzy-haired little black girl asleep in the flower-patterned daybed in the corner. Cicely's child. The gorgeous black girl who worked Keno at Caesar's. Well, Merrillee thought, little wonder what's keeping *her* mother. Then felt like kicking her catty self. Lot of room to talk, Merrillee. You sound just like Mrs. Tallon, the same way she's going to talk about you when you walk out tonight.

She left Jessie dressed in pajamas and fuzzy pink houseshoes—she always did at this hour; Jessie would go back to sleep as soon as they got home—and picked up the small white overnight case by its leather carrying strap. A quick glance around the room located only one of Jessie's toys strewn about, the Astro Barbie that Jessie had been playing with when Merrillee had left for work. She stuffed the doll into the small suitcase and snapped it closed. Then she took Jessie by the hand and tiptoed out of the nursery to the front room.

Mrs. Tallon looked like an elegant twig standing next to Size. Merrillee couldn't remember ever seeing anybody that big before. A few blubbery fat men perhaps, but nobody that was all muscle and sinew like this monster. Merrillee had stood by Merlin Olson once when Susan Roehmer's modeling agency, where she'd worked part-time in college, had sent her out to hostess a publicity party for the L.A. Rams. But she didn't remember even Merlin Olson being *this* overpowering. Even Mrs. Tallon looked intimidated. But not too intimidated to send a haughty, down-the-nose glance in Merrillee's direction when she came in with Jessie.

Jessie's soft little hand tightened its grip. "Wow, Mom! It's a *big giant.*"

"Jessie! Shh!"

"But it *is,* Mom. Just like Jack and the Beanstalk."

Merrillee thought that Size's neck reddened under the Beatle locks. But he acted as though he hadn't heard as he went on to Mrs. Tallon, "Listen, don't make out no receipt to me. Make it out to"—turning to Merrillee—"what's your name, doll?"

Jesus Christ. Talk about *embarrassing.* Timidly, Merrillee said, "Mrs. Tallon knows my name, Mr. Size."

Mrs. Tallon kept a straight face, though the corners of her thin-lipped mouth twitched, as she sat down behind a varnished antique desk—French Provincial. She took a long, check-size receipt book from the top drawer and sat primly as she filled one out, the pen in her bony hand making a thin moving shadow under the desk lamp.

As Mrs. Tallon wrote, Size put his hands in his pockets and crossed one ankle over the other. "That's the way I like things. Nice and official. I wouldn't want nobody getting any wrong ideas about me paying this lady's bill up here."

The pen paused in mid-stroke, then went on writing. Merrillee felt her shoulders hunch closer together as she mentally measured the distance between her white sandal and Size's shin, wondering if she had another swift kick left in her. From below her on the left, Jessie's tiny voice said, "The big giant's paying Mrs. Tallon? Wow, Mom. He's your *friend*!" Merrillee squeezed the little hand tighter, not saying anything.

Mrs. Tallon tore the receipt off, smirked at Jessie, and handed the receipt to Merrillee. Then she said to Size, "Thank you, sir. And not to worry. Nobody is getting any wrong ideas."

Merrillee knew that her face was crimson as they turned to go. Jessie pulled away from her. "Mr. Giant! Mr. Giant! Do you know about Jack and the Beanstalk?'' The she cupped her palms over her mouth and giggled. Merrillee thought about strangling her.

Size looked down at the little girl, puzzled, seeing her for the first time. Then he gave her a big Joe Palooka grin. ''Yeah. Sure. Teaches you not to take no wooden cows. C'mon, kid, I'll tell you about it.'' Then he took Jessie's hand in his and walked out the door, Jessie's pigtails swinging on a level with his hip and Merrillee trailing behind, her mouth agape.

It was a flight down from Mrs. Tallon's to street level, and the boards groaned under Size's weight as he went down the steps, bent over and carrying on a running conversation with Jessie. Jessie tripped along in front of him, looking back and talking over her shoulder. Merrillee brought up the rear, not believing it.

The street door opened as they neared the bottom and Cicely came in, snapping her fingers hip-chick style and listing slightly. She was still in her shortie Keno outfit, and Merrillee noticed that the top two buttons were undone, showing a lot of chocolate bosom. Cicely turned sideways, giggling ''Oops'' as she let Size pass her on the stairs. Her eyes were cocaine-shiny and she reeked of booze.

As Merrillee came abreast, Cicely rolled her eyes in the direction of Size's broad retreating back. Then she looked at Merrillee and wrinkled her black button nose.

''Groovy,'' Cicely stage-whispered. ''You wanna share johns, sugar, you just let me know.''

Merrillee drove the Mustang, feeling as if she was trying to steer a capsizing boat with one oar on the high-side. Size weighted down the passenger seat like ballast with Jessie—wiggling, giggling, and squirming—sitting in his lap.

Merrillee was beginning to wonder if this was all some kind of goofy dream she was having. First Oscar and Miss Lay-Your-Husband, setting the date. Then the Spanish version of Cheech and Chong. Now this. The biggest, toughest-looking man she'd ever seen first making mincemeat of the glass-eyed mugger, then topping it off by coming across like some sort of Disneyland character, fairy tales and all.

He was telling Jessie, "And after she eats the porridge Goldilocks goes in the bedroom. Now get this, kid, it's a strange house where she ain't never been, and it ain't smart to go snooping around people's houses. You remember that. So anyway, she goes in the bedroom and there's a big mean wolf in one of the beds wearing a bonnet and playing like he's somebody's grandma."

Jessie jumped up and down, giggling, making Merrillee swerve and almost run into the side of a pickup. Jessie shrieked, "You're wrong, you're wrong. There were three *empty* beds and she went to sleep. One bed was too *hard,* and—"

"Say," interrupted Size, "you already heard this? Maybe you oughtta tell it to me."

It was daylight, about half of the sun's orange ball looming on the horizon and the thermometer rising in a hurry. They were zipping along on the freeway with the emerald fairways of the Dunes Country Club on their left, the ninth hole that doglegged gently by the freeway's access road. The tall imported desert palms that dotted the course cast long shadows which were shortening gradually as the sun rose in the sky. Fairway sprinklers shot fine sprays that glistened and formed rainbows.

Out of the corner of her eye Merrillee was conscious of Jessie's squirming form and the yellow freeway stripe rolling next to the Mustang's hood, as she said sweetly, "Where would you like me to drop you off, Mr. Size?"

"*Mah*-umm! I want the big giant to come to my house," Jessie said.

"The big gi—Mr. Size is tired, darling. He needs his rest."

"Well, he can sleep in the cat's room."

"Huh?" said Size. He was looking to his right, at the flat roof of the Union Plaza Hotel in the distance as it towered over downtown Vegas.

Merrillee couldn't help laughing. "We had an old Tom that sort of adopted us. He took over the spare bedroom for a while. He was visiting all the ladies in the neighborhood so I, you know, had him fixed. Guess he didn't appreciate it too much, he disappeared the next day. But it's still the cat's room. Sort of a title, like the Presidential Suite."

"Yeah?" said Size. "Yeah, well, that'll be fine."

Merrillee said, "I beg your pardon?"

"Well, I need a pad for a while. So why don't I rent it from you? If it's okay. I wouldn't want to get in the way of your business or nothing."

Size lifted a corner of the drapes to peek through the window of the motel room to make sure the Mustang was still there. It was, Merrillee's chiseled features and soft hair behind the wheel, the hood vibrating visibly as the engine missed. Sonofabitch needed a tune-up. It was idling beneath the faded green neon sign that said GREEN'S TOURIST COURT. The sign was on a tall aluminum pole, a smaller red sign hung beneath it, a letter chipped away: ACANCY. Beyond the Mustang was the two-lane blacktop that was the rundown portion of Las Vegas Boulevard, away from the Strip. There was a washateria across the road that had slot machines along one wall. Size turned from the window and looked over his gear once more.

There wasn't much to it. The whole mess fit nicely into a zip-up canvas bag with the Nike logo on the side: a couple pair of faded jeans, size 34, 36 length, loose-fitting legs to let his thighs have room; two spare knit shirts, a green Hogan and a tangerine Polo, both XXL. The Luger. Old bastard, Size had picked it up eight years ago in one of Pecos Jimmy's pawn shops. He really went for the WW II gun's heft and feel, its kick that he felt all the way to his toes, but he'd finally given up hunting ammo for it. The Luger now fired nine-millimeter shells from an elongated clip that held twelve rounds, a modified rig that let people know that the owner knew what he was doing and wasn't fucking around. He checked the chamber. The gun was empty.

He wrapped it in the nylon shoulder rig and dropped it in the bag, where it landed atop spare sneakers—blue Adidas running shoes, size 13D. Size was wearing his other pair, white canvas Athletixx. He then zipped up the bag as he gave the room a final once-over.

He checked out the Nevada temporary driver's license in his pocket, looked at his snapshot, his own mug stern-faced under the Beatle wig. Galletto. Jesus Christ, how come he couldn't ever remember the name? He'd gone through so much crap in Albuquerque to get the name to begin with that he oughtta have it written on the insides of his eyelids. Two days of prowling through county records to find the birth certificate of somebody his own age who'd died when he was a baby, a big hassle with the social security woman who wanted to know how come he was just now applying for a card, old as he was. The birth certificate and social security card had made getting a New Mexico license a breeze; then the Nevada folks had made him get another picture taken when he traded the New Mexico license for a Nevada. No big deal. But he'd had to fuck around so much getting the name that he sure as hell ought to remember it. Ought not *ever* to forget it. He put the license away.

Running across the broad like he did was a pretty good break. Staying in this fleabag motel was giving him the willies—shit, the Feds were all the time nosing around dumps like this. They didn't have much else to do. But renting the room from the broad was going to give him a perfect spot to lay low while he took care of business.

Size was about to decide that the broad was on the level, that she really wasn't a hooker after all. At least he was beginning to hope not. For the cute little girl's sake, Size hoped Merrillee was Mother of the Year in disguise. Smart little bugger, reminded him of his sister's little girl. Or the way his sister's little girl used to look. Jesus Christ, he hadn't seen her since—hell, his sister's girl might be in high school by now.

* * *

Merrillee watched Jessie for a moment, now curled into a pink-jammied ball in the backseat, asleep with a miniature thumb just inches from her mouth. The same backseat where the glass-eyed black man had tried to—God, put it out of your mind, Merrillee. It didn't happen.

She felt the quiet cough-miss of the Mustang's idling engine, felt it vibrate in the steering wheel as she bent to lower the volume on the radio. It was an easy-listening station—playing an orchestrated version of "Tomorrow" from *Annie*—and Merrillee grinned to herself as she tried to remember Size's exact words. What was it he'd said? Oh, yes. "Hey, you like that shoplifting music, huh? Well, it's okay for a change."

What kind of a guy was this, anyway? A thug? Probably—Merrillee could put two and two together. She wasn't *that* dumb. A thug on the run, and Merrillee Rogers in the process of letting him move right into her house, having just met the guy. What would the ladies and gents out at Crystal Dunes Country Club think? Probably not much, probably wondering if Oscar was even going to settle up the bill he owed there. Merrillee supposed that was one bill that Oscar *would* pay. She'd run into Amanda Dunn, the club manager's wife, in the Safeway. Amanda had casually mentioned—casually hell, she'd come right out and said it—that Oscar's name was posted on the bulletin board as a no-pay membership. He'd pay to get his name off the board, if Merrillee knew Oscar at all. Image around town, you know.

Merrillee couldn't figure out what was getting into her. Letting a total stranger move into the house. To boot, a guy who'd been living here at this No-tell Motel, a guy she'd met as she was leaving a room in the Golden Nugget and he was hiding outside in the hall. She could use the money, of course. God, could she ever. And the big man made her feel . . . safe? Warm? God, Merrillee, what are you talking about? The guy thinks you're a *hooker,* for Christ's sake. And do you blame him?

She couldn't believe the guy's reaction to Jessie.

Jessie was a little girl who was awfully love-starved, especially since the marriage had broken up. Just thinking about how much Jessie was being neglected by both of her parents brought tears to Merrillee's eyes. Her craving for love made Jessie a real clinging vine at times, and Merrillee would have expected that a high-strung child would be really irritating to a tough-looking man like Size. But no. The guy was lapping it up. He'd given Jessie more attention in fifteen minutes that Oscar had in the last six months. Merrillee couldn't figure the guy out.

He was coming now, moving lightly for a huge man, across the motel parking lot, a blue zip-up tote bag like doll luggage in his grip. He moved in what Merrillee would describe as a light-footed shamble, a half-grin on his square-jawed face. Merrillee thought fleetingly about the aftershave he was wearing. A lime, she'd noticed, really a nice scent.

She put the Mustang in gear and held her foot firmly on the brake pedal as she waited for him.

Size carried Jessie into the bedroom as if she was pure nitro-glycerine. That gently. She was still hugging the Care Bear as Size lay her atop the covers with a touch so light that the bedspread hardly wrinkled. Jessie continued to breathe slow and easy, guiltless child sleep-breaths. He glanced around the room, at the toy box with a grinning Raggedy Ann peeping at him from underneath the not-quite-closed lid; at a green, yellow, and red illustrated poster-map of Disneyland with the pointed spires of Sleeping Beauty's Castle in its center. He turned and tiptoed out, barely creaking the hardwood floorboards and soundlessly closing the door behind him.

Merrillee stood in the hallway with Size's tote bag on the floor on one side of her and Jessie's carrying case on the other. One long leg was straight, the other bent at the knee. One hand was on her hip. She was watching him with her lips parted, her hazel eyes smiling. A funny kind of look, as though he'd surprised her or something. Naw, this sure wasn't no hooker. Couldn't be.

She said quietly, "Do you have children? You sure act like you do."

The glass-paneled front door was behind her. Outside, bright morning sunlight reflected from a green lawn that was mowed like a carpet, sidewalks edged and clipped in perfect lines. The house across the street had a shady gazebo in the yard. Nice neighborhood, Size hadn't known Vegas had places like this. He said, "Me? Naw, I got no kids. I guess I like them okay, though." Feeling a little tongue-tied, standing here alone with her, right here in her house. A lot different than shooting the shit with somebody across a poker table. She smelled good. A light musk.

Her gaze dropped. Jesus, it was like she was blushing or something. Like she was hearing what he was thinking. "Mr. Size, let's establish a few ground rules. Letting a strange man move into my house isn't something I do every day. But I really do need the money. Not that—well, I don't mean to sound . . ." She trailed off, not finishing what she was going to say, then went on. "Look. Up front. I don't want this hooker talk to keep going on. I don't do things like that and never will. Let's have that understanding. I'm renting to you by the week—fifty dollars per. The money you paid Mrs. Tallon, that comes off the first week's rent. Fair enough?" She straightened now, her shoulders square in a businesslike attitude.

"Yeah. Sure. And don't worry, I was just putting you on. About being a hooker. And it's Size. Don't nobody call me 'Mister.' Look, where's the room? I could use a little shut-eye."

She pointed to a closed door adjacent to Jessie's room. "It's right there. There's a private bath. A small one, though I guess they're all pretty small to you. There still might be some cat fur around in there, but I'll get it cleaned up." Now her gaze met his squarely, openly. It looked to him as if there was a mist in her eyes. "And I want to thank you for being so nice to Jessie. She really needs that, poor darling."

"Say, don't mention it." He quickly picked his luggage up. "Listen, I'm going to bed. See you later, huh?" Then he went into the guestroom before he did what he felt like doing. Before he reached out and laid a hand against her soft smooth cheek. Wouldn't be smart. Scare the broad to death, is what it would do.

Merrillee didn't sleep very well, and when she did manage to nap she had crazy dreams. In one the man with the glass eye was in her bedroom, slapping her and tearing at her clothes. The dream-slaps were so real that she whimpered in her sleep. The dead eye was staring sightlessly at her; then suddenly it began to change shape, the whole twisted black face melting away. It was replaced all at once by Oscar's face. Oscar was stark naked and so was Miss Charlotte Lay-Your-Husband, standing there next to him. Charlotte was giggling. Her laughter made her shoulders shake and her enormous pink-tipped boobs quiver like Jell-O. Oscar took a stride in Merrillee's direction, grimacing as he raised a long black whip to hit her. Merrillee recoiled, shrinking back and sucking in her breath. Then in a flash Size appeared in the dream, standing behind Oscar with his arms folded across his chest. Only it wasn't quite the same Size—he was handsomer than Merrillee remembered and had long blond hair, straight and hanging to his shoulders like a Viking's. He was even dressed like a Viking, in a pointed steel helmet, metal armored breastplate and thigh-length toga, massive arms bare and bulging. He stepped forward and put one beefy hand on Oscar's neck, the other on Charlotte's. Then he conked their heads together like a Three Stooges scene. The two looked at Merrillee with their eyes crossed, then fell to the floor like felled trees. Jessie's tiny voice rose from somewhere saying, "Oh, boy, big giant. Do it again!"

Merrillee opened her eyes and stared at a little crack in the ceiling. It took a moment for the dream to go away, a moment for her to realize that she was alone in her bedroom. Alone. By herself in her filmy shorty negligee, nobody there to—

But Jessie's laughter hadn't faded away with the dream. Her child-voice filtered through the closed bedroom door, muffled. "Do it some more, big giant. Do it some more!"

Merrillee sat up. The digital clock on her nightstand radio said 1:12. Outside the window her yellow Daphne flowers shimmered in the afternoon heat, the damp earth under them in the bed beginning to form a dry outer crust. She got up and padded barefoot over the springiness of the carpet, cracked the door open, and peeked out. Jesus Christ.

Size was on all fours in front of the den TV. The set was on and the Sesame Street Count was watching bats fly out of a spooky castle as he said, in a Transylvania baritone, "Wahhhhhn creepy bat! Two-ooooo creepy bats! Ah—ah—ah—ah!"

Jessie was mounted on Size's broad shoulders like a miniature jockey, digging imaginary spurs into his sides with her heels. He reared up on his knees, let out a thunderous "Naaay!" that rivaled the Count in volume, then went back down on all fours with Jessie squealing and hanging on for dear life.

Merrillee shook her head, not believing it, as she went back and lay down across the king-size. Was it part of the dream or not?

Just before she dozed off, Merrillee found herself wondering about the big guy, wondering what it would feel like for him to touch her. She decided sleepily that she might like that. Had to be careful, though. God, she didn't want to scare the guy.

Size finally left Jessie watching Superfriends cartoons around two o'clock. She was hypnotized, her little legs straight out in front of her on the sofa and her gaze riveted to the screen. He made a quick phone call, then went to the door to Merrillee's bedroom and knocked softly. In a moment she said, "Come on in." He did. Took one step into the room and stopped in his tracks.

It was the way she was lying there on the king-size bed. Half-sitting, leaning on her elbow, one bare, tanned long leg straight out and the other bent sharply at the knee, foot resting on the shin. A pose. Not a conscious, for-the-camera pose, but a natural sexy pose in those thin shorty pajamas. He thought right then that she was the most beautiful broad he'd ever seen.

She said, "Yes? What is it?"

"Aw. Yeah, hey, sorry to wake you up." He felt like shuffling his feet and putting his hands in his pockets.

"I wasn't asleep."

"You weren't? Hey, I got to go downtown and see somebody. I called a cab."

"No need for that. Don't you want me to drive you?" She really looked concerned, not faking at all.

"Naw. Too much trouble. You going anywhere later?"

"Just to work. And to take Jessie to stay with Mrs. Tallon, I suppose. Around seven. How long will you be gone?" She laughed softly. "Hey, I sound like a wife or something, don't I?"

"That's okay. Listen, I'll be hanging around playing a little poker tonight at the Golden Nugget. Might be a good idea you don't let on to people that we know each other." He wanted to add, Especially not the Spanish hoods, but he didn't.

She blinked long lashes. "Well, *that's* different. That's supposed to be my line. I'm the one who should be worrying about somebody finding out a man's living over here."

He thought for a second, then decided to go ahead and say, "Listen. So you'll know. Those two guys last night, I've got to keep an eye on them. There might be some trouble and I'd feel like hell if you got mixed up in it. Anyway, I got to go now." He turned to leave.

"Size."

He stopped and looked at her.

"Size—dammit, what am I trying to say? Whatever you're going to do is your business, but—well, I don't want anything happening to you, either, is all. Does that sound funny?"

The cabbie looked as though he really wanted to say something, bad. Two different times he turned his head toward the backseat and opened his mouth, then changed his mind and kept on driving, both hands on the wheel. Size didn't think the picture looked much like him. The cab-license picture that hung suspended from the clicking meter was of a skinny, chicken-necked guy who was peering out from underneath the black plastic bill of a Yellow Cab hat, the hat about two sizes too big. It looked as though the guy's ears were the only things holding the cap up. But the guy driving was a whole lot bigger than the one in the picture, a whole lot fatter. The red-tinted skin of the driver's neck stuck out over the back of his collar in folds. There was a pimple forming on the guy's neck, one that hadn't quite come to a head. Size thought, Naw, this ain't the guy. Maybe the other guy is out knocking off a little that his old lady don't know about and this guy is subbing for him. Who knows? Who gives a shit?

Finally the cabbie said in a quick midwestern accent, "Say, Mac. You sure this is where you want to go?" Might be from Chicago, Rush Street—Billy, a guy who used to play a lot of poker in Dallas, talks a lot like this guy.

Size fished in his pocket and came up with a folded slip of paper and a brass key—the front door key Merrillee had given him. He put it away and unfolded the paper. "Yeah, I guess so. One Twenty-nine Reno Avenue, it says right here. Why? You got something against One Twenty-nine Reno Avenue?"

The cabbie braked hard and pulled to the right as a woman in a blue Olds on his left came through the intersection and turned into the lane in front of him. She wasn't looking, blonde hair bobbing in rhythm to a tune on the radio. The cabbie shot the woman the finger in the rearview mirror as he said, "It's all the same to me, pal. If you want to go to Jungle Johnny's then that's where we're going. It's just that if you're looking for a used car there's better places. Places where the speedometer reading is the for-real mileage on the heap. Or closer to it, if you know what I mean. Trust me. My brother-in-law bought a car from the shitheel one time. Jungle Johnny. You're new in Vegas—you need to know these things."

Size didn't like it, the idea that the guy might remember him and where he got out of the cab. The guy was just being nice, but—Size said, "Yeah? How come you know I'm looking for a used car?"

"Well, I'm picking you up in a cab and taking you to the car lot. I got to be Sherlock?"

"I hope not. I hope to hell you ain't."

"Huh?"

Size didn't answer for a minute, thinking, looking at the big Sears sign in Vegas Mall on his right. Then he said, "Tell you what. I'm hoping you ain't no detective and I'm hoping you ain't going to remember me. I'm hoping it a ten-dollar-tip's worth. You forget me, I'll forget you ain't the same guy what's in the picture on the cab license. Fair enough?"

The traffic light in front of them blinked to amber. The cabbie started to slow down, then picked up speed, accelerating through the intersection as the light turned red. Size looked around quickly, didn't see any patrol cars, breathed a sigh.

The cabbie said, "Good enough for me. Far as I'm concerned there isn't anybody in the backseat right now. Just a sawbuck, laying right up there on the cushion."

John Y. Brown tried to picture the way that Drumbeat Sims would say it. The very best—absolutely Number

One, Oscar-winning—salesman that John Y. Brown had ever run across. What a break for John Y., bunking down with Drumbeat Sims that last eighteen months of the federal beef at Lompoc, on the Pacific Coast. What an education.

John Y. Brown caressed the fender of the maroon Monte Carlo with his palm, then dusted his manicured hands off with light slaps. "I got to tell you, pal, I can't afford to hassle anybody today. Jungle Johnny's got real trouble." He was coatless in a white long-sleeve dress shirt, a short man whose red-and-yellow polka dot bowtie was a trademark. So was the center part in his medium-length, wet-look brown hair. "Dazzle 'em with your appearance," Drumbeat Sims used to say. "That way they might not remember what you told 'em."

The mooch was a youngster, twenty-two at the most, fair hair to his shoulders with a lot of tangles in it. His drooping moustache really needed trimming, a few long hairs growing down over his mouth. He put his hands in the back pockets of his jeans and bent from the waist to peer inside the Monte Carlo. For some reason he was looking at the padding on the ceiling. Real cagey customer. "Sure sorry to hear that. Gee, this car hasn't been in a wreck, has it?" The boy was the fidgety nervous type, his thumbs outside his hip pockets, moving in little circles.

"Wreck? Say, kid, you've been around, haven't you? That's good, it'd be a waste of time trying to put one over on you. And I sure don't blame you for asking. There's a lot of shysters around in the car business that'll try to sell you *anything* just to make a buck. But not Jungle Johnny. I've sure got plenty of trouble without that." He winked, stroking his own clipped moustache and motioning for the kid to follow as he moved a few steps closer to the Monte Carlo's nose. "Look, pal, I'm going to show you something. Now I want you to *swear*"—he raised his right hand—"that you're not going to tell anybody you found this out from Jungle Johnny. There's men in the used car biz who'd have my hide if they knew I let this out. But I *can't stand* to see people get taken. I've got your word now, don't I? No fooling."

The kid darted glances around the car lot. "Yeah? Yeah, I won't say anything. I'd be obliged to you."

"I suppose I can trust you." John Y. Brown squatted by the left front tire. It was an almost-new, factory-second Firestone with double white racing stripes that he'd helped Tucker pull off a totaled Plymouth this morning. They'd had to put a couple of plugs in it to make it hold air. "Kid, the trick is in the tires, I always say. If a car's been in a wreck that front tire is going to have ridges in the tread, 'cause it won't be running smooth to the road. Feel how straight the tread is on this baby." John Y. Brown glanced quickly underneath the fender, toward the fire wall where the frame was welded together. The welding seam was out of sight and wouldn't be visible to the mooch. Good job. Far to the rear of the dusty graveled lot a tire tool rang out as somebody dropped it on the cement floor of the body shop. That would be Tucker, still fucking around with the dented fender on a Ford pickup. In the driveway of the Kentucky Fried Chicken across Reno Avenue, a horn honked.

The kid felt the tire's tread. "Smooth as a baby's butt, right enough." He looked as though he'd just been cut in on a gold mine. This kid may as well be on his back with his legs spread. Time for Jungle Johnny to lay the meat to him. "What kind of trouble have you got, Johnny?"

"Well, kid." John Y. Brown unwrapped a cheroot, lit it with a butane disposable, puffing hard. "It's one of the oldest stories in Lost Wages. This little jewel you're seeing here was a special order, for a little lady that deals twenty-one, at the Holiday Casino. Two months it took to find this cream puff for her. And I went for the old sob story—kid, between you and me, the little lady did some of her talking to me on her back, know what I mean?

"Sure do. Lost your head over a little pussy, did ya?" The kid giggled, chewing on the long strands of hair from his moustache.

Jungle Johnny kept puffing on the thin cigar as he put his hands in his pockets and looked at his shoes. "Goddam, kid, you got me pegged. And don't think it doesn't hurt, that a sharp young man your age has got more sense in his little finger than Jungle Johnny's got in his whole body. Jesus Christ, for a man that's been around as long as I have to be dipping his wick in his own cash register—well, there's no excuse for it, none in the world. I hunted all over creation for this little jewel of a Monte Carlo, took out a bank loan to buy it for cash, and was too dumb, or too pussy-locked, whichever, to even get a deposit on it. And wouldn't you know it? The bitch loses her whole pay, lock stock and barrel, out at the Stardust. Playing *roulette,* of all the dumb-fuck sucker games. Now not only can she not buy the car, she's given Jungle Johnny the old heave-ho. Now she's screwing a *desk clerk,* works at Circus-Circus. So stuck I am. I've got a note due on the car, I got to move it. Jesus, it's tough." He made his cheek twitch, just the right nervous little jump, as he looked up at the kid.

"Well now, Johnny," the kid said, looking shrewd, "you could be in luck. Just how much have you got in the car?"

"Boy, now I really feel dumb." John Y. Brown pictured Drumbeat Sims. He put on his best I'm-ashamed-to-tell-you hangdog expression. The wrecked Chevy had come to six hundred bucks. Tucker had done the welding on the frame, not much to that. The stolen hood and fenders, spare engine parts . . . "I was so out of my head being horny for the broad that I let myself get held up for it. Thirty-two hundred, kid, plus the interest on the note I got to pay. Shit, I'd even swallow the interest if I could just—" His look changed from total despair to hopeful-maybe. This model Monte Carlo was going for four grand all over town, in the square market. He hoped the kid had been shopping around.

"You drive a hard bargain, Johnny. But what the hell, I've been in some binds myself. You got financing, if I put a thousand down?"

Bingo. Tote the note—thirty percent annual interest. "Oh, I can arrange it. Boy, you're sure helping me out, I'm not letting a little financing stand in the—"

From the open overhead sliding doorway to the body shop, Tucker yelled, "Johnny! Jungle Johnny, got a minute?"

The sun was glaring from over the body shop's roof. John Y. Brown squinted and shaded his eyes. What the fuck could be this important? Tucker's short, fleshy torso was in gray work coveralls (Jungle Johnny knew they'd be greasy); his fat hands were on his hips with a dent-puller bar dangling from one clenched fist. There was a guy standing next to Tucker that Jungle Johnny couldn't see very well. Parole officer? Naw, this was Thursday; besides, the guy was too big. Unless Johnny's eyes were fooling him the guy was damn near twice Tucker's size. Sure. The phone call that had come in this morning. The hiding-out guy.

Quickly, John Y. Brown indicated the office—a thirty-foot gray mobile home on blocks. To the mooch he said, "Tell you what, kid. I won't be a minute, so why don't you relax a spell in the office. Go ahead, help yourself to what's in the fridge. Who knows, there might even be a Colorado Kool-Aid in there."

The kid took off for the office at a brisk walk, probably worried that Jungle Johnny might back out on him. John Y. Brown approached the body shop. The closer he got, the bigger the guy standing next to Tucker loomed.

Big one, all right. A simply enormous guy wearing a tangerine-colored shirt, jeans and sneakers. Didn't seem to be an ounce of fat anywhere on the guy. The black mop-top wig was a good one; it would fool most folks. Not John Y. Brown. He'd seen too many of them. The area around the crown of the head was the giveaway, nobody seemed to be able to make that crown just right. From the fair skin and the big freckles on the hands and wrists, John Y. guessed blond or redhead under the wig.

John Y. Brown extended his hand, wincing as the

giant reached for it. Then he said as a huge paw engulfed his hand, "John Y. Brown. Pleased."

The huge guy didn't squeeze, just shook firmly and released quickly. It wasn't too surprising, come to think of it. Men who tried to turn a simple handshake into a gripping contest were really pretty unsure of themselves, trying to cover up. Most hand squeezers were easy marks, John Y. Brown had learned. Not this big bastard, this guy had plenty of moxie, knew where he stood, and didn't have anything to prove to anybody. In fact he had an open, honest gaze about him that made Jungle Johnny just a tad nervous. He just didn't have the look of your run-of-the-mill, hiding-out guy. Could he maybe be a cop? Not likely—Leon Hundley wouldn't be sending any undercovers.

The guy said, "Yeah, Size Brandon. Leon Hundley call you?"

John Y. Brown didn't want to answer just yet, so he said to Tucker, "Finish with the Pontiac, okay, Tuck?" Then as Tucker waddled away, a circle of grease darkening his coveralls over the fat right cheek of his ass, Jungle Johnny said to Size, "Well say, now. Leon Hundley. Seems I've heard the name. He a Vegas man?"

"A Vegas man? Naw, he ain't. Say, you ain't the guy—Jungle Johnny? Leon don't bullshit, so where's this Jungle Johnny?"

Jesus Christ, there ought to be a password. "Oh, I'm Jungle Johnny right enough. But you come waltzing in here tossing around names and I don't know you from Adam. Tell you what. You tell me what this Leon Hundley said to me when he called and I might remember better."

"Well, I don't know. I wasn't listening to what he said. But he might have told you that you was a nervous bastard—he'd be right about that. But what he was supposed to have said was that I needed a pickup. Half-ton, with a camper-cover over the bed. So, you got one?"

The odor of oily rags mixed with the scent of auto paint. The air compressor was chugging and somewhere a leaky hose went *ssssssss*. A Grand Prix, mid-Seventies model, was high on the lift with its exhaust pipe hanging down. The Ford pickup's nose was suspended about two feet off the floor by a yellow bumper jack. John Y. Brown glanced at the pickup's fender. Looked new, good job by Tucker. Dumb-ass was a body man and a half.

Jungle Johnny said, "Look over there. Pickups are hard to come by these days. I wouldn't have fooled with it except as a favor to Leon. A dearer friend I've never had."

Size spat on the floor, the spit bubbling on the rough concrete. "Dear friend? Leon says he got stuck paying your bond off when you didn't show up in court one time. Took two years chasing you around the fucking country to collect. So let's can the bullshit, huh? I got the fifteen hundred right here"—he slapped his pants pocket—"so let's get it over with. I got things to do."

Jungle Johnny held out his hands, palms up. "Say, just a minute. It's going to cost you more than that. For fifteen hundred, shit, I wouldn't stick my neck out." Besides, he'd told Leon he had fifteen hundred *in* the truck, not that he'd sell for that. And hell, he really did have *seven* hundred in it.

Size was looking the pickup over, his gaze traveling from the jacked-up front bumper to the covered bed. The truck was white with blue trim. The camper-cover had two screened widows in each side, louvered blinds closed so that nobody could see inside. Size closed his hands into fists and put them on his hips as he said, "You know, this is funny. I never thought there was anything wrong with Leon's hearing or his memory, and Leon said the truck was going to cost me fifteen hundred bucks. Says you owe him one." Now he cocked his head to one side and narrowed his eyes as he looked at Jungle Johnny. "Say. You wouldn't be thinking of holding me up, would you, pal? Like maybe because I'm in a bind?"

John Y. Brown tugged on both sides of his bowtie. No point in trying a sales pitch with this guy. He said, "No, I'm not holding you up. Up and down the street the truck is five grand—you know that. And I don't know anything about you, friend, and don't *want* to know anything. But I'm wagering you can't stroll up and buy a vehicle from just anybody. I ask no questions, don't have the slightest interest in what you'll use the truck for. It's got registration papers that'll pass anybody's inspection. But if you want the prick it's going to cost you three grand. Take it or leave it." He folded his arms.

Size turned his back, one muscled shoulder drooping, and didn't say anything while he gave the truck another once-over. Then he said, "That's an Eighty-one, ain't it?"

"So?"

"So that's good for you," Size said. He walked, elbows slightly bent and palms to the rear, over to where Tucker was fooling with the Grand Prix's muffler. To Tucker, Size said, "Lemme borrow this."

Tucker stopped what he was doing and watched through fat-lidded eyes as Size stooped to pick up the dent-puller bar from the concrete. Size then went to the pickup, kicked the safety on the yellow jack to the off position, and lowered the truck's nose with a series of bumpy hisses. He shoved the jack aside and went to the driver's side door, the dent-puller dangling from his hand. He thumbed the latch and the door swung open on creaky hinges.

John Y. Brown was following every step of the way, waving his short arms. "What if it *is* an Eighty-one? What's that got to—Hey! What the hell are you doing?"

Size paused, about to climb behind the wheel. "It's good for you that this is an Eighty-one, 'cause I can steal the fucker just by popping the ignition out with this dent-puller. If it was a later model I'd have to bust into the steering column. That's what I'm doing, case you don't know. Stealing the fucker." He sat in the truck, placing the dent-puller against the ignition switch and screwing the pin into the slot. Taking his time about it.

John Y. Brown put both arms at his sides and drew

up to his full five-eight. "Now *hold on.* Just an ever-loving minute. You lay one more hand on that vehicle and I'm calling the law. If you think you're in trouble now, friend, you try fucking with Jungle Johnny."

Size snickered, his bicep rippling as he kept turning the pin. "Suits me. Call 'em. Then they're going to have a close look at the engine numbers on every heap in this lot. Yeah, they might arrest me—they won't be getting no cherry. You want your whole inventory gone over, you go ahead. You need a quarter for the phone, I'll loan it to you." He began to put leverage on the dent-puller against the steering column.

Air whooshed out of John Y. Brown's lungs. Jesus Christ, where do they come from? Everybody's some kind of fucking crook these days. He stretched his hands out, saying, "Now, no need to fly off the handle. Come on, I was only testing you out. If Leon told you fifteen hundred, then fifteen hundred it is. A deal's a deal."

Size let go of the bar and slung a wrist over the top of the steering wheel. He grinned. "Naw," he said. "Come to think about it, I think Leon told me the price was a thousand."

Pinky Forester bent his knee and stood on one leg long enough to reach down and scratch his ankle. What he felt wasn't an itch but more of a burn. Hot as blazes, sweat pouring down his calves inside his pantslegs, soaking his black cotton socks and seeping into the little open sores around his ankles. Tiny holes. Needle punctures. Jesus, only two hours since he'd shot up and the Mexican brown was already wearing off; he was beginning to feel sick and miserable standing there on the boiling-hot sidewalk in front of the entrance to the Golden Nugget Hotel. Everything he was wearing felt as if it was choking him, from the beige collar that was fresh and clean just a little while ago but was now beginning to dampen and wilt, to the snug black vest with the Golden Nugget logo on the breast. Even his black polished shoes hurt and pinched his feet.

He felt the rough paper money in his pocket, thought

about counting it. Hell, he'd just gotten through counting it. A Jackson, a Lincoln, three singles. He was seven bucks short, seven little Yankee dollars away from the price of a paper. He checked his watch. Straight-up two, only another hour until Candyman packed up and went home. Pinky pictured Candyman, milk chocolate scalp glistening, snow-white fringe of hair, as he hummed and brushed lint from jackets and offered damp scented towelettes and bottles of bay rum and Old Spice aftershave in the first-floor men's across the street at the Four Queens. And peddled a thirty-five dollar paper here and there, just to guys he knew. Guy wanted Candyman to fix him and didn't know the nigger, he'd better come along with somebody that Candyman did know. Seven lousy bucks away from a one-way ticket to Feelgood City. One tip away, you find the right customer in the right mood.

Pinky watched the blue and white City Cab come around the corner, watched it lean slightly as it rolled away from the intersection, the tall red neon sign of the Fremont Hotel towering over it, watched it head in his direction and brake into the drive that swung around beneath the yellow awning of the Golden Nugget. The meter flag was up. Airport run, flat fare for the carload from McCarran International downtown. Three passengers, the driver a leather-skinned, pudgy guy chewing gum. Pinky crossed his fingers and hoped—even prayed a little, bad as he needed fixing—that this was the load he'd been looking for.

Had to be careful, size up the new check-ins just right. Picking the wrong set of luggage to tote could mean the difference between a good-size tip and none at all. Pinky dropped his hands to his sides and tried to look eager, a skinny, pimply faced kid in a bellhop's uniform, his ankles now burning like fire.

The driver huffed and puffed his way back toward the luggage compartment, stopping to open a rear passenger door as he did. The passengers began to climb out leisurely and stand on the sidewalk, taking their time about it. Pinky squinted against the glare. He was suddenly bone-dry thirsty.

The first to hit the pavement looked like money. A slim, in-shape, jogger-looking guy of about forty. Thinning hair, but a razored, high-dollar style to it. Rich clothes, a short-sleeve red Christian Dior knit shirt and navy tailored slacks. His loafers were gleaming polished alligator. The guy walked around at ease, moved like an athlete, had big strong comfortable hands that he rubbed lightly together. He glanced through the glass entryway into the Golden Nugget's lobby, then back down the street in the direction of the Four Queens and Fremont. The slim gold watch on the guy's wrist was a Piaget, Pinky would bet on it.

As Pinky watched the second passenger alight he wondered fleetingly if Charlie Pride was in town. Jesus Christ, a nigger with a gold tooth, a tall skinny one decked out in a cowboy outfit. A brown western shirt with white quilting at the shoulders, and a tan Stetson with a silver band. Sleepy-eyed nigger. Bo Diddley gone country. Still, though, you never knew. Sometimes the shines tipped better than the honkies, as if they wanted you to know they had enough green to cover up their black.

No point wasting any time with the third arrival. Some kind of dyke. A husky, broad-shouldered girl in a black sleeveless T-shirt and jeans so tight they sucked up into the crack between her legs. High black boots, not even polished. She had long black hair and came out sneering. Tough bitch. Jesus, with a Harley-Davidson tattoo yet. No tipper, bet on it.

Pinky grabbed a chrome luggage cart and felt a little withdrawal shudder as he rolled it over the curb behind the cab. The trunk was open now, tan and black suitcases in a row.

To the driver, Pinky said, "Gimme a break, pal. Which bags belong to the white dude with the gold watch?"

The driver shook his head, his jaw working on the gum. "Well, you're not going to believe this, but all three of them are together. Whaddya think, you reckon the two of them are banging that big mean motorcycle bitch? Some kind of kinko salt-and-pepper sandwich job, or what?''

Pinky shrugged his skinny shoulders and began to load the bags on the cart.

10

Junior Gomez listened to Senor Emilio Garza Burista speak in Spanish. Junior nodded his head, indicating that he was listening, and walked to the red velvet drapes in front of the window. He pulled them aside, a sudden slash of light appearing on the carpet, and watched the cars streaming along on Fremont Street fourteen floors below. Jesus, his nuts felt as though they weighed a hundred pounds. Okay when he was sitting down, but standing or walking—

Burista finished speaking, sat back in the easy chair and folded his arms. His ankles were crossed on the coffee table and his lips were pursed firmly together.

Junior turned and faced the room, the drapes falling back into place behind him. "He says he don't like the setup. You make a deal with one guy, another guy shows up. He says he'd rather talk face to face with Pecos Jimmy." He gasped, holding a hand on his belly and closing his eyes against the pain.

From where he was sprawled full-length on the red bedspread, sitting up and supported by his elbows, Slim Burdine said, "S'matter wit' you, Junior man? You hurt your back or something?" He reached up and tilted the Stetson back on his head.

"Yeah," Junior mumbled. "Must have lifted too much. Doing curls."

Beaumont Gurney leaned forward, resting his forearms on his knees. The band on the Piaget stood out against his deep tan. "This isn't like somebody showing up that you don't even know, Junior. You're just going to have to make Senor Burista understand. You make a deal with Size Brandon, it's the same as making it with Jimmy. Jimmy doesn't make eyeball-to-eyeball deals. And Size just couldn't come to Vegas. He's—he's got business elsewhere. But talking to me is the same as talking to Jimmy, just like talking to Size is the same. Six of one, half a dozen of the other.'' He was in the other easy chair, across the coffee table from Burista.

''Lay it on, bro Gurney,'' Slim said. Then, to Junior, ''Size Brandon's the only con you know? Shee-it, Junior man. You know me, way back. Know me from Ramsey II, we old homeboys.'' He fished a toothpick out of his shirt pocket and let it dangle from one corner of his big lips.

Ramsey II, Junior remembered. On the Ramsey II farm, Slim had bossed a pack of niggers that called themselves the Lobos. Baddest cats in the joint. Everybody—Aryan Nation wildeyed killers, Texas Syndicate boys—kept out of Slim Burdine's way. The whole penitentiary pissed in its pants when the Lobos went on the prowl, even the warden. Not Size Brandon, though. Big red-headed gringo was a mob all to himself. Talked quiet, got along with everybody but busted heads like coconuts, anybody tried to fuck with him.

Junior shrugged. ''I'll give it a try, it's all I can do.'' In Spanish he told Burista that Beaumont Gurney was Pecos Jimmy Fontenot's lawyer, his most trusted lieutenant.

Both of Burista's bushy eyebrows lifted as he suddenly looked to Gurney with respect. ''Ah,'' Burista said, *''consigliere.''* He bunched the short fingers of one hand together and pointed them at the ceiling, as if he'd just said, ''The spaghetti was sup-*perb*-ah.''

Yucca-baby snorted. ''Jesus Christ. This motherfucker thinks Jimmy's Don Corleone, some greaseball asshole like that.'' She was sitting on the floor with her back against the wall, hugging her knees, her heavy boobs compressed against her thighs. She tossed her head and her long black hair swung.

Gurney was drinking white wine from a long-stemmed glass. He toasted Burista, keeping his gaze on the Colombian as he said, "Let him think what he wants. Getting the deal made, that's the important thing. For you *and* for us, right, Junior?"

"Hey," said Junior, taking a quick step forward, then groaning and clutching at his midsection. He half-stumbled to the king-size bed, sinking down next to Slim. Slim sat up and crossed his legs Indian-style, still wearing his polished brown boots. Doubled-over, Junior said, "Senor Burista knows a lot more of your lingo than you think. I'm telling you, this is nobody to fuck around with. You give this dude the idea that we're in on this together, running some kind of a scam on him, it's going to take the coroner a week to cut the machine-gun bullets out of our ass."

Slim Burdine snickered at the way Junior was clutching himself. "You acting like a whore I beat up one time, Junior man. How much fucking weight were you trying to curl?"

Junior didn't feel like talking. He didn't feel like doing anything except rolling around on the floor and holding his balls. Jesus Christ, his big moment coming up, biggest deal he'd ever had or was likely ever *to* have, and him sitting here like a teenager with the stone aches. That bitch had it coming, did she—

The pain suddenly subsided and he sat up. Felt as though he was sitting on eggs, but at least it wasn't hurting anymore. Not as long as he was sitting down. Burista was watching him, expectant. Wanting to know what the gringos were saying.

Junior held up a hand to Burista—just a minute. Trying to look to Burista as if he was really making an important statement, Junior said, "It ain't the weight, Slim, it's the repetitions. Okay, so I'll try to get him to go along. I think he will if I give the word. Hell, it wasn't for me the man never would have made it through Texas Department of Corrections. If Size isn't available, he ain't. What kind of deal are we talking?" In Spanish he told Burista that the gringos were dickering some, but Junior thought he could make them come to terms. Burista shook a clenched fist—way to go.

"Well, the word we have," said Gurney, "and mind you, it's strictly secondhand, is that you can come up with"—he looked cautiously around the room—"a hundred of the 'things.' Let's call them burros, for a point of reference." He turned so that Junior could read his lips and mouthed silently, "We could be bugged."

"What's this talk about donkeys?" Burista asked in Spanish.

"Burros? How about 'French ticklers'?" Yucca-baby said, scratching her tattoo. She was always doing that, and Junior wondered if the damn thing itched. His own tattoo, the picture of the writhing snakes, had been burning lately as if it was infected or something.

"Well, whatever you want to call them," Gurney said. "So long as we don't use the C-word. Trust me. I'm a lawyer."

Yeah, thought Junior, so's Horace Ortiz. He said, "Burros, French ticklers, what the fuck? You want them, they're going to cost you fifteen—"

"Dollars," Gurney said quickly. "Don't mention a figure more than dollars. And fifteen dollars is too high, Junior. Planeloads of the stuff landing every day. Ten is the going rate, twelve-five maybe. But only if it's choice."

Junior told Burista that they were haggling over prices. Burista said not to let them get the upper hand. Treat them like the field women. Jesus, thought Junior, I'm going to have to get Burista laid in Vegas yet. He briefly pictured Burista in the saddle with the big motorcycle broad. Just thinking about it made his nuts ache.

Junior said, "Choice ain't the word. This stuff'll blow the doors off an armored car."

Slim Burdine sat up a little straighter. "Seeing is believing, bro."

Junior got the okay from Burista, then went over to the dark wood bureau. His groin began to throb before he'd taken two steps, but he gritted his teeth and ignored the pain. He saw himself in the mirror, his tight dove-gray slacks and pink, puff-sleeved shirt. Behind him was Slim's stretched-out reflection, mouth open, gold tooth glinting. This cat made Junior feel cold. Junior found the plastic baggie in the top drawer, felt the powder shift inside the bag as he turned back to them. "Free sample," he said, holding out the bag.

Gurney extended a finger toward Yucca-baby. "She's the tester."

Yucca got to her feet, yawned and stretched. Junior thought, What boobs, Jesus, twice the size of Dolores's. He tossed the bag, Yucca-baby catching it with a soft plop. Burista was sitting on the edge of his chair, watching Yucca's boobs.

Yucca-baby said, "Going to take a day."

"We got a day. Give it whatever test you want to. Ether test, chemical test, whatever. The stuff is for real," Junior said.

Yucca gave a cruel grin, looking from Beaumont Gurney to Slim, who giggled into his cupped hand. Yucca-baby said, "You seen too many movies, doll. This ain't no French Connection. Yeah, I'm going to test it. Find me a girl and toot the fuck out of it, is what I'm going to do."

"Man, I *tole* you," Dolores said. "We hit Las Vegas you on your own. So there the sign. Right there. Las. Vegas. Pop. four six five. Eight four three. So how come you not hitting the pavement?" One bare dimpled knee leaned against the door. The other brown leg was straight out, thigh muscle taut, bare foot on the brake pedal. Her toenails were painted bright pink. Both hands gripped the steering wheel.

The guy in the passenger seat adjusted his sunglasses, then looked at the sign as he scratched his head. He had beachboy-blond hair and a surfboard tan, was rangy and flatbellied, like a shortstop. "Yeah, but this is the middle of the desert. You're joking aren't you, sugar?" Beneath yellow boxer-type swimming trunks, his thigh above the tan line was milk white. He had on an orange T-shirt with MIAMI DOLPHINS in green script across the chest.

Dolores tugged at the threads on the hem of her jean

cut-offs. Her midriff was bare, her red cloth shirt tied up under her boobs. She began to wave her arms and point her fingers at the guy as she said, "I no joke. You, you're a joke. I tell you when I pick you up in Tucson. I going to Las Vegas, can't nobody ride wid me into town. I got important business."

The Buick Park Avenue sat idling on the gravel shoulder, the Vegas city-limit sign about three feet from its right front bumper. An orange and white U-Haul trailer, the small covered variety, was hitched to the Buick's rear end. Beyond the city-limit sign stretched miles of sun-baked sand, rock, and thorny cactus. A single oncoming vehicle was a speck on the horizon.

The guy crossed his legs, his tanned feet in rubber shower clogs. He smiled. Pepsodent-white teeth against walnut-colored cheeks. Slowly, deliberately, he reached out and began to stroke Dolores's thigh. She started to push his hand away, then relaxed and closed her eyes. He said, "Important, doll? More important than this? More important than feeling good, than screaming your pretty Latin lungs out? You forget last night so soon?" He kept smiling, teasing, his eyes hidden behind his sunglasses.

Dolores's breasts began to rise and fall, picking up tempo as her breathing quickened. Her voice was suddenly husky. "No—no, I not forget. You wanting to do it again? Now, right here by this road?" He kept stroking her, then his body stiffened as she squeezed him between his legs. Behind them the highway stretched empty into the distance, heat shimmering on its surface. The speck coming from in front of them grew instantaneously into a speeding Hagan Motor Freight bobtail, whizzed by on the left and shrank into a dot once more. She said, "Your name. I forget your name again."

He didn't answer, his hips gyrating and his head thrown back, his teeth clenched. Then he murmured, "Does it matter? Oh, sugar, keep on. Keep on." He touched her breast. Her hand kept squeezing him in rhythm.

She stopped him. "Wait. Wait, beach man. I got something," she breathed between wanton parted lips as she bent over his lap. He watched her, not moving. There was a light click as the Buick's glove compartment opened. Her hand went inside, groped, then tightened around something. She smiled at him as she pulled it out. Her hand came into view gripping the butt of a Smith & Wesson .38 Police Special snubnose revolver. She suddenly bolted upright beside him, jammed the barrel of the revolver up one of his nostrils and clicked back the hammer.

His mouth widened. He was suddenly rigid. He said, "Jesus Christ."

"Now like I say, *chingarro.* You hit the pavement. You pretty boy, but you no-good fuck. I get better from fat man in Juarez, you hear?" She reached across his chest, holding the gun steady up his nose, and opened the door. "You sit there three more seconds you going to have very sore nose, boy."

He held his hands out in front of him and slowly backed out of the car. She kept the S & W trained on his face. He said, "Please. Don't." She chuckled, reaching with her free hand and slamming the door. Her long dark hair bobbed up and down as she scooted over behind the wheel. The Buick's tires squealed, burning rubber as the car fishtailed back on the highway. The U-Haul trailer tilted up on one wheel, then righted itself.

The beachboy stood transfixed, hands on hips and jaw slack as the Buick disappeared into the distance. Then he shrugged, turned, put on his Pepsodent smile and stuck out his thumb.

Merrillee dropped Jessie off at Mrs. Tallon's and went to work. Don't let on that you know me, Size had told her. Sure thing, nothing to it. Like falling off a log, ignoring a man who was sleeping in your house. And who you were beginning to feel attracted to, though he didn't act as if he'd noticed you were a girl. Maybe he hadn't. Maybe you're coming across like one of the fellas, Merrillee. Now that's a pleasant thought. Maybe you should ride him piggyback and watch Sesame Street, like Jessie.

One thing that Size told her to do was going to be pretty easy. Steering clear of Junior and the other Spanish guy. Really clear. In fact, after what happened last night Merrillee wasn't sure she could keep from breaking into a run at the very sight of the guys.

She stood by the bar at the waitresses' station, getting ready to make her turn around the casino. Trying to get in the mood, painting the smile on her face. Patti was bustling next to her while Freddy the bartender made some drinks. Merrillee said to Patti, "I need a favor, no questions asked. It's important."

Patti went right on clearing her loaded-down tray, red-nailed hands moving fast, poking fingers inside the rims of empty glasses, picking them up four at a time and setting them on the bar. She kept working, Miss Perpetual Motion, as she said to Merrillee, "I don't know, girl. I draw the line at murder, you know."

Merrillee leaned an elbow on the bar. Beyond the exit from the lounge there were two half-full crap games in progress, beyond the dice tables sparse action at four blackjack tables. The rest of the huge casino was dead—white-shirted, black-tied dealers waiting with folded arms. The dinnertime lull before the nighttime storm. Merrillee said, "It isn't a big favor, really. Those two Spanish guys from last night? If they come in I want you to wait on them. I really don't want to have to talk to those two, if I can get out of it."

Her serving tray was now clear, Patti was reloading. She giggled happily as she set two frosty Tom Collins on the tray and popped lime slices on the glasses' rims. "I'm not sure I'm hearing you. The cute little Spanish-speaking guy and his Valentino buddy? The one with the black chips and the fifty-dollar gratuities?"

"Right-o, that's the ones."

"Well, Merrillee, I'm not going to say I think you're crazy because you might change your mind if I did. If you want to turn those mad tipsters over to me and call it doing you a favor—well, where have you been all my life, is all I can say.''

Merrillee wondered how Patti could be so happy all the time. Never bitchy, always looked as if she'd just showered and changed. The fresh-scrubbed look, flaming red hair shining. It made Merrillee envious as hell.

''It's not the bargain that it may look like it is, Patti. I can't go into details, but I'm warning you. Those two are dangerous and you need to watch yourself with them. Strictly hands-off, arm's length.''

''Listen, sweetie,'' Patti said, picking up her tray and turning to go, ''they don't call me 'Crazylegs' for nothing. I'll handle them, you leave it to me.'' She jiggled away, deftly side-stepping two women in the lounge's entrance and sashaying onto the casino's vast, gold-carpeted floor. Merrillee herself was pretty nimble, but watching Patti in action made her feel like Slowmotion Sue.

Her own order gathered up—three Screwdrivers and a Singapore Sling—Merrillee hustled off to deliver the drinks to four matronly women who were fighting the roulette table, playing a progression system. As Merrillee approached the ivory ball clattered and clicked over the slots, finally rattling its way to rest in the hole by a red number on the wheel. The croupier pushed a mountain of twenty-five-cent chips toward the women and they squealed in delight, clapping fat hands gleefully as Merrillee set the drinks in front of them. They forgot to tip. Or pretended to forget—Merrillee wasn't sure.

She moved around the nearly-deserted tables, taking one order from a black guy at a blackjack table; another from a man and a woman, both in their sixties or seventies, who were feeding and pumping the slot machines. She paused to write the orders down—another shortcoming she felt she had as a waitress. She'd watched in envy a time or two while Patti hip-bumped through crowds as thick as a swarm of bees, all the while flirting and wisecracking, taking seven or eight orders at once, never writing anything down, and never coming back with the wrong drink.

The poker area caught Merrillee's eye, the roped-off section with an arc of white lights on a green-painted wood frame for an entrance. She hesitated. Should she or shouldn't she? Just because she went in there and asked around for orders didn't mean that she was looking for Size. Of course it didn't. Maybe she'd surprise him, sidle up next to where he was sitting, place a small square paper napkin by his elbow. Take your drink order, sir? Bat her eyes. Watch his reaction, maybe get an inkling of how she stood with him. *Stood* with him? God, Merrillee, you hardly know the guy. She went in.

He wasn't there. First trying to look nonchalant, then dropping the charade and peering carefully from table to table, Merrillee scanned the room. No big man, no huge grinning giant anywhere among the three dozen or so hard-eyed men hunching over the poker games, guarding their cards and stacks of chips. Or sitting back and checking the baseball scores on the far wall. Merrillee went back into the bigness of the casino, a strange nagging worry inching its way into her mind.

There was nothing to it, there couldn't be. He'd just had to stop off somewhere else for a while. And what if he didn't come at all? What of it? You're acting silly, Merrillee, go on about your business.

On the way back to the lounge she very nearly collided with a man—a slender-built guy of about forty with short brown hair and expressionless slate-gray eyes. He was wearing tan slacks and a white knit golf shirt.

She said, "Oops. Pardon me, sir."

"Don't mention it," the guy said. Merrillee felt for an instant as if she'd seen him before. Slender nose, sharp features. But no. It was just that the guy was so common-looking, he might be any one of a thousand other guys. A real blend-in type.

"But as long as you're here," the guy said in a

monotone, "how about pointing me in the direction of a telephone?"

She pointed out the red house phone on the wall behind the nearest crap table, one of the deserted ones with four dealers looking bored while they chewed the fat. The guy headed in that direction. By the time she turned her order in to Freddy, she'd forgotten all about the incident. The guy was so *ordinary*.

The slender, nondescript, poker-faced man moved on, walking in a slouch, hands in his pockets. His one-track mind dismissed Merrillee the second she walked away, but he wouldn't forget her. He didn't seem to be noticing anything that was going on around him, but he was. The lights with their red and green and frosted leaded-glass shades, the bored faces of the waiting dealers, each entryway and hallway leading to and from the casino—with each glance a silent camera clicked inside his head. Data recorded and filed. Tucked away in a part of his brain where he might never need it again. But it was there in case he did.

He gave the area code and number to the hotel operator, holding the receiver loosely and looking sleepily around him as he did. As he waited for her to place his call a jackpot bell jangled among the slot machines and an elderly, white-haired woman jumped up and down and clasped her hands together.

Finally he said, "May I speak to Henry? . . . Yes'm, I know it's dinnertime, but—well it's pretty important. . . . I sure appreciate it, ma'am. And don't worry, I won't make a habit—Thank you, I'll hold on."

A full minute ticked off. He watched a desperate-looking man across the casino ask a pit boss for credit. The pit boss folded his arms and shook his head. No soap.

He switched the phone from one ear to the other and stood a little straighter. "Henry? Listen, Henry, we're gonna have to do something different. Your mom—well, I'm just not used to—" He blinked twice as he listened to the voice on the other end. Then he said, ''Yeah, well let me put it another way. I don't want to talk to your mother anymore, Henry. I'm at the Golden Nugget, Room Five-twenty. From now on you call me, okay? If I ain't in the room have me paged. . . . Yeah, Henry, they're here. All three of 'em and they're pow-wowing with a couple of spics. . . . How the hell do I know, Henry? Maybe they're taking Spanish lessons, but I ain't betting on it. What about Jimmy Fontenot, he still in Dallas? . . . Okay. . . . Jesus Christ, Henry, you come to Vegas, Gurney's gonna spot—''

His expression changed to a sneer, then immediately became bored again.

''Okay, Henry, it's your funeral. Listen, I gotta run. I'm meeting some agents from the local office out here. . . . Fuck no, Henry, they ain't taking over the case. But I gotta check in with them, you know that. . . . Listen, any word on this Brandon creep? Man, I want that motherfucker. . . . There ain't? Okay, Henry, you call me in the morning and let me know what flight you'll be on. . . . No, Henry, we don't need no fucking task force. Jesus Christ, it's just those three and two spics, okay? . . . Yeah. See you.''

Sam hung up, put his hands in his pockets, and slouched back toward the front of the casino.

Size waited until he was sure that Merrillee had left for work before he went to the tote bag and got the Luger. He couldn't explain why. It was just that finding a gun in her home might shake her up some, especially with the little girl living there. Didn't want to do anything to upset the broad. Not a nice lady like her, and her letting him stay here. A nice, long-legged lady with full soft lips and a way about her that—Naw, man, a broad like that ain't for you, never will be. Don't even think about it.

He rummaged in the pantry, shuffling aside cans of Del Monte Yellow Cling peaches and Chef Boy-ar-dee spaghetti, finally locating a plain brown paper bag. He dropped the holstered gun inside and crinkled the sack around it. He didn't have a jacket. He made a mental note to buy one of the feather-light windbreakers he'd seen in the Golden Nugget's gift shop, something he could put on to hide the shoulder rig. For now he'd have to do without.

He'd just tucked the paper bag under his arm and turned to leave when the feeling hit him. It was a feeling of—hell, he wasn't sure. But something was right about it, standing here on the red and green and white linoleum floor of her kitchen. Picturing her in here, humming as she moved around, putting away dishes or frying something in a pan on the stove. Light quick steps, her slender calves bunching as she stood on tiptoe to peer out the small window over the sink. Just thinking about her was beginning to cause funny thumping feelings under his breastbone. He thought,

Jesus Christ, man, get your act together! He carried the bag to the front door and went outside.

Dusk was turning into night as he left, a few stars twinkling into view and the light inside the gazebo across the street flashing on. He wondered what it would be like, sitting outside with her while darkness came and the air got cool. Wasn't any point in thinking about things like that, but he did anyway. He stepped quickly down the front sidewalk to where the pickup waited.

The truck was a first-class lemon. A grand? That Jungle Johnny asshole was probably still laughing, holding his sides. Giggling about the way Size had acted so tough, getting the price down to a grand and thinking he'd really pulled a slick one. The front end shimmied. The steering column creaked and groaned. The transmission slipped. But the bed was solid enough and the camper-cover didn't seem to have any cracks in it. He hoped to hell it didn't rain, at least not until he'd done what he came to town to do.

He headed for the bright lights downtown, feeling the bulge of the roll of bills in his pocket that the thousand bucks to Jungle Johnny hadn't put much of a dent in. Playing pretty lucky poker these days. One more night like last night and he could square up with Leon Hundley, wire the two grand back to Dallas that Leon had loaned him to make the trip. The pickup rattled on to the Vegas freeway as Size pictured Leon, skinny chest rising and falling in his bathrobe as he counted out the money, fondling each bill as though he was in love with it. *The money it isn't, Size, you know that. It's my image with the voters. If there's any trouble, you stole the money in a burglary, okay?*

Leon and his voters—what a combination. If Leon Hundley could make it as a politician, then anybody could. But at least Leon didn't forget who got him there, and step on his friends when he got on top the way a lot of them seemed to. The money in Size's pocket right now was living proof of what could be said for Leon Hundley. Size's eyes narrowed as he thought, Helluva lot more than you could say for Pecos

Jimmy Fontenot. The pickup bumped over the expansion joints as he steered it down the exit ramp and turned up Fremont Street toward the Golden Nugget. The avenue in front of him shone in the blazing neon lights like a desert noon.

The steering wheel vibrated under his fingertips as the engine idled in front of the Fremont Hotel and he waited for the light to change, a river of people hustling back and forth across the street in front of the truck's nose. The glittering front of the Four Queens was on his left, the glistening Golden Nugget a little farther. Just ahead on the right people streamed in and out of Binnion's Horseshoe, stopping and gawking at the million in cash in the glass case that stood in the entryway. Size was letting his gaze roam up and down the streets, looking for a likely place to park, when he saw Junior Gomez come out of the Golden Nugget and catch a cab.

It was Junior, okay. No doubt about it, fancy-pants Mexican guy in his tight britches and puffy-sleeved yellow shirt, emerging out of the casino and standing on the sidewalk. Jesus, Junior dresses up like he thinks Harry Belafonte is a Mexican. Old Junior was the only guy Size had ever met who could strut without walking. Junior ran his fingers through thick black hair, primping as he looked around. Then he held up a hand and yelled something as he went toward a row of cabs that stood at the curb—two Yellows and one blue and white Vegas taxi, drivers bent over the steering wheels as they studied racing forms. Cabbies and dealers, biggest gamblers in Nevada.

The fuck was wrong with Junior? Jesus, he was walking bent over, like his belly hurt. Maybe ate a bad enchilada—who knows? Junior said something to the driver of the Vegas taxi, the driver answering as he folded his racing form and laid it on the seat beside him. Then Junior stumbled some, grimacing in pain as he opened the back door and climbed into the cab. The taxi pulled away from the curb and joined the line of cars headed toward the lit-up front of the Union Plaza, two blocks away. The light in front of the pickup changed to green. Size eased over one lane to his left and gave the truck a little gas, following the cab. He stayed a half-block behind and out of range of the taxi's side-view mirror.

Size wasn't sure what he was doing. He didn't know if he should follow Junior or go back to the Golden Nugget and keep an eye on the Colombian. Tough when you were just one guy, trying to pull this off on your own. Shit, either way he did it was probably going to be wrong. What if Junior was just farting around, taking in the sights? You never knew. The top of his head was visible through the cab's rear window, Junior sitting slouched with his knee propped up, as the cab made a left in front of the Union Plaza, turn signal blinking and flickering. Hell, what do you do? Grimly, Size gripped the steering wheel with both hands and decided to follow the cab.

The cab climbed on to the freeway and Size shrugged as the pickup groaned and rattled up the ramp with two cars—a Caddie Eldorado and some kind of little foreign job—between it and the taxi. Hell, he'd just gotten *off* this road. He wished he was in Dallas, where he knew every nook and cranny of the town. Here in Vegas he didn't know where the fuck he was going. What if the cab led him somewhere way out in the sticks—Monkeyfuck, Egypt, someplace like that—and then lost him? He'd never find his way back. He was conscious of the brilliant lighted signs along the Strip—FLAMINGO, SAHARA, SANDS, DUNES—in the distance on his left as he stayed in the middle lane and craned his neck to keep an eye on the blue and white taxi. The cab was doing about sixty in the lane next to the median. Size kept pace with it, two cars behind and to the cab's right. The cars on the other side of the median, going in the opposite direction, flowed slowly past like dark sluggish beetles with yellow eyes.

They headed north. The pickup's A/C was blowing—Jesus, that was one plus for the heap, it was a hundred and ten around here during the day. The blower fan was bent or mounted crooked, one or the other, and was making a clattering sound. Size was beginning to shiver, goose bumps rising on his forearms, so he turned the A/C off. The fan clacked to a halt. He cracked the driver's-side window down and cool desert air rushed into the pickup's cab and whipped around inside. He turned on the radio—AM only, Jungle Johnny, you cheap son of a—and settled back to an oldie. "I'm Sorry," by Brenda Lee. The pickup rumbled underneath a huge green luminescent highway sign that said it was 450 miles to Reno.

He almost lost the cab when it left the freeway. Typical cab driver, whipping across two lanes, tires squealing, giving no signal. Size saw Junior lean sideways in the taxi's back seat, heard a Nissan that was between him and the cab beep its horn, saw the Nissan driver's bony fist shaking. Size braked, let two cars pass him on the right, then darted into the lane they'd just vacated and bumped down the freeway exit ramp. The cab was already at the bottom of the hill, turning left under the interstate. Size followed, thinking, Jesus Christ, Junior, where the fuck you taking me?

Junior got out in front of a motel. There was a sign in front with a curved arrow, a painted-over Holiday Inn sign. Now it read, NEVADA INN, POOL, VACANCY. Size pulled into the parking lot of a Wal-Mart store across the two-lane blacktop and cut the engine, watched Junior get out, still walking hunched over, and pay the cabbie. The taxi left. Junior limped past the motel office to the rear, his tall shadow in the light from a streetlamp moving along with him. He disappeared into the shadow of the building.

Size hesitated, then said to hell with it and crammed the Luger into the waistband of his jeans, letting his shirttail hang out over the butt of the pistol. He wasn't walking into any strange motel unarmed. Not after any Junior Gomez he wasn't, well as he knew that bastard. He got out, slammed the pickup's door, and jogged across the street to the front of the Nevada Inn.

The light was on in the office, a gray-haired chubby woman bent over the check-in desk writing something down. There were three gleaming slot machines on the wall by the desk, all Ballys. Size got his bearings as he looked the building over. The office was freestanding, the motel proper a two-story horseshoe with rooms on both levels, a walkway with latticed railing running around the second floor. A courtyard with a pool was surrounded by the horseshoe, the motel office at the open end, cars parked nose-in to the perimeter of the building. The cars were junkers mostly, ten-year-old Fords and Chevies, a couple of old pickups with rusty fenders. A new Buick Park Avenue with a small U-Haul trailer hitched to its rear stood out like a sore thumb.

Size patted the butt of the Luger where it rested against his hard belly as he moved between the office and the motel building into the courtyard. The moon was high, the courtyard bathed in eerie light, the globes underneath the pool's surface casting green rippling reflections on the concrete. Size smelled chlorine

There were a few squat, round-based palm trees in beds around the courtyard and little islands of clipped tiff-grass in between the concrete walkways. One guy was using the pool, a slender wet-haired youngster, straight as an arrow, who was diving. The low board bumped, sprang, and bounced up and down. The guy did a pretty good swan, split the surface of the water with barely a trace, came up shaking flying droplets from his hair, and dog-paddled toward the ladder.

Size halted behind a palm, peering around the trunk of the tree to the opposite end of the pool. Two people were sprawled on chaise longues down there, one a girl. A big-thighed broad in a string bikini, a knockout body from what Size could see. She was probably Mexican from her olive coloring; she was square-shouldered, big-titted, and flat-bellied. She was sitting with one leg straight out, the other bent at the knee, and was gesturing with both hands and chattering a mile a minute to the guy on the chaise next to her. The guy was Junior. He looked as if he was trying to get a word in edgewise with the broad, but wasn't being able to.

There was one more piece of pool furniture, an aluminum, plastic-bottomed chair that sat on the concrete next to the girl. Size waited until the slender kid bounced on the board and dived again, then walked toward the broad and Junior, taking it easy, not being in any hurry. She stopped waving her hands. Both of them watched him, not sure if he was coming to join them or just headed past them to his room. He stopped and eased into the chair, propped a foot on the rail of her chaise lounge, and gazed deadpan at Junior across her belly. Junior put his hands on his chair arms and started to rise. Green water reflections moved across his cheeks.

Size said, "Junior. How you doing, man? Keep your seat."

The broad leaned toward him, squinting. She had a pretty round face and long dark hair hanging halfway to her waist. "I know this dude, Junior? Listen, you didn't say nothing about anybody else. Who's this guy?"

"That's what I want to know," Junior said. "How you know me, man?"

"Junior. I'm hurt deep, man. You don't know me?"

Junior Gomez leaned forward, the gold medallion swinging away from his bare chest and dangling from its chain. "What the fuck happened to your hair? Man, you ain't even s'posed to be here. Somebody's bull-shitting somebody."

"So I bought the hair. That don't mean it's not me. Who says I ain't supposed to be here? You see me, don't you? You're not talking sense, Junior. You called me, not the other way around. You tell me to meet you in Vegas. So what you think, we're just bumping into each other by accident?"

The kid hoisted himself out of the water and stood on the bank. He was dripping. A trail of puddles on the concrete marked his path from the pool's edge to a small table with a beach umbrella fixed to a pole that rose from its center. He picked up a towel and began to massage his sopping hair, casting glances at Dolores when he didn't think anybody was watching him. Size needed the kid to be gone.

Junior looked puzzled. "I'm not getting this. Slim Burdine, that scary fucker. And a lawyer that claims he's Pecos Jimmy's main man—I thought that's what *you* were. Oh, yeah, and a dyky-looking broad that thinks she's at a Halloween party, going as a Hell's Angel. *That's* who says you ain't supposed to be here. Them three. Hey, you putting me on?"

Size took his foot off the chaise longue, bent over, and rested his arms on his knees. *Them three.* So they were already here. He pictured Benny Sands, black smoke pouring from the Riviera while its hood twisted and melted. "You listening to those yo-yos, Junior, or you listening to me? Hey, Pecos Jimmy ain't no dummy. Those three are strictly cover. They're downtown farting around and acting like they're here to buy something. That clears the way for me to make the deal without no interference. Anybody puts the finger on anybody, it's gonna be those three and they ain't going to be found with anything. Smooth, huh? So I followed you here. You ready to deal?" Between him and Junior, Dolores was squirming, adjusting her fanny in the chaise longue, uncrossing her firm legs, recrossing them, checking to make sure both men were watching her. Size thought, Now, *this* broad probably *is* a hooker.

Size was conscious of the diver in the corner of his vision. The boy now had his feet in flip-flops and was leaving the pool area. Just a couple of minutes more. The boy slapped concrete as he moved into the shadow of a palm.

"Deal?" Junior said. "How I'm going to make a deal on my own? I can't do nothing without Burista's okay, you know that."

"Shit, Junior, you been around. You're a smart boy. Look, you and Burista ain't keeping the stuff at the Golden Nugget, not with all those crowds downtown. You got this bimbo here, out in the sticks. Two and two says the stuff's right here, all of it. So whaddya need Burista for?" The kid was far away now, his foot-slaps barely in hearing range. Casually, Size reached under the hem of his shirt and touched the butt of the Luger.

"Hey!" Dolores bolted upright, eyes flashing sparks. "Who you calling a bimbo? Junior, I think I not like this dude. *Pendejo*—how you like that, big man?"

Junior spread his hands, palms up. "Don't mean anything, doll. The man is just—" He froze with his mouth open, then said, "What the fuck's that for?"

Steadying his elbow against his thigh and aiming the Luger at a point somewhere in between Dolores and Junior, Size said, " 'Fraid you ain't going to like me, either, Junior. Let's talk. You want to give the stuff up easy or hard? Don't matter to me, and it sure as hell don't matter to Pecos Jimmy."

"Hey, big man. *Pendejo,* that not mean nothing. I jus' kidding with you. I think you kind of cute," Dolores said. She raised a shapely leg and held it at Size's eye level.

Expressionless, Size said, "If I have to shoot Junior I'll have to blow your kneecap off, sweetie. I'd put my fucking leg down, I was you." The leg returned to its position on the chaise longue.

He watched Junior's eyes shift, first glancing at the loosely held Luger then measuring the distance to where Size was sitting. The wheels in Junior's mind were turning so fast that the whir was nearly audible. Size said, "Come on, Junior. You know it ain't worth it—don't even try. Come on, the three of us are taking a walk to this little girl's motel room. You two first, then me."

Junior glared hate. Dolores swung a pretty foot down on the cement. "It's over there," she said, gesturing in the direction of the motel office. She stood and slipped her feet into straw high-heeled sandals, one at a time. "Get up, Junior. Jesus Christ, you not going to do anything. Quit tryin' to look tough." She moved away, generous hips swinging beneath the thin strap that held the front and back of the bikini pants together. Junior got up and followed, walking stooped over. Size fell in behind them, holding the Luger in close to his chest, glancing around the courtyard. He didn't see anyone else.

As they neared the entrance to a poolside room close to the front of the motel, Size said to Junior, "What you walking so funny for? You hurt or something?"

Without looking back, Junior said from between clenched teeth, "Sorry whore came up to our room last night. Burista, he was going to get a blowjob from the bitch and she winds up kicking me in the balls when I ain't looking. Cunt. I get my hands on—"

"Shut up," Size said. "Just shut up, Junior."

"What the fuck's wrong with you, man? You asked me, I just—"

Size prodded Junior hard with the barrel of the pistol. Junior stumbled and groaned, finally righting himself. Dolores unlocked the door with a key that hung on a band of elastic around her wrist. The three of them went inside. Size gestured with the Luger and Junior and Dolores sat side by side on the pale green king-size bedspread. The spread was worn thin. Dolores crossed one smooth brown leg over the other and gave Size a sleepy-eyed, come-on look. He ignored her, pulling an armless stuffed chair away from the window and sitting down, facing them.

"Now we got privacy," Size said. "Where's the nose candy, Junior. I'm saying please one time."

"Man, you trying to get me dead? You make a deal to buy the stuff, now you going to take it? Fuck you."

Size brought the Luger up, whipping Junior across the jaw. Junior yelled and clutched his face. A red, dripping welt appeared. Dolores sucked her breath in, dark eyes wide.

"Junior. You know I can't make a deal on my own. Pecos Jimmy says get the dope, I got to get it. Jimmy says, fuck Junior up good if I have to, I'll do that, too," Size said. "Now I'm going to ask again. Where's the nose candy? If you say 'Fuck you' again, I'm going to break your arm. Third time, I'm going to break your other arm. Now, if you don't want somebody to have to hold your dick for you while you take a piss, you talk to me."

Suddenly Junior Gomez began to sniffle. Jesus Christ, Size thought, he's going to bawl. Just about the way he'd figured this pretty-boy dude back on Ramsey II Prison Farm. All strut, no gut. He remembered Junior swaggering around in the exercise yard, all the Mexican guys acting as though they thought he was really something. There'd been a shakedown in the cellblock on the day when Doc Boren—Austin hijacker, not a bad old boy—had announced to the guys that his homemade raisin wine would be ready. As the guards toted the six gallons of brew away, one of them had thrown a guarded wink at Junior Gomez. Size had seen it plain as day, but he'd never told anybody about it. Merrillee flashed in his mind, a picture of her and Junior and Burista up there in that Golden Nugget hotel room.

Tears streaming, Junior said, "Size. You know what you're trying to do to me. My ass won't be worth a plug nickel when Burista finds out the cocaine's gone. Jesus Christ, I oughtta get *something* for this. Even just a few grand." He was running a finger over the welt on his jaw. The blood had clotted and a scab was starting to form.

Dolores stood and put a clenched fist on a round hip. "Big crybaby. You make me 'shamed." Then, to Size, "Come on, big man. The stuff outside in a trailer. I show it to you, maybe you take Dolores along. Huh, baby? Maybe you like that better than you think."

Junior Gomez strained, tossed, and plopped the last five-kilo sack into the back of the camper-covered pickup. The twenty bags, each one a cellophane wrapper inside a double thickness of heavy brown paper, were stacked in two neat rows, five to a row, two bags high. Junior said, "I hurting bad, man."

Size was leaning an elbow on his knee, his foot propped on the truck's rear bumper. They were in the Nevada Inn parking lot, the truck parked rear-to-rear behind the Park Avenue and the U-Haul trailer. Dolores, still in her string bikini, had a hip firmly against

Size's hip and an arm draped across his massive shoulders. She was drinking a can of Coors. Size had the Luger pointed loosely in Junior's direction.

"It's good for you, Junior," Size said. "Hell, your balls're just like anything else. You get them sore, you got to work the soreness out. Close the doors."

Junior grunted as he banged the tailgate closed and latched the swinging camper-cover doors. The blinds on the camper's windows were closed. "I'm a dead man, Size. You fucking know that." He stood back, hunched over, panting.

Size strolled to the driver's side of the pickup. Dolores kept up with him, thighs jiggling. Size stopped, turned, and pointed the Luger at her.

She stepped back. "Hey, I going with you. Dolores give you fuck you never forget, man." She cocked one hip higher than the other and tugged at the top of the bathing suit. Her breasts squeezed together under the fabric.

Size shook his head. "Naw, you ain't. I had to keep you busy drinking beer so I wouldn't have to fuck with you while I got the dope loaded. But a broad like you I don't need. Shit, I got enough trouble."

As Size wheeled the pickup out of the lot, Dolores shrieked, "Fuck you! *Pendejo.* You big faggot, hey?" Then she turned to Junior. "You lay a hand on me I gonna yell rape. I see you get the twenty-five years this time, you do anything bad to me."

Size bent forward and squinted. Jesus Christ, same deal. The picture on the cab license was of a black guy, eyes round as saucers. The driver was white, a young guy not over thirty with close-cropped, mouse-colored hair and jug-handle ears. Size waited until they passed under another streetlamp, a moving rectangle of light passing over the dashboard toward the rear of the darkened cab, and checked the picture again. Yep, it was a colored guy all right. Looked sort of like the one who used to play in all the old Charlie Chan movies—"Feet, don't fail me now." And the driver a honkie with jug-handle ears. The fuck was going on?

Glancing at the reflection in the side-view mirror, at the hulk of the five-story parking garage that loomed behind them in the night like a chunk of black granite, the white driver said, "Let me ask you something. How much they charge to store a vehicle back there?"

Size was folding the claim stub for the pickup into a tiny square. His left Athletixx sneaker sat on the seat beside him. He poked the claim stub far up into the toe and put the sneaker on. "Lemme ask *you* something. What makes you think I got a vehicle stored back there? Just because you picked me up in front of the joint?"

"Hey, pal," the driver said, showing Size the upraised back of his hand, "take it easy. I'm not prying. If you don't want anybody knowing you got wheels stashed someplace, it's your business." He cracked his window open and lit a nonfilter cigarette, a Pall Mall. The end glowed in the darkness. The smoke was acrid in Size's nostrils.

Size flattened his sole and pressed his foot on the floorboard. The folded claim stub felt like a tiny stone against his big toe. "Well, lemme ask you something else. How come you ain't a nigger? Like the guy on the license?"

The driver tensed up. "Shit. I forgot to take the picture down. Say, you're not going to turn me in, are you?" He sounded panicked.

"Naw. Long as you don't remember me or where I got in the hack."

The driver relaxed, sighing. "I forgot about you already. You see there's some of us can't get a license. So we split time with a guy that's got a license, okay?"

"How come you can't? You been to the joint?"

The driver turned and glanced into the backseat. His right earlobe had a wart on it. "You too, huh? We're easy to spot, aren't we? Yeah, I did time."

"No foolin'? What kind of a beef did you catch?"

The driver's cheeks puffed as he grinned. "Well, to tell you the truth, I used to stick up taxicabs. Louis, he's the black guy in the picture, I robbed him one time. It's how we met. Funny how things work out sometimes.''

Size pictured Pecos Jimmy Fontenot. ''You ain't kidding, pal. You damn sure ain't kidding.''

12

Size thought about going to the Golden Nugget and playing poker, sitting right out in the open and showing Burista or Junior Gomez or anybody else interested right where he was. But he decided he'd better get some shut-eye. He had what he'd come after. Now it was somebody else's turn to start watching *him.* He hadn't had much sleep in the past couple of days. Besides, if he went to the Golden Nugget tonight he wasn't sure he could keep from making a fool of himself, gaping at Merrillee. He had the cabbie take him to the house.

He called Leon Hundley's apartment in Dallas.

Jez Radley said, "We've been worried."

"Say. Thanks, Jez. How's business?"

"Seems to be about the same. Jimmy's looking all over for you. I guess you know that."

"Who's he been talking to?"

"He sent Slim Burdine by to see a couple of people you know. I think Slim roughed up Danny Orr. I heard that he did."

Danny Orr managed the Mickey Finn's pool hall on Mockingbird Lane, where Size and Benny Sands used to play nine-ball. Danny had a wife and two kids—a boy and a girl. His wife worked at the telephone company. Size said, "Tell Danny I'm sorry, Jez, if you see him. I think me and Slim got a few things to hash over."

"I heard something else. That Slim's out of town for a while."

Size was sitting in an overstuffed chair in Merrillee's living room. Through the partially open bedroom door the corner of her king-size bed was visible. He said to Jez, "Yeah, Slim's out here. In Vegas. Say. Is Leon home?"

"He's out celebrating. The Feds didn't indict him on the I-30 condo charges and he's been out drinking the past two nights."

"Hey, that's great."

"What, that Leon's turning into a lush?"

"Naw. That he ain't been indicted. So Leon didn't make no false statement to get a loan, huh? I didn't think he was that kind of a guy."

"Well, let's just say they didn't indict him. He may have fudged a little."

"Naw, he wouldn't—Say, Jez. Get a pencil, will you?"

She put down the phone and got one. He waited, shifting the receiver from one ear to the other. He noticed a picture of Merrillee that he hadn't seen before on the mantel. Over her soft auburn hair she wore a tasseled hat, as if she were graduating.

Jez came back on the line. Size gave her Merrillee's telephone number. Then he said, "I need you to do something, Jez. I got a feeling Pecos Jimmy's going to be coming out west pretty soon. Maybe tomorrow. I need to know the second he does. Think you can find out for me?"

"Sure."

"Now, you ain't going to let Jimmy know you're doing this, are you? No foolin', Jez. I don't want you getting hurt."

"Let me handle it. And you're the one who needs to worry about getting hurt." There was a catch in her voice. "Oh, you big dumbo. How'd you get into this?"

He didn't answer, just thanked Jez and hung up. He stood and stretched, thinking about Slim Burdine and doing a slow burn as he took a couple of steps in the direction of his bedroom. As he did, a doorknob rattled and as he turned toward the front of the house the front door opened.

Size froze. The Luger, holster and all, were on his bed. Forty feet away. There wasn't any way anybody should be coming here. Not looking for him. Jesus, who—?

High heels click-clicked over the tile entry hall and Merrillee came in. She stopped dead in her tracks and sucked air into her lungs. "You frightened me," she said.

Her keys were in her hand, dangling from a big, plastic blockletter M. She was wearing snug Gloria Vanderbilt jeans and a man's white dress shirt, open at her soft throat, its tail out and draped over her slim hips. Her Golden Nugget uniform was folded over her arm.

"Hey," Size said, "you ain't so bad yourself in the scaring department. I thought you worked all night. What you doing home?" He thought he saw some green flecks in her eyes, but it might be the way the light was shining.

"Oh—oh, things weren't busy so I took the night off. Hell, that's not true. I wondered where you were, so I asked the boss if I could leave. I thought you were going to be there, playing poker."

He wasn't sure he was hearing her right. "Huh? You were looking for me?"

Her lips parted and she worked her fine lower jaw slightly to one side. She was wearing a faint rose lip-gloss. Her long lashes down, she walked slowly to the couch and sat on it. She was about five feet away from where he stood, her head on a level with his waist. She tilted her head, chin rising, until she was looking directly at him. He thought he might melt.

Tossing her waitress's uniform down beside her, she said, "Please don't make me repeat myself. If I hadn't blurted it out I'd never have gotten up the nerve to say it in the first place. I never saw you before in my life until you rescued me like some kind of dashing knight less than twenty-four hours ago. I still don't know anything about you. You've charmed my little girl out of her socks. Size, I've been married for a lot of years and I've forgotten everything I know about being coy. All I know to do is come right out, and I'm pretty clumsy about even doing that. So whatever you do, accept or reject me, please don't slap my face with it."

A short while ago, just for an instant there in that motel courtyard, Size had felt as though he could break Junior Gomez in half without any problem. Right now he wasn't sure he could break an egg with a sledgehammer. He sank down next to her. She was watching him with a steady level gaze. He'd been right. There were tiny green flecks in her eyes, mixed in with the hazel coloring.

He said, "Say, Merrillee, you—you ain't really talking to me. Are you?"

She turned a little more toward him. The width of her shoulders was about half the width of his massive deep chest. Her voice grew suddenly huskier as she said, "God, who else would I be talking to?" She bent forward slightly, her face upraised to his. Her breath was like fresh spearmint.

"Merrillee, I—" he started, then cleared his throat. "Listen, I ain't—" His tongue felt three inches thick.

She gave a sudden throaty laugh. A hint of a smile touched her lips. An earthy, wanton smile. "Well, if you don't want to say anything," she said, "then why don't you try doing something?"

The Merrillee Rogers who bedded Sizemore Brandon in the dimness of her room was a wild thing uncaged. He never would have believed it. This tall, cool, sophisticated female, now beneath him panting and gasping, her upper lip curled in lust, her eyes frenzied slits. She strained and thrust against him. She whimpered. Her long legs gripped his middle like powerful, writhing velvet ropes.

His climax was growing. Sensing it, she reached with her arms and drew his mouth against hers and pushed her tongue hard between his lips and moved it inside his mouth as he gushed into her; then held him violently against her, her flat belly writhing and her head moving and jerking from side to side on the pillow as her own orgasm shuddered through her.

At some point, he whispered, "I love you, doll."

* * *

"Somewhere skyrockets are blasting off," she said.

"Yeah. Like the Fourth of July."

Their bodies formed a T on the king-size, her soft auburn hair tickling his muscled belly. "Did you know you were saying that?" she said.

"Naw. Saying what?"

"That you loved me."

He felt his face blush in the dimness. Her legs were drawn up, one knee bent, a bare foot on the bed. Her other ankle rested on the knee. Light filtered in from the living room; her thighs were half in shadow; her smooth skin a deep golden tan. The bedside radio played an easy-listening station, an orchestra wailed "Michelle."

"You didn't have to, you know," she said.

"Huh? Didn't have to what?"

"Say you loved me. I'm not expecting any kind of commitment."

"I know you ain't. I don't know, tell you the truth."

She propped herself up on one elbow and watched him. One lock of soft hair bobbed gently on her forehead. "You don't know what?"

"I don't know—hell, you know. If I meant it or not. What I said."

She shifted, lying next to him and resting her head against his shoulder. She hooked her right leg firmly over his left, her foot between his shins. He tenderly put his arm about her, still not believing this was happening to him.

She said, "Well then. I'd watch what I told a girl, mister. You might get yourself out on a limb."

"You're a graduate, aintcha? I saw your picture in the living room."

"I love your body," she said, dragging a fingernail lightly over his chest. "Big and solid, not like one of those silly muscle-beach characters who go around grunting and flexing. Ugh, they look deformed."

"Naw, really, Merrillee. You went to college, huh?"

Her slim shoulders rose and fell. "For what it's worth I did. Not that it means anything."

"Me, too. I didn't graduate, though."

"Really?"

"Yeah. What college?"

"Me?"

"Yeah. Lemme guess—Vassar? Smith? One of them swankies, back east."

She chuckled throatily. "God, no. We couldn't have afforded that. Besides, I couldn't stand those phony snobs. I stayed right home in Los Angeles. U.C.L.A. And I had to work to do that."

"No fooling?" He rolled on his side, facing her profile. The point of his shoulder towered over her. "The Bruins, huh? I talked to those guys."

"You *talked* to them?"

"Yeah. Say, you might not believe this. But I played football pretty good at Commerce High. All-district."

"Well, I declare," she teased. "Yes, I believe it. Big as you are. God."

"Hey, I had some feelers. I went to look at most of the schools in Texas. Just a couple out of state. Iowa. Then U.C.L.A. Jesus Christ, Los Angeles was one big town. I remember we went to Universal Studios, took the tour." He lay back down flat and locked his fingers behind his head. He took a deep breath and let it out. "I guess I messed up pretty good, not taking one of them colleges up on their offer. Hell, I had a free ticket."

She stretched her leg full-length and massaged his ankle with her toes. "But you said you went to college."

"Aw. Kilgore J. C. don't count, really. I had a lot of friends around in East Texas and didn't want to go far from home. Pretty dumb, huh? We had a good team, though. Almost went to the Junior Rose Bowl."

"Almost?"

"Yeah. Howard County J. C.—that's this other Texas junior college. Bastards beat us one point. Another 'almost.' I've had a lot of 'em."

"Haven't we all." She moved again, this time lying on her stomach, scooting and wiggling until her upper body was flat on his chest and side. She made a snuggling motion with her chin against his breastbone. Her nipples were soft and warm, with tiny rigid tips. "Like I almost didn't marry Oscar. He's my ex. I was modeling part-time in college and my agent said I had a future in TV. It was a choice between Oscar and a modeling career. You never know. I wouldn't have had Jessie, though. Everything's for the best. Who tattooed you?" She traced the nail of a forefinger over the outline of the bulldog on his upper arm, over the letters USMC.

He laughed, and then realized that he hadn't been laughing much lately. It felt good, the rumbling chuckles beginning deep in his belly, lying here enjoying himself just talking to her, her lovely smiling face just inches from his in the dimness. "Hell. I couldn't tell you, I was too looped. First night outta boot camp. San Diego. Hey, you was a model? Like Brooke Shields?"

She snickered. "God, I hope not. I couldn't play a teenager's introduction to sex *one* time with a straight face, much less four or five times. But I'll brag some. I was pretty good. I've got some old bikini poses I'll put up against anybody's. My agent was toying around with a lot of different professional names for me, just before I got married. He said Merrillee Goetz just wasn't schmaltzy enough, or whatever the lingo is."

"Goetz?"

"That was me, my maiden name. I was born with the monicker. It's not so bad. I kind of liked it, German and all. What kind of a name is Size? I've never heard it before."

He turned his head on the pillow and looked out Merrillee's window. There was a row of flowers in a dark earth bed and one leafy tree silhouetted against the moonlit sky.

Merrillee said, "Did I say something wrong?"

He held the palm of his big hand softly against her hair. It was going to be hard. It might even break the spell.

She said, "What is it?"

He drew in his breath, still looking out the window,

then said, "It ain't my name. Not my last one, anyway. It's my first name. Sizemore. Brandon's the last name."

He was half expecting her to move away from him. Instead she softly brushed her palm over his real, crew cut hair. "And the red hair? That's the real Sizemore, not the Beatle?"

"Yeah."

"I'm not surprised. You don't have to tell me any more. Not if you don't want to."

He thought that over, then moved his big head and looked directly at her. Her lips were parted in a question. Filtered moonlight made shadows on her soft cheeks and slender nose. Finally he said, "Hey, look. There's this guy I used to work for. Doing things. Some things I ain't too proud of. This guy was my friend all my life. But not anymore. I came to Vegas to hurt this guy. To help myself, too, but to hurt this guy, mostly. I been to prison, Merrillee. Twice."

She closed her eyes and her lovely face saddened. "I was afraid—well, like I said, I'm not surprised. Everyone makes mistakes. Lord knows I've made enough."

"It's not just mistakes. There's a lot of stuff that—that I'm scared to death to tell you. But I'm going to, anyway. I wouldn't tell nobody else, I don't think. But I want you to know from me, not hear it around. I killed a coupla guys, Merrillee. For this guy, the one that used to be my friend."

She rolled off his chest and lay on her back. Her voice sounded tiny, like a little girl's, as she said, "I'm not sure I want to hear this."

"You don't have to. I'll shut up if you want me to. You asked me a while ago if I meant what I said when we was—you know. Well, I still don't know. But I do want to be on the square with you. I don't know why, but I do."

There was a long pause. Size listened to the faint hum of the air conditioning, felt his own heartbeat.

"Go on," Merrillee said.

There, she'd said it. Go on. Too late to stop. He

said, "Jimmy—that's this guy's name, Jimmy—he lived four doors down the street. In Commerce. We did everything together, growing up. See, I never had but one sister, and she's twelve years older. I got no brothers. And in Jimmy's family there weren't no other kids, just him. So me and Jimmy were closer than brothers, I guess." He laughed softly and wondered if the laugh sounded as bitter to Merrillee as it did to him. "Matter of fact, I guess Jimmy was the main reason I didn't go to one of them big colleges to play football. Me and Jimmy sat on my front porch in a swing one night. Sat there till dawn, drinking Pearl beer. Now, I don't know if Jimmy could make a living as a salesman or not, but he could always sell me on anything he wanted to. The little shit. Damnedest things. He wasn't going to no college, no way, and far as he was concerned I wasn't either. Jesus. I was so dumb I asked the little bastard if it was okay for me to go to Kilgore Junior College even. You wouldn't have believed it."

She kissed him gently on the shoulder. He felt a little dampness where her eyelashes had brushed against him.

"So anyway, I was going to tell you about these two guys," he said. "The first guy—well, you gotta understand what Jimmy does. He does a little—well, he's got some coin machines and jukeboxes. And some bars, too, and some other stuff. Anything that makes money. But it's gambling, mostly. The craps and blackjack, some sports bets. Shit, Merrillee, you can bet Jimmy more at one time than you can one of these Vegas casinos, what with their limit and all. So anyway, there was this guy, Joe Bob Hidy. Big cowboy, fulla bullshit. He lost a lotta money to Jimmy one night, shooting dice. Then he claimed around town that we ran in some six-ace flats on him."

"What're those? Six-ace flats?" She lifted her face, inquisitive.

"Aw. That's crooked dice. Anyway, this Joe Bob Hidy, he was gonna kill Jimmy. Tried to one night, shot three holes in Jimmy's front door. So we—well, we took care of him. Me and a guy named Slim. This colored guy. We took Joe Bob Hidy for a ride, or whatever you want to call it."

"How did you feel about it?" Now her voice was calm and steady. No accusing tone, just a straight-out question.

"I feel a lot worse now than I did then. Then it was—well, just something had to be done. The cops sure as hell weren't going to stop Joe Bob. Not that we ever would have talked to them about it anyway. It was kill him or he was gonna kill Jimmy. That was a long time ago, before I found out what Jimmy'd do for me if I needed him. Nothing—a big fat zero."

She sighed. "And the other one? The other man you—"

"Killed. That's what we did, Merrillee. He was a drug man. East Eddie Kilrain. Kind of the same deal. East Eddie didn't like to pay on football bets. He's another guy that threatened Jimmy. Hell, there were a lot of guys that threatened the little twerp. But Joe Bob Hidy and East Eddie Kilrain, they were the only two that'd really go through with anything. We done East Eddie, too. Me and Slim."

He felt her stirring next to him, felt the soft warm skin of her upper arm brush his side. Then she was still again. Her light musk perfume was on his body, everywhere he'd touched her. She sat up, fumbling in the nightstand. A butane lighter hissed and flared, then went out. The point of a cigarette glowed red. He didn't like the smell of smoke. With her next to him he didn't mind.

"Merrillee?" he said.

"Yes?"

"Hey, I wouldna told you if I wasn't starting to go for you."

"I know."

"I've had broads. Strung them along, fed them a line of shit. I ain't doing that with you."

She inhaled the cigarette and blew smoke at the ceiling. It rippled in the flow from the air conditioning and vanished in the dimness. The orchestra on the radio wailed the theme from "The Great Impostor."

"What do you think about it?" he said.

She surprised him with a soft throaty chuckle. "Right now I'm trying not to think about it at all. Later I will. A whole lot, probably. Now I'm just thinking that it's five more hours before I have to get Jessie, at Mrs. Tallon's. That's five hours we can spend together. We'll take them one at a time. I'm warning you, though. Tomorrow I might be scared to death of you."

She stubbed the cigarette out and came to him. He was conscious of the faint odor of tobacco as her tongue slid warmly between his lips.

13

Pecos Jimmy Fontenot said loudly, "Fuck no!" He pushed Suzy roughly away. She flattened against the carved-wood headboard, her eyes wide. Jimmy kept the receiver against his ear and took the white Princess phone's base from the nightstand and held it in his lap. The skin on his narrow chest was pasty white, dark hairs growing thick between his nipples.

Jimmy said, "I know he ain't. Look, Beaumont, you sure the Mex ain't putting Burista on? That Junior Gomez ain't no Eagle Scout, you know. Maybe he's trying to make a score on his own."

Suzy said, "What—?"

Pecos Jimmy put a hand firmly over her mouth, his brows knitting in a frown as he listened to the phone. He stroked his handlebar moustache. Suzy shrugged, pursed her lips, and pressed the off button on the cone-shaped plastic vibrator. The faint humming ceased. She folded her arms, her bare breasts pressing together like twin balloons. She stuck out her lower lip and blew a puff of air upward. The Veronica Lake wave flared up in the quick draft, then settled back down over her eye.

"Look, Beaumont, I don't give a fuck what Burista does to Gomez. Jesus Christ, I send a whole fucking army out there and you assholes can't put together one deal?"

He listened. Suzy stroked his shoulder. He pushed her hand away.

"Well, you don't know it, but you ain't too far from dead. Five'll get you twenty that Burista's already got some dudes on their way up there you don't want to see. And if there's any more fuck-ups you're going to have Pecos Jimmy to worry about. Jesus Christ, Size fucking *Brandon*? You stay put, Beaumont. You don't so much as stick your nose outta the room till you see me. . . . How the fuck should *I* know? I'll think of something." A high-pitched ring pealed and hung in the air as he slammed down the receiver.

Jimmy sprang out of bed and stood barefooted on the thick carpet. His ribs showed like pale white bars. The hair at his crotch was coal black. To Suzy he said, "Get dressed. We're going to Vegas."

Her lips parted. *"Vegas?* Wow, Jimmy! What do I wear?"

He paused in the doorway of the bathroom long enough to say, "Wear your fucking birthday suit for all I care. But you sit there on your ass for five more minutes you're going to get left."

She wiggled, and scooted to the side of the bed as the bathroom door slammed.

Herbert Rutherford of Muncie, Indiana, wasn't going to take any shit from anybody. Not ever again. Not after twenty-three years of looking up at everybody, including the shortest of women, saying, "Yes, sir," and "Yes, ma'am," peering at them through the bars of his teller's cage while he cashed their checks and took their deposits. The half-million in cash that was stacked neatly inside his briefcase said *that* life was all over for Herbert Rutherford. *Bright light city, here I come.*

He stood in his brand-new, dove gray, Sans-A-Belt slacks, size twenty-eight, and matching dove gray knit Etienne Aigner golf shirt, size junior-small, bought in the women's department at Bloomingdale's in Chicago; stood with his birdlike shoulders square, exactly equidistant between the two handrails on the moving sidewalk that carried passengers from the deplaning gates at McCarran International Airport to the luggage-claim area. He stood stock still as the sidewalk carried him past a shimmering electric sign that said Lola Falana was knocking 'em dead at the Riviera, hefted his leather briefcase from one small hand to the other, pictured the stacks of hundred-dollar bills swinging at his hip, and threw a broad wink at the color picture of Lola Falana in a skin-tight sequinned costume. Who knew? Herbert Rutherford might even try out a colored girl, if she looked like that one.

He grinned to himself as he pictured the fat-cheeked, puffy-jowled face of Markham Stoner, president of the First National Bank of Muncie, Indiana. Pictured Markham Stoner scratching his bald head in consternation as he said, "Herb? The original Casper Milquetoast? Jesus, who'd have thought the little bastard had the guts?"

As the moving sidewalk rolled along, Shecky Greene's voice, booming from overhead, came over the public address system. Shecky Greene welcomed Herbert Rutherford to Las Vegas and reminded him to stand to his right on the sidewalk so that people could pass him on his left. He stood even straighter in the center, murmuring, "Fuck you, Shecky. Herb Rutherford stands wherever he wants to."

The flexible moving belt vibrated as heavy footsteps approached from behind. The footsteps halted. Herbert Rutherford drew up to his full five-feet-one and rigidly stood his ground.

Behind him a tenor voice said in a Texas accent, "Move over, bud. We need to get by."

Herbert Rutherford gripped the handle of the briefcase tightly and peered over his shoulder. Behind him were a slender white guy and a tall, rangy black guy. The white guy wore a soft brown Stetson hat and a tan western-cut leisure suit, complete with brown string tie. He had a handlebar moustache. The black guy wore a black western hat with a silver band, a white western shirt with pink quilting at the shoulders, and tight formfit jeans. He had a gleaming gold tooth. Between them stood a gorgeous blonde. She was in a tight green dress that was slit up one side, showing creamy thigh. Her long soft hair had a sweeping wave in front that overhung one crystal blue eye.

Looking the black guy over from head to toe, sneering slightly, Herbert Rutherford said, "Well, if it isn't Hopalong Rastus." He turned his head to the front. Behind him, nobody moved.

Suddenly a steely hand clamped his shoulder and spun him around. The black guy put a thumb on one of Herbert Rutherford's cheeks, a forefinger on the other, and squeezed. Herb's mouth formed a compressed O. The black guy's nose was inches away. There was a fine string of saliva clinging to the gold tooth.

The black guy kept his voice low and even as he said, "Listen, sawed-off honkie motherfucker. Mistuh Fontenot says move, you move yo' ass, heah?" Then he shoved. Herbert Rutherford banged hard against the rail. The three—the white guy, the black guy, and the wiggle-butted blonde—went by.

The blonde batted her eyes at Herb. She motioned toward the retreating black guy's back. "Isn't he *rude*?" she said.

Pecos Jimmy had about decided that trying to get rid of Size Brandon was a major mistake. What had he been thinking of? Six, seven years Size had been running things without a hint of trouble. Now this. In the six weeks since Size had ducked the car bomb and gone undercover, Jimmy'd had more to do than in the previous six *years*. And thinking back on it, there wasn't any way that Size was going to testify to a federal grand jury. Not after everything he and Pecos Jimmy had been through. Size just wasn't built that way, didn't matter *what* the Feds tried to threaten him with.

Goddam it, it was all Beaumont Gurney's fault. 'Course it was. It was Gurney and nobody else that talked Pecos Jimmy into sending Yucca over to look old Size up. Gurney'd sat right there that night in the Egyptian and convinced Jimmy that Size was somebody to worry about. And Pecos Jimmy was drunk to boot. Sober he'd never have done it, would have had enough sense to know that Sizemore Brandon was one guy you didn't ever want to cross. No way.

Jimmy watched the line of suitcases and boxes travel up the conveyor belt from below, then tumble one by one onto the revolving metal carrier, as he said to Slim Burdine, ''How come Gurney didn't come to meet me himself?''

Slim had his hands jammed into the hip pockets of his jeans, his hat tilted at an angle that showed his shiny black forehead. ''Don't get me to lyin', Boss. I'm jus' the nigger, remember? You tell me Beau Gurney's in charge, I'm gonna do what Beau Gurney says to do. You tell me Beau Gurney's *not* in charge, I'm gonna do something different.''

''Well, let me think,'' Jimmy said. ''That might be the next thing I tell you, that Gurney's not the man no more. Jesus Christ. I'm telling you this Burista might look like the Cisco Kid's buddy, Pancho, but he's the most dangerous sonofabitch north of the equator. Trust me, I kid you not. Hey! That's mine, doll, the green one.''

A green leather suitbag tumbled down the ramp, followed by a matching suitcase. Suzy took short, clackety-clack steps in her spike heels, her bottom wiggling under her tight dress as she followed the suitbag around the perimeter of the moving rack. ''Get a skycap, Jimmy. God, I can't carry this.''

''Sure, doll. Sure.'' Jimmy raised a hand over his head and snapped his fingers. A huffing and puffing fat black guy wearing a billed cap started to come forward, tugging along a luggage rack. A young, sandy-haired white skycap stopped him and whispered something. The heavy black guy nodded, stood aside, and let him take the luggage rack over to where Jimmy and Slim were standing. Up and down the cavernous baggage area, conveyors rolled, skycaps hustled, bells clanged, and lights changed from red to green and back again. Near the exit, behind yellow Hertz and red Avis and green Dollar counters, pretty uniformed girls waited with folded arms.

The young skycap said, ''Yes, sir. Which bags are yours?''

Pecos Jimmy indicated Suzy. ''The broad'll show

you,'' he said. ''Oh, and listen, pal. You don't put one fucking scratch on those bags if you know what's good for you.''

Underneath the plastic bill of his cap, the kid's eyes narrowed. His neck reddened. ''You're scaring the shit out of me, Mac. Listen, I'll take care of the luggage. You just don't forget the tip.'' He turned and yanked the rack over to where Suzy was pointing out pieces of luggage with a red-nailed hand.

Pecos Jimmy's jaw dropped, his gaze following the kid and the baggage cart. Then he turned his head in slow motion to look at Slim. ''You hear that?'' Jimmy said. ''Jesus Christ, some nerve, huh?''

Slim straightened his hat on his head and cracked his knuckles, bouncing on the balls of his feet. He threw a short shadow jab. ''Want me to nigger him?''

''Naw. Can you believe—kid goes, 'You're scaring the shit outta me.' Real wiseass. Hell, he's got moxie. I like his style.'' Jimmy scratched his ear. ''So back to what's happening. Let's say for argument this Gomez is telling it like it is. You don't think there can be no mistake? About Size Brandon being the guy?''

''Don't see how, Boss,'' Slim Burdine said. ''Junior Gomez, he done time with Sizemo' twice, two different prison farms. One of the times all three of us was on the same farm. Me, Sizemo', and this Junior Gomez dude. Pretty boy, no-guts dude, I always thought. But he'd damn sure know Size. Naw, Boss, ain't no mistake. Some honkies look alike, but not Sizemo'. Not that big red-headed suckah.''

''Say, you ain't seen Size, have you, Slim?'' Pecos Jimmy looked a little suspicious. ''You and Size used to be tight. Shit, East Eddie Kilrain thought the two of you was blood brothers.''

''Yeah, Size and me was like soul bruddas once, but no more. I tell you, Boss Jimmy, I know Size. He been burned. He's not going to sidle up to nobody that's got anything to do with Pecos Jimmy Fontenot. And specially not me.'' Slim looked in the direction of the carousel. ''Luggage ready, Boss. You pos'tive you don't want me to talk to the skycap kid? About what he said to you?''

''Naw. We got enough problems with Burista, believe me. I got to talk to this Colombian before the shit hits the fan, if it ain't already. Let's go.''

Jimmy and Slim fell into step behind the skycap, who was shoving the luggage cart along in front of him. Suzy led them in a parade strut. Jimmy took a gold money clip from his pants pocket. It was stuffed with bills, hundreds on the outside. He took the wad out of the clip, thumbed through it, and fished out a ten-spot. Then he reached from behind around the skycap and stuffed the bill into the kid's shirt pocket. The kid glanced back, his head cocked to one side. The wheels on the luggage cart bumped on to the rubber mat and the automatic doors that opened into the parking lot hissed and swung outward. Desert summer heat blasted in on them. Suzy shrugged her slim shoulders, smiled to no one in particular, and paraded her way outside.

To the skycap, Jimmy said, ''You earned it, son. No hard feelings, huh? About what I said to you back there.''

The sandy-haired kid grinned. ''Hey, I toted bags for Sinatra one time. Next to him you're a piece of cake. Don't give it a second thought, pal.''

After he loaded the bags into the trunk of the rented Lincoln Town Car and shut the lid, the kid mopped his brow. His face was dripping sweat—a hundred and fifteen today, according to the radio. The kid thanked Jimmy, nodded to Slim Burdine, looked at the blonde with what he hoped wasn't a leer, and dragged the empty luggage cart back into the terminal. He felt like the fair skin on the back of his neck had been seared in the blistering heat. Jesus, he'd hate to do this for a living, especially if every customer was a horse's ass like Pecos Jimmy Fontenot.

He returned the cart to the fat black porter and gave him the crumpled ten-dollar bill. The porter's face wrinkled in a smile. He had one front tooth missing.

He said, "Any time, boss. Jist let me know." The kid showed the porter a circle with his thumb and forefinger as he left, walking briskly back toward the terminal's moving sidewalk. He shunned the moving route and hustled along on foot alongside it.

The perspiration was drying on his face and neck, making him shiver some, as he entered a huge round room, like the inside of a dome. There were triple rows of slot machines to one side, bells clanging, as men and women determinedly yanked on metal handles, some not able to wait until they got to town to place their first bets; still others pouring the last of their money down Mama Vegas's eager gullet while they waited for the plane to take them back to wherever they came from. Corridors led off at intervals around the perimeter of the vast room, signs over the entrances directing folks to different sets of boarding gates. Each tunnel was carpeted in a different color—red, yellow, or green. Smack in the center of the floor, its roof directly under the top of the dome, was a double-level indoor building. The first floor held the Nevada Restaurant. Upstairs, thick-thighed cocktail waitresses in short red skirts hustled drinks back and forth to tables in the Skyway Lounge. The kid took the escalator to the bar.

The thick blue carpet gave under his feet. He tossed his skycap's hat on a rack just inside the entrance, then gave himself the onceover in the long polished mirror behind the bar—pale blue eyes, even, young-man features, a slight puffiness under the chin, sandy hair parted on the left with a rear cowlick he'd never been able to control—and thought, No wonder they all think I'm a kid. Thirty years old, I look like Harry High School. He gave a sly wink to a willowy brunette cocktail waitress as he passed her. She ignored him. He shrugged ruefully and went through an unmarked door at the rear of the cocktail lounge, pulling a small Radio Shack cassette recorder from his pocket as he did. He unplugged the wire, set the recorder on a small oval desk, and pulled the rest of the wire out from under his shirt. A tiny mike was held to the skin on his chest by cellophane tape. He stripped it off.

From his chair on the other side of the desk, Dallas Federal Prosecutor Henry Mitchell said, "How'd it go?" He picked up the recorder and squinted at it from arm's length. Henry was wearing a black suit, starched white shirt, and a red-and-gray striped tie. Above his slightly jutted jawline, his thin mouth was in a professional smirk.

Sam, the gray-eyed, poker-faced FBI agent from Dallas, was leaning back against one wall in a straight-backed chair. He had on navy slacks and a red knit shirt. He said, "Yeah, Goalby, how'd it go? They have a big dumb red-headed creep with them?"

Agent Stu Goalby of the Vegas office flashed a boyish grin and shook his head. "Negatory on the redhead. It's Fontenot, though. I made him from the photo. Tall black man in western duds was with him. And a blonde twist that was like, wow."

"We'll need a make on the woman," Henry Mitchell said. "The black would be Slim Burdine. A dangerous animal, that one." He was rewinding the recorder. There was a tiny click and the reels stopped turning. "Well, let's have a listen." He pressed the button marked PLAY.

There were a few seconds of running-tape noise, followed by a throbbing, pulsing loud beat. *Bum-bum. Bum-bum. Bum-bum.*

Henry's brows knitted. "What the hell is that?"

Agent Stu Goalby rested one hip on the edge of the desk and leaned closer to the machine. "Jesus Christ. I don't know."

Sam snorted and lowered the front legs of his chair to rest on the floor. He bent closer, touching his fingertips together. "Shit, Henry," he said. "It's Goalby's heartbeat. This is the greatest fucking surveillance since the Carmino Family, ain't it?"

Pecos Jimmy Fontenot checked into the Golden Nugget. He harangued the desk clerk, a girl of about twenty, who finally broke into tears over Jimmy's insistence on a poolside room when there were none available; lambasted a bellhop who dropped his suitcase on the carpeted floor; then made amends by handing out ten-dollar tips all around. He dispatched Suzy, along with the bellhop, to the room—a twentieth-floor suite complete with sunken Jacuzzi and a bidet—and went with Slim to call on Beaumont Gurney.

He knocked on Gurney's door. *Rat . . . Tat-tat . . . Tat . . . Tat*—one long, two shorts, two longs—then stood back on the spongy red carpet with his hands in his pockets, first on one foot and then the other. The collar on his shirt was slightly damp, the string tie drooping some. Slim leaned against the doorjamb, crossed his ankles, and folded his arms. He chewed thoughtfully on a toothpick, his Stetson tilted back at an angle.

The door opened wide.

Through the entryway, past a short, narrow corridor with a sink against one wall, Jimmy could see the foot of the bed. Light reflected from the red satin quilted spread. There was a tufted red velvet armless chair by the bed's foot. Beaumont Gurney was seated in it. He was wearing yellow boxer swim trunks and a green T-shirt, and was barefoot. Thick tape was plastered over his mouth. His hands were tied behind his back. His eyes were bulging.

A thin, olive-complexioned Latin guy with a pencil moustache, who was wearing a loud red-flowered Hawaiian shirt with the tail outside his slacks, leaned around the doorframe from inside. In his right hand was a black Beretta automatic with a long, thin, blued-steel silencer screwed into its muzzle. He put the nose of the silencer against Slim Burdine's glistening chocolate forehead.

In clipped Spanish-accented English, the Latin guy said, "Stay cool now, shine-boy. I going to back up now, you come on in with me."

Another Latin, this one a short muscled guy with long dark sideburns and a thick corded neck, stepped out from behind the open door. He wore navy shorts along with a pink sleeveless muscle shirt, and had dark hair growing on his beefy upper arms. He held a Beretta, with a silencer just like the other guy's, in his right hand. He pointed the gun at Jimmy's midsection and beckoned with his left hand, whistling, "Here, doggy," softly between his teeth.

Goose bumps rising along his spine, Pecos Jimmy entered the room. For a second he and Slim were side-by-side in the entryway. Their shoulders touched. Then they were inside. The short, stocky Latin gestured with the pistol toward the wall. Jimmy flattened against it with his face turned sideways, seeing Slim flattening against the wall beside him. A leather shoe kicked firmly against Jimmy's inner ankle. He spread his feet apart. Thick rough hands patted him down, locating the two-shot Derringer holstered at his waist and taking it away. The hands stopped searching and moved away also.

Behind him another Latin voice, lower and more gutteral than the thin guy's, said, "You will now go inside and sit on the bed."

Pecos Jimmy took short, slow-motion steps, his hands spread apart in front of him, down the corridor to the foot of the bed. He sat down with his knee a foot or so from Beaumont Gurney's knee. Gurney's left cheek was red and swollen. Below the tape over his mouth was a thin trickle of blood on his chin.

Yucca-baby was on the bed. She'd been hog-tied, her hands bound behind her with cotton rope, the rope looped so tightly around her ankles that she couldn't straighten her legs. Her big breasts quivered under the thin fabric of her T-shirt. She looked terrified. Jimmy couldn't remember ever seeing Yucca look scared before. She said, "Tell them, Jimmy. We didn't take the stuff." There were ugly red welts on her upper arms.

Slim lowered himself into an armchair by the dark-wood bureau. The skinny Latin's Beretta stayed trained on Slim's chest. Slim looked at the Beretta casually, like it bored him to death. His jaw moved as he continued to chew slowly on the toothpick. To the Latin he said, "I gonna remember you, boy. Sometime, someplace, you one dead little spic. You hear?" The Latin sneered.

The dark stocky Latin stood at ease with his back against the wall just inside the room. He slowly lowered his pistol to his side, casting an expectant glance in the direction of the low red couch by the window.

Senor Emilio Garza Burista was seated on it. He wore gray slacks and a blue-flowered silk shirt, open at the neck. His chubby hands were clasped over his round belly. He said, in accented but perfect English, "Pecos Jimmy, the only reason you are not dead is that I think you're smarter than this. Much, much smarter, my friend. So you have ten seconds to explain to me that your big red-headed man wasn't acting on your orders." He looked at his gold watch. "I am counting, my friend." He looked heavier than the last time Jimmy had seen him.

Jimmy licked his lips. He was dimly conscious of the pleading in Beaumont Gurney's eyes. Jimmy said, "Listen, I don't know what that lying fucker Junior Gomez—"

"Junior Gomez didn't lie to me. Junior Gomez didn't talk to me. When I find Junior Gomez he and I will have a talk. You have five seconds," Burista said. The stocky Latin in the pink muscle shirt took a step forward and raised his pistol.

Pecos Jimmy said quickly, "Just a—Size Brandon don't work for me no more. Shit, Size Brandon may be in with the Feds, all I know. He went in front of a grand jury, the dirty snitch."

Burista said something to the stocky guy in Spanish. The guy lowered his gun. Burista scratched a clipped gray sideburn as he said to Pecos Jimmy, "I have no reason to believe that. But there is a lot of money involved here. We're going to make a plan, you and I, to find this big man and what he took from me. When we do, you will kill him. If you don't, I'm going to assume that he was working for you. That will be unfortunate for you, friend Jimmy."

"It'll be a pleasure. Wait'll I get my hands on the creep," Jimmy said.

Burista raised his voice. "You may come out now, my dear."

Dolores sashayed out of the bathroom, good legs flashing and round hips moving from side to side. She was wearing tight jean cut-offs and her midriff was bared by a halter. She sat down in Burista's lap and put her arm around his neck.

"God, sugar," she said. "Whyn't you tell me you could speak English all along? I got some good words to say to you tonight." She bent and kissed his ear.

14

Suzy batted her crystal-blue eyes and said to Pecos Jimmy Fontenot, "Is my baby sick? God, honey, you're pale as a ghost."

Jimmy tightened his wide leather belt to its next-to-last notch. The belt had a gleaming silver buckle; J. P. F. was stamped into the brown leather where the belt wound above Jimmy's backside. He was wearing brand-new boot-cut jeans and black-and-white zebra skin boots. His tapered western shirt was black. "Naw. Nothing wrong with me, doll. Look, me and Slim got some business, huh? You get some sun. Nice suit." He gave her a short, smacky kiss on the cheek.

Suzy did a pirouette, showing off an iridescent green one-piece that was cut about six inches above her hip joints. The suit's front was cut away in a diamond pattern, showing a sharply defined navel on a flat brown belly. "Wow, I just bought it, downstairs. Isn't it *groovy*? Slim, you take good care of my baby. You going to be gone long?"

Slim shifted his weight from one foot to the other and moved the toothpick to the opposite corner of his mouth. He kept his gaze on the carpet.

Jimmy said, "Hey, I don't need nobody to take care of me. I'm the main man, doll. I got to get my business out of the way so you and me can have a ball. Won't be long." Suzy wrinkled her nose. Jimmy and Slim left. Suzy hummed "Hit the Road, Jack" to herself as she looked around the room for her floppy sun hat.

As they waited in the hallway for the elevator, Slim said, "Boss, ole Slim's doing his best to go along 'cause that's what ole Slim's been doing for years. But you making me nervous. You done told this Colombian we going to find Sizemo'. Shit, Size might be on Mars. You don't think Burista's going to kill Gurney and Yucca we don't come up with Size, you dreamin'. Then next thing Burista's going to kill us, what you think about that?"

The elevator doors rumbled open. They entered the car. Slim pressed the first-floor button. As the car started to move, Jimmy said, "Listen, if the guy knocks Gurney off it's tough shit. I might knock off Gurney myself. Yucca—well, what can I say? What's another motorcycle bitch? But I tell you something, we're gonna find Size. He ain't gone no place. He's right here, hanging around somewhere, and he's waiting for me. You think Size hijacked these guys just for the money? No, he—"

Jimmy cut himself off as the doors opened, shooting a glance each way on the first floor. They went down the corridor toward the casino, sidestepping a man and a little boy who were ogling the souvenirs in the gift shop. Jimmy was hustling, Slim ambling, taking one step to Fontenot's two. Jimmy went on.

"Like I say, Slim, Size is pranking with me. Same shit every time he gets uptight, ever since we was kids. It's like he was hiding the dope from me. He's gonna come to see Pecos Jimmy, bet on it. You can't—what the fuck you stopping for?"

They were inside the casino. There was quite a crowd for daytime, four full crap tables in action, stickmen droning, a dozen blackjack games in progress. Four old women were squealing and clapping their hands at the roulette wheel. Slim was standing stock still, his gaze across the room. His mouth was open. The gold tooth glinted and the toothpick dangled from his lower lip.

Jimmy said, "Jesus Christ, Slim, I'm in a hurry. You space out on something, or what?"

Slim grinned, slow and easy. "Naw, I ain't. Boss Jimmy, you want to see Size Brandon? Well there he is. Big dude done found him a poker game."

* * *

Size wasn't sure if a little girl would like the toy he had in the paper bag or not. He took another look at it. It was a Transformer, a blue plastic car with foldout arms, legs, and head that turned it into a robot. He'd seen some real cute dollies and stuffed doggies in the gift shop that Jessie would probably like better. But he couldn't sit down in no Texas Hold-Em poker game with a cute little dolly, for Christ's sake. Everybody'd think he was a fairy or something. He folded over the mouth of the bag, closing it, and set it aside. Then he peeked at his two-card hand and said across the table to Denver Phil Madison, "Naw, I ain't raising. I'm just calling you," as he scooted forty dollars' worth of chips into the pot.

Size was holding the king of spades and the king of hearts. Jack-eight-four-deuce was the face-up spread in the center of the table: two hearts, one spade, one club. Sandy the dealer knocked once with his knuckle to indicate the pot was right, then quickly dealt Fifth Street. Size watched Denver Phil, saw Denver's eyes following Sandy's hands, caught a slight twitch at the corner of Denver's eye and the barest movement of Denver's Adam's apple as the final card came into view. Only then did Size take a look for himself. Queen of hearts.

Denver Phil Madison's skinny neck and head barely moved, his hawk face stone as he pushed his bet out in front of him. "Forty dollars," he said.

Size shrugged. "I don't see how I can win. I'm going to let you have it." He tossed his cards away and made a shoving motion with his palms. Sandy, the dealer, raked the pot over in front of Denver Phil.

Denver Phil Madison shook his head in disgust. He was wearing a yellow baseball cap that said RANGER TRACTOR TIRES in green letters on its peak. "Two solid days, Big Tex. Two solid days of poker and you made nary a mistake. Black hair, carrot-top, all the same. You reading my mail?"

"Naw, I ain't. I'm just making some lucky guesses is all," Size said.

Behind Size and to his right, a mellow voice with an East Texas twang said, "You should have raised the fucking guy before the last card was dealt. You had him beat. He might have got out, gave you the pot. Jesus Christ."

Size stiffened, just for an instant. Then he relaxed and picked up the paper bag, opening it once more and peeking at Jessie's little present. Without turning his head, Size said, "That's why you don't ever win playing Hold-Em. You woulda raised. Guy's drawing for a flush and a straight there's, shit, fifteen cards in that deck that can beat you." Then he swiveled his big head around and looked. "The fuck you want, Jimmy?"

Jimmy was really decked out. Shit, zebra boots and black fancy shirt, diamonds flashing from the Rolex. And yeah, Slim was there with him. He would be. Jimmy wouldn't go anywhere these days without somebody to back him up. Not long ago the somebody would have been Size. Slim was standing by Jimmy and chewing on a toothpick like Corn Stalk City.

Slim said, "How's my man, Sizemo'?"

Size nodded slightly.

"Hey, big man," said Jimmy, rubbing his palms together, "it ain't what I want. It's what you want. You need to talk to Pecos Jimmy? Say, you got a problem you need to talk to Jimmy is all. We can work it out. We always could, you and me." He grinned and rubbed the tip of his finger across his handlebar moustache. Size wondered how many times he'd seen Pecos Jimmy do that. More than a million, probably.

Size picked two poker chips, a red and a green, off the table and clicked them together between a huge thumb and forefinger. "Do I want to talk to Pecos Jimmy? Yeah, I want to talk. I got to. Right over there"—he gestured with his head toward the corridor that led to the gift shop and the elevators—"is a quiet bar. It's on the left. This time of day there won't be two, maybe three people in there."

"I know where it is," said Jimmy. "Yeah. Yeah, that's good. We can have a couple beers, chew the fat.

Come on, what we waiting for?" He took two steps, stopped, and looked expectantly at Size.

Size couldn't believe the guy. Doing all that, blowing up cars with poor old men inside, making a guy go on the run. Then, Come on, what we waiting for? Like the two of them were back in Commerce, Texas, going downtown to the picture show.

Size said, "Naw, Jimmy. You go ahead, you and Slim. Save me a seat. I want to play a couple more hands. Besides—well, I don't want to hurt your feelings or nothing. But it wouldn't do me no good to get seen with you. Might ruin my rep around the joint."

A lounge in Vegas was just the kind of background that Size had always pictured for Pecos Jimmy Fontenot. Lots of glitter, plenty of class, a long polished bar, rows of glistening bottles with shiny silver spouts corked into their necks. A long mirror on the wall behind the bar to reflect the backside of an all-business, gold-vested barkeep who was mixing three drinks all at once—a vodka gimlet, a daiquiri, and a Harvey Wallbanger. The carpeted Golden Nugget hallway just outside the entrance, faint sounds from the casino—slots whirring, stickmen droning, Keno numbers called out over the P.A. system—muted in the background. Just the kind of place where you'd look for somebody like Clark Gable to wander in wearing a tux, clicking a stack of chips in his hands, and buying drinks for a broad who looked like Ingrid Bergman, who was sitting sultry at the bar. Yeah, just the kind of a joint that Pecos Jimmy'd like.

Size felt a little out of place as he stood in the entryway and let his eyes get used to the dimness. It was the clothes that he was wearing—faded jeans, a golf shirt, his worn Adidas running shoes. Like maybe he should be coming through the rear entrance, making a delivery. The bag containing Jessie's present hung loosely from one hand and the cream-colored windbreaker that he'd bought in the Golden Nugget gift shop was neatly draped over his forearm. The Luger was at home—not *home*, at Merrillee's house—and he hoped he didn't need it. Hell, he shouldn't have any use for the gun right here in the Golden Nugget Hotel in downtown Vegas in the middle of the day. But he might—you never knew.

There was a blue-white flash of diamond-reflected light as Jimmy waved to him from a back booth. Size wasn't sure if the glint was from the Rolex on Jimmy's wrist or the full-carat stone in his pinky ring. He squinted. He could barely make Slim out, slouching in the booth next to Pecos Jimmy. Size went to the booth, his feet noiseless on the thick carpet, pulled a gold velvet-cushioned chair from an adjoining table and sat down.

Jimmy said, "Howsa man, Size? You looking good. Shaved the beard, got a haircut. Hell, you look like a kid again. Don't he, Slim?" Jimmy and Slim were both drinking draft beer from tall frosted glasses.

"Sho' nuff does. Younger'n the first day I ever seen the dude," Slim said. He took a sip of beer. The toothpick was still dangling from the corner of his lip; its tip moved up and down as he swallowed.

Size thought, So Jimmy's going to come across real palsy-walsy. Jesus, how dumb does the guy think I am? He folded his arms and crossed his big legs. Without smiling he said, "Well, yeah. I got a haircut. So like I said, what do you want?"

"Hey, it's not—" Jimmy snapped his fingers in the direction of the bar and made a beckoning motion. A diamond sparkled. A leggy brunette cocktail waitress bounced in their direction as Jimmy said loudly, "On the ball, hon. Bring my big friend a drink. Whatever he wants, huh?" There was a painting on the gold-colored wall over Jimmy's shoulder, a scared calf running away top speed from a charging horse, a cowpoke in the saddle swinging a lariat overhead.

Size glanced at the girl and shook his head. She shrugged, made a face, and returned to her station at the bar, her short skirt popping against her round hips.

For just an instant Pecos Jimmy's expression changed. Most people wouldn't have noticed, but Size did. A quick, split-second uncertainty. Then Jimmy's relaxed grin was back, even teeth flashing in the dimness as he said, "Say, you're not drinking. That's good, big man, that's good. It's too fucking early. Mom always said to me, 'Jim, you need to be more like Size Brandon. Young man's got a head on his shoulders.' Why, I remember—"

"There ain't nothing to remember, Jimmy." Size felt his upper lip curl, heard his voice quaver. "Ever since I wouldn't talk to no grand jury and you showed me how much that meant to you by trying to knock me off, there ain't no memory. No Mom, no neighborhood, no Commerce, no nothing. Only poor old Benny Sands, that never hurt nobody. Yeah. I remember Benny pretty good. Now you got five seconds to start telling me what you want, else I'm getting the fuck outta here."

"Can you—?" Jimmy started to say something, then halted in mid-sentence and lowered his chin. His face was hidden behind the brim of his Stetson as he shook his head slowly and muttered, "Jesus Christ." Then he looked up. His smile was gone. "Slim, can you believe it? I mean, can you believe the fucking guy? Shit, all my life I been the best friend he's had. Let him run things, make a lot of bread. And for what? So he can rob me. Rob me, that's what he did. Not Junior Gomez, not the fucking Colombian. Me, Pecos Jimmy Fontenot, that's who he robbed. Now he's acting like he thinks I got something to do with Benny Sands getting killed. Shit, Size, I don't know nothing about no Benny Sands. Huh, Slim?" He turned to Slim and gestured toward Size, palm up. "Tell the man. Tell him I ain't got nothing to do with no Benny Sands."

Slim tilted his hat back and chewed on the toothpick as if he was deep in thought. Then he climbed slowly to his feet, taking the toothpick from between his lips and dropping it underneath the table as he did. He stood outside the booth, hands on hips. "Slim's still yo' hand, Boss Jimmy, if you want it that way. But don't get me to telling something I don't know. I don't think I'm part of this pow-wow. See you later, Boss . . .

Size. Hang loose, man.'' He ambled slowly out of the lounge and disappeared down the carpeted hall in the direction of the casino.

Pecos Jimmy watched Slim go. His jaw was slack. ''Hey. Hey, Size, see what I get? Black sonofabitch won't do nothing I tell him to. Man, I need my buddy back. Look, Size, whaddya say we—''

''Three hundred grand,'' Size said.

''Three—? What the fuck you mean? What's three hundred grand?''

''It's what it's going to cost you to keep those Colombians from shipping your carcass out with the next marijuana load. And you're lucky as a two-dicked dog you can get out of it for that.

''See, Jimmy, right after that night at Daisy Mae's there wasn't nothing that was going to keep me from offing you. I was gonna do it, Jimmy. I ain't kidding. Leon Hundley talked me out of it. You owe him one. But all I promised Leon was that I wasn't going to do you myself. I got to thinking about the call I got from Junior Gomez and I knew damn well you was too greedy to let that deal get by. And what Burista was going to do to you if he got to thinking you crossed him. Shit, having that Burista cat do you was even better than me doing it, 'cause them Colombians would let you hurt a little before they put you away.''

Jimmy said, ''I ain't believing this story.''

''You better believe it. Far as I go, there ain't no kind of dying too bad for you, Jimmy. But somethin's happened to me the last couple days that an asshole like you wouldn't understand. It has to do with—shit, caring about somebody, and that's a feeling that'll never get through to you. So I'm giving you one chance to bail your ass out. For three hundred grand.'' Size held up three thick freckled fingers.

The look was in Jimmy's eye. He understood, all right. He wasn't going to bullshit his way out of this. He stroked his moustache with a quick jerky motion. ''You're serious, ain'tcha?''

''Serious as fucking cancer. Now you go to your room and wait for me to call you. Be four, five hours.

You've got the cash, right here in Vegas. You wouldn't come all the way out here to see Burista without it. When I call, if you don't say, 'Yeah, it's a deal,' and then talk to me about how you're gonna get the money to me—well, then I'm making another call. To Burista. Then you're one dead motherfucker, Jimmy. You know that?"

"Now hold—just a—" Jimmy bent forward, his eyes slits. "You don't give no ultimatum to Pecos Jimmy. Don't nobody do that. I'm the man gives the orders, you know I am. One word from me, *poof*!"

He made a slashing motion across his Adam's apple with the edge of his hand. "There won't be enough left of you to cremate, you fuck with me. So don't—goddammit, Size, you sit down. You don't walk away. You hear that? I'm talking to you."

Size paused. He was two long strides away from the booth, toward the carpeted hallway outside the darkened lounge. There were no other customers. The bartender and the leggy cocktail girl interrupted their conversation and stared at them. Size said, "Yeah, I am, Jimmy. Walking away. Like I should have a long time ago. You got five hours, tops, until you hear from me." He turned to go, then stopped again. "Oh, and Jimmy. So you'll know. If it was just me, I wouldn't give a rat's ass for your three hundred grand. I'd rather see Burista nail your hands and feet down out in the desert and cut off your eyelids." He held up the paper bag he was carrying. "I got something right here that's worth more'n every dime you'll ever have, and if I showed it to you you'd be too blind to see what it was. So much as I'd like to see you dead, I'm hoping you decide to deal. Not for me, for somebody else. But you'll deal, I ain't worried. You ain't got the guts to go up against Burista, he ain't some poor sonofabitch what manages a pool hall back in Dallas. So don't miss my phone call, Jimmy. We're old pals, remember?"

By the time Size made it halfway through the Golden Nugget's casino toward the Fremont Street exit, he was giggling. He couldn't help it. He pictured the look on Jimmy's face and giggled even harder. A couple he passed—a cute blonde in hip-hugging jeans and a young brown-haired college-looking guy—gave him funny looks at first, then broke up laughing themselves. Hell, it must be catching. It was as though a five hundred pound weight had fallen off his shoulders. Jesus Christ, how could he ever have—Pecos Jimmy Fontenot, what a laugh. A blowhard wimp is all Jimmy was. Size kept a tight grip on Jessie's present as he did a little hop-step out to the baking sidewalk and dodged a couple of pedestrians on his way to the curb. He hailed a cab. Jessie'd be waking up from her afternoon nap pretty soon. Hell, he might even catch "Sesame Street" with her.

Sam of the FBI lounged against the doorjamb of the casino entrance to Yosemite Sam's Restaurant with his hands in his pockets. His slate-gray eyes moved from left to right as he watched Size move across the floor, past crap tables and slot machines, toward the Fremont Street exit. He muttered to Agent Stu Goalby of the Vegas office, "What's the big dumb sonofabitch laughing at? So he got a haircut. Looks like the Mex is telling the truth. It's him, Goalby. I'm not shitting you. Goddam, I feel like it's Christmas. Now don't lose him, Goalby. I want to know where the sonofabitch is going."

Goalby ran his fingers through his hair. He kept the little-boy grin on his face but sounded a little irritated as he said, "I'll follow your man, Sam. But let's don't make it an order, huh? You're a little out of your jurisdiction here."

"Yeah, guess you're right. Okay. Will you *please* get your ass in gear, and not lose the fucking guy?" Then, glancing behind him, Sam said, "Hey, stool pigeon. You're going with Goalby. We might need a fucking witness who ain't no lawman. And don't forget whose side you're on unless you want your nuts to hurt even more'n they already do. I ain't kidding, snitch. I'll turn you slap over to Burista if you fuck up."

Junior Gomez nodded, groaned softly, and limped off toward the exit. Agent Stu Goalby fell into step beside him. The two of them followed Size out to Fremont Street.

15

Merrillee carefully cut five yellow daphnes from her flower bed, leaving enough stalk so they would fit nicely into a ceramic vase. She sniffed their soft sweet fragrance. Then she held the clipping shears in her right hand and wiped the perspiration from her brow with the back of her wrist. Las Vegas had to be the hottest town in the world. Briefly, she tried to think of something nice about living here. She couldn't. What was it the diehards liked to say? Vegas is a wonderful place to live if you can keep from gambling? Well, what everloving else was there to do in this hellhole? Drink and gamble and wonder who your husband was sleeping with. She carried the flowers up on the redwood deck, and through the back door into the house. The refrigerated air inside chilled her.

On the TV screen in the den, Ernie and Bert were yelling at each other in animated voices. Something about whose turn it was to play with the rubber duckie. Jessie sat on the couch, her wide hazel eyes riveted in place, hypnotized. She was clutching the plastic toy Transformer-robot that Size had bought for her in her lap. Size was sprawled in an easy chair, a huge leg draped over the arm. Merrillee caught his eye and beckoned with her head. He got up and followed her into the kitchen. She set the flowers on the counter and turned to him. He brushed a lock of hair from her forehead and kissed her lightly on the lips. God, she felt so tiny when she was close to him. So protected.

She said, "What would I do about the house? I can't just—"

"Hey, doll. It don't have to be right now for you.

Just me. I'm the only one needs to leave right away. Matter of fact, it'll work a lot better for us if we don't leave town together. I'll go someplace safe, then be in touch. You can take your time about it, meet me in a few months."

She put her hand in his. "It seems crazy. That I can just—just drop everything and go with you. And Jessie. A change like that will affect a child so much more. Though I don't suppose Oscar would even notice we were gone. Or if he did, it would be a relief for him. He wouldn't have to worry about paying me. God, do you think we can really do it? And that nobody's going to—well, come for you?"

"Huh? Come for me?" He looked puzzled for an instant, knitting his red brows. Then his features relaxed and he said, "Aw. You mean the cops. Well, there ain't no charges against me anywhere, not now anyway. I don't have to worry about that. And I got me another name I can use, if I have to. There's the deal with the federal grand jury. But that'll blow over. Shit, once the Feds see they ain't going to be able to use me to get to Pecos Jimmy they'll just start looking around for somebody else to put the screws to. It ain't no big deal to them."

"How will we live?" Merrillee pivoted away from him and turned to face the sink, picking up a green vase in the shape of a swordfish and filling it with water.

From behind her he said, "That's why there's got to be this one last thing I'm gonna do. It's to set us up somewhere. So we won't have to worry for a while. Hey, babe." She felt a huge hand on her shoulder. He spun her gently around and put his arms around her. He could crush her like an egg if he wanted to. She was sure of it. "You with me?" he said.

She put her cheek in the hollow of his shoulder. "God knows I shouldn't be. But I am . . . we are. Jessie and I."

Merrillee said to Size, "How long is it going to take?"

He was lying on his side on the king-size, propped

up on one elbow. She was in the center of the bedroom, buttoning tan Jamaica walking shorts over black bikini briefs. He said, ''I don't know. I gotta call a guy in''—he glanced at the clock radio on the nightstand—''a half hour or so. Tell you the truth, I don't think very long. It'll probably be over tonight. Hey, you don't think you could hold off for another thirty minutes? Bringing Jessie home?'' He was looking at her bare breasts.

Merrillee laughed. This man who acted so rough and tough was so gentle at times it floored her. No cave-man bedroom tactics. Size acted as if it embarrassed him to talk about sex. He could only hint, not ask straight-out. She fastened her bra strap behind her back as she said, ''Wouldn't I love to. I don't know if we could live through another half-hour, but it'd be worth a try. But no. It's something you learn being a single mom. Judy Baxter next door is just great about letting me shuffle Jessie off to play with her little girl for short stretches. But if I wear out the welcome the invitation won't be there next time.'' She buttoned a white sleeveless blouse and stepped into brown sandal flats. ''I'll be back with the kid in a jiff. Try to have some pants on by then, will you?'' She batted her eyes and blew a kiss in his direction as she left the bedroom.

Merrillee noticed an extra spring in her step as she went down the front walk. A spring that she couldn't remember having been there since—well, just about the time she'd found out about Oscar and Miss Lay-Your-Husband. She never would've believed it. But it was happening, and it was making her feel good. Feel wanted.

She went next door to Judy Baxter's and stood on the front porch and knocked. The sound of children's laughter drifted through the front door to her. Jessie's voice was the loudest and happiest.

In the front seat of the yellow Thunderbird a half-block up the street, Junior Gomez sat up. He'd been bent over behind the dashboard. He said, ''She look this way?'' Merrillee stood about two hundred yards away, waiting on the front porch of a red-brick house with white trim. Her arms were folded and one sandaled foot was placed slightly in front of the other.

Agent Stu Goalby fiddled with the steering wheel. He was smoking a Marlboro. ''Nope. She doesn't even know we're here. Why? You know her?'' The T-bird's engine was idling and the A/C was blowing. Goalby had been letting it run long enough to cool off the car's interior, then killing the engine, and letting the radiator cool. A pop station was playing Stevie Wonder, ''I Just Called to Say I Love You.''

''Jesus Christ,'' Junior said. ''Yeah, I know her. Listen, I get through helping you guys, you going to put me in the witness program? I'm going to need it, man. If I tell you what I'm thinking about telling I'm going to need a new name, the works. I'll be dead, you don't protect me.''

Goalby took a final drag and stubbed his cigarette in the ash tray. ''You don't want much, do you? You come babbling to us about some yo-yo from Texas that Sam's got a hard-on for—so okay, you've done all right up to now. But the witness program? I don't know. You're a Dallas office stoolie, I guess you'll have to talk to Sam.''

Junior winced as he massaged his groin. ''You get me back downtown. Then you make a call to La Tuna prison in El Paso and ask about a guy who's supposed to be there. Only he ain't there, he's here in Vegas. I can give you this guy.''

''Well, I've got to admit, it's interesting,'' Goalby said.

Junior jabbed the air with a finger toward where Merrillee waited on the porch. As Goalby looked, the front door of the house opened and she went inside. Junior Gomez said, ''Oh, yeah. To make it work just right it's going to take some bait. That broad right there. She's it.''

As Size called the switchboard at the Golden Nugget and waited for the operator to put the call through to

Pecos Jimmy Fontenot's room, he wondered what the trick was going to be. There'd be one, you could bet on it. Some kind of bullshit. Some runaround that somebody as dumb as Jimmy figured Size to be would fall for.

A broad answered on the second ring. A soft nasal voice with just a hint of an East Texas junior college twang to it. Size knew the type. She said, "Hello. Mr. Fontenot's room."

"Yeah. Jimmy around?"

"Just a moment, please." She sounded like a receptionist. Probably had been one, at some time or another. If she was typical of what Jimmy usually went around with she'd be a tall flashy blonde, not much between the ears.

There was the tinkling sound of ice in a glass. Jimmy said, "Yeah."

"You get it?" Size said. Merrillee and Jessie paraded past the open bedroom door on their way to the kitchen. Size covered the phone's mouthpiece with his palm and gently shut the door.

Jimmy chuckled. "Well, sure I got it. It wasn't no problem. Say, Size, you sure you want to go through with this? You ain't going to be safe, you know that."

"I ain't? Hell, I'm going to be safer than working for you. Now I only got me to worry about. You got all of it? Right there?"

More ice tinkled and Size pictured Jimmy taking a swig from a tall glass. This time of day he'd be drinking a Tom Collins, and the smacking noise that Size now heard would be Jimmy sucking on the lime slice. Jimmy said, "Yeah, it's here. Now we need an open spot to meet. Somewhere quiet, out in the toolies. Where you can get what you want and I can get what you got. No sweat, nobody around."

Size sat down on the edge of Merrillee's bed. Outside the window the yellow daphnes shimmered in late afternoon heat. "Someplace nice and quiet—so Slim or Yucca or somebody can shoot me when I ain't looking? Jesus Christ, Jimmy. Ain't you got a better idea? Trouble with you is, you don't give nobody credit for knowing anything. Naw. There ain't going to be any meeting out in the toolies."

"Now just a fucking minute. You saying that Pecos Jimmy Fontenot ain't a man of his word? What I say you can bank on. How you think I got where I'm at? By going around bullshitting everybody?"

"Naw, Jimmy. You got where you're at getting a bunch of dumbos like me to do stuff for you. I ain't got time to jaw about who's going to trust who. So here's the way it's going to be. You put the dough in a briefcase and you give it to Slim. I'll meet him—aw, say that bar. Yeah, the same place where we was at. At six-thirty—that's an hour from now. He gives me the money, I give him a claim check. Thirty minutes after that, if the cash in the briefcase tallies up, I give you another call, tell you what the claim check's for. It'll get you the nose candy." There was one blackened cigarette butt in the ashtray on the nightstand. A faint lipstick smear was on the white filter. Size emptied the ashtray into the wastebasket.

Jimmy said, "So now I'm gonna trust you with three hundred grand? You and Slim? How the fuck I know you and the nigger won't go south with the money and the coke both? Maybe sell it in Dallas, huh?"

"Jimmy. You know 'cause I'm telling you. Me, Size Brandon. Me and Slim are the only two guys in the world ever shot one hundred percent straight with you. And I don't sell dope, you know that. You know I'll do what I say 'cause that's the way I do things. And you'll send Slim. You'll send him 'cause you're scareder of Burista than you are worried about me. I'll meet Slim in an hour, Jimmy. Don't fuck around on me, huh?"

Beaumont Gurney's shoulder sockets ached. So did his wrists. So did his head. The sock that was stuffed into his mouth tasted like the glue on the tape that was sealing his lips. He wished he'd never heard of Pecos Jimmy Fontenot. He wished he'd never even gone to law school in the first place.

Gurney was still tied in the red velvet chair. It was

now against the far wall of the hotel room where the two ya-hooing Pancho Villas—the skinny Latin and the short, muscled one—had moved it a little while ago. Yucca-baby was asleep on the floor with one wrist handcuffed to a leg of the bed. She was snoring. Tiny black hairs sprouted from her underarms. Dolores and Burista were on the king-size, he in tan boxer underwear and she in red bikini panties and push-up bra. They were passing a joint back and forth. The two thugs had gone out somewhere.

Dolores held the roach between a thumb and forefinger and pointed its end in Gurney's direction. "Hey, big lawyer-man. You like mari-jew-wana? Man, this good *shit*!" She took a drag and French-inhaled.

Gurney said, "Urrff. Umph." Meaning, fuck you.

Burista's feet were crossed at the ankles. His soles were grimy. His hands were clasped on his round belly. He glanced at the Colt .38 automatic that lay within arm's reach on the pillow. "I should shoot this fucking lawyer. All lawyers. A great man, greater than me even, was asked how to make the world a better place. He answered that first he would kill all the lawyers. He was right. So what you think, big lawyer? Should Emilio Garza Burista let you live, or kill you?" He picked up the gun and sighted down the barrel, aiming at Gurney's nose. Gurney closed his eyes.

The mattress quivered as Dolores bounced up on her haunches. "No. Not kill him now. First we finish this joint and then I give you blowjob. I want this big lawyer watch me give you blowjob. It turns me on for him to watch. Maybe I even pee on him, what you think?"

Burista looked thoughtful as he sucked hard on the joint, round cheeks puffing. The sickly sweet smell of the Colombian weed was everywhere. Gurney wondered dully if a hit of the marijuana would make the pain in his shoulder go away.

The bedside phone rang. Yucca-baby moaned softly and stirred on the floor as Dolores grabbed the receiver. " 'Allo?"

Her face screwed into a frown. She sat back against

the headboard and pinched the phone's cord between her fingertips. She listened, then said, "What you want? Hey, man, you got nerve calling here. You want to be dead?" She thrust the receiver at Burista. "It that fucking Junior Gomez. *El chingarro.*"

Burista said something in Spanish into the phone. He listened. His eyes widened, then narrowed. He looked at Gurney as he spoke in Spanish again. Gurney caught "*muerte.*" Dead. Dolores's eyebrows arched slightly. She looked from Burista to Gurney as she listened. Burista hung up, stood, and struggled into his pants—beige double-knit with wide short legs and a huge waist. He said something in Spanish to Dolores. She looked uncertain as she got out of bed and wiggled into her cut-offs and red halter top. Her lips were parted and her dark eyes big and round, as if in fear. Gurney felt cold pin pricks at the base of his spine.

Burista finished dressing, putting on polished tan loafers and a pink Polo pullover. Then he said loudly, "Pedro! Ramiro! *Andale!*"

The door to the suite opened and the two Latin thugs came in. The skinny one regarded Gurney with a half-smirk. His silenced Beretta hung at his side, held loosely in his right hand. Burista barked orders in Spanish—Gurney's breath caught in his windpipe as he heard "*muerte*" again—then firmly took Dolores by her arm and led her outside. She threw a parting wide-eyed look at Gurney as she disappeared into the hallway. The door closed quietly.

The short Latin's upper lip curled. He took two quick short strides and stood over Yucca-baby. He nudged her ribs with his toe. She moaned softly and stirred. Grinning as if he was enjoying himself, the stocky Latin shot her twice in the head. His arm jerked. The silencer spit orange flame. *Psst! Psst!* Yucca jerked once violently, then relaxed, and was still. Her final breath came in a long sigh. Dark blood oozed into her hair.

The thin Latin faced Gurney and raised his pistol. Gurney tried to yell, but couldn't. The sock and the tape muffled any sound he could make and his throat was constricted in terror. The Latin's hand recoiled. The first slug thudded solidly into Gurney's forehead. The flat slap of the bullet was the last thing Beaumont Gurney ever felt.

Henry Mitchell sat on the edge of a desk in the FBI's Vegas office and dusted his palms together. The slap of his hands was a little too loud. He needed more practice, to get the sound reduced to a light feathery brush. It was a subtle, impeccable move that Henry had seen F. Lee Bailey make in a New York courtroom just before he approached the jury with his closing argument. Style.

Mitchell pinched the bridge of his nose with a manicured thumb and forefinger as he said to Junior Gomez, "Is the trap baited?"

Junior took his hand away from the phone's receiver. He'd just hung up. He buttoned the third button of his green satin shirt. The gold Cabeza de Vaca medallion on his chest disappeared from view. Junior said, "Huh?"

"Is the trap baited? What did our man say?" Henry was wearing a navy suit, white shirt, and maroon tie. He didn't wear solid black anywhere except in the courtroom. Too much power for everyday wear.

"Oh. I dig. Yeah, well he didn't say much. But he's going. On his way, right now." Junior was sitting in a straight wooden chair with a slatted back, against the wall at the end of the desk. A tan metal paper-shredder was next to him. He leaned an elbow on it.

Agent Stu Goalby sat behind the desk in a swivel chair, his feet propped up on the desktop. He was reading a U. S. government memorandum that the secretary—a squat, gray-haired woman in granny glasses and black lace-up, low-heeled shoes—had brought in. He offered the memo across the desk to Mitchell, saying, "Read this over, Mr. Mitchell. Just your initials will do. We're letting you call the shots on this one because it's your case. But if we're going to put innocent citizens in danger I want my file documented as to who gave the order, sir. I'm sure you understand."

Mitchell took the memo and looked it over. Hesitantly, he said, "My initials?"

"Yes, sir, right down there at the bottom," Goalby said. "I'm sure there won't be any problems, but you never know."

Mitchell adjusted the knot on his tie and cleared his throat. "Yes, of course. Tell you what, Agent. I've got a call in to my chief prosecutor back in Big D. Jesus Christ, I'm sure it's okay. Emilio Garza Burista, right here in Vegas. What wouldn't I give to have seen the look on that La Tuna warden's face. As soon as the chief gives the okay, I'll sign for you. Fair enough?" The memo fluttered down to rest faceup on the desktop.

Goalby cocked his head to one side. He licked his lips. He opened his mouth to say something.

From across the ten-by-fifteen office, Sam said, "Fuck, Henry. I'll sign it. Lemme have it." He got up from the low cloth divan and crossed the tile floor. He borrowed Goalby's black pushbutton U. S. government ballpoint and scribbled his name on the bottom of the memo. As he handed the memo to Goalby, Sam glared at Mitchell. Goalby checked the signature, then added the memo to his file.

16

Size decided to drive Merrillee's Mustang downtown to the Golden Nugget for his meeting with Slim Burdine. He wanted to leave the pickup—and its payload, lined up neatly in double thicknesses of paper underneath the camper cover—right where it was for the time being, and he didn't want to chance any more taxi drivers getting a good look at him. He'd discarded the Beatle wig and his crew-cut red hair stood out like quills. The dye was gone from his busy eyebrows; they were again their natural fire engine color.

He told Merrillee at the front door that he didn't want her to go into work tonight.

Her soft forehead puckered in concern as she said, "I don't know, Size. I left early last night. They're going to start wondering what's wrong."

He took a moment to watch her, trying to memorize every smooth clear inch of her face. He touched her graceful neck. "Look, doll. If this comes out the way I think it will you ain't going to be working there no more anyway. There's guys downtown at the Golden Nugget that I don't want within a mile of you. Not just the spics, either. Some other guys, too. Besides. If you're gonna be my—my girl, I don't want you working as a cocktail waitress. You got too much class."

She laughed softly. "Well, if you don't beat everything I ever saw. Don't get me wrong, I love your wanting to protect me. It gets me right down to my toes. But here you're going off to deal with no telling what kind of characters, on no telling what kind of business—and you're worried about me being a *cocktail waitress*? Talk about double standard. Criminy."

"Yeah? Well, maybe that's what it is," he said. "But that's the way I feel. Listen, you and Jessie stay put until I get back, okay? And you won't go to work?"

She looked dubious, but said that she wouldn't. Size kissed her gently on the lips and went down the sidewalk and started the Mustang. She was still on the porch as he left, the long perfect brown legs, soft auburn hair reflecting sunlight like a halo. Size remembered dreaming about broads like her. He thought that if he'd always had Merrillee he probably never would have been in trouble with the law. Might have gone to medical school, been a doctor or something.

Downtown he parked the Mustang in the self-service garage next door to the Golden Nugget. He got out of the car and closed the door. He was wearing his new windbreaker, the Luger holstered snug against his rib-cage. His footsteps echoed off the parking garage's bare concrete walls on his way to the elevator. Downstairs he exited into the searing heat. There was a crowd, there always was in Vegas. Across the street in the sportsbook, perhaps a dozen people waited to get their bets down.

Size checked his watch as he went through the Golden Nugget's rear entrance. He was fifteen minutes early. Good, he wanted to be waiting when Slim got there.

There was a different bartender, this one a tall, soft-looking black guy with receding salt-and-pepper hair. He was picking up bottles one by one from the counter underneath the back-of-the-bar mirror, checking the level of the whiskey, then writing something down on a spiral pad. The leggy brunette cocktail waitress was gone. In her place was a short peppy redhead with thighs that were fleshy but firm. The four-to-midnight, swing shift crew, part of the twenty-four-hour Vegas action. There were two other customers, both seated at the bar—a young guy who looked out of place in a suit and tie and a slender, thirtyish blonde in leopard pants. Size thought she was probably a hooker. The young guy beckoned timidly in her direction. She slid expertly two stools over and sat by him. The bartender ignored them.

The redhead jiggled over to Size—he'd flopped into the same booth where he'd met with Pecos Jimmy earlier—and put a small square napkin down in front of him and smiled expectantly. He started to order a beer, then changed his mind. He tried plain quinine water, the drink that Benny Sands used to order when he was on the wagon. It tasted like medicine.

Size didn't have long to wait. At 6:25, Slim sauntered into the lounge carrying a brown leather satchel. He slowly looked around, as if he had all the time in the world, then spotted Size in the booth. With his free hand, Slim tilted his Stetson to show his ebony forehead. Then he shot Size with an imaginary pistol, his index finger serving as the barrel and his thumb as the hammer. Grinning, Slim strolled over and sat in a chair across from Size. He put the satchel on the carpet by his right boot.

"You making a gutsy call, Sizemo'," Slim said. "I thought about it myself, lotsa times. You got more insides than Slim, big honkie." The waitress started to come over, but Slim sent her away with a casual wave, then said to Size, "So here we are. Couple dirty ole dogs, huh?"

Size picked up his glass and made circles in the frost with his thumb. "You shouldn't have let him try to do me, Slim. It's what killed poor old Benny, nobody trying to stop Jimmy. Wasn't no call for it, you know that. You going to leave the satchel?"

Slim leaned forward and put his elbows on the table. His eyes narrowed. "You hold yo' fuckin' horses, boy. Blowing up yo' car wasn't none of my play. I sight near quit Jimmy that night, right there. It was Yucca and that dope freak Tommy—shit, you already know that. I tole Jimmy straight-out you didn't talk to no grand jury."

"I can't take you off the hook for it, Slim. You still riding shotgun. Like I say, you leaving the satchel?"

Slim gave a little snort, then shoved the satchel underneath the table with the toe of his boot. Size picked it up and put it on the seat next to him. It felt heavy. Slim said, "Sho, I still riding. What else I'm going to do? Guys like you and me, we get in a rut, bro'."

Size looked at his folded hands, then back at Slim. The lights from the bar and the hallway were behind Slim, his expression hidden in shadow. Size said, "Slim. You ever had a good woman?"

"What's good? I had a coupla whores didn't knock down anything. That's good, I reckon." He chuckled silently, his head bobbing slightly up and down. "It's a broad, huh? Shit, I mighta guessed. Ain't nothing going to do in a man like you, 'ceptin' a broad."

There wasn't much that Size could say to that. He fumbled in his pocket, his bicep squeezing the holstered Luger through the fabric of the windbreaker, and handed Slim a small pasteboard claim check. Size had torn the writing off the end. He said, "The stuff's in the bed of a pickup. It's under a camper-cover. I'm going to call Jimmy in a half hour and tell him where the truck's parked. If the money tallies, I'm going to call." He patted the satchel. Visible over Slim's right shoulder, an old man with a walker went down the carpeted hallway in the direction of the casino. In the distance, the P. A. announcer was calling out a string of Keno numbers.

Slim stuffed the ticket in the pocket of his jeans without looking at it. "You know, the money's going to add up, Sizemo'. Shit, bro', Slim brought it to you."

"Yeah?" Size almost grinned. "Yeah, it's going to tally. I might not even count it. The half hour's to make sure nobody's following me when I leave here." He took a quick sip of the tonic water, then set the glass down and kept his gaze on it as he said, "You going to come for me?"

Slim reached in his breast pocket for a toothpick and let it droop from the corner of his lips. He regarded Size through half-lidded eyes. "Maybe. If not me, somebody. Pecos Jimmy's gonna send a cat, you can bet on it. I been thinking about it. If Jimmy tells me to—hell, I'd be lying if I told you what I'd do. I might tell Jimmy, fuck off. Then I might come, depends on how I feel. I know the man looks for you's got trouble. He wouldn't have no chance, 'cept for your broad.''

Size raised his eyebrows. ''What you mean?''

''If it's just you, just Size Brandon, I don't know anybody's got a chance, man. Unless it's me, I might have a pretty good one. But you going to be looking out for the broad, more'n you are yourself. That's going to make it easier for whoever wants you. Them lady friends can get a man dead.'' He moved the toothpick from one corner of his mouth to the other. ''Between you and me, I'm all for you, babe. Hey, man. You my pool-playin' buddy. I don't want nothing happening to you.''

It surprised Size a little. For a second he thought Slim was putting him on. But no, Slim was dead serious. But that wouldn't keep him from coming, balls-out, if he set his mind to it. Size gripped the satchel by its handle and stood. ''Don't bother tryin' to follow, huh? You'll be wastin' your time.''

''Hey, don'tcha think I know that?'' Slim said. ''Besides, following you won't get us the nose candy. That's the main thing. You sho had Jimmy figured, man. Only one knows how scared Pecos Jimmy is of that Burista cat is Jimmy's laundry man. You stay cool, Sizemo'. Keep yo' head straight, you might make it.'' He winked and touched the brim of his hat in a salute.

Size took a step in the direction of the exit, then paused. ''You, too, man. Shit, who knows? One day I might show you a couple combinations on the nine ball you ain't learned.''

Size left, shuffling along in a slight swagger, carrying the satchel as though it was loaded with feathers. Slim watched him go, then got up. He pointed a goodbye index finger in the direction of the redhead. She wrinkled her nose at him. Slowly, casually, Slim strolled out of the cocktail lounge and down the hall toward the casino. He was shaking his head and chuckling to himself.

* * *

Jessie squealed, "Higher, Mom!" Then, feeling the ropes slacken and grow taut at the top of the swing's arc, she yelled breathlessly, "That's too high, Mom! That's too *high*!"

Merrillee caught her daughter around the waist, then made the swing's arc a little smaller. "How's that, darling? Better?" Jessie squealed and giggled that it was.

They were in the backyard, Merrillee's bare feet in cool mown grass. She tried to remember the last time she'd played with Jessie here. She couldn't. Oscar had erected the wooden swing set when Jessie was three. Merrillee had forgotten what a pleasure the backyard was as the sun set and cool dusk gathered, the six-foot stockade fence shutting out the rest of the world. She and Jessie hadn't had much privacy lately.

The shift boss at the Golden Nugget hadn't been happy about Merrillee's not coming to work, especially, he'd said, since he'd had to cover for her the night before. She felt a twinge of conscience about the guy's annoyance, but right now she had more important things on her mind.

She'd made up her mind to quit vascillating about Size. Face it, she was falling for the guy. Above everything else, more important even than what he'd told her about himself, she had no doubt that she could believe every word the big man said to her. That mattered so much. And yes, she might be letting herself in for a lot of heartache. But more so than with Oscar? Hell, Oscar couldn't even keep his wedding vows, how could anybody believe anything else he had to say? No, for better or worse, the die was cast where Size was concerned. So quit worrying about it, dummy, she thought.

"Mom! You're not pushing," Jessie said. She was pumping with her legs, trying to swing higher.

Merrillee came out of her trance and gave Jessie a little shove, sliding into the effort with a stepping motion. As she did, the gate in the stockade fence creaked and swung open.

Merrillee was so busy with her thoughts and pushing Jessie that it took an instant for the sound of the gate to register. It was as if the sound of the gate opening was in the background, not in the same yard with her and Jessie.

Finally she looked. Two Latin guys were standing there, one thin, the other short and barrel-chested and wearing a pink sleeveless muscle shirt. The skinny guy was watching her with an expression that she could only describe as an oily leer. He was pointing a pistol at her. There was a blue steel extension attached to its muzzle.

Merrillee gasped. In a reflex action she caught Jessie on the backswing and hugged her daughter to her chest.

The thin Latin's eyes were like lumps of dull coal. He gestured with the pistol. "Let the keed down slow, missy. Do it now." His thick Spanish accent was a monotone.

Slowly, Merrillee lowered Jessie to the ground. Jessie stepped out of the swing and clutched Merrillee's hand. Her hazel eyes were wide as saucers. "Are they bad men, Mommy?" She hadn't called her mother "Mommy" in over a year. "Mom" sounded more grown-up, she'd said.

"Shh. It'll be all right, darling. You mind Mommy," said Merrillee, praying that her tone had a lot more conviction than she felt right now. Panic welled in her throat like bile. The burly thug was holding his hand behind his back. Now he brought it into view. He had a pistol with a silencer, just like the other guy's.

The thin Latin said something in Spanish that Merrillee tried to decipher but couldn't. The muscular guy listened, adjusting the hem of his shirt with his free hand. He was wearing navy shorts, his legs like hairy tree trunks, and brown leather sandals. He nodded to the thin guy and went back outside the gate. The thin guy stepped closer.

"You going to take me on a tour of your house now, missy. You some good-looking broad, so don' make me mess you face up none." Only his jaw moved. His lips under his moustache stayed in place, like a talking dummy.

Merrillee kept a tight hold on Jessie's hand and moved up on the redwood deck toward the back door. The Latin kept the gun at waist level as he followed. Jessie began to make choking sounds, then burst into tears.

"What is it, Mommy?" Jessie said between sobs. "Make him stop, Mommy. He's scaring me."

The Latin took two quick heavy steps on the deck and grabbed Jessie's arm. "I said be quiet, little girl," he hissed.

Merrillee turned to face him, fire in her eyes. She was conscious of the pistol in his grasp, but right now even the gun didn't scare her. "You take your hands off her. If you don't, so help me I'm going to scream at the top of my lungs."

He locked gazes with her for an instant. Then he glanced away. He released his hold on Jessie, stepped back and leveled the pistol. He was looking at Merrillee now, but his tone lost some of its authority as he said, "Then you keep her quiet, missy. Inside now. Move."

In the den, Merrillee stood stiffly erect on the carpet and rested her hands on Jessie's shoulders. Jessie's sobbing had subsided, but her little shoulders were trembling. The Latin kept the pistol ready as he stepped into the kitchen and looked around, his dark eyes moving from side to side. Then he went to the bedroom door. He waved the gun. "This looks good enough. You and the keed go sit on the bed. Stay where I can watch you, huh?"

She hesitated. "Look, I don't have much money here. There is some jewelry—"

"Shut up, missy! You making me tired."

Goose bumps rose on Merrillee's forearms as she took Jessie and sat next to her on the bed. The Latin stayed in the bedroom doorway, alternating his gaze in the direction of the back door, then at the bed where Merrillee and Jessie sat. Jessie's eyes now had a dull glaze, as if she was in shock. Merrillee hugged her daughter's shoulders. Oh, God, honey, if Mommy could just—

The sound of the back door opening came to her.

A voice that sounded vaguely familiar to Merrillee said something in Spanish, the sound muffled slightly by the wall that separated the bedroom from the den. As he listened, the thin guy in the bedroom doorway lowered his gun to his side, his expression one of respect—or was it fear? He stepped aside. A short and pudgy Latin came into the bedroom, stopped, and grinned at her.

At first glance Merrillee didn't recognize the guy, just realized that she'd seen him somewhere. He scratched a clipped gray sideburn. His fleshy arms were bare beyond the sleeves of his shirt. Then the scene from the other night flashed in her mind—the pretty-handsome one, Junior, rolling and groaning and clutching at his testicles, the pudgy little man babbling at her in fearful, incoherent Spanish—and a tingling sensation darted upward from the base of her spine. The nape of her neck felt pricked by a hundred icicles.

He said, "Are you comfortable?" in perfect but accented English. His mouth was smiling, but it was the grin of the dead. His eyes were like black holes in his face.

Now a woman came in to stand beside him, a full-bodied Mexican girl in tight jean shorts and a breast-hugging halter top. She had a full pouty mouth. She was half a head taller than the guy, and she put her arm around his waist. "Hey, baby. Who this chick?"

The guy started talking to her in Spanish—Merrillee remembered that he hadn't spoken any English the other night—and the girl's dark eyes widened as she glanced back and forth from him to Merrillee. Still babbling a rapid stream of Spanish, he took a short step and swung his pudgy leg in a kicking motion. The girl began to giggle, hugging herself, her shoulders heaving, her breasts jiggling.

The girl said to Merrillee, "You let Junior have it in *gonad*? Hey, girl, you *okay*!"

The pudgy guy's expression grew solemn. "I am

not a man who holds grudges,'' he said in English. ''So I will be benevolent. I want what your large red-headed friend took from me. Then I am prepared to—is it to 'let bygones be bygones'? Is that what you Americans say?''

The Mexican girl stuck out one round hip. ''Best for you to listen to him, sweetie. That monster red-headed guy, he your boyfren'? Man, he took a lotta cocaine the other night.'' She pointed a red-nailed finger at Burista. ''You not know this guy, chick. But I gonna tell you. You not be okay for long, you don't come up with his toot.''

Merrillee scooted a little closer to Jessie and hugged her daughter tighter.

Size went out on the Strip and made the call from Circus-Circus because he'd never seen the place before. He left the satchel with the money inside locked in the Mustang's trunk, strolled leisurely out of the parking lot, up the huge stone steps, and through the hissing electronic glass doors out of the fading afternoon heat into the coolness of the carpeted lobby.

He spent a good half hour just wandering around, looking at the trained doggie act, deciding that the magician, who was sawing a girl in half, was doing it with mirrors. He craned his neck and stared goggle-eyed at the flying trapeze act. A short dark girl with huge muscular thighs, wearing a red sequinned shorty costume, did double somersaults from one rope swing to the other. Two guys in faggy-looking tights who lifted weights a lot stood on the launching platform, flexed their pectorals, and flew high above the crowded casino floor. Man, wouldn't little Jessie go nuts in here?

The extra fifteen minutes he took on purpose, picturing Pecos Jimmy Fontenot huddled by the phone in his hotel room, sweat beading on his forehead. Hell, let Jimmy worry for a while. He had a lot of worry coming to him.

It was almost eight o'clock when he went back into

the lobby and used the wall phone by the check-in desk. He could see through the glass entryway into the parking lot. The sun was setting fast and the shadow from Circus-Circus's massive bulk extended nearly all the way to Las Vegas Boulevard. Size held the receiver close to his ear, kept the cut-off button depressed with his forefinger and glanced around him. The desk clerk, a tall thin girl in a lavender Circus-Circus employee's outfit, had an expression similar to any other desk clerk in any other luxury hotel anywhere in the world. Bored to death. She was thumbing through a *People* magazine with a grinning cover photo of Princess Di in a filmy blue dress; next to Di's waist was a headshot of Prince Charles. Size thought that Bonnie Prince Charlie looked mad as hell. He released the button, dialed the number of the Golden Nugget, and leaned his big shoulder against the wall while the other line rang. He was suddenly tired.

Pecos Jimmy said, "Man, where you been?"

"It's at Five-thirty-two Nevada Lane, Jimmy. That's a storage lot. The stuff's in the bed of the pickup, under a camper-cover."

"Slow down. What's the address again?"

"I'll give it once more, and you better get it. Five-three-two Nevada Lane. The claim check you got is for the truck. And this is the last time you're gonna hear from me. Let me alone, Jimmy. You fuck with me, you ain't going to like it."

"Size, you sonofa—"

Size hung up, feeling a lot better. He was thinking about the Flying Whatchamacallits on the trapeze as he called Merrillee. He was gonna bring her here. Jessie, too.

After the third ring, Merrillee said, "Hello?" Size caught the barest tremor in her voice and a tiny alarm went off inside his head.

"Merrillee? Hey, you like the circus?"

There were ten long seconds of silence. Finally she said, "Someone wants to talk to you. God, darling, please don't—" He heard her sharp intake of breath, picturing the phone snatched from her hand. She'd called him "darling." The fear in her tone made him forget that.

A syrupy male voice with a Spanish accent said, "It's a shame we haven't met. If you will bring my belongings to me here we can have a nice friendly chat. If you do not—well, then, I am afraid that this lady and this little girl who are with me are going to have some hard times."

Size gripped the receiver until his knuckles showed white.

"Heat?" said Pecos Jimmy Fontenot. "*Heat!?* Man, you ain't seen no heat like I'm going to put on that big red-headed sonofabitch. I mean it, Slim. He's dead. He don't know it yet—he's still walking around. But he's fucking dead."

A slow-moving elevator was lifting them from the ground floor to the third level of the parking garage at Five-three-two Nevada Lane. The elevator walls were pale yellow. The paint was chipped. Jimmy looked at the green receipt he'd gotten from the attendant. He tore it into tiny pieces and let them flutter down to rest on the floor. "Jesus Christ, couldn't the big dumb bastard pick a cheaper place? Remind me to check on this parking racket. Might be something to muscle into."

Slim had his shoulder against one wall and his hands jammed into his back pockets. His Stetson was tilted sideways. His gaze on the toes of his boots, he said, "Boss Jimmy, I wouldn't be countin' Size dead. You think it's going to be easy finding somebody to go up against his mean ass? Shee-it. It be harder than you think it is."

The doors opened and they walked on to smooth concrete, footsteps echoing. The garage's levels were slanted, rows of cars and trucks headed nose-in to bare, unpainted cement walls. From somewhere below a horn honked. Its sound reverberated.

The blue and white pickup's rear was visible about halfway up the ramp, between a green Eldo and a yellow Porsche. The attendant had given the truck's keys to Jimmy, and he took them from his pocket and jingled them as he and Slim approached.

Slim said, "How come we don't leave the truck where it's at? Shit, Burista can come and get it easy as we can."

Jimmy stuck the key in the lock that opened the camper-cover. "I'm thinking. First I want to make sure the powder's here. And maybe we better get the shit to Burista before he—Jesus Christ, it ain't even locked. Talk about dumb—" He turned the handle and the camper's door swung open.

Size Brandon sat up from behind the fastened tailgate, extended the Luger, and put its barrel against Jimmy's nose.

Jimmy froze. "Jesus Christ. Now I seen fucking everything."

Slim kept his bored expression but moved fast, bending from the waist, grabbing his pantsleg below the knee. Size pivoted his shoulder, keeping his arm extended, and swung the Luger to his right to point at Slim's kneecap. "You're kidding, ain't you? Take it out slow and give it here."

Slim hesitated, figuring his chances, then shrugged and grinned. He raised his pantsleg a little at a time, dug inside his boot and came out with a two-shot Derringer. He held the two-barreled pistol gingerly and handed it to Size, grip first. Then he stood and spread his hands, palms down. "Sizemo'. How you doing? Boss Jimmy was jes' talking about looking you up, man."

Size tucked the Derringer in his waistband and rose up into a crouch. Behind him, heavy paper bags were visible, lined in neat rows in the pickup bed. He swung a leg over the tailgate and put his foot on the rear bumper. Keeping the Luger trained on a point between Jimmy and Slim, he climbed down to stand on the ground. "Hey, Jimmy. I'm gonna borrow the truck." He held out a big freckled hand.

Jimmy shrugged and handed over the keys. "This

is crazy. Craziest fucking thing I ever seen. Man, how come you called me in the first place? Whyn't you just take the coke and haul ass? You just wanted to stick me up, or what?''

" 'Cause something happened I ain't got time to tell you about. Both of you, now, you put your hands on that wall over there.'' Size waved the Luger.

Jimmy and Slim looked at each other, then back at Size. Slim had a crooked grin on his face. Jimmy in the lead, they followed Size's direction to the bare concrete wall at the pickup's nose and flattened their palms against it. Slim's shoulders were shaking in laughter. He murmured, ''Well, I'm a sonofabitch.''

Pecos Jimmy kept his gaze on the blank gray wall in front of him and listened. Size's faint rubber-soled footsteps retreated, then came closer again. Something dropped on the concrete between Jimmy's feet, something that landed heavily.

Jimmy turned his head to one side. ''What the fuck was that?''

''It's the satchel with your money,'' Size said. ''Hell, I ain't *robbing* you, for Christ's sake.''

Jimmy started to turn around but felt the Luger prod his back and turned his face back to the wall. ''You're shitting me. You're sticking me up and you're gonna give my money back. Jesus Christ.''

''Just shut up, Jimmy. Just 'cause I don't want to rob nobody don't make me crazy. You just stand there and play like a fucking statue.''

The footsteps retreated again and the pickup's door opened and slammed. Its engine coughed, then roared into life. Tires squealed and echoed as Size backed out, put the truck in forward gear, and peeled out for the exit.

As the sound of the truck's engine receded, Jimmy turned. Slim was watching the pickup disappear around a curve, headed down to the first level. Only the squealing sound of its tires remained. Slim looked at Jimmy, the gold tooth in his wide-open mouth glinting.

"He's absolutely fucking nuts," Jimmy said. "Shit, he belongs up there with Hinckley. That's where Size belongs, right there in the same cell with the guy who shot the president."

17

Size had thought long and hard before he decided to turn the money over to Pecos Jimmy. Jimmy'd think that was pretty dumb, giving the money back. So what else was new? Hell, Jimmy thought that *everything* Size did was pretty dumb, had thought that way ever since they'd shot marbles together in a dusty country schoolyard back in Commerce. Size didn't care what Jimmy thought anymore.

But giving the money back had to do with Merrillee. And Jessie, too—hell, he'd already begun to think of them as his family even though he didn't figure he really had the right to. The money was for them, not for him. Without them Size didn't want a penny of it. If anything happened to Merrillee or to Jessie, Size was going to kill Jimmy. It was that simple, and there wasn't anything going to stop him. If he could somehow get them out of this—he was actually *praying* about it, that's how bad he wanted them to be okay—then he'd go to Jimmy and take the three hundred grand back again. Jimmy wouldn't give it up easy, of course. But Size would get it, you could bet on it. He steered the pickup off the freeway on to Merrillee's street, keeping a firm grip on the steering wheel.

The truck bumped and rattled over asphalt repairs in the pavement between well-mowed lawns. In the daylight, the grass in Merrillee's yard looked to him to be greener than that in the others, but in the growing darkness the lawns were all the same color. Two sprinklers—a pulsating rotary and a vascillating golf course Lawn King shooting a twenty-yard spray skyward—were turned on in the block. A black Cadillac limo was pulled to the curb in front of Merrillee's. Its rear windows were pitch black and a chrome antenna sprouted from the center of its trunk. That would be Burista's rental car. Hell, Burista probably didn't know there was any other make. Size resisted the impulse to slam on the brakes and go charging through the front door with the Luger ready, but gave the pickup a little gas and kept on going. He wanted to give the neighborhood the once-over. You never knew.

There were a few more cars in the block, parked in driveways. A couple of houses past Merrillee's, a yellow Thunderbird sat idling at the curb. Its nose was pointed in the direction from which Size had come. There was a guy sitting behind the wheel. Size slowed as he went past and squinted into the T-bird's interior, but he couldn't make out the driver's features in the dark. He went on by and watched the Thunderbird in the pickup's rearview. Red lights brightened and dimmed as the guy hit the brake pedal, then let off. Might be something, might be nothing. Size came to the end of the block and turned right.

There was an alley bisecting the side street, and Size herded the pickup on to its narrow surface. He moved slowly, alternating between the brake and gas, steering around trash cans. Once he had to stop for a big black tomcat who took his time, stared at the pickup, then moved on. Each house had a high wood fence in back. They were all alike. Jesus, how was he going to—? Air escaped from his lungs as he recognized the top parallel bar on Jessie's swing set. That's how. He continued up the alley, drove back around to the front of the house, pulled to the curb behind the limo and cut the engine. He got out, started to lock the door, then changed his mind. He gave the butt of the Luger a final pat through his windbreaker and ambled up the sidewalk to the front door. He rang the bell.

Sized glanced up and down the street, then turned and looked at the house across the way. The gazebo was dark. Funny. He was pretty sure there'd been a light on over there last night. Suddenly, from somewhere off to his right, a cricket started a high-pitched buzz. It startled him and his hand jumped involuntarily toward the Luger. The handle turned and the door behind him opened. He relaxed and faced it.

He took one step toward the door, then stopped. A skinny Latin guy with black sideburns and a pencil moustache was framed in the glow from the overhead hallway light. An Uzi was cradled in his thin right arm, its snout pointed at Size's midsection.

The guy took his time about looking Size over from head to toe. "Man, they said you were big. They weren't shitting. Come on in and grab some wall, kitty-cat."

"Kitty-cat"? Jesus Christ. Roman Polanski, the midget in *Chinatown*. Cut Jack Nicholson's nose. He ignored the Uzi and spread the front of his jacket open. "I got one Luger, kitty-cat. And I ain't grabbing no fucking wall. Where's Burista?" Slim's Derringer was still tucked in his waistband, around to one side, out of sight.

It worked. The guy hesitated for an instant, then held the machine gun against Size's belly and back-handed the Luger from its holster. He hefted the pistol in his left hand, glanced at it. Then he lowered the machine gun and pointed the Luger. "Hey. Nice piece. Old but nice." He raised his upper lip and bared his front teeth in a weird-looking grin.

For a second Size couldn't figure out what the fuck the guy was doing. Then he got it. "Jesus Christ. Al Pacino, *Scarface*. You been practicing the jerky-looking grin, right? You been to too many movies, pal. Next you'll be flipping a fucking nickel. George Raft. Cut the bullshit and show me Burista, huh?"

The guy looked disappointed. He shrugged and gestured with the pistol toward the den. Size shook his head and mumbled as he went by.

Burista was seated on the couch with his legs crossed. He held a Coors in one pudgy hand. Dolores was snuggled close to him, her legs drawn up under her. She looked at Size with her eyebrow arched and ran her tongue tip over her parted lips.

Size said, ''Hiya. What happened to Junior? He run out of money?''

She yawned. ''You still *pendejo,* big man.''

Burista said something to the skinny guy in Spanish—Size caught the name Ramiro. Ramiro nodded, shrugged, and lowered the guns. He went back to guard the front door. He didn't look happy about what Burista had said to him. Burista said to Size, ''We meet at last. You've been trouble to me. Did you bring my merchandise?''

Size glanced toward the bedroom door. ''Mr. Burista, the only reason your boy out there ain't wearing that Uzi for a necktie is 'cause I ain't seen Merrillee yet. Now if I don't see her in about ten seconds some shit's going to start that you ain't going to like.''

Burista was a man who wasn't used to being talked to like that. He frowned, started to get up. Then he relaxed and smiled. ''Have it your way for now. She's fine. So is the little girl. You want to see them? Please. Go on in.'' He raised a chubby arm and gestured toward the bedroom. As Size walked in that direction, Burista said, ''I'm humoring you. After you see her you are going to give me what is mine. Otherwise it is you who won't like what's going to happen.'' Size didn't act as though he heard. He went into the bedroom, his heart thudding against his breastbone.

Merrillee was sitting with her back against the headboard of the bed, her long brown legs stretched out. Jessie was asleep, lying on her side with her head in her mother's lap. There was a half-smile on Jessie's baby face, like a cherub. Merrillee lips parted in surprise, her gaze flickered to the far corner of the room.

Another Latin guy was seated in the corner. He was straddling a chair, his arms crossed on top of the chairback. He was a chunky, burly guy. His expression said he thought he was a lot tougher than he was. He started to rise.

''I think your mother wants you,'' Size said. ''Out in front.'' Then he raised his voice and said, ''Hey, Burista. You want to talk to this dude, don't you?''

The guy rose all the way to his feet and took a long

stride in Size's direction. He was sneering. Size snorted. "Jesus Christ, what movie *you* seen?"

From the other room, Burista shouted in English, "All right, Pedro. Leave them for a while. You have five minutes, Mr. Brandon."

Pedro kept on sneering. He swaggered past Size and out the door, his shoulders rotating around his spine. When Pedro was gone, Size sank down on the edge of the king-size. The mattress sagged under him. He reached out and touched Merrillee's smooth cheek. Jessie stirred slightly, but kept on with her slow, even breathing.

"We ain't got long. They didn't hurt you?" Size said.

Merrillee squeezed his hand as it lay alongside her cheek. "No. So far, we're fine. Whatever is happening? My God, they came right in the backyard and— The thin guy out in front has carried enough guns in here to start a war. Who *are* they?" She sounded more angry than scared.

Size hung his head. "I shouldna let you get mixed up with me. Seems everything I try to do gets screwed up. They ain't nice guys, I'll tell you that. I swear to God, babe, I don't know how they found you."

She pinched his chin between her thumb and forefinger and raised his face to a level with hers. "Hey, stop it. I'm the one who threw in with you, remember? Nobody forced me to. Are we going to be able to get out of this? The three of us?" She stroked Jessie's hair.

His gaze steadied. "Yeah. We're going to. I got something they want. As soon as I give it to them they'll go away."

"Do you know they will? How do you know they won't just take whatever it is and then—" For the first time there was fear in her voice.

"They'll go," Size said. "You gotta understand these kinda guys. They don't think no more of killing somebody than swatting a fly. But they ain't crazy. It's just business with them. They got no reason to kill us once they get what they want." He leaned forward and gently kissed her, then stood. "It'll be over in a minute, babe. Hang tough, huh?"

He went to the doorway and signaled Burista. In a few seconds, Burista's round head appeared around the doorjamb. He smiled at Merrillee, then raised his eyebrows to Size. Size went over to stand by the bed. He carefully arranged a lock of hair on Merrillee's forehead, then said to Burista, "See that? I'm gonna take one of your coolies out to the truck and load the stuff into your car. If anybody's so much as moved that hair on her head when I get back, you got trouble, pal."

These guys Pedro and Ramiro were a couple of pieces of work. First the skinny guy, Ramiro, told Size and Pedro to stay inside the house while he checked out the lay of the land. Then he went out on the porch, a Latin guy peering up and down the street carrying an Uzi in the crook of his arm. Jesus Christ, this was supposed to be a nice quiet neighborhood and here's a guy walking around on the front porch carrying a machine gun. Size figured it would be a miracle if he and Pedro make it to the pickup without somebody calling the cops. Ramiro came back inside and said with a satisfied look that the coast was clear. Size and Pedro walked down the front walk, side by side.

Pedro was a horse of a different color. Figured he was Franco Columbo or one of those other famous body builders, flexing his pectorals and jutting his shoulders as he strutted along. At least the guy had sense enough to put the Beretta in his pocket, Size had to give him that much credit. But the clue to being a good sidekick to a guy like Burista was to blend in with the scenery. Make those witnesses look you over, then say, I can't be sure, Judge. Hell, anybody got one look at this Pedro could make the guy if you lined him up next to the whole fucking cast of *Ben Hur.* Come to think of it, Pedro stood out next to Burista about like Size Brandon next to Pecos Jimmy Fontenot.

Out of the side of his mouth, Pedro said, "I will remember you, big man. When this is over you gonna see me again.'' His English was a lot worse than either Ramiro's or Burista's and he hesitated a lot, as though he was trying to remember what the next word was supposed to be.

Size laughed suddenly, a deep rumble that started deep in his belly. ''Hey. That's great. You going to see me, huh? Maybe we can shoot some pool.'' He slapped Pedro on the middle of the back, and was a little surprised when Pedro didn't fall down. Hell, Size thought, I knocked the living shit outta the guy. Pedro just grunted softly and kept swaggering. He had to be faking.

They came to the end of the walk and went to the pickup. Size started to open the camper-cover, then hesitated. It was really dark now, the desert moon hadn't peeked over the roofs of the houses as yet. Size checked out the street. The gazebo across the way was still dark. In one direction the street was empty; about half the houses had lights glowing in the windows. When he looked the other way, Size could barely make out the outline of the yellow Thunderbird, still parallel to the curb. Its lights were off. Size couldn't tell if the engine was still running or if the guy was still behind the wheel.

He said to Pedro, ''Look, I'm wanting this over just as bad as you. But before we go to toting bags of cocaine back and forth, let's have a looksee at that car down there.''

Pedro pulled some hair on his moustache. ''If we must. I will go behind you. My hand is on my pistol, big man.'' He jammed his fist deep in the pocket of his shorts for emphasis.

''Yeah?'' Size said. ''Well, okay, bring up the rear. Don't get shook up and shoot yourself in the knee, Pedro. I need you to help me load the dope.'' He left Pedro and moved casually toward the Thunderbird. His elbow brushed by his waist and touched the handle of the Derringer. Pedro followed a couple of paces to the rear.

They passed by the pickup and around Burista's limo, walking single file in the street. When they were about ten feet past the Caddy, the T-bird's lights suddenly flashed on. Its engine raced and it zipped away from the curb. It screeched to a halt beside them. The driver's-side window was sliding down on electric rollers. A bare arm extended out the window and pointed a gun. In the dark it looked like a Colt Python .357 revolver, but Size couldn't tell for sure. A tenor male voice from within the car said, "Freeze, assholes. FBI."

The passenger door of the T-bird banged open and a second guy emerged. He was slender and wore a white short-sleeve shirt. He laid both arms across the roof of the car and pointed a pistol with both hands. "Like he said, gents, don't move. Hey, Brandon. I liked you better with the beard."

Size narrowed his eyes and peered. Jesus Christ, it was the FBI from Dallas, the one he'd cuffed to the toilet. The fuck was this guy doing here? Size spread his hands, palms down. "Hey. There's a little kid and—"

Pedro whipped his Beretta out. They weren't expecting it and their surprise gave him just the time he needed to get away with it. The silencer gave two short hisses, like a rattler, as Pedro shot the driver in the cheek and dead center in the nose. The back of the guy's head disappeared and a dark mess splattered the top of the seatback. The guy went limp, the Colt Python banging once against the door and clattering on the pavement. Pedro high-tailed it back toward the house, yelling something in Spanish between harsh heavy breaths.

Sam's gun went off, a loud blast that hurt Size's eardrums. His head snapped back as the bullet whined six inches away, throwing off sparks as it ricocheted off the sidewalk close to Pedro's thudding feet. Then Pedro was in shadows on the front porch. The door opened and slammed. Another shot rang out, this one from behind Size and to his right. Quick flame spurted from the darkened gazebo across the street. A slug thudded into the wood frame surrounding the front door of the house.

There was the faint tinkle of breaking glass, then the Uzi came to life. Rapid machine gun bursts split the night air and spurts of flame squirted across the lawn. Size lunged, grabbed the dead FBI's pistol and ducked around behind the T-bird. He said to Sam, "Get down, you dumb shit." The slender FBI crouched next to him as slugs from the Uzi whanged against the Thunderbird.

"You okay?" Sam said.

Size cocked his head to one side. "Yeah, I guess." The fuck was this? Hiding behind a car and shooting the shit with an FBI.

Sam pointed his gun. "You're under arrest, case I ain't told you."

That sounded more like it. Size handed over the dead FBI's pistol. Sam took it and leveled both weapons like Two-gun Pete. "You want to waive me reading your fucking rights? We'll get our asses blowed off, screwing around out here."

Now sirens howled. Two black-and-white police cruisers careened up the block and screeched to a halt. A dark van came from the other direction, red rooflight flashing. Uniformed Vegas cops unloaded from the cars. One guy had a riot gun, the others with what looked like carbines. The cops spread out, taking cover behind cars.

Size said, "Hey, man. I wasn't kidding. There's a little kid and her mother in there. You going to fuck around and get them killed?" His heart felt like it was in the pit of his belly.

There was the barest flicker in Sam's steady gaze, like he was trying to look directly at Size but couldn't quite bring himself to. Sam said, "We thought the lady was at work and the kid was with the babysitter. Listen, see that van over there? The sliding door's open, around on the other side. You take off and get inside the van. I'm right behind you. If you even look like you're going to run off, I'm going to shoot you in the leg."

Size narrowed his eyes. Why the hell would they think Merrillee was at work? And how'd they know to bring all these cops out here? The guy was lying, you could tell that by looking at him. Cool off, Size told himself. Blowing your top ain't going to help Merrillee. He nodded to Sam, rose to a crouch, and ran around behind the van. The sliding side door was open and he climbed aboard. Sam clambered inside behind him. At the front of the house, the Uzi barked and spit fire into the night. There was a *pinggg!* from one of the carbines as the cops returned the fire.

The interior of the van was fixed up like somebody's living room. There was rich blue carpet on the floor and walls. Four black padded leather chairs were anchored to the floor. In the wall opposite the sliding door was an oval tinted window about two feet wide and four feet high. The house was visible through the window and the spurts coming from the machine gun looked blue-green.

The federal prosecutor from Dallas—Mobley? Naw. Mitchell, that's it—was seated in the armchair closest to the window. He was wearing a white shirt, dark suite, and striped tie. He raised an arm and rapped his knuckles on the window. ''Bulletproof, Mr. Brandon. You're hard to locate. Please sit down.''

Size shrugged, sat down by Mitchell, and crossed his legs. It was all he could do to keep his lip from curling as he looked straight across the van at Junior Gomez. Prancing little dip in a satin shirt and skin-tight pants, sitting there as though he was one of the boys. Which he was, now. Sam sat next to Size and the four men now formed the corners of a square.

Mitchell propped his elbow on the padded arm of the chair and scratched above his eyebrow. ''Come on over, Mr. Brandon. It's the only way. Tell you what. We'll put a year cap on it, let you plead to a misdemeanor. And I don't mind telling you, I'm going against the FBI. Sam here wants to put you away for quite a spell.'' Over his shoulder, Merrillee's porch light went on and cast an eerie greenish glow through the tinted window.

Size clenched and unclenched his hands. ''You fucking guys take the cake. You got a man outside with his head blowed off and a girl and a little kid in trouble that're worth ten times the lot of you put together. And all you want to do is sit around and talk about somebody stooling somebody off. You think everybody's a piece of shit like Junior Gomez?'' Junior winced as though he'd been slapped. Size went on. ''Well, all you're going to get from me is a promise, Mister Fed. That if anything happens to that lady or that little kid—Jesus Christ! Oh my God.'' He looked past Mitchell through the window and got a preview of what it must feel like to die.

Pedro came out on the lit front porch. He was carrying Jessie, hugging her to his chest with one burly arm. He was holding the Beretta against her temple. Even from this distance Size could see her eyes. They were big and round. She wasn't moving, her body rigid with fear. In her tiny hands was the toy robot Size had given her, clutched in a death grip.

Pedro stood on the porch and held Jessie for a full half-minute. He yelled some things, his neck cords standing out and his teeth baring in hate. The scene through the tinted window in the sound-proof van was like some silent horror film. His message delivered, Pedro backed slowly through the front door. As Jessie's baby face disappeared from view, it seemed to Size as if she was looking directly at him in fearful, wide-eyed pleading. His stomach turned over. Tears stung his eyes. He made a silent promise to Jessie and Merrillee, though he didn't have the slightest idea how he was going to keep it. But he was going to.

Mitchell leaned over inside the van and knocked on the back of the driver's seat. The driver turned around. He was a round-faced, pleasant-looking guy of about thirty wearing a shirt and tie with no coat. The folds of his neck hung over his collar. The brown leather strap of a shoulder holster was fastened across his chest.

Mitchell said to the driver, ''Get on the radio, Agent. Under no circumstances are we going to endanger those innocent citizens' lives in there. Did the FBI know that those people were in the house? Who in hell authorized—'' He stopped in mid-sentence and his eyes widened in shock, then his mouth twisted in fear.

Size had risen to his feet and was bent from the waist over Mitchell. His monstrous left hand was steadying the prosecutor's jaw. In his right hand was the Derringer, its short double-barrel against Mitchell's left temple. There was a faint *click-click* as Size cocked the hammer with his thumb.

Sam had been holding the two pistols in his lap. He started to raise the Colt Python. On the other side of Mitchell, Junior Gomez looked as if he was about to throw up.

Size turned his head, kept his grip on the Derringer, and said to Sam, ''Go ahead. You can't stop me before I get him. And believe me, buddy, I don't give two shits about me right now.''

Mitchell said, ''My God, Sam. Please.'' His lips moved and his eyes rolled, but the rest of his body was stiff and rigid.

Sam hesitated as he gave Size a searching look. Then he slowly lowered the Colt. ''Naw, I don't guess you do, big boy. I don't guess you do give a shit.'' Then he looked at Mitchell and chuckled softly, as if to himself. ''Be brave, Henry. Try not to crap in your pants, huh? Hell, you might have to give an interview.''

Size took his left hand from Mitchell's jaw and held it out to Sam. ''Gimme the Colt. Then lay the other revolver on the seat and go to the back of the van.'' He swiveled his big head and looked toward the driver. ''Don't do nothing funny, pal. That government paycheck ain't worth it.''

Sam gave the Colt to Size, stood, and put the other gun on the seat—a .38 S & W revolver, snub-nose. He backed up slowly, against the van's rear doors. ''Jesus Christ, this is where I came in with this big sonofabitch. At least there ain't no toilet in here.''

Size jammed the Derringer into the waistband of his jeans, shifted the Colt Python to his right hand and scooped the .38 off the seat with his left, making the entire transfer in one deft flowing motion. He kept the .38 trained on Mitchell, took one step backward and pointed the Colt at the driver of the van. "Okay, now you two get back there with the other guy. I'm going to borrow your wheels and I don't need no funny guys riding along. You"—he indicated the driver—"come up outta that seat slow and keep your hands where I can see 'em.

The driver half-smiled, raised his hands above his shoulders, and moved deliberately between the seats and toward the rear. Size stopped him, jammed the .38 in his waistband next to the Derringer, and stripped the driver of his gun. This one was a Llama .380. Size thought, Jesus Christ, what a bunch of guns, huh? The three Feds—Sam, Mitchell, and the driver—were now standing side by side, backed up against the van's rear doors.

Junior Gomez sat forward. There was a twitch in one of his olive cheeks that he couldn't seem to control. "Man, you're not *leaving* me! Not with this crazy bastard. I got more stuff to tell you." His gaze shifted wildly back and forth between the Feds and Size.

Size drew back the Colt and started to bust Junior across the mouth. Then he stopped. Hell, the scumbag was too pitiful to hit. Size said, "I ain't got time for you, Junior. You get on back there with the rest of the assholes. Get those doors open, Mr. FBI."

His shoulders sagging with relief, Junior scrambled to join the others. Sam pulled on the rear door handle. The double doors swung outward. The loud barking and spitting noise from the machine gun inside the house invaded the van's interior. Size felt a slight breeze flowing across his cheeks.

His face now pasty white, Mitchell said, "We could all get killed out there."

Size gestured with the Colt. "Yeah, you could. Tell you what, I'll give you a tip. When I hit the street I'd run like hell if I was you."

The four men left the van. Sam and the driver hid behind the yellow T-bird, Agent Stu Goalby's dead face now grinning at them through the passenger window. Junior made a mad dash for one of the black-and-white police cars. A cop lowered his carbine long enough to hold the door open as Junior dove into the back. Mitchell stood frozen in the middle of the street for a moment. Then the Uzi *rat-a-tatted* a stream in his direction and Mitchell took off like a man jabbed with a hot poker. He dove into the black-and-white after Junior.

Size slammed the doors, climbed forward, and sank into the posh leather driver's seat. The Derringer and the .38 were digging into his waist so he dropped them on the passenger seat and laid the Python and the Llama down beside them. The van's engine was running. Size shifted into forward gear and slammed the accelerator to the floor. The van shot between two police cars, side-swiping one and then careening wildly down the block. Size cussed under his breath and fought the wheel, feeling one tire bump the curb before he got the van straightened out. He reached to the dash and flipped on the lights, the rushing pavement a blur in the stabbing beam as he turned the corner and whipped into the alley.

The van bumped and rocked on its springs as he steered up the alley. The front bumper rammed a metal trash can; something wet and sticky plastered itself against the windshield. The top of Jessie's swing set loomed over the fence top on his left. Size jammed on the brakes, grabbed the Colt and the .38, and hit the ground running. Blood pulsed in his temples. His breath whistled between his teeth. He was moving purely on instinct now, his eyes sending racing images to his brain that he didn't fully understand. He hesitated before the stockade fence long enough to cram the pistols into his jeans, then grabbed the top of the fence and vaulted over it. Behind him, a shotgun blasted. Pellets ripped into the top of the fence and a few of them lodged in his ankle as he went over. He didn't even feel them. He charged around the swing set toward the redwood deck, his feet now thudding on grass-covered sod. The moon had risen and Merrillee's yellow daphnes were a ghostly shade of blue.

From the top of the fence behind him a deep male voice yelled, "FBI. Halt!"

Size ignored the order and lunged across the redwood porch toward the back door. A shotgun blast split the cooling night air. The porch shuddered and splinters flew from redwood planks. Size hit the glass-paneled door with his shoulder like Lawrence Taylor blasting a Cowboy running back. The door crashed open. Size rolled on the thick den carpet and dug into his waistband. The grip of the snubnose slapped his palm and his fingers wrapped around it. He came up on one knee, the .38 held in both big hands, extended and ready. His breath sucked in. He was conscious of the faraway *chug* of the compressor that ran the air conditioner.

The lights were off. Moonlight slanted in through the windows and made parallelograms of ghost-light on the carpet. The couch was visible, along with about half of the TV, its blank screen vacant and staring. On Size's left the bedroom door was closed and artificial light streamed through the crack at the bottom. He listened to the racing beat of his heart, straining his ears for any noise, any sound to tell him that Merrillee and Jessie were okay. Aside from his own heartbeat he didn't hear anything. As his eyes grew accustomed to the dark the table and cabinets in the kitchen began to take familiar bulky shape.

Somebody was running from the front of the house, coming his way. Heavy footfalls jarred the floor. A stocky silhouette charged into the den. Pedro. Size took cover, diving behind the couch as Pedro snapped off a shot. There was a noise like a hissing serpent and flame spurted. A window that overlooked the porch broke into pieces, glass tinkling. Pedro was steadying the Beretta, getting ready to better his aim, when Size suddenly stood bolt upright and shot him in the head.

Size had to admit, it was a pretty lucky shot, considering the dark and all. He really didn't even aim, just rose to his feet with the .38 leveled in both hands and squeezed the trigger. The S & W bucked and jerked his hands skyward. It went off like a big firecracker. Pedro flew backward through the air and rammed into the wall that separated the den from the kitchen. He slid down the wall into a crumpled heap, then was still.

Size didn't have the time to check Pedro over, he knew that. He wanted to look inside the bedroom, even took a step in that direction. As he did, Ramiro's tenor voice yelled from somewhere in the front of the house, *"Pedro! Que pasa? Quien es?"*

Size steadied the .38 and crept through the darkness toward the sound of the voice. An image of Jessie flashed in his mind—her wide pleading eyes when Pedro held her on the front porch a little while ago. That score was settled. Now for the bastard with the Uzi.

He didn't have long to wait. He'd made it halfway through the dining room to the hallway that led to the front door in one direction, and to Jessie's room and the guest bedroom in the other, when he heard Ramiro coming. Ramiro's footsteps were light and tappy, like a kid's. There was a long mahogany formal dining table in the center of the room. Size took a deep breath and crouched behind it. Ramiro came in from the hallway and halted in his tracks, his head rotating from side to side, his ears cocked. Size could barely make out Ramiro's skinny outline in the darkness; a stray beam of light from the den glinted fleetingly on the barrel of the Uzi. The only sounds were the faint hum of the refrigerator in the kitchen and Ramiro's even breathing.

Ramiro said, *"Orale! Quien esta aqui?"* There was a faint tremor in his voice.

A heavy glass ashtray was on the dining table about a foot from Size's face. Slowly, carefully, keeping one eye on Ramiro and the other on the ashtray, he reached for it. His fingers closed around cool heavy molded glass as Ramiro pivoted slowly in his direction, the machine gun held ready. Mentally, Size shrugged. What the hell, he'd seen it work for Hopalong Cassidy with a rock.

He heaved the ashtray into the den. It flew end over

end through the doorway, crashed against the wall, and thudded on the floor next to Pedro's body.

Ramiro opened fire with the Uzi. It chattered and spit bursts of flame. Pedro's body jerked and twisted. Size straightened, planted his feet, and shot Ramiro through the chest, then steadied the pistol and fired again. Ramiro pitched violently sideways and sprawled on the floor. The machine gun fell at his side. Size was left alone with the smell of burning gunpowder.

Size moved. He charged back through the den to the bedroom, tripping over one of Pedro's outstretched legs, nearly falling headlong, righting himself. He threw open the door and went in. A silent prayer raced through his mind.

Merrillee was seated on the edge of the king-size with one smooth brown leg crossed over the other. Jessie was sitting big-chief-Indian style at Merrillee's side. Merrillee smiled weakly and touched the soft lock of hair on her forehead. "It's still there," she said. "Nobody's touched it. My goodness, don't you knock?"

Jessie bounced up and down and clapped her hands. "Wow, big giant! Just like *Superfriends*!"

Burista was huddled in the far corner of the room by Dolores. Her clenched fists were at her waist and one round hip was cocked higher than the other.

Burista held out both hands toward Size. "I got money, big man. I got a lot of money."

Size didn't hear. He was too busy putting one arm around Merrillee and the other around Jessie and hugging the daylights out of them.

Henry Mitchell was down on his haunches behind a black-and-white Vegas police car. He was saying, "—and he's known in some circles as *'El Gato Grande Malo.'* That's 'The Big Bad Cat.' His organization is worldwide. We think he's here to deliver two thousand kilos, though it could be even more. Say, you fellas have hookups to the wire services, hey?"

The reporter glanced up from his note taking. He was a chubby young guy wearing wire-frame glasses, a white short-sleeve shirt, and dark tie. "Well, yeah. *Vegas Sun-Times,* we've got our own computer and everything." He rolled his eyes.

A white mobile news van was a half-block up the street. A cameraman stood to one side, shooting video.

A policeman yelled, "Get ready, men. What the hell is that?"

The porch light winked on. Emilio Garza Burista came haltingly out the front door holding a broom in his chubby hands, straws pointing down. Something white fluttered from the broom's handle. Burista was waving the makeshift flag slowly back and forth. On Mitchell's left, someone said, "Fuck. I think they're panties."

In a low serious tone, Mitchell said, "*El Gato Grande Malo.* So we meet at last." The reporter put a hand over his mouth and snickered.

Dolores followed Burista out on the porch. She walked carefully, moving her feet in dainty half-steps, as if she was modeling underwear.

Merrillee brought up the rear, clutching Jessie's hand. She moved with purpose, her back straight as a ramrod, her gaze steady and her auburn hair in slightly tousled waves. She was firmly gripping a pistol and aiming it at a point between Burista's shoulder blades. Jessie's chin was tilted upward and she was watching her mom like a worshipful fan.

Dolores stopped, squared her shoulders, and stood at attention. She said loudly, "We giving up now. Don' shoot, cops."

Mitchell stood up behind the police car's fender and cupped his hands around his mouth. "Don't move yet, men. You—on the front porch. Where are the others?"

Merrillee answered without taking her gaze from Burista's back. "Inside. They're all dead, I think." Jessie yanked her mother's hand and started to say something. Out of the side of her mouth, Merrillee said, "Hush, Jessie."

"All right, men. Move forward with caution." Mitchell went around the police car and up the walk. One blue-uniformed cop stood and watched Mitchell and scratched behind his ear. Then he shrugged, gave a come-on wave to the others, and followed. Sam rose from his crouch behind the Thunderbird, trotted across the yard, and fell into step beside Mitchell.

"Hey, Henry," said Sam, "don'tcha think you ought to cool it? Jesus Christ, you're stepping on some toes, going around giving orders to these local cops. That one guy back there's a captain, shouldn't you let him call the shots?"

Mitchell showed Sam a crooked grin. "I can't help it, Sam, I'm just a take-charge kind of guy. Always have been, I guess. Look, don't worry. When it's all said and done I'll smooth their feathers. Trust me." He winked.

They stepped up on the porch. Mitchell faced Burista and studied him, looking first at Burista's shoes, then letting his gaze raise contemptuously until they were eye to eye. Mitchell said, "End of the road for you, El Gato."

Dolores looked confused. "*El* who?"

The cop with the rifle came up on the porch. Mitchell stepped back, put his hand on the cop's elbow, and kept looking at Burista as he said, "Cuff this man, Officer. Take him and the girl downtown and keep them on ice. I'll be having a long, shall we say, 'chat' with them later." Then he stepped toward Merrillee. She lowered the gun to her side. "You're safe now, Mrs. Rogers," Mitchell said. "We'll take over now. My, what a cute little girl." He beamed at Jessie. She wrinkled her nose.

Sam paused, about to go inside the house. He said to Merrillee, "Excuse me, ma'am. That big red-headed guy. He in there?"

Merrillee licked her lips, then said quickly, "In the backyard, I think. It all happened so fast, I'm not sure." Her long lashes lowered.

Sam nodded and went inside with Mitchell goose-stepping at his heels. The cop held the rifle in the crook of his arm, faced Burista, and lifted one side of his mouth in a wry half-smile. "You got me, pal," he said. "The guy might be the fucking attorney general himself for all I know. I just work here. Here, hold out your hands.''

Burista frowned. *''Con permiso? Yo no hablo ingles, el jefe.''*

Sam took one last look around the bedroom, then said to the young patrolman, ''I don't think there's a helluva lot to do in here. I don't guess we should touch anything, the lab boys will want to bag up some stuff. But it's pretty cut and dried. We've got, shit, the two stiffs out there, and the Colombian, Burista. And the lady's our witness. Whatcha think, son?''

The plastic bill on the cop's hat was nearly touching his nose, like a marine's cap. Sam wondered fleetingly if the kid shaved every day yet. The cop said, ''Looks to me like you're right on target. Let's close this room off and move on.''

Sam nodded and went into the den. The kid put on one cloth glove and closed the door to the bedroom quietly. Sam paused, felt his breast pocket for a cigarette, then decided he didn't need one. He looked around. The Vegas cops had covered Pedro and Ramiro with old green army blankets. An Uzi machine gun was on the dining room floor, lying next to one of the bodies. Sam pictured the pistols and one rifle he'd just seen in the bedroom closet. These boys had figured on having some shooting to do.

Merrillee and Jessie were seated at the dining room table talking to a tall, thin, all-business cop who was taking notes. The little girl was giggling. The chubby reporter from the *Sun-Times* was at the table also, sitting across from the cop. Sam appraised Merrillee—soft, face-framing auburn curls, perfect even features, full mouth forming a permanent question that her hazel eyes said she already knew the answer to—and thought, Class act, this broad. Wonder how she fits into all this. He shrugged and went through the back door to the redwood deck, pausing for a second to look at the shattered window adjacent to the door. On the porch, one of the redwood planks was blasted nearly in two. Mitchell was in the backyard, his arm extended and his hand resting on the bark of a stubby palm tree. The backyard light was on; the grass reflected brilliant green. Mitchell was flanked by the rifle-toting police captain and the chubby Vegas FBI agent who'd driven the van. Sam sauntered over to them.

Mitchell was saying, "—and I agree that it's befuddling. But he didn't go over the fence, one of our boys out back would have seen him. A man that size—" He trailed off, brushing dust from his lapel, then added, "Maybe El Gato knows something."

The cop looked as if he was going to laugh, then his expression grew serious. He was sniggering slightly as he said, "We'll have to ask El Gato. He and his girlfriend will be arriving downtown about now. Along with the Mexican guy—your snitch, what's his name?"

Sam stepped closer. "They're gone? Listen, who's guarding the front of the house?"

"Why, nobody is. You fellas said to take them downtown. Hell, we've got to search the grounds, I don't have enough men to—" The captain was looking at Mitchell.

"Now wait a minute, Henry," Sam said. "Jesus Christ, I don't know. Gomez said Brandon's been shacking up with the broad, how do we know she—"

They stared at one another in silence as a starter chugged in front of the house. An engine coughed and raced. Tires squealed.

Sam turned and headed for the back door. Over his shoulder he said, "Don't look now, Henry. But I think you might have fucked up again."

Sam sprinted to the end of the front walk and came to a halt. Mitchell collided lightly with him from behind. The two stood with hands on hips and watched the pickup's taillights disappear from view around the corner. The truck was fishtailing.

Sam folded his arms. "He's got the fucking dope, Henry. Hell, we didn't even get a look at the stuff. How you think we're going to make a dope case without no fucking dope?"

Mitchell became very interested in the toes of his shoes.

The mobile news crew was gathered around the white van across the street. One guy was holding a flashlight and reading from a paperback book. Sam yelled, ''Hey. You see who drove that truck away? Big red-headed guy?''

The man looked up and switched the flashlight off. ''Yeah. Boy, is he a monster. I didn't think the FBI hired them that big. Isn't there a weight limit?''

18

The skinny kid in the Golden Nugget bellhop uniform squinted his eyes and said, "Well, just how you going to make it worth my while? I can lose my job for that kind of shit." He shifted his weight nervously from one foot to the other and touched a pimple on his cheek with a forefinger.

Size thought, junkie, probably a skin-popper. He glanced at the blue and white pickup that sat double-parked in the street, motor idling, then let his gaze wander to the huge neon sign on the Fremont Hotel, a half-block away. Crowds were streaming back and forth on Fremont Street. High above the neon glow, the sky seemed pitch black. Size said, "I'm going to give you that truck and what's in it. Shit, you won't need no job."

"Yeah, I'll bet," said the kid. "I'll bet you're a narc, got all kinds of microphones up your ass."

"Man, you sure got me pegged. I'm a narc, okay, a D.E.-fucking-FBI, just dying to turn over a hundred kilos of eighty percent pure, just so's I can bust a bell-hop. I ain't made a good bust lately. Jesus Christ," Size said.

The bellhop folded his arms and lifted one skinny shoulder. "Lemme get this straight. You're going to let me drive off with a hundred kilos just for giving you a guy's room number. Say, you haven't escaped from no mental joint, have you?"

"Look, I'm trying to make you rich, you want to stand around and be a funny guy. I'll tell you that the truck's going to have a hot sheet on it, you don't want no cops stopping you while you're driving it. You can take it out on Reno Avenue to a guy they call Jungle Johnny. He'll take care of the truck. Going to cost you your ass, but you can afford it with what you got in the truck.'' Through the glass entryway, Size could see a dark-haired female desk clerk filling out a registration card for a fat man in overalls.

The bellhop said, ''Who's the guy? The room number you want.''

''Fontenot. From Texas. Dallas. Want me to spell it?''

''You must be kidding, big man. That dude? Kind of short, dresses like the rhinestone cowboy? Hangs with a scary black cat, don't he?''

''That's the guy.'' Size jerked his head toward the pickup. ''Your motor's running, kid. You don't want no parking ticket, not in *that* rig.''

The kid took short jerky steps to the curb, then paused. ''It's a suite, number 2610. And listen, I don't think you're crazy. I *know* you are, fucking around with those two dudes.''

The suite wasn't locked and Jimmy wasn't there. The girl was. She was about what Size had figured—tall and blonde, filled the skimpy bathing suit like a Sea'n'Ski ad. She was on a stool in front of a white carved wood vanity, brushing her hair with long, firm strokes. Her back was to the door. She didn't turn around.

Size waited for a second, then finally said, ''Hey.''

She looked at him over her shoulder. Her shining hair was swept over one eye in a Veronica Lake wave, and she'd been crying. Her mascara was streaked. There was a red swollen welt under one eye. It would blacken and turn purple in a day or so.

She sniffed. ''Tell him I'm hurrying. I'll be gone soon. Just please, don't beat me up. I'll just die if you hurt me any more.''

Size felt his face soften and his shoulders droop slightly. It wasn't the first time. Jimmy always needed a broad to take it out on. It was part of the deal. But hell, she was grown. Didn't anybody hog-tie her and drag her along.

"I ain't here to beat you up," he said. "But if you're smart you'll go, fast as you can. You got any idea where he went?"

"He said he was going to Mr. Gurney's room with Slim, I think. I wasn't paying that much attention, not after he—" Her bare shoulders began to shudder and heave and she covered her face with her hands. "Why would he *do* it? I didn't do anything. Oh, hell. He didn't even leave money for me to get home."

Size rolled his tongue around in his cheek and watched her cry for a moment. Then he reached in his pocket. He counted out five one-hundred-dollar bills and dropped them on the vanity. "Here. This'll get you where you're going. Where's Gurney's room?"

She looked at the money as though she was in a daze. Then she scooped it up and clasped it to her chest as she told him Gurney's room number. Size turned to go. From behind him she said in a tiny, little-girl voice, "It hasn't always been this way, you know. Why, I used to be an Apache Belle."

He paused with the door open. "Hey. You were? I seen them one time, in the Cotton Bowl . . . Good luck, huh?"

Her lips were forming the beginning of a smile as the door closed behind him.

Size relaxed and let the Luger hang limply by his hip. There was an empty stuffed chair next to the one where Beaumont Gurney sat, his wrists still bound and tape plastered over his mouth. Gurney's chin rested on his chest and his left cheek was against the point of his shoulder, his eyes still open, though they'd never see anything again. Size avoided looking at Gurney. He stepped around the dead lawyer, moved the empty chair nearer to the center of the room, and sat down. He let his gaze linger for a moment on the Harley-Davidson tattoo on Yucca-baby's hefty upper arm; then turned his attention to his last visit ever with Pecos Jimmy Fontenot.

Jimmy didn't look too bad being dead, not compared with some others that Size had seen. The sneer was gone and Jimmy's expression had softened into a sort of smile. His hands were clasped over his belly-button as if he was ready for his funeral. Size couldn't help it, he hoped that Jimmy'd have a nice one, that somebody'd get up with an organ in the background and sing "The Old Rugged Cross." That had been Jimmy's mama's favorite. Blood the color of cranberries was beginning to clot above and below Jimmy's folded hands.

Well, Jimmy, Size thought, you finally got to where there was nobody to run interference for you. Had to happen sooner or later. Size knew that; hell, he probably would've wound up killing Jimmy himself. It was just that he was going to miss the guy.

The door that led into the bathroom was at Size's back. It opened, with just a barely audible click of the turning knob, then an almost silent swinging on oiled hinges. Finally, a presence in the room that Size felt more than he saw or heard. Two muffled footsteps on padded carpet, then nothing.

Size leaned forward, the Luger dangling between his knees. The diamonds glittered around the face of Jimmy's Rolex. It was a quarter to twelve. Without turning around, Size said, "I guess you're going to get smooth away with it. Yeah. They'll figure Burista for all three of 'em."

"I thought about it lots of times," Slim said. "Shit, Sizemo', I tole you that from jump street, down in the bar."

Size swiveled his head, taking his time about it. Slim was wearing his Stetson tilted away from his forehead and his gold tooth was moving up and down on a toothpick. He hefted the satchel of money in his left hand. His right elbow was bent and he held a Donleavy .32 automatic pointed loosely in Size's direction; Size thought it was the same gun Slim had carried when they'd done East Eddie Kilrain. "Jimmy's broad's gonna know," said Size.

Slim glanced fleetingly at the ceiling. "She still up there?"

"Naw, she ain't. She'll be nigh to McCarran by now. Shit, Slim, that broad ain't going to be no trouble for you. She ain't going to talk to no law."

"I don' s'pose she is. What about my Sizemo'? You going to take your share, you go your way, Slim go his?"

Size thought that over. Time was, he would've gone for it in a minute. Finally he said, "I don't guess I am. That money ain't mine. It ain't yours, either. It's for somebody else. Somebody that wouldn't want me to have no part of killing somebody. Not for money anyway."

The disappointment on Slim's face was real. And there was puzzlement, too, as though he and Size weren't even speaking the same language. Slim said, "Your broad, huh? By God, she got you. Hey, guess she done broke up our pool game, buddy." Then the .32 jumped in his hand as he shot Size in the lower back, through the ribcage.

It didn't hurt as much as Size had always thought it would. Just a quick burning sensation before his side went numb. The bullet tore out through his stomach. He was aware of a quick, warm stickiness. He lurched sideways, pitching and rolling on the carpet, the Luger barking and spitting flame. One bullet caught Slim in the chest; another tore his eye away. He dropped the satchel, staggered, and fell on his face. His Stetson fell off. His leg twitched. He stopped moving.

Size labored to his feet, his breathing heavy. The numbness was going away; in its place a dull throbbing ache. He stooped and picked up the satchel. Jesus, it was heavy. He gritted his teeth and went into the bathroom.

Wasn't no way that wrapping one little package should be so hard. Pain razored through his side as Size tugged on the final flap of thick brown paper, held it in place, and secured it with a strip of Scotch Magic Tape. He lifted the package in both hands—Jesus

Christ, the damn thing couldn't have weighed more'n twenty pounds, but just picking it up made him feel as though somebody'd kicked him in the ribs—and shook it. The box he'd gotten from the gift shop girl was about six inches longer than the satchel, and the package rattled. He couldn't help it, it would have to do. He glanced past the counter out the gift shop window. A skinny teenage kid and a girl with braces on her teeth were strolling by, hand in hand.

He pulled the lapel of his windbreaker away from his body and looked down. The towel he'd gotten in the bathroom upstairs was doing a pretty good job of soaking up the blood; he couldn't see any seeping through. His windbreaker covered up the hole that Slim's bullet had ripped in his shirt. The Polo—wouldn't you know it? His favorite. He took a ballpoint and wrote Merrillee's name and address on the package, then walked to the gift shop counter. He had to close his eyes against the throbbing ache a couple of times on the way.

THe girl at the counter wasn't much more than a teenager. Her sandy hair was tied at both sides of her round pleasant face in doggie ears. She wore tight jeans stretched over wide, full hips. She said, "I hate to charge you for a whole roll of paper, you've used so little."

It seemed to Size that the girl's image wavered some. He blinked. Then he fished a ten-dollar bill from his pocket and laid it on the counter. "Stamps. I'm gonna need a book of stamps." A bubble of air popped somewhere around his middle. At the same time blood welled up in his throat. He swallowed it. Jesus, just a few minutes more and he could find a spot to cop some z's.

She reached under the counter, laid a booklet of twenty stamps on the counter, then cocked her head in question. "Are you all right, mister? Jeez, you look a little pale."

Size mumbled that he was okay. He licked the stamps and put them on the package while she rang up the sale and brought him his change. He said, "Can

I''—he swallowed some more blood—''can I mail this around here?''

''There's a box at the curb, just outside the hotel door.''

Size nodded and left. He clutched the shop's doorframe, leaned on it for seconds, then gritted his teeth and went on. The girl watched him go, then picked up the phone and called the county emergency number.

It couldn't have been over thirty feet from the Golden Nugget's side entrance to the blue mail box at the curb, but it seemed to Size that with every step he took it got farther and farther away. He collided with a balding fat man in a tan suit, stumbled, righted himself, and moved painfully on. He was staggering now, tears clouding his vision, the pain roaring upward through his chest and around into his shoulder blades. A yellow cab idled at the curb. The driver was staring at him.

The packaged tumbled down the chute and thudded on the bottom. Size leaned on the box, sighed, and grinned an ear-to-ear grin. He thought, Jesus, what a job, huh? A siren wailed in the distance.

He decided to go back up to Jimmy's room and lie down. Be good as new in a while. Fit as a fucking fiddle. He went back into the hotel, his feet now dragging with every step. Blood began to soak through the towel and dribble on his windbreaker.

He fell down just inside the entrance. A woman screamed. She sounded miles away. He tried to get up, tried again, then relaxed. Hell, the carpet was soft enough. Good a place as any to rest.

There was a huge stuffed dog in the window of the gift shop. It had big blue friendly eyes and lopsided ears. A grin was painted on its face and Size thought it looked just like Benji. As a red haze filtered over his vision and images darkened and blurred, Size thought, Man. Wouldn't Jessie go *crazy*? I got to get her one of them dogs.

Look for A.W. Gray's big new novel,
IN DEFENSE OF JUDGES,
at your bookstore beginning June, 1990,
in hardcover from E.P. Dutton.

IN DEFENSE OF JUDGES

A novel by A.W. Gray

Marvin Goldman, clad in black, his starched white cuffs glistening, his goatee combed into a near-perfect triangle, said, "And the evidence will show that . . ." Then he took long, purposeful strides in a line parallel to the railing that separated the jury box from the courtroom.

Bino Phillips thought, That's one . . . two . . . three . . . four of 'em, Marv. Four big ones. Now turn. That's it, not too fast. Now. Point. *Point* at the dirty fucker. *Presumed innocent,* right?

Goldman pivoted, his eyes narrowed, raised his right arm, and held it straight as a ramrod. His index finger extended, his nails buffed and manicured, he said, *"This Man."* And then he paused, and during the pause a pin dropped on the carpet would have sounded like the beginning of an avalanche.

Bino thought, What man? *Weedy?* Not my Weedy, not on your life. He reached over and clasped Weedy Clements's shoulder, at the same time favoring the jurors with his best it-ain't-so look. Seated in the front row of the jury box, a Mexican guy who was wearing a pink sportcoat yawned.

"Devised a scheme," Goldman went on. "A scheme, a plan, an artifice. A scheme that . . . worked well for a while. A scheme that resulted in the importation and sale, over a period of four years, of six tons of Colombian gold marijuana. That's *six tons*, ladies and gentlemen. Enough to put all the schoolchildren in Dallas on a permanent, festering high. And that . . ." Goldman's shoulders drooped and he shrugged. "But enough. Our case will speak for itself. And after the evidence has spoken and you prepare to do your duty as jurors there will be only one choice for you to make. To con-*vict*. Justice . . . must be served. I thank you." Goldman marched to the prosecution's table, poured himself a goblet of water from a chrome pitcher, and sat down.

Judge Hazel Burke Sanderson, her iron-gray hair stiff as papier-mâché, glared in the direction of the defense table. Bino wasn't sure whether the scowl was intended for Weedy Clements or for Bino himself. Probably both. Hell, this wasn't even her courtroom, the old—Bino wondered for about the tenth time since he'd come to court what had happened to Emmett Burns, the judge who had been scheduled to try the case, and whom Hazel Sanderson had replaced at the last minute. If he knew old Hazel, she'd probably read on the docket that Bino Phillips was the lawyer for the defense, had gotten together with Goldman, and muscled Judge Burns out of the way. "Does the defense wish to make an opening statement?" Hazel Sanderson said. "Mr. Phillips?"

Weedy raised his arm and beckoned. Bino bent his head and leaned closer. In a hoarse stage whisper, Weedy said, "What the fuck's a 'festering high'?" Weedy was short and blocky, with long, thinning brown hair combed straight back on a head that was shaped like an anvil, and was attached to his body by a thick neck which looked to be about an inch long. He was wearing a blue suit. Bino thought that Weedy looked about as at home in a suit as Charles Bronson in a ballerina costume. Visible behind Weedy, the two U.S. marshals who had escorted him over from the county lockup lounged in chairs that were backed up to the rail.

"I don't know myself, Weed," Bino said. " 'Festering' has something to do with a sore. Sometimes Goldman gets all wound up and gets stumped for words. Maybe he just made it up as he went along." He smiled and nodded in the direction of the bench, though showing Hazel Sanderson a genuine-looking smile took some doing on Bino's part. "If the Court please, Your Honor. We do have a brief statement."

Bino stood to his full six-foot-six and glanced out at the twenty or thirty spectators in the courtroom. Dodie was in the front row with a spiral notebook in her lap and a ballpoint pen in her hand. She was wearing a blue business dress that stopped a couple of inches above shapely knees. Her blond hair flowed softly to her shoulders. Seated beside her, Half-a-Point Harrison was thin as a skeleton and looking worried. Usually, nothing worried Half except point spreads that didn't create enough action on both teams, and every other Tuesday when the grand jury met. Dodie flashed Bino an encouraging smile. Half clutched his windpipe and gagged silently.

Bino adjusted the knot on his red-and-silver-striped tie, then went around to the jury-box side of the defense table and sat on its corner. He left his charcoal-gray coat unbuttoned and spread his palms out on the table behind him in his best folksy posture. At the prosecution's table, Marvin Goldman rolled his eyes. The clean-shaven FBI agent who was sitting next to Goldman leaned over and said something. Both men snickered.

"You-all are going to hear some bad things about my client Mr. Clements here," Bino said. "Some real bad things. Because it's the government's job to make Mr. Clements look bad, just like it's my job to make him look as good as possible." Twelve heads moved as one of the jurors gazed at Weedy. Bino tried to read something in their expressions. He couldn't. One girl—a General Services Administration secretary, Bino recalled from the juror list—was chewing gum, and the Mexican guy in the pink sportcoat didn't look as though he could stay awake through the opening statements. If Goldman were to kick him right now, the

Mexican would probably snap wide awake and holler, "Guilty!"

Bino swept a lock of snow-white hair away from his forehead and sat up a little straighter on the table. His hands now resting on his knees, his expression more intense, he said, "But it really doesn't matter if what I say about Mr. Clements is true, or if what the U.S. prosecutor Mr. Goldman over there"—here he looked at Goldman, who stared straight ahead in the direction of the bench—"says about him is true. What matters is guilty or not guilty. Now, I didn't say guilty or *innocent,* and there's a big difference. After the prosecution says what it's going to, and after I say what I'm going to, Judge Burns—excuse me, Judge *Sanderson.* This is Judge Burns's courtroom, but he couldn't be here today so Judge Sanderson is sitting for him. Anyway, when we're all through blowing our trumpets, the judge is going to give you an instruction about how the prosecution has to prove its case beyond a reasonable doubt. You've all heard about reasonable doubt on lawyer TV shows, I know that, and the bottom line is that I don't have to prove Mr. Clements is innocent. I'm not even going to *say* that Mr. Clements is innocent. Heck fire, look at him. His nickname is *Weedy,* for goodness' sake."

He glanced in Weedy's direction. Bino'd have to say this much for Weedy, the guy was keeping a poker face even though his toes were probably knotting. Goldman's upper lip was beginning to curl, which meant that he didn't like Bino telling about Weedy's nickname before Goldman himself could get the monicker in front of the jury. Score one for Bino. Now even the jurors were looking interested, shifting around and scooting forward in their chairs. The girl from the General Services Administration had stopped chewing her cud. The Mexican's eyes were wide and round. Score two for Bino. He raised one finger in a teaching attitude and went on.

"But the government hasn't charged Weedy Clements with smuggling a little marijuana, or even with *selling* a little marijuana. If they had you'd all be at home and Weedy would've already pled guilty and be at Bastrop or El Reno or Big Spring or one of those other nice places the government has. But no. No sirree. They've charged Weedy with *conspiracy.* They've got to prove—beyond a reasonable doubt, mind you—that Weedy got together with some other folks and plotted. That he said to one guy, okay, you buy the marijuana, and to another guy, okay, you bring it over the border, and so forth. But that isn't all the government has to prove, not by a long shot. If Weedy just gets together with some friends of his and plots, that isn't against the law. There's got to be an overt act, somebody he's plotting with has got to go out and do something shady to further the deal. That's what we're talking about here. Conspiracy. Ladies and gents, I don't care if Mr. Goldman shows you a full-color picture of Weedy Clements in between two bathtubs, one filled with marijuana and the other with hundred-dollar bills, if there's nobody else in the photo with him they ain't proved a thing."

Here Bino paused long enough to throw the jury a broad wink, and for an instant thought that the girl from the General Services Administration was going to wink back at him. There he heard Judge Hazel utter a disapproving gasp. That was okay with Bino; if the judge was getting pissed off it meant that he was putting across to the jury just what he wanted to. Fired-up now, Bino said, "Remember it, folks. Above everything else you're going to hear in this courtroom, remember. Conspiracy. We'll do our best to make it interesting for you-all." He got up quickly, circled the table and went back to his seat, conscious of Dodie beaming at him from beyond the rail and feeling pretty proud of himself. Clarence Darrow, Melvin Belli, Racehorse Haynes, bring 'em on. When Bino Phillips was on a roll he didn't take a back seat to anybody.

Judge Hazel leaned forward and clasped her hands, then bent her head to regard them for a moment. She raised her gaze slowly, her thin lips pursed, her wire-frame Martha Washington glasses perched on the slight hump in her nose. "Theatrical, Mr. Phillips." Then, to the jurors, "Ladies and gentlemen, I fear that jury selection and opening statements have wasted the morning. We'll break for lunch now. You're to return promptly at one. And remember—you're not to discuss this case with anyone, including yourselves." She banged her gavel, tossed a curt nod in Goldman's direction, and made her haughty exit by the judge's private door. She didn't so much as glance in Bino's direction.

Weedy made a fist, protruded his middle knuckle and thumped Bino on the upper arm. Showing a craggy grin, he said, "What a lawyer. Main man, huh?" The two marshals had come forward and now stood behind Weedy's chair, one on each side. They both wore tan Stetsons and brown cowboy boots, western-style suits and black string ties.

Bino rubbed his arm where Weedy had frogged him. "You don't need a main man, Weed. You need Houdini, but I doubt if *he* could get you out of this. Jesus Christ, your own *brother* is going to finger you. You want a trial, we'll give 'em one, but you ought to think over what I said about copping a plea. With the regular judge in the courtroom we might've stood a chance, but wait'll you see *this* woman in action once the testimony starts. Goldman's a lazy bastard at heart, he might still make a deal." The marshals were fidgeting, shifting their weight from side to side.

Weedy's features twisted, and Bino thought, just as he had for years, that Weedy Clements was the only guy in the world who could actually, physically, get his nose bent out of shape. "My mama didn't raise no copout artist," Weedy said. "Fuck 'em. Tell 'em to crank it up."

Bino expelled a long breath. Jesus, what was it with these guys? Weedy Clements was a two-time loser, you'd think he'd been dragged through enough courtrooms to know the score. Bino guessed it was the hope that springs eternal, or whatever they called it. He said, "Whatever goes, buddy. Like you say, fuck 'em." He raised his gaze to the two marshals and said to Weedy,

"Here's your keepers. I'm going to grab a burger. See you at one." He brightened. "Hey, I saw them bringing the food over. Ham and cheese. You'll probably eat better in the holding tank than I'm going to." The marshals took Weedy away, each of them taking one step to his two as he hustled along between them.

Bino looked toward the exit as he approached the railing gate. Dodie waited by the rear courtroom door with one spike-heeled foot slightly in front of the other. Half was back there, too, reading—Jesus, was it? That's what it was, okay, Half-a-Point Harrison was standing near the exit from the federal district court reading a racing form. Bino shook his head and started to go through the gate. As he did, Marvin Goldman brushed in front of him, stood aside like a theater usher, and swung the gate open. He made a sweeping bow.

"Great opening statement, buddy," Goldman said. "I don't know what you're going to do for an encore, but your opening had them on the edges of their seats. I can't match you in bullshit, Bino. No way can I. Only in hard facts and evidence."

Bino cleared his throat, more as a stall than anything else. Applauding Bino's opening statement was something that the U.S. prosecutor would rank right along with carrying out the garbage. But Goldman had put just enough barb in his congratulations so that Bino was now supposed to yodel, beat on his chest, and start laying out to Goldman what evidence the defense was holding to rebut the government's passel of witnesses. Bino wasn't falling for that one. Not old cagey. Besides, in Weedy Clements' case, Bino didn't know that he *had* any evidence.

He showed Goldman a bland smile and said merely, "Thanks, Marv." Then he went past Goldman and through the gate, turning his head to hide a grin. He'd gone a couple of steps up the aisle when he turned back to Goldman, snapped his fingers, and said earnestly, "Hey. What happened to Judge Burns? He sick or something?"

Well, Goldman had taken *his* shot, now Bino was

trying one of his own. If the U.S. prosecutor came back with something wiseass and off-the-wall, Bino was going to know that the last-minute change in judges was in fact a Federal shenanigan. Which would tell him that maybe, just maybe, the government's case against Weedy Clements wasn't all that they were building it up to be. Bino cocked his head and waited for an answer.

Goldman's reaction was a surprise. His gaze averted, not looking directly at Bino, Goldman said, "I've got nothing to do with it, buddy. Nothing at all. Judge Burns . . . well, you'll find out soon enough. I can't talk about it."

Bino knew Goldman well enough to know when the prosecutor was lying—which was pretty damned often—but this time Goldman wasn't. In fact Goldman was just a little bit shook. Bino was bursting at the seams to ask more, but knew better. He moved on up the aisle toward Dodie. His white eyebrows were knitted in puzzlement.

Bek's Hamburgers was a cafeteria-style, order-'em-and-rassle-to-grab-'em hamburger joint located in the tunnel that connected One Main Place to Interfirst Tower, First Fidelity Plaza, and points beyond. Bino stood in the entryway and craned his neck in search of a table while leggy secretaries in spike heels and businessmen in Brooks Bros. or Hart, Schaffner & Marx suits—all of the suits navy or gray, one solid color or the other—strolled up and down the corridor, peered in shop windows, and pretended not to notice one another. Inside the restaurant, Hispanic teenagers in red and yellow uniforms, each one wearing a paper chef's hat with the Bek's logo on its crown, fried greasy burgers, cooked sizzling baskets of fries, and spooned mounds of chili onto open-faced sandwiches. One older black man, wearing a uniform identical to the teenagers', yelled out orders and shot frigid glances in the direction of whichever Mexican wasn't spooning chili or turning patties fast enough to suit him. Bino recognized one lawyer who was seated at a table for two in the far corner, in a little raised area that was wide enough for a row of two-seater booths in addition to the tables. The lawyer was Frank Bleeder, a classmate from South Texas College of Law. Old Bleed 'Em and Plead 'Em was ignoring his cheeseburger and fries and talking a mile a minute to a tall redhead who was seated with him. Bino gave the redhead a quick once-over (not being too obvious about it, mainly because Dodie was standing at his elbow and he could feel her breath on his neck), and got an overall view of skin the color of milk, a trim figure that was likely to cause a few collisions in the hallways, and wide blue, let's-party eyes. Bleeder, a big guy who'd grown one helluva pot belly since Bino had last seen him, whose hair was graying, and who had a good ten years on the redhead, zoomed in on Bino and gave him the thumbs-up sign. Bino lifted a hand to shoulder level and waggled his fingers.

Dodie shook Bino's elbow. "There's one over there," she said. "Right there in the center. Wow, it's been vacant ever since we've been standing here. When you get through looking up everybody's skirt, let's eat. God, I'm famished."

And there *was* an empty table. There it stood, its top made of slatted blond polished wood, standing out like a sore thumb and looking lonely among all the other identical tables, which had two, three, and four people crowded around them. "Damn. Don't know how I missed it, Dode," Bino said. He stepped aside and extended his arm. Dodie sniffed a little sniff and led the way. Half-a-Point, who had been off to one side studying his racing form, folded the form under his arm and strolled along behind her. Bino brought up the rear, shooting another glance at the redhead and thinking that she was a little out of Frank Bleeder's class. By a couple of miles or so.

Finally seated, Bino studied the menu. It was encased in laminated plastic and featured a cartoon character, a chubby little guy wearing the Bek's uniform and chef's hat, in several poses: frying a burger, cleaning off a table, and running like hell to deliver a take-out order. There was a pad of order blanks on the table, held inside a wooden slot with a pen attached to it on a chain. Bino took one blank and wrote down a Number Four—hickory sauce, relish, and mustard—for himself, then hesitated. Finally he decided to cut the onions. He wouldn't mind breathing a little onion breath in Goldman's face, but he never knew when he'd have to get close to the jury box in order to make a point. Dodie checked out the supply of Certs breath mints by the cash register, then told Bino she'd have a chili and cheese. Bino wrote that down, then said to Half, "How 'bout you? I'm buying, suit yourself."

Half had taken a paper napkin from the holder and was wiping down the table with little circular strokes. "Onions. I love 'em. I been dreaming about 'em. But I already got enough heartburn fooling with these ponies. Saladburger. Well done. *Super* well done. Bino, you tell those cooks that if I see a spot of pink in the center I'll have the law down here raiding the joint. Bet half the help around here is wetbacks, I can smell 'em a mile away."

"Wait a minute," Bino said. "What's this *me* tell 'em stuff? What's wrong with you telling 'em yourself? How come it's always me that's waiting in line?"

"I wait sometimes," Half said. "When it's my turn."

"Hold on. When *is* it your turn? Once, I can remember once. We were in high school. You waited in line for hot dogs at the Mesquite Rodeo, only later I come to find out that the hot dog guy owed you and Pop money from betting on football. You waited in line so you could dun the guy when he gave you the hot dogs. Maybe one other time in our whole life. I tell you, Half, I'm sick of always waiting in line."

"And you're both making *me* sick," Dodie said. Her eyes were probably bluer than those belonging to Frank Bleeder's redhead, though not quite as wide. "Please, no more 'back to Mesquite' stuff. Here. *I'll* go. I need some bucks, boss. Come on, fork over." She stood and held out a tiny hand, palm up. She was making Bino feel a little guilty, but what the hell. He'd be damned if he'd stand in line. Half could starve to death before Bino'd stand in line again. He handed Dodie twenty dollars. Hips swaying, she folded the twenty along with the order blank, went over and stood hesitantly beside the serving line. The line extended almost into the corridor outside, men in suits and women in business dresses, holding money, waving credit cards. A young guy, thirty or so, clean-shaven and with an I'm-a-banker look about him. took a plastic tray from the stack and slid it along the counter, then got a load of Dodie and did a double take. He stopped and said something to her. She showed him a grateful bat with her eyelashes, took two trays for herself, and cut in line ahead of the guy.

"She's getting one helluva lot better service than you could," Half said. "From now on she's elected. Who's the guy?"

Bino was keeping a close eye on the eager beaver who had let Dodie in line, not really blaming the guy but watching him anyway. "How'm I supposed to know?" Bino said. "He's a guy that wants to hit on Dodie."

"Not *that* guy. I'm talking about the dude with the redhead, the one you waved at. Lawyer, ain't he? I've seen him down at the courthouse. He acts like a real asshole, from what I've seen."

Bino glanced over to where Bleeder sat. The redhead was now bent forward and apparently reading old Frank the riot act, her hands balled into fists on her full round hips. The fun look was now gone from her eyes. Bino said, "It's not a good idea to go around talking about other lawyers, Half. It just doesn't look good."

"Okay, so I won't talk about him. *You* talk about him. Who's the guy?"

"Frank Bleeder."

"Jesus Christ. *That's* Bleeder? Yeah, I've heard about him. From some guys wish they *hadn't* heard of the guy. He's a jail jockey. Hangs around down at the county and buddies up to the prisoners' wives and mothers. He gets 'em to up him a little front money, then that's the last they ever see of him.''

Bino felt a strange sadness. ''Too bad. Too bad there's a whole lot more like that. Yeah, that's old Frank. Wasn't always. But is now. King of the court appointments.''

''King of the what?'' Half said.

''Court appointments. You know, bugs this judge and that judge to death. To get rid of him the judge appoints him on indigent cases; hell, Frank has more of those than anybody in town. Bim-bam, thank you, ma'am, the guy goes off to the pen and Frank gets a check from the county. There's some funny stories going around about how he gets all those court appointments, but don't ask me to repeat any of 'em. I'm taking enough of a chance talking about another lawyer, but I'm sure as hell not saying anything about how a *judge* takes care of his business.''

''I read you,'' Half said. ''There's things you don't *want* to know. Jesus, Bino, how's a guy like that ever get to be a lawyer in the first place? If he was a bookmaker and got a reputation like that, somebody'd tar and feather him.''

Across the restaurant, Bleeder was now leaning back in his chair with his palms facing the redhead. Frank was defending himself about something, his jaw working nonstop. The look on the girl's face said that Bleeder wasn't doing a very good job of talking his way out of whatever it was that he was trying to talk his way out of. Bino pictured a much younger Frank Bleeder, flat-bellied and with hair the color of licorice, pleading, tears in his eyes, turning a jury to mush and saving a black boy from the electric chair. The black kid had done okay. He'd gone to school in prison, earned early parole, and now ran a youth center on the south side of town, saving a lot of ghetto youngsters from jail and much, much worse.

Bino cleared his throat. ''With that particular guy it was a lot of work to be a lawyer. He didn't have it easy, and I'll tell you something, Half. Fifteen years ago I'd see Frank Bleeder stand toe to toe with some of the ballsiest prosecutors in the state and make 'em holler uncle. Late sixties he took on some cases I didn't think anybody could've won. But Frank did. And he wasn't just in it for the money. Back then if Bleeder didn't see something in a guy he was going to represent, he'd tell him to take a hike."

Half fished a packet of Rolaids from his inside coat pocket and popped one of the white tablets into his mouth. His pencil mustache was beginning to show some gray. "We talking about the same guy? Bleeder? What in hell happened to him?"

Bino shrugged. "Who knows? He had a nasty divorce once, but that was three marriages ago and the others don't seem to have bothered him any. Might be liquor, but I don't remember ever seeing Frank when he was drunk. At least not any drunker than I was at the time. Maybe he just quit caring. A lot of 'em do, you know. Being a lawyer is a lot like being a cop in ways. You see this turd and that turd, every day another turd, and not all of the turds are the guys charged with the crime. After a few years of finding out that the whole fucking justice system is a game, and that both the good guys and the bad guys are playing it . . . well, some people take the easy way out. Tell you what, I bet old Frank makes a lot more money today than he did when he was practicing law for real. If money's any way to keep score. I've heard around that he takes a lot of Vegas trips. Gambling high as a kite, from what I understand."

"Damn, maybe he likes to bet on football," Half said. "What's the guy's phone number?"

"You'd be wasting your time. Betting football's too slow for a guy like that. Bet on a team and then wait for a week, three or four days at least, to find out how you came out? No fucking way. Not when he can make the same bet on the pass line, let 'em roll and then bet some more. A guy like Frank is looking for fast action."

Bino sensed, rather than saw, Dodie's hip on a level with his shoulder. She was standing beside the table balancing two trays, one in each hand. "Did I hear somebody say, 'Fast action?' I swear if you make me stand here any longer I'm asking for a tip.'' One tray was stacked with wrapped sandwiches, the chili on Dodie's burger soaking the treated paper. On the other tray were three white plastic cups with interlocking lids, straws poking through holes in the lids like upright candy canes. Frost had formed on the sides of the cups, a few large drops rolling down and making rivulets.

Bino hustled to his feet, balanced the tray of burgers on the box-shaped metal napkin holder, then set one drink in front of Half, one at his own place, and one before Dodie's empty seat. ''Quick trip, babe. How'd you get through the line so fast?''

She sat down and crossed her legs. ''I've got ways. Cost me a phone number. Wow, I wonder whose number it was.''

They ate. Dodie took itty-bitty bites, laying her sandwich down and chewing slowly between each one. Half opened his sandwich, inspected the meat like a USDA sleuth, then shrugged and ate the burger in four big gulps. Bino took his own time, drinking icy Coke through a straw between each bite. Dodie's dimpled knee was just inches from his thigh. He didn't think she was doing it on purpose, but it bothered him. The first time with Dodie had been two years earlier and had been something of a lark. The second occasion had been only weeks ago, and that time he'd needed her badly. Neither of them had talked about it since, but . . . She caught his eye fleetingly, shifted in her chair so that her knee pointed away from him. Her cheeks flushed slightly.

Half spoke a little faster than normal, ''What's the story on Weedy? You going to be in trial the rest of the year or what?''

Bino hesitated. Half had forced it, like somebody who was changing the subject, even though nobody was talking about anything. Could it be that he knew about Bino and Dodie? Probably not, at least not for sure, but the three of them had spent too much time together for Half not to snap that there was something going on.

Finally Bino said, "I hope to hell not. I got to say I thought Weedy Clements was smarter than this. It isn't like he's never been around. I've seen Goldman's witness list and I don't guess there's anybody that knows Weedy that isn't going to testify. But the silly bastard won't make a deal, no way. What can I do about it? Hell, I can't *make* the guy plead guilty. I don't know what Weedy thinks is going to happen, but trying this case? Shit, he's going to be lucky if he gets out of jail before the turn of the century."

"Well, talk to the guy," Half said. "Jesus, I got a lot to do without sitting around court watching Weedy Clements go down the tube."

"I've *already* talked till I was blue in the face. You think I *want* to be in trial? Hell, nobody's covering the office. Which reminds me, Dode, you checked the answering service? We get any calls?"

Dodie laid down her burger and rolled her eyes. She swallowed. "Smokes, can't I finish eating first?"

"That's the trouble," Bino said. "Everybody's sitting around eating and stuff, nobody's taking care of business." The look on her face made him feel like biting his tongue off. "Hey, I'm uptight, okay?" he said. "Take your time, Dode."

She made a sour little face. It was a *cute* sour little face, but anybody that didn't know Dodie was pissed just didn't know her very well. "Never mind, boss, I've lost my apetite." She stood. "On my way, massa. Want me to check the cotton crop too?" She went off in the direction of the pay telephone, her backside twitching from side to side.

Half watched her go, then said matter-of-factly, "You been giving that little girl a lot of shit lately, Bino, and I don't see that she's done anything that calls for it."

This lunch wasn't going too well. It wasn't going worth a shit, matter of fact. Now *Half* was getting on Bino's case. A lot of cracks went back and forth between the two of them, cracks that didn't amount to a hill of beans. But the number of times in their lives that Half had let him have it for real? Bino could probably count them on one hand. He drank some Coke. "Well, maybe I have. Maybe I been fucking up from here to El Paso. Look, maybe I better go on back to the courthouse by myself, okay? Take Dodie back down to the office, giver her a few hours to cool off. Hell, I don't need the two of you, I got Goldman and Hazel Sanderson to fight. Jesus, not to mention my own client. Old Hazel, the last time I tried a case in her court she wound up turning me in to the bar association. This time she'll probably throw my ass in jail for contempt. Hell, I . . . Never mind. I'm taking off, maybe I can talk sense to Weedy, I'm not doing too good with my own people." He got up and tossed his wadded paper napkin on the table.

"Well, suit yourself," Half said. "You ain't going to bother me none, I been bitched at by guys which are a helluva lot tougher than you. But while you're fucking around town, you better think a few things over, Bino. I mean, this ain't you, the way you're acting. Dodie Petersons come along about once in a decade, and I don't mean just broads which *look* as good as her. You better think about what I'm telling you." He turned away and directed his gaze to the far wall.

Bino took a half step forward, drew in his breath to say something, then slowly let it out. Half was right on the money, of course. But what good was it going to do to . . . ? What the hell. Bino spun on his heel and made for the exit, feeling like ten kinds of an asshole but not being able to do anything about it. Maybe later. He hoped so.

He'd made it about three-quarters of the way across the restaurant, squinting to read the clock in the Zale's jewelry-store window across the corridor from Bek's, when there was a loud crash on his right. Glass shattered and tinkled. A hush fell over the crowd. Bino stopped in his tracks. He turned and stared.

The redhead stood looking down at Bleeder, hands on hips and eyes blazing. Old Frank didn't look too happy himself. The gal had dumped his lunch on him.

Greasy meat coated with melted cheese and French fries slipped and slid in his lap over a bed of droopy lettuce and squishy tomato. Bleeder was watching the redhead with fear in his eyes, like a guy up for sentencing. Bino was conscious of the piped-in music outside in the corridor. "Jingle Bells." Happy holidays.

The girl said something to Bleeder, then made tracks, heels clicking. The flesh around her eyes was red, puffy, swollen. Her mascara was streaked. Bino stood there with his mouth open like a fly trap as she headed straight for him. She didn't even see him. Jesus, this girl was going to walk straight through him as though he was Topper's ghost. Only he *wasn't* a ghost, and if he didn't get the hell out of the way she was going to run over him. He closed his mouth and started to step aside.

He wasn't fast enough, and she plowed right into him. As she uttered a soft, startled, "Oops," her red hair tickled his chin and the fragrance of face powder drifted into his nostrils. He fell back a step, then caught himself. Her blue eyes widened. Her red lips parted. Her chest rose and fell in rapid succession. Bino got another, this time much closer view of milk-white skin, a full mouth that ought to be smiling, and long, long legs that were meant to be shown.

He said lamely, "My fault."

She looked for a second as if she was going to start bawling again, then said, "Oh, I'm so . . . *sorry.*" With a small sob from somewhere deep in her throat, she brushed past him. Her pale calves flashing, she left the restaurant and disappeared down the corridor in the direction of the Elm Street elevators. Bino thought about going after her; nobody should be wandering around alone in her mental condition. Just as he started to move, a heavy hand dropped onto his shoulder from behind. He turned.

He hadn't had a closeup look at Frank Bleeder in a while, and Bleeder's appearance hadn't taken a turn for the better. His cheeks and jowls were beginning to sag, and his entire face was an unhealthy red. In the old days Frank's hair had been a real attention-getter;

it had been coal-black with a sheen about it. Bleeder was graying now, and his hair was dull and limp. There was a scabbed-over nick on his chin where he'd cut himself shaving. "Hey, Bino, no big deal," Bleeder said. His voice was hoarse, maybe from too many cigarettes, maybe from yelling for too many sevens and elevens that never seemed to come. "Just a little boy-girl hassle is all, nothing to it. She'll be okay."

Bino glanced down at Frank's clothes. There was a greasy stain on Bleeder's pants leg and a slice of tomato still clung to the hem of his coat. Mentally, Bino had an instant replay of Dodie, her butt twitching as she stalked away to use the telephone. "No sweat, Frank," Bino said. "Happens all the time. Hell, I nearly got a plateful of lettuce in my lap awhile ago myself. Would've served me right, come to think about it."

Bino was beginning to think that Weedy Clements's brother favored Marvin Goldman a whole lot more than he favored Weedy. Bino wasn't sure *why* he thought the brother resembled Goldman, so he looked both of them over again. Well, the brother had a goatee and mustache like Goldman did, but the brother's hair was sandy red where the U.S. prosecutor's was coal-black with little touches of silver mixed in. And where Goldman was slim, trim, and fit, did a lot of jogging and worked out with the weights, the brother was built like a fireplug. Yeah, the brother was *shaped* like Weedy, so what was it? Bino snapped his fingers. Sure, that was it. It was the way that the brother was *pointing* that reminded Bino of Goldman. Weedy's brother was pointing at Weedy in exactly the same manner in which the prosecutor had pointed. As though Goldman had rehearsed the guy or something.

"And are you positive?" Goldman said.

"Yep. I guess I know my own brother," Weedy's brother said.

There was a stirring in the jury box as an elderly woman in a print dress leaned forward and squinted in Weedy's direction, then did the same in the direction of Weedy's brother. She settled back in her chair, her gaze now on Goldman. Bino felt a faint spark of hope. Maybe the juror felt the same way that Bino did, like maybe Goldman had slipped his own brother in as a witness in place of Weedy's brother.

"Please let the record reflect," Goldman said, "that the witness has identified Andrew Clements, the defendant." He leaned against the witness-box railing and folded his arms. "And what, if anything, did the defendant say? If you recall."

"Well, he told me to stack the weed in the back end of the pickup. Tell you the truth, I didn' want to. I mean, the stuff had been out in that field for a week and it had been raining like hell. It stunk. You ever smelled wet marijuana?"

"I confess I haven't," Goldman said. Bino suspected that Goldman had smelled plenty of weed, though, when it was rolled into a joint and burning at one end.

"Well, you ought to sometime," Weedy's brother said. "Anyhow, I told Weedy I didn't want to load it, but he said for me to get to piling the bales or it was gonna be my ass."

"*He* told you that?" Now it was Goldman's turn to point. Counting two points by Goldman, plus one apiece by the other two witnesses who had already testified, Bino figured that this made six points at Weedy so far. And they were just getting started.

"Yes, sir," Weedy's brother said.

"The defend-ant."

"Nobody else."

Weedy leaned over close to Bino and whispered, "I didn't have no idea he was gonna say *this* shit. Call King's-X. I think I wanta make a deal."

"That's what I been telling you all along," Bino said. "But it might be too late, this trial might be too far out of hand. I'll give it a shot, Weed, it's all I can do." Bino caught movement in the corner of his eye. A pink-cheeked man wearing a dark green suit had come into the courtroom. He paused, came through the railing gate, and laid a thick folder on the prosecution's table. Then he stepped back and nodded at Goldman. Goldman returned the nod. The new guy wasn't a prosecutor, his suit was the wrong color. Probably an FBI who was new on the job and hadn't learned how to dress as yet.

"Well, do *something,*" Weedy said. "Hell, they're barbecuing me. Stick a fork in me, I'm done." He glanced at his brother and curled his upper lip.

Bino stood. "Your Honor . . ."

Judge Hazel took her glasses off and blinked. "Are you objecting, Mr. Phillips? We have a witness here."

"No, Your Honor. I want to have a word with Mr. Goldman. In . . . private."

"Irregular, sir," the judge said.

Bino grinned, feeling slightly foolish. "How 'bout it, Marv?"

Goldman shrugged and spread his hands, palms up. "I've got the time, Your Honor. If the court does."

"Well, be quick about it, Mr. Phillips. I'm warning you." Judge Hazel replaced her glasses on her nose and produced a small gold watch from the pocket of her robe. Weedy's brother adjusted his position in the witness chair. Goldman strolled over beside the prosecution's table and waited expectantly.

Bino came over to Goldman and tapped his index finger on the file folder that the man in the green suit had brought in. "What's this stuff?" Bino said to Goldman. "We already had discovery, you know, you can't run in a bunch of crap out of left field."

"Extraneous and irrelevant, my boy," Goldman said. "Doesn't even have anything to do with this case. What is this, anyway? You're calling time out in the middle of direct examination to ask me about this file? The proper procedure is for you to make a motion—"

"I know the fucking procedure, Marv. My client wants to make a deal. One count, he'll cop to it. Five-year max."

Goldman scratched his cheek with his index finger. "Okay," he said.

"Or two counts at the most. He can't . . . *huh?* What'd you say?"

Goldman sat on the corner of the table. He was grinning. "I said, 'Okay.' One count, five-year cap. You want to try for two?"

Bino couldn't have been more surprised if the U.S. prosecutor had unzipped his fly and started pissing on the table. Bino said lamely, "What's the deal, Marv?"

"Well, if you *got* to know, the deal is that file there. The one you were asking about. Something's come up, and to tell you the truth I got no more time to fuck with Weedy Clements. Bigger fish to fry, or whatever you want to call it."

While Goldman's herd of civil-service-pool typists were upstairs fixing up Weedy's plea-bargain agreement, Bino used the pay phone in the hall. He punched in his own office number, then stood and listened to the clicks and rings as he gazed down the corridor past the courtroom entrance—ceiling-high door, stained and carved, with a glassed-in vestibule on the left for government witnesses and FBI agents to lounge around in and shoot the shit—to the end of the hallway. There was a plain vanilla entryway down there, identified by gold lettering over the door as the U.S. attorney's trial headquarters. Bino wondered briefly how much it would cost for a defense attorney to have, in addition to his main office, headquarters outside every courtroom in town. Naw. Never be able to afford it. He'd already counted six rings, and just as he'd decided he'd called the wrong number and was ready to disconnect and try again, Dodie picked up the phone on the other end and said, "Lawyer's office."

"What took you so long?" Bino said. "I was getting worried."

"I was on the other line. Worried about what, massa? We-uns is heah."

He shoved his free hand into his pocket and closed his eyes. "Say, Dode, I've been meaning to tell you. You don't know how much I appreciate the . . . job you're doing."

"No, you don't," she said.

"Hey, not true. You're number one, I've said it all along. Let's call a truce, huh?"

There was crackling static on the line, accompanied by the sudden clatter of Dodie's typewriter keys. "What's to call? You're the boss, I'm the secretary. No big deal. You want your phone messages? And by the way, how come you're not in court? What'd you do, throw poor Weedy to the wolves?"

A plump woman in her forties, wearing a pink slack suit, came down the corridor lugging a stack of papers, did a column-right, and went into the courtroom. Probably Weedy's copout deal. "I don't get it," Bino said. "I'm *in* court. Where do you think I am?"

"Well, *I'd* of probably started looking for you at Joe Miller's Bar. But I didn't tell the judge that. He called for you."

"*He?* The judge is a woman, Dodie. Judge Sanderson."

"Wow, you're right. Score one for you, I'd forgotten. The judge that called was Emmett Burns. That's why I thought you weren't in court."

Bino thought, Jesus Christ. Now his head was going around in circles. Judges just didn't call lawyers out of the blue, not lawyers who had cases pending in the judge's court. Not *defense* lawyers, anyway. And Emmett Burns wouldn't be calling *either* side, the guy was too straight-arrow. Besides, Emmett Burns wasn't Weedy Clements's judge anymore, was he? Bino said, "What'd he say?"

"Well, after he said, 'Is Mr. Phillips in?' and I told him you weren't, he left a number. It's right here. Gee, I should have noticed before, but this exchange isn't a downtown number. He must be at home. You want it?"

Bino fished a pad and pen from his inside breast pocket and cradled the receiver between his jaw and shoulder. "Okay. Shoot."

The number was an Oak Cliff exchange, and Bino had a fleeting image of nice old homes nestled among the elms and sycamores and winding mossy creeks near Stevens Park Golf Course. Bino thought about trying again for a truce with Dodie, then decided he'd better let the water settle some more. He thanked her, disconnected, and tried the Oak Cliff number. Marvin Goldman was now standing in the courtroom entryway motioning to him. Bino held up one finger in Goldman's direction as, over the phone, Judge Emmett Burns's calm and cultured tenor voice said hello.

"Bino Phillips, Judge."

Emmett Burns would be all business, at least that's the way he had always come across. Bino figured Burns to be around sixty, but the voice over the phone belonged to a man twenty years younger. The judge said, "I've already mailed you a retainer, Mr. Phillips, which is going to be sufficient for me to start calling you Bino. I live at four seven eight Crystal Hills. The street intersects Hampton Road just south of I-30 and winds around to Colorado Boulevard. Can you come by around seven?"

Burns wasn't really asking, he was telling, and there was enough authority in his voice to make Bino snap to. "Yes, Your Honor. I'll be there."

"Emmett will do, if you're going to be my lawyer. And the retainer puts us in an attorney-client relationship. Which means you're not to tell anybody about this."

Goldman was now waving like a third-base coach sending the runner home. Bino said, "Absolutely. I'll see you then."

Judge Burns disconnected.

As Bino approached the courtroom entrance, Goldman said, "Jesus Christ, hurry up. The judge has already got her panties in a knot over all this plea-bargain shit. You're the only guy I know with enough nerve to keep a judge waiting."

ABOUT THE AUTHOR

A.W. GRAY has played poker at Binnion's World Championship and driven to South America with golf star Lee Trevino. He has lived in Memphis, Los Angeles, and New Orleans, and currently makes his home in Fort Worth, Texas. His first novel, *Bino,* is available in an Onyx paperback edition. His new novel, *In Defense of Judges,* has just been published in hardcover by E.P. Dutton.